About th

Mark Robson was born in Wanstead, Essex, in 1966, and was raised, for the most part, near Carmarthen in West Wales. In 1982, he gained a scholarship to join the Royal Air Force as a pilot and he is currently serving at RAF Brize Norton, Oxfordshire. His first book *'The Forging of the Sword'* was largely written during tours of duty in the Falkland Islands. The long quiet hours maintaining the constant vigil of the Quick Reaction Alert Force proved to be an ideal breeding ground for flights of fantasy, mainly because the wet and windy weather of the Falkland Islands prevented flights of anything else! Subsequent books have been inspired by the wave of encouragement by readers. Mark now lives in the Midlands and is married with two children.

By this author:

The Darkweaver Legacy

Book 1:	The Forging of the Sword	*ISBN 0953819000*
Book 2:	Trail of the Huntress	*ISBN 0953819019*
Book 3:	First Sword	*ISBN 0953819027*
Book 4:	The Chosen One	*ISBN 0953819035*

Forthcoming Titles

Imperial Spy	*ISBN 141690185X*
Imperial Assassin	*ISBN 1416901868*

Imperial Spy - April 2006

Femke, a gifted and resourceful young spy, is entrusted with a vital foreign mission by the Emperor. It appears a simple task, but nothing is straightforward when your enemies are one step ahead of you. Framed for two murders while visiting the neighbouring King's court, Femke finds herself isolated in an alien country. As the authorities hunt her down for the murders, her arch-enemy, Shalidar, is closing in for his revenge...

For up to date information on future releases see:

www.swordpublishing.co.uk

THE
CHOSEN ONE

Mark Robson

SWORD PUBLISHING

THE CHOSEN ONE
ISBN: 0-9538190-3-5

First published in the United Kingdom by Sword Publishing

First Edition published 2003
Reprinted 2004
Reprinted 2005

Published by Sword Publishing,
9 Wheat Close, Daventry, Northants, NN11 0FX.
www.swordpublishing.co.uk
info@swordpublishing.co.uk

Printed and bound in Great Britain by Technographic, Kiln Farm, East End Green, Brightlingsea, Colchester, Essex, CO7 0SX.

For you, the readers,

In particular: Hannah, Marianne, Jess and Louise, for their enthusiasm and constant emails. Thank you all for your encouragement and positive feedback. I hope you find this worth the wait.

Acknowledgements:

To Nigel and Georgina at 'Words and Publications' for their success in turning my manuscripts into books – without them, The Darkweaver Legacy would have fallen at the first hurdle.

To all the proof-readers. I still expect to see 'C- See me' written at the bottom of every script – especially given the amount of red ink you throw around!

To my wife, Sarah and my daughter, Rachel, for their patience and understanding.

'... and it will come to pass that in the time of the ascension will the Chosen One arise. Eternal damnation shall be at His left hand and lasting peace at His right. He shall wield the Keys of the World to determine its fate, and though the faithful may clear the way, only the Chosen One shall walk the final road. The road to the abomination shall be His alone to tread. If any but He and the Key itself doth tread the path, then the World shall end. All paths for the Chosen One lead to the final road. The Key will choose the time and the Chosen One shall know no other choice. Eternity for all nations shall reside in His hands.'*

– Extract from *The Oracles of Drehboor*.

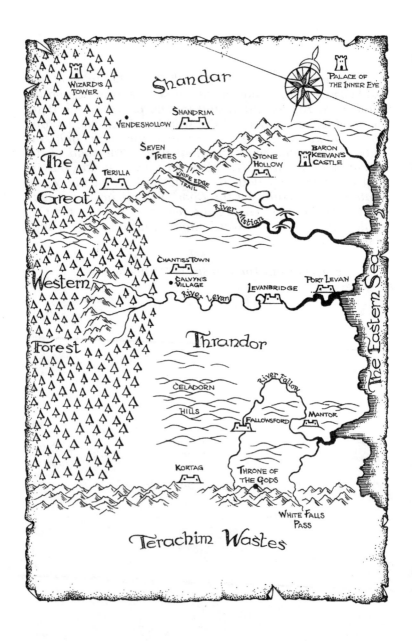

PROLOGUE

High Lord Vallaine, Sorcerer Lord of the Inner Eye, started in his seat at the sound of a sharp double knock at the door to the Emperor's study. In the blink of an eye, Vallaine's appearance changed from his own unmistakable wizened features to the more distinguished and imperial bearing of the Emperor of Shandar. If testimony was needed to endorse Vallaine's skill as a Sorcerer, then the fact that none of the Imperial House Staff appeared to have noticed any change in the Emperor since Vallaine had killed and replaced him, spoke volumes of his subtle powers.

'Shand send that this is good news,' Vallaine muttered under his breath. He inhaled slowly and deeply. 'Come in,' he ordered, his voice composed and his intonation identical to that of the dead Emperor.

The last ten days had not been easy for Lord Vallaine. Just about everything that could go wrong had turned into an unmitigated disaster. To begin with, Commander Chorain had been mysteriously murdered before Vallaine had been able to question him about the military defeat in Thrandor. Next, Bek, the Thrandorian arena fighter who Vallaine had intended to employ as an assassin, had been badly injured during a challenge bout before he had somehow disappeared from under the security guards' noses immediately after the fight. Vallaine had set spies to watch the place where the Thrandorian fighter's compatriots had been known to be hiding out, but they too had given Vallaine's people the slip. All in all, High Lord

Vallaine had good reason to feel that events were conspiring against him and his frustration was such that he was ready to start heads rolling if anything else went wrong.

The door to the Emperor's study opened and a young woman entered. A huge barrel-chested man followed closely behind her and, on seeing him, Lord Vallaine slowly curled his lips upward in a smile reminiscent of a dangerous predator lazily remembering an easy kill and an ample meal.

'Ah, Femke, once again you have lived up to your reputation for getting things done efficiently. Be assured that you have my deepest gratitude for finding and bringing Barrathos to me so swiftly. You will be richly rewarded for this service,' Vallaine said, his voice all but purring with satisfaction.

'It was my pleasure, your Imperial Majesty, but if you have nothing further for me right now, then, with your leave, I will retire and get some rest, for the journey was long,' Femke replied wearily.

'Of course, Femke. Go. Sleep well. I'll probably have a new task for you tomorrow, so rest with my blessing.'

'Thank you, Imperial Majesty. Should I report to you at a particular time?'

'No, Femke, go and rest. I'll send for you when I'm ready,' Vallaine answered in kindly tones.

Femke dropped her head forward in the appropriate nod as she curtsied before backing towards the door, but Vallaine's sharp perception noted that when Femke's head rose again there was little tiredness in the young woman's eyes. Femke was a woman after his own heart, born to a life of deceit and subtle manipulation. Femke suspected something about him, of that much Vallaine was sure, but what she had deduced and what she would do with any knowledge that she gathered, the Sorcerer Lord did not really know. Femke was a dangerous unknown quantity in the game that Vallaine was playing. The time might come when she would have to be removed from the playing board, but at present the clever spy was far too useful an asset to sacrifice. No, the trick would be to keep her off balance and so busy that her own games and suspicions would not have time to be played out. Vallaine smiled to himself as the door closed behind her. He had more than enough tasks to keep Femke busy.

Dropping his guise as the Emperor, Vallaine turned his attention to Barrathos, who displayed no surprise at the sudden change of Vallaine's appearance from Emperor to High Lord of the Inner Eye. The big man was already nervous though, and was slowly rubbing his huge palms together in a subconscious effort to remove the sheen of sweat that coated them.

'What have you called me here for, Lord Vallaine?' Barrathos asked, his deep voice resonating slightly despite the décor of the chamber.

'To employ your skills, Barrathos, why else?' Vallaine said simply, his sunken eyes glittering with a wicked enjoyment at the big man's discomfort. 'Despite the incident with the Gorvath, you are still the most competent Wizard that I know and I wish to summon some demons. I have put your past failure where it belongs – in the past. Now I need your abilities again, Barrathos, only this time I can afford no failures.'

Vallaine did not think it wise to add that in fact Barrathos was the *only* Wizard that he knew. Wizardry was the least practised of the arcane arts for good reason; primarily, the inherent dangers involved in attempting to control demons put off all but the stoutest of heart and the most foolhardy. The unfortunate fact was that eventually a Wizard was almost inevitably tempted into summoning a demon more powerful than he could actually control. Any mistake when handling demons usually proved to be a fatal misjudgement, as the demon would normally devour the Wizard in question. Aside from further reducing the number of practising Wizards, unsurprisingly this also served to decrease Wizardry's popularity as a choice for study.

'Did you say *demons*?' Barrathos asked incredulously.

'Yes, you heard correctly – demons, plural. One might not be enough to tackle the task that I have in mind.'

'Lord Vallaine, you saw the devastation caused by one Gorvath and the dangers involved in summoning such a powerful entity. Now you suggest that I am to summon more than one such demon. Are you truly serious? Or have you simply brought me all this way to mock me?'

'Oh, you can bet your last sennut that I'm serious, Barrathos,' Vallaine responded, stepping forward to close the distance between them.

Despite towering over Vallaine, Barrathos instinctively backed away from the Sorcerer, as one would step back from a venomous snake, or a dog that was growling with its hackles up. Barrathos was obviously not willing to risk Vallaine's bite, be it verbal or sorcerous and he quickly began to concede to the Sorcerer Lord's demand.

'What exactly did you have in mind, Lord Vallaine?' he asked, his apprehension of the answer as plain as his fear of the Sorcerer.

'Well...' Vallaine began, his eyes automatically flicking upwards as considered for a moment. 'I think that three demons should be sufficient. Obviously not Gorvaths – I am not so unrealistic as to demand that, but something deadly. What do *you* think?'

'All demons are deadly in their own way, Lord Vallaine. Much in the same way that humankind has its strengths and weaknesses, so do demons. Will we have supporting minds to control them like we did with the Gorvath?' Barrathos asked thoughtfully.

Vallaine shook his head. 'Just you and I,' he answered.

'And all you want is to send them to kill someone?'

'Yes, but it's not just anyone. These demons are to kill the young man whose soul we fed to the Gorvath. He is resourceful and dangerous, so we need to be sure that whatever you summon will be more than a match for him.'

'It would help to know how the Gorvath was killed,' Barrathos suggested pointedly. 'Is there any way that this person could have engineered the freeing of his own soul, do you think?'

Vallaine thought for a moment. He had not been one hundred percent certain that the Gorvath had been killed at all until now. Indeed, his worst fear had been that the soulless Lord Shanier had simply double-crossed him to further his own ends and that the whole Thrandorian debacle had, in fact, been a result of Vallaine's misjudgement. Now he felt somehow further vindicated of responsibility. After all, how could he have possibly anticipated both the escape of the beast and the fact that someone would actually be able to kill such a powerful creature before it chose to return to the demon realm of its own accord? The combination of circumstances still seemed unbelievable, even though he knew them to be true.

'To be honest, Barrathos, I'm not really sure what Lord Shanier is capable of any more. He has deceived me once. I will not underestimate him again.'

'In that case, I suggest that I summon two Naksa demons and a Krill. The Naksa are hunters by nature and they generally bond into partnerships of two or three to track prey anyway, so that will work well. They are deadly killers, possessing both speed and physical power, but they are not overly intelligent. I'm told that any more than two or three Naksa hunting together will often turn on each other and fight until only the strongest remain, which is probably why they never group in larger packs. Adding a Krill to the power of the Naksa will bring guile and cunning to the group.'

'A Krill? I believe I've heard of such a demon before. Isn't that a shadow demon?' Vallaine asked, his voice betraying his curiosity.

'Yes, that's right,' Barrathos nodded. 'They have large and powerful bodies, but can melt away into shadows and remain unseen with surprising ease. Once summoned, the Naksa demons wouldn't be difficult for me to control, but the key would be handling the Krill. A large Krill may prove troublesome in the same way as the Gorvath we summoned. If we're successful, however, the Krill, being of a higher order in the demon realm than the Naksa, will become the natural leader of this hunting party. Yes, it would work well,' the Wizard said slowly.

He paused for a moment and scratched absently at his scalp. Suddenly regaining his focus, Barrathos met Vallaine's eye with more conviction than he had yet shown the Sorcerer.

'If we are really going to do this, then your aid will be required, Lord Vallaine. I have successfully summoned both Naksa and Krill on my own in the past, but have never attempted to control a mixed group. It will be up to you to control the Naksa whilst I deal with the Krill. The Naksa are ferocious creatures, but their minds are not complex. I don't think that they will pose you too many problems. You saw what happened with the Gorvath when it escaped our control before. I hardly need to tell you that if we lose control this time, then we will both die in seconds. Are you sure that you really want to risk that?'

Barrathos already knew the answer, but he asked the question anyway. When Vallaine nodded his affirmation the Wizard sighed in resignation, though in his heart he was not as downcast as he made out to Vallaine. He was far more confident about this multiple summoning that he had been about calling the Gorvath.

'Very well,' Barrathos grumbled, taking a deep breath and squaring his shoulders. 'Do you have anything that belonged to the young man? Preferably something with his scent on it, but that is not strictly necessary.'

Vallaine grinned with chilling malice. 'Yes, I have just the thing,' he said.

'Good,' the Wizard replied. 'Then we can begin.'

CHAPTER 1

Calvyn stared up at the gently billowing canvas roof of the tent and wondered quite how these old men that he was travelling with were going to be of any use in stopping Selkor. Calvyn had once witnessed Selkor bring two opposing armies literally to a standstill, ride casually into the middle of the battlefield, take what he had come for and then ride off again. These old fellows could not even manage to put up a tent properly, either with or without the aid of magic.

A flicker of light from outside the entrance flap of the tent drew Calvyn's attention. It was only a momentary flash and Calvyn wondered for a second whether he had imagined it. He was still not overly happy with the Magicians' insistence that there was no need to mount a watch during the night. After all, what would they do if someone crept up to their campsite and stole their horses whilst they slept? Unable to ignore the light, Calvyn sat up and counted the dark slug-like shapes of the bodies wrapped sleeping in their blankets. He had just finished his count, confirming that no one was outside, when a distant rumble of thunder growled and crackled ominously, providing Calvyn a reason for the flash.

'A storm – that's all we need,' Calvyn muttered, silently offering thanks once again to Derra for the training and habits that she had ingrained in him whilst he was a recruit in Baron Keevan's army.

The Magicians had scoffed at his insistence of mounting storm lashings over the tent every night, but he had ignored

15

their comments as, aside from Lomand, none of them displayed any real knowledge of camp-craft whatsoever. The five Grand Magicians had done nothing constructive to help during the evenings that the party had camped out, leaving Calvyn, Jenna and Lomand to do all the work whilst they sat around the fire and argued. All they seemed to do was bicker amongst each other about anything and everything. In particular, they constantly found new nuances to debate over the wisdom of embarking on this journey at all, and Calvyn wished fervently that they would just stop all the arguing and concentrate on getting to Mantor as quickly as possible.

Someone snorted loudly and rolled over. There was a short pause and then the sound of gentle snoring began to drift through the tent. Calvyn laid back down and pulled his blankets back around his shoulders. Winter was really setting in and even with the warmth generated by eight bodies in the tent, the air still had a distinct nip in it. The snow line in the Vortaff Mountains to the south of their path had been progressively lowering almost on a daily basis. Calvyn was certain that the group would encounter winter conditions before long, even down here on the low ground. It would be interesting to see how the old men coped, he thought, as he closed his eyes and tried once more to drop off to sleep.

With his eyes closed and his body relaxed, Calvyn would normally fall asleep within a few minutes, but tonight his mind was too active to allow sleep to come easily. Another roll of thunder rumbled in the distance, and a slightly stronger gust of wind caused the canvas of the tent to flex first outwards and then snap back inwards again. Calvyn ignored it, but then found that his ears picked out the soft sound of Jenna breathing next to him. Even with the unidentified snorer generating noise elsewhere in the tent, Calvyn found that he could definitely pick out Jenna's slow, rhythmic breaths coming from the roll of blankets next to him. The sound was soporific, almost to the point of being hypnotic, but instead of lulling him to sleep, Calvyn found that it simply triggered even more thoughts and pictures in his overactive mind.

Jenna loved him. That had been a revelation. Even more of a shock, perhaps, was the discovery that he returned that love. Everything that had confused him about his feelings for Jenna had suddenly made perfect sense when viewed in this light. It was just amazing that he had not seen it before. Calvyn had missed Jenna terribly since his soul had been returned to him, but not for one instant had he considered why that should be. He had just accepted the feelings and moved on. It had only become clear why he had missed her so much a few days ago, when Jenna had found him at the Magicians' Academy and declared her love for him in an emotional storm of hugs and tears. He was in love and it felt wonderful.

There had been a lot of news for them to catch up on since being reunited, and they had taken it in turns over the last few days to tell their stories. Calvyn could only marvel at Jenna's bravery, both during her journey to free Perdimonn from his rocky prison in the Vortaff Mountains, and her subsequent hunt for the incredibly dangerous shape-shifting demon that had taken Calvyn's soul. Of course, Jenna had modestly played down the danger in both quests, but Calvyn could read enough between the lines of her tale to know that she had faced many dangers with a stout heart. Many would have baulked at travelling alone into the Vortaff Mountains, let alone tracking a deadly demon with no real idea of how they could kill such a beast. Jenna had done both and succeeded where many would not have even dared to try. He felt extremely fortunate to have won the love of such a woman.

For Jenna's part, after recovering from the initial shock of discovering Calvyn's unexpected rise to the nobility, she rejoiced with him over his good fortune. As a Knight of the Realm of Thrandor and personal adviser to the King, Calvyn's status had changed immensely since Jenna had last seen him. He had been trained as a Sorcerer and had received training towards becoming a Magician as well, both of which would have made Jenna very uncomfortable a year ago. Times and attitudes were changing fast though and, with the King's blessing on Calvyn's abilities, Jenna was not about to take issue over them.

The battle for Kortag, when Calvyn used his newfound powers of sorcery resulting in the destruction of both the Terachite Tribal Army and the Shandese Legions, was a story that he had related to Jenna quietly, when there was little chance of being overheard by any of the Magicians. Calvyn still had no idea whether the Magicians knew anything of the recent events in Thrandor, or how they would react if they found out that he had been responsible for the deaths of tens of thousands of Shandese soldiers. No matter how impartial Magicians were with regard to the nationalities of their students, that sort of personal history was sure to polarize their views of him. Relationships with the Magicians were strained enough, without any more prejudice being introduced.

Another gust of wind, stronger this time, caused the canvas of the tent to flap and flutter again. Almost immediately afterwards a crack of thunder caused Calvyn to reopen his eyes. The storm was much closer this time and obviously moving at a fair pace. No one else had stirred at the sound, so Calvyn decided to have a look outside on his own. Silently he rose and picked up the cloak that he had been using as a pillow. Carefully, he unrolled it and drew it around his shoulders. If the storm was going to pass over them, then Calvyn was not about to let it do unnecessary damage to their equipment.

Like a shadow, Calvyn tip-toed around the sleeping bodies and, unfastening the entrance flap, he ducked under it and stepped out into the night. No sooner had he re-fastened the tent flap than the sky behind him blossomed with light. Calvyn did not turn quickly enough to actually see the lightning, but he did not need to see it to learn where the storm was. As he looked eastwards towards the sea, a vast wall of cloud obscured the night sky and he did not have to wait long for the sky-splitting sound that followed in the lightning's wake.

The temperature had dropped markedly since sundown and the breeze that was picking up in strength was now bitterly cold. Calvyn rubbed his hands together briefly, blew into them and then drew his cloak even tighter around his body as he crept around the tent. Everything seemed secure, but he did manage to work a little more tension into the storm lashings, which made him feel that braving the elements had been worth the effort.

Lightning flashed again, leaping across the sky from cloud to cloud in a rapid chain reaction. This was not just a single storm, Calvyn realised grimly, it was a line squall: a whole string of thunderstorms marching inland like the battle line of some marauding army, all brandishing their weapons and shouting their war cries with impossibly loud voices.

The horses were stamping nervously and tossing their heads in obvious agitation. Calvyn walked over to where they were tethered and patted Hakkaari reassuringly on the neck.

'Calm down, it's OK,' he said soothingly. 'It's only a bit of wind and rain.'

Hakkaari was plainly not convinced and continued to roll his eyes and stamp in alarm at the now frequent flashes of light and corresponding crashes of thunder. A freezing blast of wind caught Calvyn a little off guard. Storms generated their own wind – Calvyn knew that much, but he was not prepared for the sudden change from cold breeze to freezing gale in a matter of seconds. The next hour or so would not be a lot of fun for anyone, man or horse, caught out in the open, Calvyn decided. Leaving the horses attached to their current pickets would be cruel and the animals might hurt themselves attempting to get free, so he elected to get them at least under the shelter of the nearby copse of trees.

Working swiftly at the knots of the tether rope, Calvyn untied Hakkaari and led him into the trees. Quickly securing his horse within the dubious shelter, Calvyn raced back for the next horse and the next, but he was rapidly running out of time.

'What do you think you are doing?'

The shout made Calvyn nearly jump out of his skin, coming as it did from just behind him.

'I'm getting the horses under cover, Master Akhdar. They're terrified of the storm and I can't say that I blame them. It looks as though it's going to be a bad one.'

'You should have woken the rest of us. If you had, then you wouldn't have wasted your effort. Now, start fetching the horses back out here to the pickets. I'll send Lomand to help you.'

'But, Master...'

'Just do as you're told, Calvyn,' Akhdar ordered firmly.

'Yes, Master.'

Moments later the rain struck: a great curtain of water driven by the wind that soaked everything in its path within seconds. Even under cover of the trees, the rain sheeted through. With all the deciduous trees having long since shed their leaves, the green needles of the pine and larch trees that had offered some visual cover let the water through like a sieve. Cursing the task for one of madness, Calvyn untied the first of the horses and turned to lead it back out to the picket in the open.'

'It only appears madness because you are not thinking like a Magician,' Lomand chided reprovingly, his deep voice and unexpected presence causing Calvyn to start for the second time in as many minutes. 'You're thinking like a soldier, not as one who would manipulate his surroundings with magic. Let's move the horses and you will see what I mean.'

Calvyn nodded, suitably chastised, and began coaxing the skittish horse he was leading back out into the open. Master Akhdar was waiting for them, calmly standing between the tent and the picket, encased in a personal bubble of magical energy. The rain was not touching him at all and the howling wind did not so much as stir the tail of his cloak. Calvyn understood instantly. The shield that

Master Akhdar was using was a variation on the protection shield that Calvyn had used at the battle for Mantor. It was a simple enough spell, but if the Magician intended to shield the horses from the rain by such means, then he would need to draw an enormous amount of magical energy to do so, Calvyn thought sceptically.

Lomand emerged from the trees behind Calvyn leading both Hakkaari and the remaining horses with apparent ease. Calvyn's fingers were so cold by now that he found it all but impossible to tie a secure knot in the lead rope. Lomand quickly secured his two horses and came to Calvyn's aid, giving him a kindly smile as he finished off the job.

'Now, watch and learn, young Calvyn,' Lomand instructed pointedly.

Lomand nodded at Akhdar, who acknowledged with a brief nod of his own. From beneath his cloak, the snowy-haired Grand Magician drew out a staff, the top of which was shaped like a hand clutching a huge red gemstone. Calvyn recognised it instantly as the Staff of Dantillus and gasped as he realised that he was about to see it used. The Staff had been an icon of power amongst Magicians for some three hundred and fifty years or more and few were allowed to use it.

Akhdar closed his eyes and held the staff upright in front of him with his right hand above his left. Calvyn could see the Magician's lips moving and his thick white eyebrows were drawn together in a look of intense concentration. Suddenly, Akhdar opened his eyes and Calvyn instantly flinched as a wave of magical force exploded from the top of the Staff. The wave passed right through everything in the campsite, only to form a huge shimmering bubble of magical energy many paces in diameter. Calvyn shuddered as he tried to shake off the feeling of the wave passing through him and then looked around to find that the fury of the storm was now beating in vain against the wall of magical power.

Akhdar lowered the Staff and gave Calvyn a quick smile.

'Now maybe you'll lay down and get some sleep,' the Grand Magician said kindly. 'We will be perfectly safe here until I dispel the shelter and I have no intention of doing that until morning.'

'Yes, Master,' Calvyn replied meekly, combing his wet hair back from his forehead with his fingers. 'I was only trying to help.'

'Very commendable, I'm sure,' Akhdar replied. 'But wholly unnecessary.'

Akhdar disappeared back into the tent whilst Calvyn flipped his cape off his shoulders and started to shake off the excess water. It was no use. The cloak, along with absolutely everything else that Calvyn was wearing, was sodden. Even without the freezing wind and rain, Calvyn was chilled to the bone and soaked through to the skin. There was nothing else for it, he would just have to pull his spare dry clothing from his pack and get changed. If he tried to sleep like this, he was bound to fall ill.

Setting to work, Calvyn started to wring out his cloak in order to hang it out to dry, but after a moment he stopped. Lomand was watching him with a strangely puzzled expression.

'What's the matter, Lomand? Am I in your way?' Calvyn asked irritably.

'No, not at all,' the Magician replied, scratching absently at the back of his neck. 'I was just wondering what you were doing, that's all.'

'What does it look like? I'm setting my things out to dry, of...'

He was going to finish 'of course', but it was at that moment that he noticed that Lomand's clothes all appeared perfectly dry and yet only a few minutes before, Lomand had been as wet as he. More magic! It had to be.

'OK, Lomand, would you *please* show me how you did it,' Calvyn sighed, exasperated at having been made to look a fool twice in quick succession.

'You mean that you honestly don't know?' the big man replied in surprise. 'I had heard rumours that you were way ahead of the other Acolytes when it came to spell-casting.'

'Maybe in some areas,' Calvyn said, trying his best not to let his irritation get the better of him. 'In others... well, my horse would probably fare better than I.'

Lomand laughed and then stifled his voice with his hand as he remembered that others were trying to sleep.

'Here, let me do it for you this time,' he offered. 'I'll teach you the spell tomorrow whilst we ride if you like.'

'Thank you, Lomand. I would really appreciate that, and if there are any other simple spells that you would be willing to share, then I would be most glad to learn those as well. The Masters are all too pre-occupied with the journey to think about progressing my education right now.'

Lomand waved one of his shovel-sized hands with a seemingly negligent flick and a spatter of water hit the ground behind Calvyn. Automatically, Calvyn's hands moved down his body to confirm what he already knew was true – his clothes were bone dry.

'I'm sure that there are one or two that I can teach you,' Lomand said with a smile. 'As you say, I doubt that the Masters will mind *too* much.'

Calvyn grinned and then glanced up, as lightning struck the dome of force above them and writhed across the surface as if searching for a way in.

'It's quite alright,' Lomand assured him calmly. 'The magic attracts the lightning for some reason, but it can do no harm to us here. Come, let's get some sleep.'

Lomand raised the entrance flap of the tent and Calvyn ducked under it and made his way carefully back to his pile of blankets. Some of the Masters had not stirred at all throughout the whole episode. Others were obviously awake, but were probably wishing themselves asleep. Calvyn ignored them all and swiftly wrapped himself back up in his blankets and forced himself to relax.

Just as he settled, he heard Jenna whisper quietly to him. 'What happened?'

'Tomorrow,' he replied softly. 'I'll tell you tomorrow.'

When morning came, there was little evidence of the storms from the night before. The sky was a glorious blue, and bright white puffs of fair weather cloud simply punctuated character into an otherwise unblemished firmament. Calvyn and Jenna observed with intense fascination as Akhdar performed the counter-spell to disperse the bubble of magical energy above them, and before long the party was underway again.

Calvyn and Jenna rode in their customary position at the back of the party, each leading one of the two packhorses. The five Grand Magicians all rode in an ever-shifting gaggle in front, chatting and debating over many subjects. Initially, Calvyn had found that listening to them was informative and interesting, but after several days of the same, it now grated on his ears like the incessant bickering of bored children who simply argued for the sake of something to do. Calvyn had wondered for a while whether the constant changing of position might be based on some sort of point scoring from the arguments. It had taken Calvyn almost a full day of observation and silent analysis to decide that in fact there was no real rhyme or reason for all the swapping around, so he put it down to a lack of travel discipline.

Lomand did not really take part in the debating or the shifting of position and tended to ride behind the main group, but in front of Jenna and Calvyn. Today he changed that habit and dropped back to ride between them. Calvyn had already managed to give Jenna a brief account of the events of the previous night, so when Lomand joined them, neither were overly surprised.

'So, Calvyn, shall we begin our lessons?' Lomand asked, smiling with encouragement.

'That would be great, Lomand. Thank you,' Calvyn replied enthusiastically.

'And what about you, young lady? Are you about to change your mind and begin to learn about magic?'

'I... I...' Jenna spluttered in astonishment. 'You're serious? I thought that you were teasing me when you mentioned it at the door to the Academy.'

'Absolutely I'm serious. There is something about you that I noted that day, when you first arrived at the door. I can't promise you that you'll be able to progress far during our journey, but I believe that you have the potential to learn.'

'I don't believe it! And I was sure that you were just having a joke at my expense,' Jenna said, her voice distant in wonder that the Magician was obviously quite serious in his proposal to teach her.

'I never joke when it comes to teaching magic, Jenna. Magic is a serious business. You found the Academy unaided – that alone would have gained you admission to be assessed. You quite plainly have received messages sent by magical means. Many would not be able to hear such messages no matter who was sending them. That tells me that you have both a good imagination and a sensitivity to magic that would probably make you a strong candidate for admission to the Academy no matter who was assessing you.'

'But I'm a girl! All the Acolytes that I saw were boys,' Jenna pointed out.

'That's because the girls undergo their training in a different building,' Lomand replied with a grin. 'It was discovered centuries ago that the girls proved to be just too big a distraction to the boys during their classes, so we segregated them.'

'What?' Calvyn exclaimed a little louder than he had intended.

'Ah! Something else that slipped you by, Calvyn? I must say that I was a little surprised that you didn't get involved in the plots to visit the girls' block, but then you were a bit intense with your studying in your short time there, weren't you? The Academy has trained many female Magicians over the years. In fact it's quite unusual not to have at least one lady on the Council. Their abilities are often more diverse than the men and they frequently develop subtleties in the use of magical power that will baffle even the best male Magicians.'

'Naturally,' stated Jenna with a grin. 'How to baffle a man is one of the first lessons that a girl learns at her mother's knee.'

Lomand laughed loudly at that, whilst Calvyn grinned a little ruefully. Inwardly, he was almost willing to accept that Jenna was only half joking this time, as he had never really understood girls. Jenna had certainly always managed to keep him guessing, and Calvyn had often not been able to tell when she was just fooling around from when she was deadly serious.

'I think that you would take to it very well, Jenna,' Lomand chuckled. 'Very well indeed. I will not pretend that you will be ready to start casting spells any time soon, but if you wish, then I will run through some of the introductory classes whilst we ride. The Masters will be pleased, because Calvyn missed out on the majority of those classes and has already broken more rules of Magician etiquette in his short time with us than most ever manage...'

'But, Lomand...' Calvyn protested.

Lomand held a hand up to silence Calvyn and gave him a reproving look.

'Of course I will not renege on my promise to teach you more spells, Calvyn. There will be more than enough time as we ride to mix and match the lessons. Jenna is going to have to spend a lot of time in meditation, learning clarity of thought and mental precision if she agrees to learn at all. Don't worry – I will load you up with plenty of practical exercises to back up the theory. I think that you will find me every bit as hard a taskmaster as your regular teachers. Now, Jenna, what's it to be? Will you join your young friend here in his quest to become a Magician?'

Jenna leant forward to look across at Calvyn for some guidance.

'No, young lady, do not look to Calvyn for an answer. This must be *your* decision,' Lomand instructed her firmly, his bass voice almost growling with its depth.

Jenna was flummoxed. Becoming a Magician had never

been a personal goal and she was reluctant to commit to it as, in theory, she still had an obligation to complete her bonded time in Baron Keevan's army. Yet it would help her to understand Calvyn better and to share in something that he considered a most important part of his life. If she was serious about sharing her life with Calvyn as her partner, then understanding his abilities and even sharing some of them would make the partnership more equally balanced.

If there was one thing that Jenna was certain of, it was that she loved Calvyn. The only question was, would Calvyn want her to share in his pursuit of magical abilities, or would he perceive her acceptance as undermining him? Jenna did not really know and it was possible that if she made the wrong decision, she ran the risk of driving a wedge between them before their newfound level of intimacy had a chance to settle.

'If I were to accept your offer, Lomand, what would you advise that I do about my bond to Baron Keevan?'

'An interesting question,' Lomand agreed. 'But let me ask you some in return. Should I hold open an offer for someone who has already broken one bond? Have you got the commitment to follow this through to the end, or will you dash off the moment another more exciting adventure comes along?'

'That's not fair! Jenna was...' Calvyn exclaimed, rapidly rallying to Jenna's defence.

'I wasn't asking you,' Lomand interrupted, not so much as looking at Calvyn. 'Jenna is capable of answering her own questions – more than capable unless I'm much mistaken.'

Jenna nodded, her brain racing through possible answers like a squirrel skipping at speed from branch to branch, sometimes running for a moment but mainly in flight from one stop to the next. Eventually, realising that to show any more hesitation would display an unacceptable degree of indecision, Jenna replied.

'I will not deny that I have broken my bond to Baron Keevan, Lomand, though it has always been my intention to return and face the consequences of that action. As to whether I would break another bond, well, if faced with identical circumstances, then yes, I would make the same decision. That said, I could hardly be accused of seeking out adventure. The adventure most definitely came in search of me and I merely reacted in what I considered to be the most appropriate manner at each throw of the dice that fate cast.'

Lomand looked thoughtful for a moment and then his face slowly broadened with a smile.

'A good answer, Jenna. Honest and to the point. You see, Calvyn? This is one young lady who does not need to hide behind a protector. However, you've still not answered my original question, Jenna. Will you undergo the training to become a Magician?'

Jenna did not hesitate this time. 'Yes,' she said positively. 'I will.'

'Excellent,' Lomand enthused, slapping his broad thigh with delight. 'Then we can begin. We will start, I think, with etiquette. Whilst I'm sure that most of this will come naturally to you, Jenna, your boyfriend here needs lessons desperately.'

Jenna chuckled along with Lomand, partly to humour the big man and partly at hearing Calvyn referred to as her boyfriend. It sounded nice, she decided happily. Also, Calvyn was smiling with what appeared to be genuine pleasure at her decision, which gave her confidence that she had made the right choice. With a light heart, she settled back into her saddle and listened attentively as Lomand began to teach them.

Over the next hour and a half or so, Lomand chatted through a whole host of rules and niceties that applied to Acolytes committed to becoming Magicians. The time passed amazingly quickly for both Jenna and Calvyn, as Lomand proved to be an entertaining teacher. Many of the points that he raised were emphasised with funny anecdotes and stories that often had all three of them laughing together. Calvyn had not seen this side of Lomand before and decided that the big man was a more entertaining and effective teacher than any of the Masters.

It was shortly after lunch that the sky gradually began to cloud over again. At first it was just the white horse tails of the really high level cloud, then slowly but surely, more layers pushed their way in from the east and it was not long before the sunshine of the morning seemed a distant memory.

Jenna was lost in her first mental discipline exercises and Calvyn was busy learning new spells when the cloud finally lowered such that it touched the ground and settled around them in a thick wet fog. Before long the forward visibility had reduced such that those at the front of the party were little more than dark shadows to those at the back.

'It's no use,' Akhdar stated loudly enough for all to hear. 'We'll have to stop and sit this out. Trying to navigate safely in open countryside in this weather carries risks that I'm not willing to take, no matter how urgent the journey. OK, let's set up camp. Here will do as well as anywhere.'

'Why won't he just use magic to lift the fog, Lomand? Surely Master Akhdar could do that using the Staff?' Calvyn asked as they climbed down from their horses and began to unload the tent from the packhorses.

'Messing with the weather is a dangerous business, Calvyn. The ramifications are huge. There is no way to predict what knock-on effect there might be. Lifting the fog here might set patterns of air in motion that could lead to natural disasters on a worldwide scale. As a rule, Magicians never mess with the weather unless it really is a last resort.'

'But what about last night?' Calvyn asked with a tinge of surprise.

'The spell that Master Akhdar used last night did not affect the weather, Calvyn. It merely cut us off from it. There is a subtle difference.'

'But couldn't he do the same again now?' Calvyn persisted.

'To what end? The bubble would hold the fog off, it is true, but the fog isn't threatening us in any way. It's merely hindering safe navigation. To create a moving bubble that would follow us wherever we went would require an extremely complex spell and I don't see how that would benefit us greatly. It would still be nigh on impossible to navigate anyway, unless of course you have a spell that would help us to find our way safely through this soup?'

Privately, Calvyn felt that he could probably develop something that would work, if given a little time. Outwardly though, he shook his head and continued unloading the horses. Inevitably, the bulk of the work of setting up the tent fell to Calvyn, Jenna and Lomand, but this time Calvyn found that he did not really mind. Putting the tent up kept them moving and was far better than sitting around arguing over the best road to take southward into Thrandor. Calvyn was pleased to find that the spell that Lomand had taught him to expel water was easily mastered and so he practised it several times as he worked.

Once the tent was erected and suitably fastened down, Calvyn and Jenna built a couple of makeshift shelters next to their fire using spare tent poles and blankets. This allowed them to remain relatively dry without having to stay inside the tent. By careful positioning of the shelters, yet another trick learned from Derra, the heat of the fire evaporated most of the water droplets in the air within the shelters, thus keeping the misty fingers of the fog at bay.

Most of the Magicians simply unpacked their blankets and settled themselves into the tent to sleep, but Master Jabal joined Lomand, Calvyn and Jenna by the fire. Calvyn was pleased that it was Jabal rather than one of the others, for he felt that of all the Grand Magicians, Jabal was the most open-minded and approachable. True, Master Akhdar had that wise and kindly visage and he had been pleasant enough to Calvyn in his short time at the Academy, but Calvyn had always felt that he had to be on his guard when talking to him. Master Chevery had been outright hostile to Calvyn from the moment that they had been introduced, and he had not really had much contact with Masters Ivalo and Kalmar, so he did not really know them well enough to make a comparison. Master Jabal was certainly quick to join in with their conversation.

'So, I hear that we have another Acolyte to welcome into the fold,' he started, smiling warmly at Jenna. 'It seems that Brother Perdimonn has suddenly decided to fill the Academy with his protégés.'

'Oh, I'd hardly say that, Master Jabal,' Jenna replied quickly. 'I don't think for one second that Perdimonn ever had any intention of sponsoring me to the Academy. I mean, why should he? I displayed no interest in becoming a Magician to him and in the time that I travelled with him he did not encourage me into the practice of magic in any way.'

'Really? Yet he gave you a magical object to use, didn't he?'

'Well, yes – but I had to push him hard to get it and what he gave me was not really what I wanted,' Jenna admitted defensively. 'I'm surprised that he mentioned it to you, because I wouldn't have thought it significant. He set off to find you with important news of Selkor, so I would have thought that our brief travels together would have been low on his conversation agenda.'

'Perdimonn gave you a magical artefact?' Calvyn asked in surprise. 'You didn't mention it before. What did he give you?'

Lomand sighed heavily, his disappointment obvious, and Jabal chuckled openly.

'I think that he's a lost cause, Lomand,' Jabal laughed, his eyes dancing with merriment. 'But I'm sure that Calvyn will enjoy your remedial etiquette lesson later.'

Calvyn's face flushed to a deep red of embarrassment as he realised that he had interrupted the Master's conversation. He bit his lip and then apologised to Jabal for his lapse.

'Apology accepted, Calvyn,' Jabal nodded, still smiling. 'As it happens, Jenna, I echo your rash young friend's curiosity. Perdimonn didn't mention either you or the gift that he gave you as far as I can remember. That Perdimonn

31

gave you a magical object at all was a guess. You see, old habits die hard. I have been doing sweeps for magical items for so long that I did one out of habit earlier. My spell should have found nothing, for I excluded all the items that I was aware of, like the Staff of Dantillus and Calvyn's sword, for example. To my surprise, however, something triggered a response and I narrowed it down to you. As I found it unlikely that you possessed a magical item before you encountered Perdimonn, it was a simple extension of logic that he gave you something – an object of power.'

Jenna shrugged her acceptance of his explanation.

'I wanted Perdimonn to give me a weapon: a magical spell, or something that I could use to kill the demon that had consumed Calvyn's soul. Even when I pressed him though, Perdimonn refused my request.'

'That isn't really surprising as Perdimonn is a pacifist,' Jabal commented, his eyes keenly observing Jenna's reactions as he spoke. 'Even if he had agreed, a magical weapon would not have helped you against such a creature. It is said that certain demons are immune to magic – particularly the more powerful ones. So what did he give you?'

'This,' Jenna replied, pulling out the little silver arrow charm that she still wore on the leather thong around her neck. 'He made it for me.'

'He made it? Hmm... interesting. May I have a closer look?' Jabal asked, quite obviously intrigued.

'Of course, Master Jabal.'

Lifting the loop over her head, Jenna collected it into her hand and handed it over to Jabal for him to look at. The Magician studied it minutely and in silence for quite some time before looking up again.

'Well it's pretty and cleverly made, but I cannot discern its purpose,' Jabal admitted, handing the charm back to Jenna.

'It was made to guide me to the demon so that I could kill it and free Calvyn's soul,' Jenna explained, holding up the charm and spinning the arrow as a partial demonstration.

'The arrow always pointed in the direction of the Gorvath, which made it possible for me to catch up with it quickly.'

'Ah, I see!' Jabal exclaimed enthusiastically. 'A sort of quest compass – very clever. Trust Perdimonn to come up with something so ingenious.'

What neither Jabal, Jenna, nor anyone else noticed, however, was that before Jenna replaced the pendant around her neck, the arrow came to rest pointing firmly north-eastwards – directly towards Shandrim.

CHAPTER 2

The mood amongst the Warders was sombre as they took stock of their position. Ever since Morrel had joined them a few days ago, the four had been tracking towards Mantor as fast as they could travel. The problem was that Mantor was not exactly an ideal safe haven and not all of the Warders were convinced it was wise to go there.

'What difference does it make where we go?' Perdimonn snapped, his exasperation at the other Warders' indecision, combined with his fatigue, bringing his irritation to the surface. 'We could go to the far shores of the Eastern Sea and Selkor would follow. We need to choose somewhere to make a stand. Mantor is as good as anywhere.'

'But we cannot fight him, Perdimonn. Our vows...' Rikath protested, the pitch of her voice rising with anxiety.

'... allow us to act in self-defence, providing that we don't compromise the Keys in doing so,' Perdimonn interrupted firmly. 'Listen! Selkor already has your Keys. He fooled each of you by pretending to be me, when none of you had any reason to suspect foul play. He can't use that trick with me, so he is likely to be far more direct in his approach this time. We just need to be prepared to face him.'

'That's easy enough to say, but what can we actually do?' asked Morrel, Warder of the Key of Air. 'After all, Selkor does seem to hold all the master cards in his hand.'

Perdimonn looked across at the short, blocky man and smiled knowingly.

'Not *all*, Morrel. Selkor still needs the Earth Key to

become the Chosen One and I have no intention of letting him have it. I still have a couple of aces up my sleeve and I'm sure that if we put our heads together, we'll find that we have a few more good cards to play as well.'

Perdimonn had always felt Morrel a strange choice as Warder of the Air element. Somehow it just did not seem right to have someone with such a solid appearance warding the most intangible of the elements. Appearances were often deceptive though and where Morrel was very suited to his element was in the way that he thought. Flighty and changeable were not the first words that sprang to mind when seeing Morrel for the first time, but Perdimonn knew only too well that he would have to work hard to keep Morrel going in the same direction for any length of time.

Rikath, on the other hand, suited the Water element very well. Flexible, powerful when angered, and equally soft and welcoming when tranquillity prevailed, Rikath had all of the qualities of the oceans that she served and loved. More importantly, in Perdimonn's view, was the quality in her that made her follow things through to the very end. Just as the incoming tide would stop for no man, so Rikath, once motivated in a direction, was as inexorable as the pull of the moon on the water. If he could just get Rikath started in the direction that he wanted her to go, then Perdimonn was sure that she would become his staunchest ally.

Finally, of course, there was Arred. Mischievous, volatile Arred. Probably the most capricious of the four of them, with his flaming ginger hair and his ready bright enthusiasm, his welcoming smile and his wicked sense of humour, Arred could flare faster to roaring anger than any of the others. He looked so harmless with his tall, reed-like frame and his impulsive smile, yet he too could be coaxed to direct his devastating power to do good, rather than the damage and devastation that were so often attributed to his element.

'So are you going to tell us what these aces are that you are holding on to, old friend?' Arred asked, his eyes predictably bright with anticipation.

'In a moment, Arred. Firstly, I want to make a few things clear. The whole idea behind going to Mantor was to give the Council of Magicians somewhere to meet us. We will need their power if we are to successfully deal with Selkor. Agreed, I could have chosen somewhere else that might have been a more suitable confrontation ground, but assuming that we were all travelling at a similar speed, then Mantor came out as a good halfway meeting point. Our biggest single problem at the moment is to keep Selkor off our backs long enough for us to meet up with Akhdar and the others before we have to turn and face him. Does that make sense so far?'

Perdimonn looked each of the other Warders in the eye in turn and all of them gave him the nod that he was looking for.

'Good,' he continued. 'In that case I'll pull out my first ace.'

Perdimonn paused for a moment and gave Arred an encouraging grin, his blue eyes twinkling with the same sort of mischievous amusement that Arred often displayed.

'Time,' Perdimonn stated boldly.

'Time?' Rikath asked, her surprise evident. 'But Selkor has been using time against us since the start of this!'

'Exactly!' Perdimonn said forcefully. 'And now it's going to stop.'

'Nice,' Arred agreed with a grin. 'A fine trick if you can pull it off, but you admitted yourself that he gained his time manipulating skills from you in the first place. What makes you think that you can suddenly take them away from him again?'

'*I'm* not going to – *we* are,' Perdimonn replied with a chuckle. 'Listen, this idea might be crazy, but I have a seriously strong hunch that it isn't. I think that I can stop Selkor from messing with time providing that you all give your unreserved help. It won't be easy, but I think that it's possible.'

'Stop fiddling around the note, Perdimonn! What is it that

you think we can do?' Rikath asked irritably.

'I think that I can tie time permanently to the Earth Key.'

'What?' exclaimed Rikath and Morrel simultaneously.

Arred said nothing, but a wide smile spread across his face as Perdimonn's proposal sank in. Then he began to laugh. Slowly at first and then building to a belly laugh that reverberated amongst the rocks and dust around them. There was something infectious in that laugh that spread unbidden smiles across the faces of the other Warders like fire taking hold in a dry forest. Morrel and Rikath looked back and forth between Perdimonn and the now helplessly laughing Arred, plainly torn between perplexity and amusement at Arred's laughter and astonishment at Perdimonn's claim.

'Ha, ha, ha! That's priceless, old man. Absolutely priceless!' Arred guffawed, completely unable to stop laughing.

'You're serious?' Rikath asked Perdimonn, disbelievingly. 'You really think that you can anchor time in that way?'

'Well, let's just say that I'm *fairly* confident that it will work, but we will have to work in concert. All four Keys will be needed and we will need to work fast if we are going to be effective, because Selkor is probably hard on our heels as we speak.'

'What would you have us do, Perdimonn? I, for one, have never attempted to manipulate time and wouldn't know where to start,' admitted Morrel dubiously.

'Are you willing to try this then?' Perdimonn asked in return.

The other three Warders looked around at one another, Arred still sniggering to himself, and one by one they nodded their support. Perdimonn took a deep breath and began to explain what it was that he wanted. Essentially, he was going to get each of the Warders to unlock the power of their element and pour it into a pool of energy such that Perdimonn could take the whole unfathomable mass of power and pour it into a relatively simple spell of binding. The difference with this spell was that rather than being a binding that tied something on a local basis, it bound on a universal scale. As such, the power required to complete even the simplest binding was beyond imagination. To bind time was hardly a simple undertaking and so the outcome was far from sure. Each of the Warders would perform a simple spell in sequence, unlocking their elements and making the total sum of their power sources available for Perdimonn to channel into the final spell. In theory, the only way that Selkor could then unlock the effect of the spell would be to reverse it, and that would require him to have access to all four Keys at once.

The Warders listened attentively as Perdimonn spoke and gradually their faces began to display signs that their favour of his plan was growing. Arred, naturally, looked the most enthusiastic. Perdimonn was sure that the Warder of Fire would need little encouragement to use his Key again. It had been plain to Perdimonn that Arred had been making use of his Key more often than was necessary, and probably more often than was prudent. Perdimonn knew only too well from his recent experience at Kaldea, when he and Arred had joined forces to stop any further volcanic eruptions, that the rush of god-like power experienced when unlocking such a huge power source was liable to be very addictive.

'You know,' Arred said, wiping tears from his eyes as he finally managed to get his laughter under control, 'if you manage to do this, Perdimonn, Selkor is going to be seriously upset with you. I mean *seriously* upset.'

'I'll get over it. Your point is?' Perdimonn asked, unable to prevent a smile at Arred's brightly grinning expression.

'People who are that mad make mistakes,' Arred replied innocently, trying to keep his voice serious and failing miserably. 'Tarmin's teeth! He'll be so mad he'll be apoplectic, particularly if you stick a sting in the tail of your spell.'

'A sting?' Morrel asked suspiciously. 'What sort of a sting?'

'Oh, nothing that would break our vow of pacifism,

Morrel,' Arred grinned wickedly. 'Just something that would backlash on anyone trying to manipulate time with enough power to give him a nasty headache for a while.'

Morrel frowned, but Perdimonn and Rikath laughed aloud.

'Arred, you're a genius! That shouldn't be difficult at all in comparison to the rest of the spell. What about something like this?' Perdimonn chuckled and he sketched out a quick sequence of runes into the dusty ground in front of him with his staff.

The other three Warders gathered around and looked at the spell that Perdimonn had scratched into the dust.

'It should work well enough,' Rikath conceded with a shrug. 'What's the matter Morrel? Don't you agree?'

Morrel looked at the spell, his face a mask of concentration as his eyes ran backwards and forwards across the lines of runes. That he was troubled was obvious, but the nature of his inner conflict was unclear to the others. They waited patiently as he struggled to articulate his problem.

'Are you sure that we're not actually attacking Selkor here? I mean, we *know* that he's going to try to manipulate time again, so aren't we just setting a trap for him? That puts us on the offensive in my mind and I don't know that we should go down that route.'

'Oh, come on, Morrel! Ease off on the ethics a little, will you?' urged Arred, exasperation clear in his voice. 'It's not as if we'll actually do him any harm.'

'No, Arred,' Perdimonn interrupted, his tone serious. 'Morrel is right to question the morals of this, because each of us should always consider the implications of our actions – especially at the moment. Every decision that we make, every step that we take, is crucial to the future of the world around us and we should never take that responsibility lightly. Let us each consider this action carefully for a moment or two longer, but then we must make a final decision, for I feel that time is running short.

All levity washed away at Perdimonn's words and the four

Warders fell silent as they thought through the situation and the proposed plan of action. The gentle breeze brought no real comfort from the dry heat of the Terachim Wasteland and no sound of any living creature disturbed the silence. If any reminder was needed of the devastation that could be caused by a magical disaster, then they were standing in the middle of it. Another legacy of Darkweaver's time, the Terachim was not a naturally formed desert and made a sobering setting in which to consider a potentially world-changing magical undertaking. A little dust devil, no more than a few feet high, swirled gently out from between two rocks no more than twenty yards away from where they were standing. The movement caught Morrel's eye first and the others glanced around in mild alarm as they noticed his eyes tracking movement.

'Enough,' Perdimonn stated finally. 'What is it to be? Do we try for the feedback spell, or just the binding spell? Alternatively, of course, we could do nothing, but I think that we're agreed that we must attempt something.'

'Well, I say that we go the whole way and give Selkor a headache,' Arred said firmly. 'As far as I'm concerned the whole thing is a defensive measure anyway. It's not going to stop Selkor, or even really hurt him. The best we can hope for is to slow him down a little.'

Perdimonn nodded, unsurprised by Arred's opinion, but inwardly winced at the Fire Warder's initial choice of words. There was little doubt that he would have voted for anything that hindered Selkor, no matter how outrageous. It was all down to the other two now. Perdimonn met Rikath's gaze first.

'What about you, Rikath? Do you agree with Arred?'

'Yes,' Rikath sighed reluctantly, and glanced across almost apologetically at Morrel. 'I do. It is necessary to slow Selkor down and I think that this is a good, non-aggressive way of accomplishing that goal.'

Morrel grunted sourly at that and shrugged.

'I take it that you are unlikely to have changed your opinion, Perdimonn?' the stocky Warder stated more than asked.

Perdimonn kept eye contact with Morrel and shook his head slightly.

'Very well, then I agree. Let's do it and get moving again before we all bake out here.'

Perdimonn was actually quite surprised that Morrel had agreed to the whole plan so quickly, particularly after his earlier questions. However, unpredictability was a cornerstone of the man's personality, so Perdimonn took Morrel at his word and pressed on with things before the Warder of the Key of Air had a chance to change his mind.

'Alright then, this is what I want you to do. Firstly, I need each of you to memorise this spell,' Perdimonn began, rapidly scratching out the symbols in the dust. 'What we will do is to each work the spell in sequence, fitting our individual Keys into the spell here at the sixth juncture. Morrel, you will go first, then Rikath, then Arred, and finally I will complete the spell by adding both my element and the binding to tie the whole effect to the Earth Power. I will also try to tag the other spell onto the end to complete the backlash effect. Remember, the spell must be focused with each element working in concert, so we will all aim our spells at Morrel's. Any questions?'

There were none. Each Warder knew enough to understand perfectly what Perdimonn was attempting to do.

'Very well, then let's begin.'

The four Warders each took up a position about a pace apart in a slightly concave line facing inward. There was no further chat, Morrel just launched silently into the spell and as he reached the crucial sixth juncture and activated his Key, he raised his right palm forward in front of him. A visible glowing stream of force burst from his hand and terminated at the focal point of the group in a shimmering haze of sky-blue power. Then Rikath raised her hand and added a stream of green power into the haze. Arred joined her quickly, adding an orange-red stream of force and the focal point of the power streams pulsed and buzzed as it tore at the very fabric of space and time. Finally,

Perdimonn began his part of the spell and added the binding and backlash elements before raising his hand and sending a stream of brown-gold force to blend with the others.

Perdimonn's power stream joined the multi-coloured aura and the burning focus of the power streams swelled outwards as if it had drawn in a huge breath. Then in the blink of an eye, it collapsed inwards until it formed a tiny point of blinding white energy before exploding silently in a white wave of magical power.

For an instant the universe seemed to jolt, as time stood still and then – nothing.

The four Warders lowered their hands, the power streams having cut off at the instant of the silent magical wave and three sets of eyes turned to Perdimonn expectantly. Perdimonn's expression took on a look of extreme concentration for a moment and then settled into one of satisfaction.

'It's done,' he said simply.

*　　　*　　　*　　　*　　　*

Femke slipped through the crowd like an eel weaving its way through thick pondweed. Somehow, nothing seemed to hinder her as she moved rapidly through to where the spy wanted to be, which, as usual, was right in the thick of things. This was the biggest gathering that she had heard of yet and the general buzz was one of anger and recrimination for the military losses in Thrandor. The whole tone of this was turning ugly for the Emperor, and Femke wanted to know who the prime organisers were. There was always the chance that there were no main leaders of this mob, but even if no one was really leading the rallies now, someone was bound to step in and take advantage of the situation soon.

One theme that was consistent throughout the crowd was that everyone blamed the Emperor for the disaster. Femke had spotted some of the Emperor's agents trying to shift the blame onto the Sorcerer Lord, Shanier, but their words were falling on deaf ears. So much so that one of the agents was actually beaten by several of the nearby men in the crowd for suggesting that anyone other than the Emperor should take the responsibility.

Emotions were running high, and without a vent for those emotions it was only a matter of time before the crowd exploded into some sort of action. Everywhere that Femke looked, anger and bitterness had united the people in a way that would never normally be seen in Shandrim. Washerwomen were standing next to merchants of obvious standing, teachers conversed with those who swept the streets and farmers, lots of farmers, mingled with the city folk as if they met every day. This sort of singleness of purpose spelled the end for the Emperor's reign unless he acted quickly, dynamically and decisively. A crowd like this did not just represent a pebble rolling down a mountainside, it was a large boulder that was picking up momentum with every turn and triggering other falls as it went. Very soon the Emperor would be facing a landslide on a huge scale unless he could somehow apply a deflecting force. The only consolation for Femke was that she had given him fair warning.

Moving on through the mass of people, eyes constantly scanning for anything unusual, Femke suddenly caught a glimpse of a familiar figure moving through the crowd with similar ease ahead of her. It was Shalidar, the Emperor's top assassin, and he was moving with what appeared to be a real sense of purpose. To Femke's mind that could only mean one thing – Shalidar was closing in for a kill.

'This could prove interesting in the middle of this many people,' Femke muttered to herself as she changed tracks to follow the deadly killer. Not that the crowd would not offer suitable cover to effect a clean escape, but it could equally make an escape difficult if the hit went wrong. Femke had never witnessed Shalidar at work before, though she had heard much of his skill from others. If what Femke had heard was true, then she could easily miss him make his kill and then blunder into the aftermath before she knew it, particularly if, as she suspected he would, he made his hit on the move.

As Femke tracked Shalidar, her mind raced. Was his target the main leader of this rally? If so, then where had he got his information? Certainly the Emperor had many spies at his disposal and it was always possible that one of the others had beaten her to discovering who the key people were in these rallies. It was unusual though, for Femke had all of her sources of information working at this and so far they had turned up nothing. Femke had not built her reputation as a top spy by being second to know anything, so playing catch up at the information game was not something that she was either used to, or happy about.

Quick as Femke was at manoeuvring through the crowd, Shalidar was quicker and he was slowly getting away from her. Gritting her teeth with determination, Femke tried to pick up her pace.

'Excuse *me*!' exclaimed a well-dressed woman pointedly, after accidentally colliding with Femke.

Shalidar's head turned despite the loud background buzz of the crowd noise and Femke ducked down, pretending to pick something from the floor as his eyes scanned the people behind him.

'Sorry,' Femke mumbled to the lady, despite the fact that the collision had not been her fault.

'I should think so too,' the woman said, in a very high and mighty voice. 'You should... how rude!'

The woman did not finish her sentence, for Femke had already slipped into the crowd again, melting away as swiftly as water poured on dry sand.

'Who are you after, Shalidar?' Femke whispered to herself as she regained a discreet distance behind him. The way the assassin was scanning the crowd ahead, Shalidar had evidently not acquired his target yet. Despite this, he still moved with apparent purpose and surprising speed. Femke would have expected the man to slide along quietly and not draw any attention to his movement. Granted, he was moving smoothly and creating no real disturbance as he went, but at the speed that he was slicing through the crowd, Shalidar could not hope to go completely unnoticed.

'What are you thinking of?' Femke mused silently. 'For a man with such an awesome reputation, you just aren't acting like a top professional killer.'

Suddenly, the assassin changed direction and Femke thanked the gods that she had not moved up to flank him, or he would have spotted her for sure. 'Has Shalidar spotted his victim?' Femke wondered, looking into the crowd ahead of him. The spy could see no one that stood out among the people ahead of Shalidar, but then she did not really know what she was looking for.

All the way through the mass of people, Femke kept expecting Shalidar to focus in on someone and make his move, but she was to be surprised again, for Shalidar was not aiming for anyone in the crowd. Instead, he made his way to a doorway and, after a swift glance around at the crowd, he knocked twice and entered, closing the door behind him.

'Damn!' Femke cursed, grinding her teeth in frustration. The assassin had obviously not been on a hit after all and yet his behaviour had piqued Femke's curiosity such that she was unwilling to just let this chance encounter go. Whatever the Emperor's top assassin was up to, Femke felt that it was well within her remit to investigate it. After all, information was her business and things in the Imperial Palace had been very strange over the last few weeks.

Femke could not shake the feeling that something strange had happened to the Emperor. He had changed somehow, and the change gave her the creeps. Maybe whatever Shalidar was up to was linked to the weird feeling that she had about the Emperor. It was a long shot, but one that the spy was not about to relinquish easily.

After waiting a few moments to be sure that Shalidar was not going to reappear in a hurry, Femke made her way surreptitiously up to the door. It was plain, with no indication of who lived or worked behind it. Femke moved casually past the lower floor window adjacent to the door, but the internal shutters were closed, giving no clues as to what lay inside.

This really was most intriguing, Femke decided, as she moved a short distance away from the door to avoid her interest in the building from becoming overly conspicuous. A crowd, hundreds strong, maybe thousands, milling in a middle class quarter of Shandrim talking nothing but treason and Shalidar just happens to turn up, weave his way through the crowd and enter a building in the exact same area where the rally is taking place. Coincidence? Femke did not think so for one second, but what did it mean?

Someone a little further down the street started to speak out in a loud clear voice and the general buzz of the crowd dropped to a muted murmur as the people began to listen to what the man had to say. Whoever was speaking had a powerful voice that carried easily through to where Femke was standing and beyond. The man's voice spoke passionately of the losses that the people had suffered and the events that had led up to those losses. It spoke of better times before the Emperor had messed with borders that would have been better left as they were. Certainly, the Thrandorians had been in the wrong for raiding Shandese trade caravans and creating trouble in the borderlands, he stated vehemently, but sending an army to invade a country required proper military planning and a tough and capable military leader to command the troops. Sending Sorcerers to run an army simply showed a lack of appreciation for the realities of life and clearly demonstrated the Emperor was not fit to rule, the voice exhorted. It was time that the Emperor stood down and made way for someone worthy of the position – someone who would make Shandar strong again, so that no Nation would dare to interfere with her trade or her borders – someone who was in touch with the feelings of the people and the day-to-day needs of the man on the street.

Femke was terribly torn. Whoever was speaking was quite obviously a prime mover in these rallies, but from her present position she had no chance of tying a face to the voice. If she moved now though, she might miss Shalidar leaving and she desperately wanted to know what he was up to. What to do? It was a tough decision and Femke hesitated to choose between the opportunities.

The speaker was expertly playing the crowd with his rhetoric and Femke twitched several times as she tried to decide what to do. The man was building up to something, probably the name of whomever the speaker supported as the next Emperor, Femke decided. At least she would take that much away from this event, she reasoned – but she was wrong. The city militia chose that precise moment to arrive and ruin everything.

Just when Femke felt that the speaker would name his preferred choice for Emperor, panic set the crowd in motion as the militia arrived in force to break up the gathering. Femke cursed her luck and with a last rueful glance at the door that she had been monitoring, the spy let herself be swept away in the crowd until she reached a suitable back alley to slip away into. Getting to the alley was no sinecure either, as Femke had to work very hard indeed to twist and turn her way across the flow of people in order to reach the entrance. It was very much like swimming across a fast flowing river, aiming into and across the flow in an attempt to avoid being swept past her target.

Breathing hard as she broke free of the crowd, Femke assessed her position. There was no hope of discovering the identity of the speaker under current conditions. That would be a job for tomorrow. Someone would know who it was and Femke would find out one way or another. There was a good chance, however, that Shalidar might not leave that building for a while. He would not want to get tangled up with the militia any more than she did, so he might well sit out the commotion in the hope of slipping away quietly a little later. It was certainly worth a bit of effort on her part to see if her hunch was correct, she decided.

Gritting her teeth and sucking in a deep breath, Femke launched herself into a run. The alley led to a dead end, but Femke had known that when she had chosen it. There was no alleyway in Shandrim that Femke did not know. In her profession it was always useful to have a few back exits up your sleeve and Femke had spent years learning every inch of Shandrim for just such an occasion.

The wall at the end of the alley was about ten feet high, but it caused her no problems. Femke launched herself up at it, catching the top with her fingers and pulling herself up with ease. A quick walk along the top of the wall to the right and a nimble jump to catch the rooftop above, and within seconds Femke had pulled herself up and onto the roof of the building.

Nimble as a cat, Femke ran across the gently sloping rooftops, leaping from surface to surface with ease and moving quickly back in the general direction of the building that she had seen Shalidar enter. Being above the streets proved a huge bonus as the spy kept a good overall picture of what was happening in the streets directly below her. Initially, she was one street removed from where all of the action was happening, but Femke did not wait long to rectify that. As soon as she came to a lower roof, Femke lowered herself over the edge until she was hanging by her fingertips before dropping to the street below.

Despite picking a lower roof, it was still a fair drop to the pavement and Femke landed hard, her feet and legs taking the majority of the shock of impact. With a grunt, Femke picked herself up quickly and sprinted across the street to look for a way up onto the next line of rooftops. It was not difficult to find. Femke went up the side of the first house that she came to with the ease of a spider, her fingers seeking out handholds and her feet finding toeholds that most would not even see. Seconds later and she was skimming over the rooftops again, doing her utmost to keep low as she went. If the militia spotted her, they would chase her for sure. After all, what possible legitimate reason could anyone have to be up there? More than likely they would shoot first and ask questions later and Femke had no desire to be stuck full of crossbow bolts.

Dropping to all fours, the spy crawled across the last couple of buildings before worming her way down to the edge of the roof overlooking the door that she wanted to watch. The whole street was still crawling with militia men, some mounted, but most just strutting about in their uniforms like male peacocks displaying their feathers.

'Good,' Femke breathed. 'He won't have left with that lot around.'

Easing back from the edge just a little, Femke tried to make herself as comfortable as she could. It might be a long wait and she did not want to be hampered by cramps if she had to move again in a hurry.

Time passed slowly, minutes reluctantly dragging into hours as the afternoon grudgingly ticked away. Slowly but surely, the militia dispersed. Eventually just two footmen remained. Quickly bored, they wandered up and down chatting and generally just whiling away the afternoon until their watch was up.

Life in the street was slow to return to normal. The first few folk to walk past stepped quickly, with frequent apprehensive glances towards the militiamen as if expecting to be stopped for no reason. As the afternoon wore on though, so folk became bolder again and by the time fog descended in the late afternoon, people were moving to and fro in what Femke judged to be an everyday fashion.

The fog was a mixed blessing for Femke. It reduced the chances of anyone spotting her up on the roof, but it also made it more difficult for her to see who was moving around on the street below. Also, the fog brought a real chill to the air. A cold wet chill that numbed her flesh and made her bones ache. It was not long, after the thick, wet mugginess descended, before Femke started having thoughts of giving up on Shalidar and heading back to her room in the Palace for a nice hot soak in the bath. The colder that she became, the more frequently the thoughts surfaced, but Femke was tenacious in the extreme and she continued lying there, with her teeth chattering, firmly determined not to let the day be a wasted effort.

Finally, the door opened and a figure stepped out onto the street. The figure was wrapped in a dark cloak with a deeply cowled hood, making it impossible for Femke to visibly confirm whether the figure was indeed Shalidar. It no longer mattered. The person knew what was in that building and, more than likely, what Shalidar was up to. That was enough for now.

Forcing herself up onto her haunches, Femke watched long enough to note which direction the figure began walking in and then started scrambling as silently as possible across the rooftops to try to get ahead of her quarry. The biggest need now was to get down to street level quickly if she was to have a chance of tracking him successfully whilst remaining undetected. The nearest safe drop to the ground was several buildings ahead, so the spy knew that she would have to move very quickly if her predetermined plan of action was to work.

Even as she started to run, her brain analysed the figure's gait and decided that it was definitely not Shalidar. The walk belonged to a man: no woman walked that way. Also, the man's walk was positive, but not that of an assassin, or at least, certainly not that of Shalidar. The Emperor's top assassin always walked on the balls of his feet, stepping lightly, as most predators did. However, this figure was more flat-footed, moving precisely, but not with the sort of precision that Femke would relate to an assassin. It was more like... military! That was it, she decided. The man was in the military. But what unit would he be from and why would he be meeting with Shalidar?

Femke was literally flying along now, forcing her stiff, reluctant muscles and her cold-clogged brain into overdrive as she sprang from roof to roof. Then, in mid-flight, the world seemed to stop. For a heart-stopping moment, Femke saw a flash of white light and for an instant it felt as if she was just hanging, suspended in space between two buildings, high above the ground. With an equally surprising suddenness, her momentum returned and her leap across the alley ended abruptly with her crashing, completely unbalanced, onto the rooftop that suddenly raced to meet her. With no time to recover, Femke fell onto her stomach and started to slide out of control towards the edge of the roof. Falling from this height would almost certainly prove fatal, so survival instincts overrode any thoughts of concealment. Femke scrabbled desperately for a moment to gain some sort of purchase and then spread her limbs, thereby increasing the friction with the surface across which she was sliding.

Briefly, Femke's right foot caught on the narrow flat ledge that marked the edge of the roof before sliding over into space. The slight catch of her foot marginally slowed Femke's descent, but it also slewed her body as she slid slowly over the edge. Somehow, Femke managed to slap her left forearm across the narrow ledge and catch hold with the fingers of her right hand, leaving her dangling high above the alleyway in precarious fashion.

Normally, with that amount of purchase Femke would have swung herself back up onto the roof with ease, but cold and shaken as she was, it seemed all that she could do just to hang on. Gasping for breath, Femke tried to swing her right leg up to the ledge and her right hand momentarily lost grip, leaving her swinging, with only her left forearm across the ridge. Growling with effort, Femke regained a hold with her right hand and forced her right foot up the wall until it made the ledge. Painfully she hauled herself, shaking with effort and fright, back up onto the roof. Chest heaving as she gulped great mouthfuls of air, Femke sat in shocked silence for a moment, wondering what on earth had happened during that simple jump. Something very strange was about her best description.

Thoughts of following the cloaked man were forgotten. The spy was shaken, bruised and bleeding from several nasty scrapes and grazes. Femke was a realist. She was in no fit state to effectively trail anyone. The Shalidar mystery would have to wait, she decided glumly, and carefully easing herself back onto her feet, the battered spy started making her way slowly back to the Palace.

CHAPTER 3

'Eloise, check the door,' Derra ordered sharply, glancing around at the same time to confirm that her weapon was within easy reach.

Bek groaned with pain as Derra continued to briskly re-strap his wound. Derra was certainly competent at basic medicine, but Bek might have wished for a more sympathetic nurse. The Sergeant had not offered him so much as an acknowledgement that he was even suffering any pain and she simply treated him, as she would do any other task that needed completing, with practical efficiency.

Bek could hear someone climbing the wooden stairs towards the room in which Derra, Eloise and he were hiding. They had been here for more than a week now with only a couple of incidents of near discovery. Derra must have heard the person come in through the door downstairs, Bek realised, still wincing at the Sergeant's firm ministrations. It irked him that there was little that he could do in the event of a fight, but he still felt as weak as a newborn babe and he doubted that he could stand up for more than a minute or so unaided, let alone swing a sword.

'It's OK, Sergeant. It's just Fesha,' Eloise informed them with a hint of relief in her tone.

'Good,' Derra replied, allowing no emotion to touch her gravelly voice. 'Let's see what news he brings this time.'

With a final, business-like pull at the ends of the bandage, Derra neatly tied off the knot and tucked away the ends. Once more she drilled Bek with her famously hard gaze and raised a threatening finger to him as he gingerly lowered his tunic back down over the freshly bound dressings.

'Don't mess with it, Bek. No prodding or poking this time. You're only slowing down the healing process and as far as I'm concerned that is tantamount to self-inflicted injury and a punishable offence. As I'm able to award a suitable level of punishment, I suggest that you bear that firmly in mind and leave it alone.'

'Yes, Sergeant,' Bek replied meekly. He knew that he was already in a whole dung heap of trouble over his refusal to leave the arena when Derra and the others had tried to free him the first time. He was gratified that despite his disobedience, the Sergeant had not given up on getting him out. He had told them to leave him there, but Derra had absolutely refused to do that. Bek had not yet worked out quite why that was, but he suspected that it had to do with her sheer stubbornness when it came to pursuing goals. The Sergeant had come with the mission to free Bek and Jez from the arena and she had not been about to go back to Thrandor whilst Bek was still alive.

Bek just wished that Jez could be here with him. The easy-going young Private had always maintained that a rescue party would be mounted and though Bek had humoured him in that belief, he had never truly expected anyone to come. Unfortunately, the rescue had come too late for Jez. He had been killed in the so called 'games' by the top-ranked fighter, Serrius, and though Bek had avenged Jez in the arena by defeating the Shandese fighter, rage still burned in Bek's heart at Jez's death. Fesha had tried to discover whether Serrius survived the wound that Bek had dealt him, but the wiry little Private had not managed to discover any news of him.

Bek did not care about Serrius any more. The Shandese fighter could live or die as far as Bek was concerned. His revenge against Serrius was complete, but Calvyn – Calvyn was a different matter entirely. Calvyn, or Lord Shanier or whatever he chose to call himself, had sent Jez and he to the arena in the first instant. The next time Bek met Calvyn it would be with a sword in his hand and, fit or not, Bek intended to honour the oath that he had made the day that Jez had died.

Eloise had told him that Calvyn had originally set out with them on the rescue mission, but when Bek had asked her where Calvyn was now, Eloise did not really know. She had some vague notions about a magical message and having to go to a city called Terilla, or some such place, but the imprecision of her answer led Bek to believe that Calvyn had simply deceived Eloise and the others yet again. Bek told himself firmly that Calvyn was a master of hiding his true intent and refused to believe that he was now somehow good again. There was no other rational explanation for the facts as Bek saw them. Somehow, during his training at Baron Keevan's Castle Calvyn had managed to fool everyone into thinking that he was nothing but a normal young man looking for a career as a soldier. Looking back though, it was obvious that Calvyn had always had his own agenda.

Even from the very beginning, Calvyn had quietly used magic and sorcery to gain everyone's trust. The ointment that he had handed around the dormitory healed blisters faster than Bek had ever seen, the light that Calvyn had made in the dungeon to tie Bek into secrecy and, of course, the sword. Bek now even questioned Calvyn's motives for fighting Demarr at Mantor. Maybe the whole fight with Demarr had been a cover to get the amulet for the other Magician, Selkor. He was Shandese as well, Calvyn had said as much after the battle. It all fitted. By defeating Demarr, Calvyn had prevented Thrandor from being overrun by a force that would have been more difficult for the Shandese Legions to defeat, and so prepared the way for the invasion from the north. Devious in the extreme, Bek decided grimly, but whatever Calvyn's grander motives were, Bek intended to see that the man he had once considered his best friend, paid dearly for Jez's death in the arena.

Eloise opened the door briefly and allowed Fesha to step

inside before she shut and bolted the door behind him. The wiry little man with his mischievous air and his quirky smile had kept them all well supplied with food, medical supplies and information since he had brought them here on the day of Bek's fight with Serrius. Somehow he had also disposed of the body of the guard that he had killed that day as well. Fesha was apparently both creative and resourceful. Once again his eyes were smiling, which Bek instantly read to mean more good news.

'Good to see you sitting up, Corporal,' Fesha said brightly as he shucked off his cloak.

'Never mind the pleasantries, Fesha,' Derra growled. 'What's going on out there?'

'Chaos,' Fesha stated simply, grinning from ear to ear. 'Pure unadulterated chaos.'

'What do you mean?' Eloise asked suspiciously. 'They're not searching for us again are they?'

'No, no!' Fesha laughed. 'Far from it! In fact, I don't think that there's any further danger of specific searches for us. The militia are going to be way too busy for that.'

'What have you been up to?' Derra growled, her suspicion obvious.

'Me? Nothing!' Fesha answered innocently, trying to look hurt by the implication, but his dancing eyes gave off nothing but amusement at the fact that his companions thought him capable of causing widespread disruption across Shandrim. 'The Shandese people though, well that's another story.'

'Go on,' Derra prompted impatiently.

'They're mounting rallies and protests all over the city. It seems that the news of the Shandese defeat at Kortag has finally started to filter through to the populace here. The people are, shall we say, not overly pleased with their Emperor right now. To be perfectly honest, Sergeant, we couldn't ask for a better opportunity to make our move out of here. Even the weather is on our side. I don't know if you have looked out of the window in the last half hour, but there's a real soup of a fog descended on the city. With everything else that's going on, if we can get to the city boundary without getting stopped, then we should be able to get well clear of Shandrim by nightfall.'

Derra considered that for a moment and then shook her head.

'No. By the time we get the horses and equipment here, there won't be enough daylight left to get far enough from the city to be safe if the fog lifts. I agree that it is a good opportunity, but if these rallies are just beginning to build, then they won't die out overnight. There will be other chances,' she said regretfully.

Fesha just grinned and then winked at Eloise slyly.

'Well, Sergeant, I did actually consider all that and so I brought the horses and equipment with me. They're in the alleyway opposite,' he said casually.

'So why didn't you just say so, Fesha?' Derra growled, her eyes narrowing dangerously. 'Let's cut the chat and get going while we have the chance.'

'I think that's what I just said,' Fesha whispered to Eloise.

'I heard that, Private,' Derra grated. 'Don't push your luck!'

'What about "Thank you, Fesha. You did really well"?' he grumbled to himself as he and Eloise gently lifted Bek to his feet. Bek heard the comment and grinned. The Private had a lot to learn if he expected outright praise from Derra. The Sergeant did notice when things got done well, but said little. When things were not done well, or not done at all, then Tarmin help the person responsible. From what Bek had seen so far, about the only thing that Derra could criticise Fesha for was his manner. Whilst it was obvious enough that the little Private got under her skin, Bek knew Derra well enough to see that she would not be blinded by that one factor. Fesha was very competent – extremely irritating and arrogant maybe, but very competent.

Bek would be more than a little glad to leave this room, as all it held for him was memories of pain. The bare, whitewashed walls were clean enough but, aside from the insides of the permanently closed plain wooden shutters, they gave no relief to the eyes. The little room held only one small bunk, a stool, a wooden chair and a very small wooden table. The floor was bare and the wooden flooring was dark with age and wear. The small floor space was utilised as a sleeping area at night for whichever two were not on watch. The last member of the party sat on the chair next to the door to listen out for any signs of people entering the building.

Derra, Eloise and Fesha had all been out on errands at various times, but since Fesha had left Bek alone on that first day to fetch the two women, there had never been less than two people with him at all times. After the first couple of days, Derra had sent Fesha out more and more. This was mainly because he proved more successful at foraging supplies and gathering information than the others. However, Bek believed that Derra found the chatty little Private irritated her intensely when they were together for any length of time, giving her further cause to want him out of the cramped living space. Bek found him amusing, but could easily see why Derra limited her own exposure to Fesha's wit and repartee.

Fesha and Eloise half carried Bek out of the room and over to the top of the narrow stairway that led down to the ground floor. There was no room for even two abreast down the stairs, but there was a handrail that offered some support. Bek's legs felt incredibly weak after more than a week of enforced bed rest, and his thighs were actually trembling slightly just with the effort of standing up. He was not about to admit that weakness though, particularly in front of Eloise.

During his protracted period of enforced idleness, Bek had found his eyes following the raven-haired beauty more and more. To begin with, when there was some doubt over Bek's chances of surviving the wound that he had sustained during his fight with Serrius, Eloise had been tenderness personified. Although her face could hardly be called angelic, Eloise did possess a beauty that seemed to transcend that of most women. Being tended gently by such beauty in the midst of a sea of pain brought feelings that Bek was unaccustomed to. He had always been attracted to Eloise, but then most of the men in Baron Keevan's army had been similarly attracted, he reflected ironically. It just seemed that somehow the depth of that attraction had reached a new level over this period of convalescence. The strange thing, however, was that the stronger Bek became and the more certain his recovery from his wound became, the more distant Eloise seemed to act. Bek did not understand why, but he was certain he was not imagining it.

The feeling of Eloise against his side, as she had helped him walk for the first time since the injury, had set Bek's blood pounding through his veins. He leaned heavily against the rail at the top of the stairs and took a couple of deep breaths.

'Do you think you can manage, Bek, or should we rig up something to help you down?' Fesha asked tentatively.

'No, I'll be fine,' Bek replied steadily. 'Just give me a moment.'

Bek felt anything but fine. His heart was pounding, his legs were trembling and he felt dizzy, as if he was about to pass out. Derra emerged from the little room carrying the remains of their possessions and supplies in her arms and looked at him sharply.

'Just stay there a moment, Bek. Let me take these things downstairs first, then I'll come back and help you down,' Derra ordered.

'I don't need help, Sergeant. I can make it down on my own,' Bek said stubbornly.

Derra stopped and drilled him with one of her hardest stares.

'You will do as I tell you, Corporal. Don't add any more insubordination to your tally, or I'll strip you of your stripes faster than you can blink,' she grated fiercely. 'Fesha, take some of this off me. Eloise, keep an eye on the Corporal here and don't let him do anything stupid.'

Fesha grabbed an armload of blankets from Derra and

rattled down the stairs at pace. Nobody messed with the Sergeant when she used that tone, and whilst he was not on the receiving end of it for a change, Fesha was not about to give Derra a reason to move her focus onto him.

Derra followed Fesha down the stairs with more decorum, leaving Eloise alone with Bek for the first time. They stood in silence, looking anywhere but at each other's eyes. Bek was not so much struggling for something to say as struggling to stay upright. Battling quietly with his quaking legs Bek realised that he was fighting a losing battle, and with a groan he started to slowly collapse, still clinging doggedly onto the support rail for all he was worth.

Almost before the groan left his lips, Eloise was there, her arms supporting some of his weight and gently lowering him to the floor.

'Why is it that you men have to act so tough all the time?' she asked him gently, as she propped him in a sitting position against the wall.

'Why did you want to become a soldier?' he asked in reply, twisting his lips in a sardonic smile. 'I act tough because I'm expected to act tough. I must be tough because I'm First Sword, remember?'

'How could I forget?' she replied, her voice heavy with sarcasm. 'You wear the title like a challenge. You could just put a sign around your neck saying, "I'm First Sword – go ahead, try and stick a blade through me." Oh, I'm sorry, I forgot – someone already did that, didn't they?'

'I still won though.'

'And what good did it do you? You're lucky to be alive. The fight was unnecessary. If you had just come with us when we came for you the first time, then we'd probably be safely back in Thrandor by now and you wouldn't have played pincushion for Serrius.'

'Yes,' thought Bek silently. 'Safely in Thrandor, but I would never have forgiven myself for breaking my oath. I have held my word, Jez. Tarmin help me, I have held my word and I will not fail to finish what I've started.' Aloud, he just grunted, letting Eloise make of that what she would.

How could he hope to explain it to her? Calvyn had somehow bewitched all of them into thinking that he was on their side. All this talk of Shandese unrest and plotting against the Emperor was probably the normal state of affairs in a country that encouraged the looting and invading of neighbouring lands.

Derra and Fesha came back up the stairs and Derra looked at Bek with the nearest that he had seen yet to compassion on her face. 'Come on, let's get you outside and on a horse,' she said briskly. 'At least the weather gives us a good excuse to ride with our hoods over our heads. Hopefully nobody will recognise you. I think that you'd better double up on a horse with someone else until you've regained a bit more of your strength.'

'He can ride with me,' offered Eloise, and Bek's heart leapt at the thought of riding double either with Eloise's arms around him, or with his around her.

'No,' Derra disagreed with a slight shake of her head. 'Fesha is lighter. It makes more sense for Bek to ride with him.

For a moment, Bek felt a surge of anger and hatred towards Derra for denying him the chance to ride with Eloise before common sense told him not to be so petty. Derra was just being her usual, practical self and Bek was allowing his growing infatuation to cloud his judgement, he told himself firmly. Despite his resolution, he could not help the final thought that crossed his mind that, small though he was, Fesha could not weigh much less than Eloise.

Derra and Eloise helped Bek down the stairs, one in front and one behind, while Fesha disappeared outside to bring the horses across the street. Bek moved slowly, one step at a time, but by the time he had reached the bottom of the stairs he found that rather than sapping energy from his legs, the movement seemed to be restoring strength. His muscles were obviously stiff and incredibly weak, but the movement of blood through them appeared to be acting as a restorative.

Mounting a horse proved more painful, even with the boost from Derra to shunt him up into the saddle. Bek gasped with pain as the movement pulled at the wound in his side and he was not surprised to feel the warmth of a fresh flow of blood into his bandaging. Bek held loosely onto the sides of Fesha's tunic as he settled himself, then he drew his hood over his head and waited for the others to ready themselves.

Derra and Eloise finished packing the last of their things into the saddlebags and loaded the bulk of them onto the spare horse. Within a few minutes they were underway and Bek started to work at moving with the rolling gait of their mount to prevent any further pulling at his wound. It was not easy to accomplish when sat behind someone riding with a conventional rhythm, but Bek gradually settled into a movement that minimised his pain without bothering Fesha.

Fesha and Bek rode alongside Derra, with Eloise behind them leading the packhorse, the clopping of the hooves on the stone streets sounding strangely both echoing and yet muffled in the thick fog. Bek had no concept of how big the city was other than by the size of the crowds that he had seen in the arena, but Fesha appeared confident in his ability to navigate them through the murky streets, so Bek decided not to worry about keeping track of their route.

A sudden voice in the gloom ahead called out almost precisely the words that Bek dreaded hearing most.

'Halt! Identify yourselves and state your business.'

Two uniformed figures gradually emerged from the fog like ghosts materialising from nowhere. They were militiamen on foot and appeared almost as apprehensive at seeing mounted folk as Bek felt about seeing their uniforms.

'We are visitors here in Shandrim, sir. We came to visit with relatives, but the city is not what we were expecting. People running through the streets being pursued by your compatriots has made our homes in the country seem much safer and more comfortable places to be right now. We are cutting our stay short. You city folk are welcome to

Shandrim,' Fesha said loudly in an accent that he knew to be typical of the southern Shandese countryside.

'Very well, you might as well go on your way,' the militiaman said with a sneer, quite obviously thinking them cowardly and not worthy of his concern after all. As they moved to pass though, he stopped them a second time and Bek's breath caught in his throat as he thought the game was up. 'Tell me, good countryman, why do you ride double when you have a spare horse? Don't tell me that your fellow countryman cannot ride?' he asked suspiciously.

'Oh, that's just because our other horse is showing signs of going lame,' Fesha replied easily. 'If you watch her walk, you'll see that she is favouring her left rear leg. The fetlock on her right is obviously tender, so we're just keeping her load light until she's recovered.'

Bek held his breath as he realised the gamble that Fesha was taking. The confidence of Fesha's voice carried weight, but Bek knew he was bluffing, counting on the militiaman knowing little of horses and their care. The militiaman waved them forward, obviously content with Fesha's answer and, as they goaded their horses forward into a slow walk again, Bek could only marvel at the casual way in which Fesha had lied to them. His accent had been all but perfect from what Bek could tell and his answers had come out so naturally that Bek had found that even he had wanted to believe them. Within moments the fog had swallowed them once more into its surreal world of swirling shapes and shadows and the immediate danger of discovery was past.

The streets seemed to go on forever. Whether it was luck, or that the city militia were busy elsewhere, they would never know for sure, but they did not encounter any more uniformed men as they rode through the city. There were occasional other passers-by, and each shape that emerged from the fog brought an instant of doubt, but all just hurried on their way, eager to get to wherever they were heading and completely disinterested in the riders.

'Are you sure that you know where you are going?' Derra asked Fesha eventually, voicing a concern that was uppermost in Bek's mind as well. 'I feel like we are going in circles.'

'Positive, Derra,' he replied confidently. 'I came this way to avoid some of the main streets where the militia would be most likely to be patrolling and also some of the more unsavoury districts of Shandrim. If we had strayed into one of those areas in this weather, then our chances of leaving it alive, or at the very least with our horses and equipment, would have been slim.'

'Fair enough,' Derra conceded grudgingly. 'But how much further have we got to go in order to clear the city?'

'Oh, not far. It should only take about...'

A flash of white light washed over them and for a stomach lurching instant the world stopped. Then it started again.

'... five minutes,' Fesha finished, his voice trailing off into silence.

'Tell me that you all felt that too,' Derra said, her voice uneasy.

'I did.'

'Absolutely.'

'Me too.'

'Well what in Tarmin's name was it?' Derra wondered aloud.

'Never mind what that was, what is *that*?' Fesha asked, cocking his head to one side slightly, like a dog listening.

In the distance ahead of them sounded a growling howl, the like of which Bek had never heard before. Another, slightly lower pitched voice joined it and shivers set Bek's spine tingling like a vibrating string on a minstrel's lyre.

'If they're dogs, then they've got voices like none that I've ever heard,' shuddered Eloise from behind them.'

'They sound... evil,' Fesha murmured, his voice uncharacteristically subdued.

All of a sudden, there was a barking roar and the howling cut off abruptly. The four riders looked at one another uneasily, the final unasked question unnecessary. None of them knew what would make the last sound either, and it went without saying that they did not want to find out.

'Do I need to ask which way we're heading tonight, Fesha?' Derra asked, her voice firm again, but unconvincingly so.

Fesha shook his head. 'We're going that way,' he said, pointing in almost the exact direction of the frightening howls.

'Why did I just know that you were going to say that?'

*   *   *   *   *

'What are you doing out there?' Akhdar called angrily from the tent.

It was still only late afternoon and not even beginning to get dark despite the thick fog. Jenna had just tucked away her silver pendant and the conversation had turned to their lessons, which caused Calvyn's face to redden once more after his very recent breach of etiquette. The bright wave of magical energy washed over them, causing everything to freeze for an instant before returning to normal.

'That was nothing to do with us,' Jabal replied, his face draining of colour until it threatened to blend with the fog. 'That was... well I don't know what it was.'

Seconds later the other four Grand Magicians had joined the group around the fire. Conversation and speculation erupted into a heated discussion almost immediately.

'Time stopped and yet I was aware that it had stopped. How could that be?' asked Kalmar, plainly puzzled.

'Nonsense!' Chevery disagreed heatedly. 'If time stopped then everything would stop. Everything! That includes thought, Kalmar.'

'I don't know that I can quite agree with you there, Chevery,' interjected Master Ivalo thoughtfully. 'In theory...'

'Gentlemen, please!' Akhdar interrupted forcefully. 'Whilst theorising on the nature of time is undoubtedly a worthy subject for debate, let's try to keep on track here. That wave of magical force was of a high magnitude. As none of us caused it, then I suggest that it was probably not a local phenomenon, which in turn implies that someone has unleashed a spell requiring an enormous amount of energy.

I need hardly remind you that the magnitude of energy required to work on that scale is beyond any of us here without the aid of the Staff of Dantillus. It would probably be beyond us even with the Staff's magnifying powers. That limits the possibilities of who caused this effect to a very short list. I have three initial questions. Who? Why? And what exactly did that wave do?'

'The first is easy,' Chevery said condescendingly. 'Selkor. It must have been.'

'*Must* have been, Chevery? Why *must* it have been?' asked Jabal mildly. 'Any one of the Warders is capable of acting on a worldwide scale if they felt the need. The strange thing about the wave though was that it appeared to affect time. None of the elements individually control time, so I doubt that any individual Warder could alter it in a substantial way. I suppose that the Earth Element would have the greatest influence over it, but that is sheer conjecture. In any case, I cannot imagine Perdimonn messing with time on this scale. What could he possibly hope to achieve? Is it possible that the wave is actually a side effect of a clash of elemental powers? If Selkor were to use an elemental Key as a weapon and a Warder drew on the same element to block him, could it be possible that the resulting conflict would cause such a wave?'

There was a solemn silence for a moment at the thought of a conflict on such a scale. It was obviously a fear that had been discussed in the past. That Selkor might use one of the powers as a weapon had been a serious possibility since he had gained the Key of Fire, but nobody had reconciled what would actually happen if two such powers were raised against one another.

'If there has been such a conflict, then anything is possible,' Akhdar said thoughtfully. 'I didn't get any such sense of conflict from the experience of having the wave pass over me though. It was more like time was...' The old Magician's voice trailed off and everyone waited expectantly.

'Shifted?' Calvyn offered and then winced as he realised that he had once again spoken out of turn with the Masters.

'Shifted! Yes, that's it! Thank you, Calvyn, that's it precisely. I don't know how, or why, but I think that someone has shifted the whole framework of time in some way.'

Lomand caught Calvyn's eye with one eyebrow raised in a question. Calvyn shrugged and pursed his lips in a silent apology and Lomand shook his head slightly in a show of obvious disappointment.

'Master Akhdar? If I may speak for a moment?' Calvyn asked politely, watching Lomand out of the corner of his eye as he spoke. Lomand just smiled and chuckled silently in resignation.

'Why? Do you have some insights for us on the propagation and manipulation of time, boy?' Chevery sneered dismissively.

'Peace, Chevery. The young man did not ask you. Go ahead, Calvyn. What is it that you want to say?' Akhdar asked, frowning sternly at Master Chevery for his rude interjection.

'Well, Master, Perdimonn has manipulated time in the past on a local basis. He did it when we encountered Selkor about a year ago.'

'Really? What exactly did he do? Did he cause a wave like the one we just saw?' Akhdar asked, plainly very interested now in what Calvyn had to say. Everyone else appeared equally interested at Calvyn's claim, including Master Chevery, whose eyes gleamed with what Calvyn saw as a sort of avarice as he waited for Calvyn to speak again.

Calvyn related the story of the encounter with Selkor and the conversations, as accurately as he could remember them. He explained, as Perdimonn had to him, the nature of the spell that the old Magician had used and the way in which he had used it to fool Selkor into backing down and leaving the marketplace. The Grand Magicians listening displayed a mixed response of wonder, horror and incredulity at Perdimonn's brazen bluff and the manner in which he had employed it.

'What if one of you had bumped something by accident?'

Chevery choked, obviously stunned that Perdimonn would take such a risk.

'Well, if my understanding is correct, Master Chevery, then the results could well have been very messy,' Calvyn replied with a perfectly straight face.

'Messy indeed,' Akhdar said thoughtfully. 'It was a bold move and obviously one that Perdimonn had planned carefully as a fallback option. It was also incredibly risky, not only in that one of you might have been killed or at the least seriously injured, but it might also have given Selkor another weapon for his arsenal. If Selkor somehow learned from what Perdimonn did and managed to duplicate it, then with the power sources that he has at his fingertips now, there is no telling how he might manipulate time to further his goals. That knowledge in Selkor's hands hardly bears thinking about. Thank you for sharing your story, Calvyn. Although it brings little comfort, your tale does give us a lot of food for thought. It also, I fear, brings us no closer to deciding whether this time shift, if that indeed was what it was, was wrought for good or ill.'

'Is there anything that we can do here to affect what has been done?' Jabal asked pointedly.

'No,' Akhdar replied thoughtfully. 'Probably not, but knowledge is power, Brother Jabal. If we could understand the true nature of what was happening, then maybe we could better prepare ourselves to face the consequences.'

The discussion continued for some time, the Masters each putting forward various ideas and theories about the nature of time and how this strange wave might have affected it. Calvyn, Jenna and Lomand kept quiet, listening to the exchanges with interest but not really having anything further to input. Eventually the light began to wane and the fog seemed to clamp its grip around them even tighter. One by one, the Masters retired to the tent to sleep. Akhdar went first and the others followed in fairly quick succession afterwards. Master Jabal was the last to leave.

'Goodnight all,' he said jovially as he struggled up to his feet. 'We old folk need our sleep if we're to have enough energy to argue again tomorrow!'

The Master chuckled as he left and Calvyn instinctively smiled at Jabal as the three remaining by the fire wished him a good night in return. The Grand Magician walked stiffly to the tent and carefully bent to duck under the entrance flap before disappearing inside.

'I like him,' Jenna observed quietly, smiling fondly as she spoke. 'He isn't like the others somehow. More like an old uncle or something.'

'Master Jabal is a very special man,' agreed Lomand in his deep bass rumble, also keeping his voice very low. 'Any young would-be Magician would do well to learn from his good sense of priorities. That is not to say that each of the other Masters isn't special too in his own way. Each of them has qualities that stand them apart from your average Magician. If you observe them closely you will learn much.'

'If they are all so special, then why do they insist on arguing over every tiny point?' Calvyn asked in a hissed whisper that said much of what he thought of them.

'Well, maybe that's a part of what sets them apart,' Lomand replied with an amused smile. 'Despite Jabal's parting quip, I doubt that they really see it as arguing. They see it more as a way of establishing facts and collating information. Each Magician is very knowledgeable in his own field of magic and some of that knowledge overlaps with that of the others. They debate points to establish the best information available so that they can use it to best advantage.'

What Lomand said made sense, but Calvyn could not help thinking that they were in fact just a bunch of cantankerous old fools who each thought they were better than the rest. If Perdimonn had not placed such importance on getting them to Mantor as soon as possible, Calvyn would have taken great pleasure in just riding off and leaving them to their debates. 'How would *that* sit with Lomand's etiquette lessons?' he wondered with a grin.

The fact that Akhdar held the Staff of Dantillus also weighed heavily in Calvyn's mind. The Staff was the one tangible thing that Calvyn felt most certainly would be of use in any confrontation with Selkor. Having seen the Staff used, Calvyn itched to try a spell with it, but he knew that the chances of him being allowed to use such a powerful icon of magic were non-existent. Still, he could always dream. Dreaming had never hurt him to date, he mused. Even in class when he had been less than fully attentive, his mind had generally been running a sort of subconscious recording of what the Master had been talking about. Certainly his memory had functioned enough that he could answer questions when asked.

The flames dancing on the logs were subtly hypnotic as he allowed his mind to drift in thought. The magical wave, the Masters, Selkor, the fog, Jenna, Bek and Jez, Derra, Fesha and Eloise, the King, Perdimonn, magical mind-messages, a whole host of thoughts and images washed through him as he allowed himself to sink into the jumbled collage. The tapestry in the Great Hall, Sorcerers, the Gorvath, spell-casting, the Oracles of Drehboor, Darkweaver's amulet, the battles at Mantor and Kortag all flashed through his mind in a rapid sequence of images. What was his mind subconsciously searching for? The more that he realised that he was looking for something, the more illusive that thing became. He allowed himself to drift again. The light spell, the translocation spell, Perdimonn's grimoire, the...

'Calvyn? Are you alright?' Jenna asked, tapping his arm gently to get his attention.

'Ahh!' he breathed in quiet frustration. It had been there, just tantalisingly out of reach. Whatever it was that his mind had been searching for had been coming to him. He had felt the proximity of the answer to a question that he could not define. Now it was gone again.

'What's the matter?' Jenna asked with concern, placing an arm gently around Calvyn's shoulders.

'Nothing,' Calvyn replied with a gentle smile. He leaned against her and rested his head on her shoulder for a moment before twisting to weave his own arm around her back. 'Absolutely nothing at all.'

CHAPTER 4

Selkor strolled through the desert as if he was out for a leisurely walk in the countryside on a pleasant afternoon. He had manipulated time such that he was moving at three times that of his surroundings. To risk moving at a higher speed was unnecessary, particularly as he had no specific destination or timescale to work to. The pressure in his mind was his only goad. Inner voices urged him to press forward to the ultimate goal with all speed, holding an eagerness and anticipation that almost left a taste in his mouth.

All he needed was to gain the final Key of Power and his quest to become The Chosen One would be complete. That in turn would enable him to complete the goal that would secure his place in history for all time. The question was, where would Perdimonn run to? Selkor already knew that the old Magician was abroad again. It was for that reason that Selkor had felt it necessary to collect the other three Keys in such quick succession. If Perdimonn had somehow managed to warn the other Warders that he was coming, then finding them and robbing them of their precious Keys might have proved terribly tedious. The Earth Warder was the least predictable of the four, but short of locking himself away indefinitely, Perdimonn would not be able to avoid another confrontation forever. One way or another, Selkor knew that he could track the old Magician down, and even if Perdimonn did elude him, Selkor had the feeling that with the Ring of Nadus, Darkweaver's amulet and three of the four Keys, he probably had enough power at his disposal to achieve his goal without the Earth Key.

'Ah, Perdimonn,' he muttered aloud. 'Where *will* you go?'

The sun beat down from a cloudless blue sky and the desert baked in the heat. By all rights, Selkor should have been roasting in his black outfit, complete with high leather boots and a thick black cloak, yet he did not break a sweat. Within his little time bubble, he had cooled the air with a simple spell and, for all he cared, the temperature outside his little sphere could double and not bother him one iota.

It was because he was in the time bubble that Selkor actually saw the wave of magical energy coming towards him. Even seeing it at a third of its actual speed, Selkor only had time to flinch before it struck and stripped the time bubble from him in one terrifying heartbeat. It was all Selkor could do to let out a single, strangled scream of pain as his little artificial sphere was ripped away, for it was as if his body was struck by a million little lightning bolts simultaneously. Every nerve ending in his skin fired pain signals into his central nervous system at once, and he collapsed to the ground, writhing and jerking as his brain threatened to overload at the excess of input.

After about thirty seconds or so the worst of the pain subsided and the shaking, jerking motions of Selkor's body settled, leaving him flat on his back and staring unmoving at the clear blue sky above. The heat of the desert sun and the temperature of the ambient air had him pouring sweat within no time, but initially he could not bring himself to move.

Every part of his body hurt. Indeed, even the thought of moving brought more pain. Yet he could not just lie there, for he knew that if he did nothing, the spectre of death would be quick to step in and leech the last ounce of life from his body. For a short while Selkor was beyond caring, but before long the prompting voices in his mind started to override his pain. Slowly, he rolled over onto his belly and forced himself up onto all fours. He paused for a moment, panting with effort, and then pushed himself up further until he was kneeling.

'Well done,' the voices congratulated. 'You are strong. You can do it. You must do it. You have to get the last Key so that you can open the door. Then you will be able to rest. Your fame and glory will be eternal. As The Chosen One all will bow before you. Get up. Move onwards. Don't stay here. Only death lives here. Move onwards.'

With an anguished cry of pain, Selkor forced himself up to his feet and he staggered across to lean against a nearby rock. Even as his body contacted the rock he felt another jolt of pain, like a heavy static shock that zapped him with a considerable discharge of energy. He jerked in response and cried out again, but he remained leaning heavily against the rock.

His face a smeared mess of sweat and dust, with a small trickle of blood at the left corner of his mouth, Selkor snarled at the sky in a primal outburst of anger and defiance that ended with him spluttering and choking.

'What in the name of everything unholy was that?' he croaked, spitting dust and wiping his mouth with a sleeve so dirty that it merely added more grime to his dishevelled appearance. Whatever that wave was, it must have been magical in origin or it would not have disintegrated his spells, he reasoned logically. If it was magic and powerful enough to floor him as it had, then it must have been Perdimonn or one of the other Warders that had sent it.

'It couldn't have been those bungling idiots at Terilla. Their minds are not powerful enough to hurl magic all this way, which means that it must have been you, Perdimonn,' he called out into the empty desert. 'It will do you no good. I will find you sooner or later. I will become "The Chosen One". It is my destiny.'

The empty desert echoed his words, but if anyone heard them then they declined to offer any indication or acknowledgement. Selkor grunted irritably at the silence and, pushing away from the rock, he doggedly braced himself with his feet widespread. Even the thought of using magic was abhorrent in his current state, but it was necessary if he was going to avoid being overcome by the desert heat.

Weaving the web of runes in his mind, Selkor once again wrapped himself in a cocoon of cool air. Inhaling deeply through his nose, Selkor breathed out a huge sigh of relief at escaping the thought-sapping, broiling heat of the desert atmosphere. Even that small victory was double edged though, for his sweat soaked body quickly started to shiver as the moisture on his skin cooled rapidly.

'The sooner that I get out of this stinking desert, the better,' he muttered, brushing his hair back over his head in a combing motion with his fingers.

If Selkor had been thinking rationally, he might have stopped to consider the properties of the magical wave before he attempted any further magic. Instead, incensed by having been blasted unexpectedly from his feet by an unseen adversary and with his thought processes dulled by pain and general discomfort, Selkor did not think before attempting to re-instate his time distorting spell. The results were as spectacular as they were painful for Selkor. Even as he released his spell, Selkor's eyes widened and bulged slightly in fear and anticipation, as the realisation dawned on him an instant before the magical feedback began that he was about to undergo the torture a second time. Sure enough, the Shandese Magician was hit from every imaginable angle by a myriad of tiny bolts of energy and his body seemed to literally crackle with them as he collapsed screaming and writhing on the ground again.

Selkor stayed down a long time. His arms hugged at his body in an apparent attempt to squeeze out the pain as he rocked slowly from side to side, his screams dying away to gentle groans and whimpers as the initial effect subsided. When he did finally manage to drag himself back to his feet, his face and hands were smeared with blood and dust, and his eyes were flashing with silver as he took a deep breath and hurled a stream of curses at the top of his voice into the uncaring, empty wasteland.

Falling silent for a moment, Selkor stood, head down,

shoulders slumped and arms hanging loosely at his sides. He looked for all the world like a man defeated. Battered, bloodied and filthy, one could have been forgiven for thinking that Selkor was ready to lie down in the desert and die. If this had happened at a different time in the Shandese Magician's life, then maybe he would have, but at this instant Selkor was far from ready to die. Like a tiger slowly lifting its head above the long grass to get one careful last look at its prey before leaping to the kill, so Selkor's head rose and the only death in his strangely silver tinted eyes was the death that he intended to deliver to his enemies.

*   *   *   *   *

Sleep had brought the answer to Calvyn's mental collage of images. As is so often the case with such tantalising brain-teasers, his subconscious mind had worked at the problem overnight and when he awoke the next morning, the answer popped into his mind as if he had been completely blind not to see it before.

It was strange because Calvyn did not even know what the problem was that he had been trying to solve. The question came to him along with the answer but, as it happened, both had already become irrelevant shortly after dawn. Calvyn's idea provided a way of navigating safely through the fog, but by the time that everyone was awake and had packed up the gear onto the horses, the fog had dispersed of its own accord.

The solution involved another simple combination spell, utilising two of the spells that he had learned over the previous couple of days. A very weak version of the protective shield of force that Akhdar had used could be feasibly erected over a huge area, as the shield would not require much power because it was not really to protect so much as to offer a boundary. The water-repelling spell that Lomand had taught him could then be added into this to literally repel the fog from the air within the barrier. Calvyn was quietly disappointed when the fog cleared, as there was no longer a reason to propose the spell, but he noted down the combination of runes into his grimoire while it was still fresh in his mind.

The whole of the following week of travel was fairly uneventful other than a growing feeling of unease that Calvyn and Jenna could not resolve. It was as they passed to the north of Shandrim that Calvyn began to experience a growing sense of dread that either something terrible had happened, or was going to happen imminently. Jenna apparently shared his feelings and although they talked about it briefly, neither could place a finger on what exactly was wrong.

'It must be something to do with Bek and Jez, or Derra and the others,' Calvyn told Jenna when he tried to define the feeling. 'The sensation definitely began when we passed Shandrim. Something bad has happened to them. I'm sure of it.'

'You're just feeling guilty for leaving Derra to manage the rescue,' Jenna disagreed. 'They're all safely back at Baron Keevan's Castle by now, you'll see,' she assured him confidently. Yet her own heart mirrored the dread felt by Calvyn. A darkness seemed to haunt them like a shadow, yet none of the Magicians seemed to show any signs of being aware of it.

Calvyn felt strongly enough to speak to Lomand about it, but whilst the big man listened carefully enough, he dismissed it as being Calvyn's overactive imagination. Instead of acting on Calvyn's feelings, Lomand simply tried to swamp them with a sea of learning. Almost every minute of the journey from then on was spent in study. Occasionally, Master Jabal dropped back to join them and took an active part in the teaching. The Grand Magician was an excellent teacher. He was able to bring subjects to life with demonstrations and illustrations that were both amusing and very apt, and both Calvyn and Jenna enjoyed his lessons immensely.

Not far north of Stoneshollow and well inside the northern border of Thrandor, they stopped for a midday meal at a tiny hamlet. Calvyn and Jenna were both glad of the break, particularly as, with the availability of a village tavern, they would not be called upon to cook the meal.

The little taproom in 'The Stonecutter's Rest' was warm and homely enough. As they entered, a log fire crackled in the large open fireplace and a thin haze of pipe weed smoke mingled with the smell of the log fire. Three villagers and the Innkeeper, distinguishable by his apron, were all sitting at the tap bar with lit pipes in their mouths and clay pots of ale on the bar in front of them. The ceiling was low and crossed with a dozen thick wooden beams, but the thick walls were all made of the local cut stone, glued together with a form of mortar.

A huge brute of a dog lay in front of the fire, but whilst his eyes followed the group into the room, the dog did not expend so much as the flick of an ear in effort to show any further interest in them. Talk amongst the four at the bar ceased the moment that they began to enter and the locals' eyes goggled as they took in the five old men in their dark cloaks, followed by one who could have passed as a giant from the legends of minstrels. Lomand did not just have to duck to get through the door, he had to duck under every beam in the ceiling as well. Calvyn and Jenna entered last and the Innkeeper seemed to eye them with even more suspicion than the others.

'Probably because of the strange company we keep,' Calvyn thought with a smile.

The Innkeeper withdrew his pipe from his mouth and got to his feet. Shuffling quickly behind the bar as if it offered him protection, the red-faced, rotund fellow looked distinctly uncomfortable with this sudden influx of customers, dressed as they were in outlandish garb and looking distinctly foreign. Calvyn noticed that one of the customers made a subtle hand movement, which he recognised as being a local hex supposed to ward against evil. Calvyn could not stop the corners of his mouth from rising up into a smile at that gesture as he wondered if any of the others had noticed it.

'What can I do for you good people today?' the Innkeeper asked, trying to sound jolly and welcoming. His tone lacked any conviction, but Akhdar, who was the self appointed spokesman for the party, did not make anything of it.

'Seven pots of your ale for the men please, good Innkeeper, and what will you have Jenna?'

'The same will be fine, thank you,' she answered, trying to emphasise her Thrandorian accent.

'Eight pots of ale then please, and food for the same. What do you have to eat today?'

The Innkeeper looked a bit flustered, but he kept himself together and stammered out that there was some roast left over from yesterday's joint, but not enough for eight. However, there was plenty of winter stew to feed them all, and fresh bread and butter to go with it.

Akhdar diplomatically accepted that eight portions of the winter stew would be fine and politely asked if there were any tables that the Innkeeper would prefer them to use, or could they sit as they wished.

'Oh, help yourselves to tables, sir,' the Innkeeper said, still obviously very uncomfortable and trying to work himself up to something. 'Beggin' yer pardon, sir,' he said nervously in a rush. 'But might I see how you'll be payin' for all this? It's just, I don't take no foreign coin as a rule.'

Akhdar smiled and reached into a pocket.

'I trust that this will be acceptable?' he said, spilling a small handful of gold and silver coins onto the bar.

The Innkeeper's eyes went wide at the sight of so much money. 'Oh yes, sir! Most acceptable, sir,' he said, suddenly all smiles and brightness and obviously mentally adjusting his prices to ensure that he would relieve this stranger of as much of the money as possible before the party left.

Calvyn was mildly surprised, because he noted that all of the coins that Akhdar had put on the bar were Thrandorian. There was not a Shandese sen, senna or sennut among them. Quietly he wondered where the Magician had acquired so much Thrandorian currency, but then the Magician's Academy was probably not without considerable resources, he decided.

The Innkeeper began dipping out jars of ale, which Calvyn and Jenna collected from the bar and distributed amongst the Magicians. The five Masters pulled chairs around one table, whilst Lomand settled himself at another nearby. Once they had handed out the pots of ale, Calvyn and Jenna joined Lomand whilst the Innkeeper bustled off out of a back door from the bar that presumably led to the kitchen area. He was not gone long, and when he reappeared it was with a large bowl of stew in each hand and a woman following behind him similarly laden. The woman, who apparently was the Innkeeper's wife, was stout and hard-faced, and the smile that she gave the Masters as she placed the bowls on the table looked forced. Spoons were produced, and the Innkeeper and his wife made another couple of runs to the kitchen to fetch more bowls of stew, some bread, butter and knives. Within a very short time the whole party was eating and drinking, still being watched surreptitiously by the three locals. The men had returned to puffing away on their pipes, with their heads leaning close together and they spoke almost in whispers at the bar like some sort of farcical conspiracy group.

The Masters, true to form, began a discussion over food and Taverns, with which they quickly became deeply involved to the apparent exclusion of all else around them. Calvyn, Jenna and Lomand ate initially in silence, but Calvyn had been considering the troubling feelings of dread and imminent danger that he and Jenna had been experiencing for some days and decided to offer up a solution.

'Jenna, how long do you think it would take to ride to Baron Keevan's castle from here?'

Jenna paused in the movement of lifting a spoonful of stew to her mouth and looked thoughtful for a moment.

'About four or five hours, I suppose,' she said with a shrug. 'But we're not going there are we? I thought that we were taking the main road south from Stoneshollow to

Levanbridge because it's the quickest way to Mantor.'

'That's true,' Calvyn said slowly. 'It's just that I was considering asking you to take a detour and catch up with us. We might discover more of what happened at Shandrim and we would know if the rescue party has returned. Maybe then these worries about Bek, Jez and the others might go away. Would you mind going?'

'Well no, I suppose not,' Jenna replied hesitantly. 'But what if they won't let me go again? I don't have your rank and status, Calvyn. At the moment I'm just a Private who is absent without leave. I could be detained and punished for that.'

'There is no chance of that, Jenna,' Calvyn assured her positively. 'As I told you before we left Terilla, the Baron was there when I told my story to the King. He knows what you've been doing and I'm sure that he understands just how critical a role you played in recent events. If you tell him that you are working for me for the time being and mention Selkor in the same breath, I feel sure that he'll give you whatever assistance he can. Have a think about it.'

'All of that is irrelevant, however,' Lomand interrupted, giving Calvyn a very direct look and pointing at him with his spoon. 'You are *both* Acolytes now. That means you do what I, or any of the Masters, tell you to do. At the moment, as far as I'm concerned, that does not include disappearing off on unnecessary diversions on a whim. You might have rank and status here in Thrandor, Calvyn, but whilst you remain an Acolyte I don't care whether you are a Knight, a King, or the Emperor of Shandar, you will do as I tell you, or there'll be trouble.'

'But, Lomand...'

'No buts, Calvyn,' Lomand ordered firmly. 'Neither Jenna, nor you, go anywhere without the permission of the Masters or myself. Understood?'

'Yes, Lomand,' Calvyn sighed, resignation in his tone and his disappointment evident.

After a suitable pause, Lomand grinned at Calvyn broadly. 'I did only say, "as far as I'm concerned" though, so you may ask the Masters if you wish.'

'Thank you, Lomand,' Calvyn said gratefully and then proceeded to work on finishing his meal.

If Jenna did not wish to go to the castle, Calvyn had no intention of forcing the issue, so he let the subject lie and waited to see if Jenna raised it again. Calvyn knew Jenna well enough to have a fair guess at how she reacted to events. He was certain that the idea of going back to Keevan's castle would play on her mind and that she would have made a decision on what she wanted to do long before the day was out.

Calvyn was not wrong.

Jenna pulled Calvyn aside before they left the Tavern and gave him a resolute look. Meeting Jenna's gaze, Calvyn once again lost himself in Jenna's large brown eyes and melted inside. Her eyes really were most distracting, he decided, as he realised that she was actually talking to him.

'... talk to Jabal. He will listen to us,' she finished, awaiting his response.

Calvyn gave a thoughtful 'Hmm,' as if he were thinking.

'You didn't hear a word that I just said, did you?' she accused him in a loud whisper.

'Not much,' Calvyn admitted with a wry smile. 'Did I ever tell you that you have the most beautiful eyes?'

Jenna smiled instantly with pleasure and leaning forward she gave him a quick kiss.

'Yes, but you can tell me again as many times as you like,' she whispered in his ear. 'Now, as I was saying...'

'Talk to Jabal. Ask him to give you permission to go. He'll listen to us,' Calvyn pre-empted. 'I guess I must have been listening subconsciously after all.'

Jenna punched him playfully on the shoulder and he pretended to be hurt. The game carried on until they walked outside to join the others.

'Thanks again,' Calvyn called back over his shoulder as they exited the tavern in an attempt to establish a reason to the Masters as to why they had been slow to leave.

The Magicians were already mounted and the two

Acolytes received hard looks for their tardiness. Up and down the one street of the tiny hamlet, curtains twitched as curious locals peeked out at the party of strangers. Other less covert villagers were standing in their gardens and watching them openly. The Tavern would see plenty of trade tonight, Calvyn thought to himself with a grin as he swung up into Hakkaari's saddle. Their short stop here would keep the locals in gossip for weeks.

Jenna mounted her horse smoothly and then heeled the chestnut mare forward until she had closed alongside Master Jabal. The Magician looked across at her, obviously a little surprised that she wanted to speak to him in particular.

'Master Jabal?'

'Yes, Jenna? What can I do for you?'

'Well, Master, Calvyn and I have been experiencing a sense of foreboding ever since we passed Shandrim and we think that it might be related to our friends who we know to be held prisoner there. With your permission I would like to make a slight diversion to visit the Baron's castle where Calvyn and I trained.'

'Where is this castle and what good can you gain by going there?' Jabal asked thoughtfully.

'The castle is about four to five hours ride east of here, Master Jabal, and if I went, then I could at least confirm whether any of our friends have returned. It would only take me a day or two to catch up with you again. At the very latest I would be back with you by Levanbridge,' Jenna replied.

The Master appeared thoughtful for a few seconds, considering the request. His eyes went distant and he appeared almost in a trance as he deliberated, but then he shook his head in denial.

'No,' he said apologetically. 'Letting you disappear off right now would not be a good idea. I have a bad feeling about letting you go. It would be wrong. Making the trip just for information is not a worthy enough reason. It achieves nothing. What would you do if your friends were not there and there had been no word of them? Would you then want to form another rescue mission to go to Shandrim in search of them? Equally, what if they are there at the castle? What would you have achieved? Nothing! No, I think that it would be better if you stayed with us for now. If you go off on this trip I fear that something bad will come of it.'

'But, Master, I could...'

'No, Jenna. The answer is no and that is the end of the matter,' Jabal said firmly.

Jenna bowed her head in acceptance and reined in her horse to drop back level with Calvyn and Lomand. Calvyn met her eye and raised an eyebrow inquisitively. Jenna shook her head very slightly and Calvyn frowned deeply in response. Calvyn had no desire to get into trouble with the Magicians, but at the same time he was becoming increasingly anxious for news from Derra and the others about what had happened at Shandrim. Something was going to have to give way soon, or he felt that he might be forced to clash with someone.

It was Lomand who diffused Calvyn's growing sense of rebellion and he did so with one simple question.

'Calvyn, why are we going on this journey?'

Calvyn was both annoyed with Lomand and yet pleased that the big man had restored his sense of perspective at the same time. Of course, the priority was to reach Mantor and help Perdimonn against Selkor. If they did not do that, there was no telling how many lives might be lost as a consequence. The fates of Bek, Jez and the rescue party were important to Calvyn and Jenna, but in the great overall scheme of things, he could hardly lend too much weight to it.

Calvyn sighed heavily and the frown slowly seemed to drain from his face.

'Yes, Lomand, you are right. Tell me, are you sure that you're not reading my mind by some method that I can't detect?' he asked with a wistful smile.

'No need,' Lomand replied in his normal bass rumble. 'It

was written all over your face. Try to keep your mind on the things that *really* matter. When you do that, the path to tread is always clearer.'

They were out of the village by now and the Magicians picked up the pace to a steady trot as the road ahead was clear. The rolling countryside marched by steadily as they held the faster pace for quite some time and both Calvyn and Jenna found themselves thinking about the last time that they had made the journey south to Mantor. It had been a long march to battle, knowing that they were outnumbered and not knowing for a large part of the journey if Mantor was even still in Thrandorian hands. How things had changed since those simple days of being newly appointed Privates in Baron Keevan's army. This time they made the journey to face a battle against a single enemy and yet that one man posed a threat somehow greater than the entire Terachite army ever had. Magicians and magical artefacts, Warders and magical Keys of power, all complicated matters in ways that twisted reason and reality into a web of confusion and possibilities. A simple battle, horrific as battles were, might be preferable to this, Calvyn thought grimly. He would have been pleased to realise that Jenna's thoughts all but mirrored his own.

'Ow!' Jenna exclaimed suddenly, clutching at her upper chest and grimacing in pain.

'Are you alright?' Calvyn and Lomand asked, almost as one.

'Yes, I'm OK. It's just that the arrow on this charm that Perdimonn made me keeps catching at my skin. I guess that I'll just have to wear it outside of my tunic for a while. I don't think that Perdimonn designed it with bouncing along on the back of a horse in mind,' she said with an apologetic look at the others for her outcry.

Reaching down inside the neck of her tunic, Jenna pulled the silver arrow pendant out and then rubbed gently at the sore area where the arrow had jabbed. It was not easy to do whilst riding along at a trot, so it was not surprising that Jenna did not look down as she did it. Looking down might have given her the answers to several questions, as the arrow swung constantly to point straight back through her body, often balancing the point against her chest to do so.

Jenna had never really considered horse riding as one of her greater skills. She found it took much of her concentration to watch the road ahead and try to raise and lower her body in a rhythm that did not have her descending bottom meeting an upcoming saddle in such a way that quickly became painful. Providing that she kept a measure of concentration, Jenna found that she could achieve that much, but she was certainly not an accomplished horsewoman and not confident enough to try to do other things at the same time.

The Magicians pushed along at a good pace for the rest of the day, but as night fell there was no sign of a nearby village or town to lodge at and Akhdar finally called them to halt. They set up camp next to a copse of trees just off the road. It was a good site, offering plenty of fuel for a fire and fresh water from a large stream that ran along the other side of the stand of trees. Calvyn, Jenna and Lomand had the tent up and secured very quickly, having established a slick routine for these basic tasks. Before long the fire was going, windbreaks were set, a large pot of dahl was simmering and a meal of bread, cheese and salted meat was handed around. Also, rocks were placed around the fireside ready for warming their feet in the tent later in the evening.

Jenna and Calvyn ate in silence and Jenna sensed that Calvyn was still worrying over Bek, Derra and the others. Indeed, Jenna felt her anxiety levels rising just sitting next to him. When she had finished her food, Jenna decided that she would walk down to the stream and wash away her travel grime. The moon was virtually full and offered plenty of light for night walking, so she told them where she was going, got up, and moved clear of the pool of firelight.

It took a few minutes for Jenna's eyes to begin to pick out much detail. Once her eyes adjusted to the lower light level, she stepped out more briskly, allowing her thigh muscles to stretch out some of the cramps that she felt after days of constant riding.

The woods were eerily silent as Jenna walked between the trees and threaded her way down towards the stream. When she stopped and listened, Jenna could still make out the sounds of the Magicians chatting around the fire. Otherwise all was silent, and Jenna found herself moving as soundlessly as she could as an instinctive reaction to the intense quiet around her. Gedd had taught her a lot about moving quietly through trees and Jenna found that she was justifying her stealthy movement as some overdue practice. The woodsman would have been amused at that, she thought wryly. The truth was, she was just plain spooked for some reason, but no matter how hard she told herself that this was Thrandor, and the chances of anything harmful being in these trees was so remote that it was almost unthinkable, the more uneasy she became.

Slowly, Jenna became aware of the sound of running water and she smiled at the thought of a decent wash, even if it was in icy cold water. What she would not give now for a steaming tub of hot water and a bar of pure soap to wash with! Even the thought of it sent a thrill of pleasure down her spine. As it was, she would be content with her piece of travel soap and a cloth that would pass for a flannel so long as the water was clean running.

Moonlight filtered through the trees, casting ghoulish shadows as Jenna carefully eased her way down to the water's edge. Even though the deeper sections of water looked black in the silvery light of the moon, Jenna could see from where water flowed over rocks near the surface and in shallower runs that it was running clear. Sitting down on the bank she eased off her boots and socks, and with a slight gasp at the icy temperature she dangled her bare feet into the water.

Despite being freezing cold, it felt really good to let the water cleanse the day's travel dirt from her feet, and after sluicing them around for a minute or so and wriggling her toes in pleasure, Jenna decided to start soaping herself down limb by limb. It was far too cold to strip and climb completely into the water, so she pulled her feet from the stream and knelt by the water's edge. Unwrapping her piece of soap from the cloth that she used as a flannel, Jenna leaned forward and dipped the soap and the cloth in the water. As Jenna rubbed the soap and cloth together to build up a good lather, the dangling silver arrow charm caught her attention. It was moving most strangely, suspended as it was on the leather thong.

'It's almost as if the needle is hunting between two targets and is unsure which to choose,' Jenna mused silently, falling still and watching the strange motions of the arrow. Then the arrow began to vibrate and the cloth and soap tumbled from her hands as the shock of recognition at what was happening finally struck home.

CHAPTER 5

Femke waited outside the door to the Emperor's private study, as the feeling of unease filled her once more. Only a few weeks ago Femke would have relished the opportunity to report her findings to the Emperor and feel the glow of satisfaction that bringing new information to him gave her. Why the spy now found herself dreading these report times was still a mystery to her, but a mystery to which an answer was beginning to take shape in the back of her mind. It was still not an answer that Femke could access, which was most frustrating, but she knew that she had enough of the puzzle pieces to solve the conundrum. It was now just a matter of time and juggling those pieces around until they started to slot into place. All it would take was the appropriate trigger and everything would make sense, she was sure of it.

The assassin, Shalidar, was one of those critical pieces that just did not fit, no matter which way she turned it. After recovering from her fright on the rooftops the previous week, Femke had trailed him successfully for two full days to no avail. The assassin had not gone back anywhere near the area of town that she had tracked him in before. More than that, he had not spoken to anyone with an even remotely military bearing. Shalidar remained an enigma that Femke did not really have the leisure to solve, yet she was determined that any spare time she did have would be dedicated to trying.

The Palace ran normally, if nervously, which was not

really surprising given the circumstances. The demonstrations in the city streets continued to grow in size and frequency, and Femke had now identified at least three different faction leaders who had notions of becoming the next Emperor of Shandar. The way that she felt about reporting to the Emperor at the moment, Femke wondered whether any one of them might be more comfortable to work for. Treasonous thoughts were not good for a long life in the spy business though, so Femke firmly shuttered them in the back of her mind.

The door to the Emperor's study opened and one of the Emperor's serving staff held the door open and waved her inside.

'The Emperor will see you now, Ma'am,' he said formally, bowing his head as she passed and then stepping outside before closing the door behind him.

The now familiar chill ran down Femke's spine as she met the Emperor's eyes and she used her curtsy to break that eye contact, bowing her head as she attempted to maintain her composure. Scrolls and books littered the surface of the Emperor's desk, along with sheets of notes, some written in the Emperor's bold hand, but many more written in a scratchy, spidery script that she did not recognise. Strangely, one of the top note sheets in that strange handwriting appeared only half written. Who would give a half written report to the Emperor, Femke wondered?

Femke took the details in, as an artist would freeze a moment in time into a picture on canvas. The way the papers were arranged, the quill and inkpot slightly left of the middle of the desk, the map of Shandar with its beautiful depth of shading laid open over the pile of scrolls on the right side of the desk and the crystal goblet, half full of red wine, standing right in the middle.

Although it only took a moment to assimilate the details of the study, Femke sensed that she had taken too long over her cursory look at the desktop. The Emperor gathered and shuffled all of the papers together in an apparently casual fashion, but Femke did not miss the fact that he deliberately ensured that one with his own handwriting was at the top of the pile. He was hiding something in there that he did not want Femke to be aware of, but then he was the Emperor and she was a spy. What the Emperor held in his study was his own affair, she reasoned silently. After all, Femke was supposed to be spying for him, not on him.

The Emperor got to his feet and his eyes glittered with that recent coldness that bothered her so much as he asked her to give her report.

'Your Imperial Majesty, the demonstrations continue to increase in size and frequency. One of yesterday's rallies, organised by supporters of your younger brother, Governor Maritsa, ended in a riot. There were several militiamen badly injured and probably twice as many of the rioters sustained injuries during the clashes. There have been at least four people killed this week in conflicts on the streets of Shandrim, and the number of fatalities look set to rise steeply unless something can be done to subdue the populous.'

'Maritsa is a fool,' the Emperor interrupted coldly. 'But you are right, he is a fool with a following. Have you found out who else looks set to offer challenges yet?'

'Yes, your Majesty, there are at least two more that I know of and both are also Governors.'

'What a surprise!' the Emperor said sardonically. 'Go on, Femke – the names?'

'Governors Sammanis and Daraffa, your Majesty. It appears that both have substantial numbers of followers here in the city, and unless you move to thwart them soon then I fear that they will gather many more. The mood of the people is not kind towards your rule, your Majesty. The militia are working hard to contain the troubles, but there are signs of sympathisers within their ranks as well.'

The Emperor reached across the desk for the goblet of wine and lifted it to his lips. He took a sip and he smiled at Femke with a confidence that the spy was sure she would not feel in his position.

'I have always had the deepest respect for you and your

abilities, Femke. You're resilient, resourceful and clear-spoken. I really admire that, which is why I'm going to assign you to a particularly special and important mission. More of that in a minute, however, for I can read your unspoken implications as well as any written report, child. You wonder why I haven't simply squashed any thoughts of rebellion with an iron fist before it had a chance to gather pace. Well, believe me, I've thought about it. It's irked me intensely to all but ignore the pathetic rabble-rousing tactics of my would-be rivals and the whining of the weak-willed commoners who have lost family or friends in that battle in Thrandor. After all, it was they who joined the military and accepted the Imperial Senna. The military is there to fight battles. People die in battles – it goes with the territory, I'm afraid. Well, the waiting is over and it's proved its worth, because by my actions I've forced the real threats to my reign to bring their plots into the open. Now that I have the names that I was looking for, I can move to crush all of my challengers in one fell swoop. At the same time, I'll show the people just what the military is here for and what they're capable of.'

The Emperor paused and took another sip of his wine. Just that small motion sent another shiver down Femke's spine. Maybe the Emperor was losing his mind, she thought suddenly. Maybe that was why he was making such strange decisions and sending these chilling feelings through her body. If the Emperor was losing his sanity, it would explain all of the strangeness that she had felt in coming to his study to report over the past few weeks. Yet, as she met his glittering gaze, Femke did not so much see insanity in his eyes as cold, calculating evil, and that assessment frightened her more than the idea that he was mad. Why would she think that the man was evil? He had never done anything that Femke could point at and justify the feeling. Maybe it was she who was losing her mind, Femke thought grimly.

'When you return from your mission, Femke, it will be to a different Shandrim. Tomorrow I will set in motion the movement of seven entire Legions of troops into the area and institute a conscription order that will empty the city of able-bodied men. Let the women and children protest if they will, but their men are either going to join the military or hang from the city walls. Maritsa, Sammaris and Daraffa will hang regardless for their treason.'

'So that's why Shalidar was meeting with the military fellow during the rally,' thought Femke, slightly disappointed that she had not worked it out sooner. 'The Emperor has been using him to communicate with the military leaders prior to them entering the city in force.'

'Would you like me to call for Shalidar when I leave?' Femke asked, attempting to show the Emperor that she had been aware of his military intentions all along.

'Why would I need Shalidar?' the Emperor replied, looking genuinely puzzled. 'The military can flush out the Governors and do the hanging. I don't think that I'll need an assassin's services for that.'

'Oh, I don't know,' Femke answered, feeling terribly foolish. 'I just thought that you might need his services. I obviously wasn't thinking straight, your Majesty,' she finished lamely.

Now Femke was really confused and the unnerving stare of the Emperor's penetrating eyes was not helping her to think straight at all. If the Emperor was not using Shalidar in connection with the military, then what game was the assassin playing? Just when Femke thought that his part of the puzzle had fallen into place, she had discovered that the whole intrigue was more complex than ever.

'General Surabar will handle these petty insurrections. Then, once the rebels have been suitably dealt with and the conscripts gathered, the combined forces will move to invade Thrandor properly. This time there will be no mistakes. Thrandor will be taken and held as it should have been the first time,' the Emperor stated, his tone conveying his total confidence in both General Surabar and the outcome of this grand plan.

Femke was not surprised at the Emperor's confidence in

Surabar. The General had a legendary reputation as both a commander of men and as a strategist. Only a handful of men were ever awarded the rank of General, as normally Legions were led by Commanders and if more than one Legion was committed to an action, then the Commanders worked strategy by consensus. The overall plan was then executed with each Commander leading their part of the agreed strategy. The only break with the traditional chain of command in recent history had been the unprecedented decision to allow Sorcerers to lead the invasion force into Thrandor. Somehow, Femke could not see that mistake being repeated in the imminent future.

'For you, Femke, I have a task both vital and extremely difficult. I am not sure where it will take you, so I suggest that you take plenty of provisions and I will authorise a suitable amount of gold to help you along the way.'

'Gold, your Imperial Majesty? I have never needed extra gold to carry out my duties before,' Femke said in surprise.

'Yes, well, I've never really sent you all that far afield before and this mission might change that. I want you to find the Thrandorian fighter, Bek, who disappeared from the arena. Find him and help him in any way that you can.'

Femke was shocked.

'Help him, your Majesty? Help him to do what?'

'He is going to try to find and kill the Sorcerer Lord, Shanier. Help him to achieve that goal and then bring me a token so that I know for certain Bek has succeeded. The Thrandorian fighter has a gold ring that I gave him. When he has killed Shanier, bring me the ring from Bek's hand as a token that the task is complete.'

Femke was truly surprised, curious and hurt all at the same time. This sounded more like a job for an accomplished assassin like Shalidar. Femke was primarily a spy, whose proven area of expertise was intrigue in Shandrim. Why was the Emperor not sending him? Also, why the token? Did the Emperor no longer trust her to tell the truth? Was that what he had been hiding in that pile of reports? Was there a new spy around that Femke knew nothing about who was filing reports to the Emperor that were undermining her position? Femke had a myriad of questions that she would love to have asked the Emperor, but of course she could do nothing of the sort. The Emperor had given her the assignment. Now it was up to her to prove once again that he could trust her to get things done successfully.

'It will be done as you order, your Majesty,' she affirmed simply. 'Will there be anything else, your Majesty?'

'No, Femke. That will be all. Good luck and may Shand speed you on your way.'

Femke curtsied and backed to the door, her mind in turmoil. The situation in the Palace was becoming stranger day by day. Exiting the room silently, Femke nearly jumped out of her skin as she turned from the door only to find herself literally face to face with Shalidar.

'I'm sorry,' he apologised in his whispering, breathy voice. 'I didn't mean to startle you. Is his Imperial Majesty in a good mood today?'

'As good as he normally is,' Femke answered, trying to brush off the fright he had given her and moving to sidestep him.

Shalidar put out an arm and stopped her.

'Sent you off on another mission has he?' he breathed, obviously amused by something.

'What? How did you...'

Shalidar laughed softly and shook his head.

'Don't tell me that you haven't worked out what's going on yet?' the assassin mocked, his eyes dancing with amusement. 'And I thought that you spies were supposed to know everything!'

Femke shook free of his arm and pushed past him brusquely. Standing around to be mocked by Shalidar was not at the top of her 'to do' list, so she did her best to ignore him as she strode away down the corridor.

'Oh, and Femke,' the assassin called after her, his voice rasping as he raised the volume from his normal low whisper. 'Don't bother following me again. It'll do you no good.'

Femke did not look back, or even pause in her stride, but inside she was seething. He had known she was following him. That was why he had not led her to anything useful. Steaming mad with Shalidar for obviously knowing information that her sources had not managed to unearth, and for his having deliberately led her on a wild goose chase for two days, Femke's mind ran through the worst set of expletives she knew.

Femke had always known that Shalidar was an exceptional assassin, so when he had led her on such a meaningless run around town, she should have guessed that he had known that he was being followed. 'Was she losing her touch,' she wondered? Why was she being sent out of Shandrim again and why would the Emperor confide that information in an assassin before he had even told her? If the Emperor had wanted someone to follow and aid this Thrandorian, Bek, then why had he not sent someone after him when the fighter had first disappeared? For all Femke knew, the Thrandorian could be dead. After all, the fighter, Serrius, had run him through by all accounts.

'Too many questions and no forthcoming answers,' Femke muttered despondently. With a shrug, she set off towards the Imperial Treasury to collect the gold that the Emperor had said she was to take. At least there would be no need to live like a pauper on this job, she realised. If the Emperor was seeing fit to open the Imperial Coffers for her use, then she might as well make the most of it.

*   *   *   *   *

'Well, there it is,' Perdimonn said with satisfaction. 'Mantor, capital city of Thrandor.'

'I thought that it would be bigger for some reason,' Arred commented, eyeing the distant walled city with a degree of disappointment.

'Yes, well it was until recently. The nomad clans of the Terachite Wastes sacked and burned the newer part of the city that used to sit in the valley. It looks as if the people have not had a chance to clear the debris and rubble yet, let alone begin rebuilding. Have any of you been here before?' Perdimonn asked hopefully.

None of the other Warders had been and not one of them looked overly enamoured with the prospect of visiting now. Each had been used to a solitary life, at peace with the world and the element that they warded. Cities did not normally feature on their agendas for anything.

'Not to worry,' Perdimonn said brightly, determined not to be put off by the other Warders' negative responses and distinct lack of enthusiasm for their destination. 'We shouldn't need to be there for long anyway.'

'Perdimonn? Why are we still going to Mantor at all?' Rikath asked suddenly. 'There is no need any more. You are now the only person who can manipulate time. We could stay ahead of Selkor for evermore if we wished. Every time he gets close, you could just slip away from him again. You have very neatly blocked Selkor from ever being able to learn your Key and therefore he can never become 'The Chosen One', so why do we still need to stop in Mantor? All you are doing is giving Selkor a chance to catch up with us.'

Perdimonn sighed. In some ways he agreed with Rikath's assessment of the situation. It was true, he could now prevent Selkor indefinitely from ever becoming 'The Chosen One' by doing exactly what she had described, but that was not all that was at stake. There were a lot of other considerations to be taken into account.

'You're right of course, Rikath. We could just run away and hide, but I don't think that would be a good idea. I need not remind you that Selkor presently holds more potentially destructive power in his hands than Darkweaver ever had and we cannot just run away and hide from that fact. We still don't know why Selkor wants all this power. I doubt that he's gathering it without a reason. Someone has to face him down, Rikath. The only people equipped to do that are the Magicians' Council and ourselves, and probably only then if we do it together.'

'Face him down to what purpose, Perdimonn?' Morrel

asked, his voice dubious. 'We can't harm him, or take the knowledge back that he has learned. Why provoke a confrontation?'

'As I just said – to find out why he is doing this. If Selkor's only motivation were that history should record him as 'The Chosen One', then I wouldn't be concerned, but vain though Selkor is, I somehow doubt that vanity is the driving force behind all this. There is more to this than simple ego, Morrel, and you know it. You're right, we can't kill him, but if we can discover his true motive then we can try to formulate a measured plan. If that plan proves to be running away for the rest of our lives, then so be it. Personally though, I'm not happy with anyone roaming the world with the sort of power that Selkor now holds. Once I know what he plans to do with that power, then I'll be willing to listen to suggestions as to what we should do next. If the consensus is to leave well alone, then I'll go with the verdict. My gut instincts tell me that leaving him alone will not be an option though, so I have prepared a few alternative ideas.'

'Really?' Arred asked, his eyes lighting with interest. 'Another of the aces up your sleeve?'

'You could say that,' Perdimonn replied, but his face was grim. 'The prime ace is not an option that any of us will be able to take lightly though, so I'll not speak about it unless we're faced with no other option.'

The four rode in silence for the next half an hour until they had crossed the Fallow Bridge and were approaching the city gates. Now that they were closer, the work on clearing the destroyed remnants of Mantor that lay outside the main city wall could clearly be seen. People seemed to shift within the rubble like a mass of busy ants working together to rebuild their broken homes. Fascinating as it was to watch the mesmerising streams of people swarming around the outer city, Perdimonn was focused on entering the main gates.

'Where will we stay in the city, Perdimonn?' Arred asked, as they rode slowly up to the open gates.

'Before we worry about lodgings I'd like to go and have a talk with Malo,' Perdimonn answered thoughtfully.

'Malo? Who's he, an old friend?'

'Hardly!' laughed Perdimonn. 'Though I did know his father. Malo is the King of Thrandor. His palace is at the top of the hill.'

'The King!' Rikath exclaimed in surprise. 'Why would we want to talk with him?'

'Well, it is his kingdom, Rikath,' Perdimonn answered reproachfully. 'And his city as well. He really ought to know what might happen here shortly.'

'So we're just going to stroll up to the Palace, knock on the gates and say "Oh, hello there. Go and fetch the King would you please? We've just dropped by for a little chat," are we? From what little I remember of civilization and rulers, getting to see a king isn't that easy,' Arred pointed out sarcastically.

Perdimonn looked across at Arred and grinned.

'Well, I might not quite use those words exactly, but in essence, yes, that is precisely what we're going to do. If the guards prove obstructive, then we might need to persuade them to co-operate. It shouldn't prove overly difficult. These people have lived without magic for two hundred years. Even something simple will convince them that we're for real.'

'Something simple,' Rikath laughed merrily. 'Ah yes, Perdimonn, something simple. I look forward to this. I've got a sneaky suspicion that your perspective might just be a little out of line here.'

'What do you mean, Rikath?'

'Oh, we'll see,' she laughed. 'Something simple! Ha, ha, ha!'

They rode up through the city, taking the most direct route to the palace gates. The streets were busy but not extraordinarily so, and the Warders made their way two horses abreast at a steady walk. In the lower streets, market stallholders and street hawkers called out to them extolling their wares, but as they climbed the hill towards the Palace, the Warders also climbed through the various social class areas. Before long, the street sellers and open stalls were left behind and the houses that lined the streets grew steadily grander in design and quality of finish. The numbers of people on the streets gradually thinned out as well, until by the time that they reached the road that ran around the Palace walls, the four riders were virtually on their own.

Riding up to the great golden coloured gates of the Palace, the group noted the Royal Guards standing smartly at the entrance.

'Leave this to me,' Perdimonn instructed the others.

'Whatever you say, old man,' Rikath agreed with a smug expression that spoke volumes for her amusement.

Perdimonn frowned at her slightly, but then cleared any irritation from his face as he approached the guards. As one, they snapped to attention and sloped their weapons such that they crossed in a symbolic blocking gesture.

'Halt!' the nearest of the two ordered. 'Who are you and what is your business at the King's residence?'

'I am Perdimonn, a Magician. My companions and I seek urgent council with the King of Thrandor.'

'You openly declare yourself a Magician, sir? Are you not aware of our laws regarding magic in Thrandor?' the older of the two guards asked, sounding mildly surprised.

'I am well aware of the laws of this land, Corporal,' Perdimonn answered him, noting the rank stripes on his epaulettes. 'I am not seeking to flaunt your laws, merely to bring urgent news to the King. Besides, your law prohibits the *practice* of magic in Thrandor. I merely stated that I was a Magician. Does *being* a Magician break your law?'

'I'm sorry, sir, but I cannot just march you and your friends into the Palace because you claim to have a message for his Majesty. Frankly, claiming to be a Magician does not help your cause either, so I suggest that you go on your way, sir,' the Corporal suggested politely.

'Is your Captain available, Corporal?'

'He's in the guardroom, sir, but I can assure you that he

will be no more amenable than I. Indeed, he is more likely to arrest you for your claim of being a Magician.'

'Really? Is that so?' Perdimonn said, his voice lowering. 'Then I suggest that you fetch him out here quickly, or I might just do something that will bring the King himself running.'

The Corporal blinked in surprise. The old man was still smiling and his bright blue eyes still twinkled with brightness and amusement, yet the words had carried a compelling power in them that he could not ignore. Unable to stop himself, the Corporal walked reluctantly across to the guardroom and disappeared in through the door.

When he reappeared, the Corporal was followed by a sharp-eyed Captain who looked at the strange-looking party of four with a penetrating gaze. He saw a plainly dressed old man, a gawky looking fellow with a shock of red hair, a short, stocky man with an intense expression and a strangely attractive, dark-haired woman dressed in an unusual sea-green dress. Not your everyday group of visitors to the Palace, he thought to himself as he approached the old fellow who appeared to be their spokesman.

'Thank you for coming out to see us, Captain,' Perdimonn began pleasantly. 'As I tried to explain to your good Corporal here, we need to take council with the King over a matter of the utmost urgency. Now, if you would be so good as to guide us into the Palace, we can speak to the King and be on our way.'

'Is that right?' the Captain enquired slowly, not quite sure if the old man was being serious.

'Well, that would be the easiest way,' Perdimonn affirmed, his blue eyes sparkling with their usual contained merriment.

'And if I won't take you into the Palace?' the Captain asked, his mouth twitching into an amused smile.

Perdimonn's face hardened a little and he shook his head slightly.

'That would not be such a good idea, Captain. I am in

good humour today, so I would try to limit the damage that I would wreak on my way through to see the King but, one way or another, I will see him before this day is done.'

'What sort of damage, sir? My Corporal tells me that you claim to be a Magician. Do you know the penalty for using magic in Thrandor?'

'Magic like this?' Perdimonn asked, and he concentrated for a moment, holding out the flat palm of his hand towards the Captain. A small sphere of white appeared in his hand and began to glow more and more brightly.

'Oh very good, sir,' the Captain said blandly. 'And I suppose that you can make coins disappear and do tricks with pieces of rope as well, but that will not get you in to see the King. Please, sir, do yourself a favour and go about your business. I have no real desire to see you locked up unnecessarily.'

'Listen, Captain, I suggest that you listen to me, and listen carefully. I have no desire to cast down those gates, or to flatten the Palace wall, because your people have got enough work to do rebuilding Lower Mantor. They don't really need me to knock more of the city down, when a simple few words with the King would be enough to prevent any unpleasantness,' Perdimonn said coldly, closing his hand on the ball of light and extinguishing it.

'Flatten the... ha, ha, ha!'

The Captain burst out laughing as he looked at the old man and then at the huge, thick wall that ran off around the extensive Palace grounds. 'That's a good one – flatten the Palace wall! Well, I have to say that you've provided me with a real first today. I've had people try to use no end of different ploys to get into the Palace before, but this is the first time that I've had anyone threaten to level the wall if we didn't let them in. Thank you for the entertainment, old man, but I suggest very strongly now that you be on your way.'

Perdimonn looked down at the flagstone that the Captain was standing on and smiled as he decided to up the stakes a little.

'Stand very still, Captain. Whatever happens, do not move. I would hate to see you hurt,' Perdimonn instructed the immaculately dressed officer.

Muttering a spell under his breath, Perdimonn pointed at the Captain's feet and there was a loud crack, followed by a grating sound of stone on stone. The Captain's jaw dropped in amazement, as did those of the two guards, as the flagstone that he was standing on rose out of the pavement on a square column of earth and rock. The column grew until the Captain was standing some twelve feet above the pavement, looking down at the guards and the Magicians below.

'What the...?'

'Now then, Captain. When I decide to bring you back down from there, will you please tell the King that we await an audience with him? It's that or I flatten the walls and walk in unannounced. What's it to be? I promise you that if the King does not want to speak to us, then we will be on our way, but I have a feeling that he will want to hear what we have to say. However, if you decide not to be a good fellow and do as I ask, then you will be responsible for an incident the like of which Thrandor has not seen in two hundred years.'

To be fair to the Captain, he did not panic and he did not lose all sense of dignity. He remained standing and thinking on the column for what seemed like an age to the other two soldiers. He was so still as he contemplated the situation that he almost appeared a statue atop the unusual pillar, and when he finally spoke it was in a calm and reasonable voice.

'Very well, sir, you have made your point. I should have my men place you under arrest right now, but I too wish to avoid unpleasantness. Lower me down and I shall bring your request for an audience to the King. You have my word on it.'

Perdimonn nodded and, with another series of grating sounds, the column gently retracted back into the earth until the flagstone was back perfectly aligned with the rest of the pavement. The Captain stepped off the flagstone and looked back at it, as if it was a snake about to strike.

'Interesting trick,' he observed with a wry expression. 'Corporal, go and get some men from the guardhouse to take care of the horses. Gentlemen, my Lady, if you would just leave your horses at the rail, my men will see that they are groomed, watered and fed. Private, open up the side gate, please.'

Whilst the Captain organised things swiftly, Rikath wandered over to Perdimonn with an amused smile.

'So does threatening to cast down the Palace wall count as doing something simple?' she asked with a quiet snigger.

'Well, it was a straightforward enough idea, so you could call it that. I guess they weren't quite as easily impressed as I'd imagined they'd be,' Perdimonn admitted with a rueful grin.

'The pillar was a nice touch,' Rikath said, trying to keep her voice down so that the busy Captain would not hear her. 'That will probably live in street legend for centuries.'

'Thanks. I kind of liked it too,' Perdimonn admitted, and then they both fought to keep their faces straight as the Captain gestured for them to precede him through the side gate and into the Palace grounds.

Before they knew it, the Warders were walking up the broad stairway to the huge wooden doors at the front of the Palace. Veldan, the Head Butler, was quick to intercept them as they entered the great hallway and he insisted on walking with them into the inner recesses of the Palace.

As they walked down the hallway, Perdimonn nudged Rikath and pointed at the great tapestry depicting the fall of Darkweaver. He said nothing. He did not need to. The picture showed three Magicians facing down the figure in black, with four other figures standing in the background. Rikath silently pointed it out to the other two Warders and all four of them wore grim faces as they followed Veldan and the Captain into the corridors beyond the great hall.

When they reached the waiting area outside the King's private study, Veldan turned to the Captain and asked for the visitors' names. The Captain, not wishing to show that he did not even know that much, merely swept his hand around in a gesture to the Warders for them to introduce themselves. Perdimonn smiled at the old butler and his eyes sparkled with that blue inner humour once more.

'My name is Perdimonn, Veldan, and these are Rikath, Morrel and Arred. We are... Magicians who need to bring tidings of a grave nature to the King,' Perdimonn announced, his eyes looking anything but grave.

'You look strangely familiar, Perdimonn. Have we met somewhere before?' Veldan asked, his eyes searching as he combed his memory for the answer.

'It's possible,' Perdimonn conceded. 'This is not my first time here at the Palace, though it has been some years since my last visit.'

'Indeed? Very well then, I shall think on it,' Veldan said, clearly disturbed that he could not place where he felt that he knew Perdimonn from.

The old butler knocked at the King's study door and waited for the faint 'Come in' before working the big metal handle. Veldan stepped inside and closed the door behind him. Perdimonn and the others could hear nothing but the low mumble of voices through the thick wood, until the word 'Magicians' being exclaimed by the King in a loud voice carried through to the corridor. There was a little more mumbled conversation, and then silence and the door reopened.

'The King will see you now,' Veldan announced. 'Your Majesty, the Magicians Perdimonn, Rikath, Morrel and Arred. Would you like the Captain to remain here, your Majesty?'

'No, Veldan, that shouldn't be necessary. Please send for Anton though, I would value his presence at this meeting.'

Veldan bowed and left, closing the door behind him. King Malo looked at the strange group before him and shook his head slowly.

'Forgive me, Lady Rikath, gentlemen, a year ago I did not believe that magic was real, and here I have not one, but four people claiming to practise the forbidden arts. Not only that, but they claim to have business with me for some reason. This is all very strange for me to comprehend. I hope that you understand? Please do take a seat.'

The King gestured to a line of comfortable seats around the side of the room and with a bow, each of the Warders moved to one and sat down. Malo looked thoughtful.

'Perdimonn, I have heard that name before,' he said slowly. 'Calvyn mentioned you, I'm sure he did.'

'Most likely, your Majesty, Calvyn and I travelled together for some time and our fates seem intertwined for some reason,' Perdimonn said with a smile. 'He's a good lad.'

'That he is,' the King agreed warmly. 'I would give much to have him back to advise me now on what to say to four Magicians.'

'Well, your wish should be fulfilled very shortly, your Majesty, because Calvyn is on his way here even as we speak. Unfortunately, however, so is Selkor, of whom I'm sure that Calvyn will also have spoken. The problem is that I'm not sure exactly who will arrive first.'

CHAPTER 6

General Surabar walked into the Emperor's study with the confidence of a man always at ease with his circumstances. The salute that he gave the Emperor was smart, but somehow the action conveyed a slight air of casualness born from the knowledge that he was here to provide an invaluable service which the Emperor could get from no one else.

'General, it's good to see you again. Please, take a seat,' welcomed Vallaine, forcing himself in his guise as the Emperor to suppress his irritation at what he saw as the General's arrogant over-confidence.

In fact, Vallaine had never met Surabar before and so he knew that he would have to tread very carefully in this meeting. The General was venerated as some sort of military god by the Legions. The list of his accomplishments spanned several decades, and Vallaine knew that if the General left the meeting with a personal goal then it was as good as achieved already. What Vallaine needed to do was to ensure that the General left with the goal that Vallaine wanted him to have. Nothing else would be acceptable.

'Drink, Surabar? I've got some of your favourite brandy here if you'd like a drop,' Vallaine offered, moving across to the drinks cabinet with his own glass in his hand.

'No thank you, Imperial Majesty. It's a little early for me,' the General declined, choosing a chair with its back to the wall and sitting down neatly into it.

'The man even sits like he's on parade,' thought Vallaine irritably, as he topped up his glass of wine. 'Shand, how I hate the military!'

Outwardly he smiled and pulled a chair around slightly so that he could talk to the General without having to crane his neck, or sit awkwardly. It crossed his mind that the General had chosen the chair deliberately for that purpose, but he stamped on the idea swiftly. It would not do to allow himself to become visibly irritated. This was too important.

Vallaine took a moment to assess the General as he sat down and took a sip of his wine. Surabar looked like a man in his early fifties and yet Vallaine knew that he must be over sixty, just from the length of the man's military career. He was clean-shaven with chiselled features, short cropped silver-grey hair and very light grey-blue eyes. His shoulders were broad and his waist narrow. Everything about him exuded military precision and order and Vallaine found that he instantly hated him for it.

Surabar eyed the Emperor with a similarly assessing gaze and as their eyes met, Vallaine felt for a moment as if the General could see straight through his illusion.

'Thank you for coming so quickly, General. As you've no doubt heard, there have been disturbances on the streets of Shandrim recently. The city militia are not able to cope with the scale of these disturbances, so I would like you to bring in the Legions and restore order to the city.'

Vallaine fell silent and waited for the General's response. Surabar simply sat looking into Vallaine's eyes and the Sorcerer's heart began to pound. Did Surabar know who he really was? Had he somehow discovered Vallaine's secret when none of the Palace staff had an inkling that anything was out of the ordinary?

'Is that it?' the General asked, his expression unchanging. 'You have called for a General and seven full Legions of troops to restore order to the city, your Majesty?'

Vallaine smiled and took another sip of his wine.

'It might appear an overkill, General, I agree, but that is merely the first small step of what I have planned. First I would like you to secure the city. At the same time, I would like you to enforce a conscription order to enrol every eligible man in the city into the military. The conscripts will need to be given an intensive basic training programme to prepare them for the final part of the plan, which is...'

'To invade Thrandor,' the General anticipated.

'Correct, General – to invade Thrandor. Do you foresee a problem with that?'

The General took his hands from his knees, interlocked his fingers and deliberately cracked his knuckles. His eyes seemed to rove aimlessly around the room for a moment, as he apparently lost himself in thought. Vallaine watched and waited for a response, but although he was half expecting it, when Surabar's eyes snapped back into focus and looked straight at Vallaine, the Sorcerer's breath still caught in his throat. Vallaine could not understand it. Surabar possessed no powers of sorcery or magic that the Sorcerer Lord could discern and yet the man's mere presence made Vallaine nervous.

'I'm not sure yet, your Imperial Majesty. You have already sent five Legions into Thrandor, with Sorcerers leading them, I understand.'

The General's tone was bland and not confrontational, yet Vallaine could feel the distaste in Surabar's words. He had no illusions about how Surabar felt about Sorcerers leading Legions.

'From what I understand, your Majesty, a bare handful of men returned from that venture. What makes you think that seven Legions, even augmented by conscripts, will do any better?'

Vallaine swallowed and bit back his anger. He understood perfectly what the General was leading towards, but he needed the man's support, so he kept a firm grip on his temper and said the words that Surabar obviously wanted to hear from him. Vallaine's only satisfaction was that when this was all over and Thrandor was subjugated, there would be no further need for the General's services. Surabar would then meet with an unfortunate 'accident', he thought gleefully. Shalidar would no doubt savour the chance to kill such a notable figure.

'Allowing Lord Vallaine to appoint Sorcerers as the leaders of that force was a mistake,' Vallaine answered, keeping his voice firmly under control. 'I should never have allowed it to happen. I'm sure that if I had appointed a military leader of your stature the first time, then this whole unfortunate situation would not have occurred.'

The General nodded, his expression still bland but thoughtful. Vallaine, though, was inwardly seething. Did this man have no respect for the fact that he was the Emperor? Oh, how he wished to reach out with his mind and squash this General's spirit like an over-ripe fruit. Vallaine knew that if he wanted, he could have Surabar writhing on the floor in helpless agony and begging for mercy in the blink of an eye – yet for now the man was inviolate. The Sorcerer Lord needed Surabar and his command over the Legions far more than he needed to salve his own damaged ego.

'Very well, your Imperial Majesty, my troops will begin restoring order tomorrow. It will be a few days before we will be ready to begin accepting conscripts. There is no point in starting the conscription process until we have the appropriate equipment, clothing and accommodation for them. I will issue the orders to begin the preparations immediately. Obviously there will be a large cost to this endeavour, your Majesty. Can I assume that funds will be made available to arm and equip the conscripts with appropriate equipment?'

'Definitely, General. I will notify the treasury staff as soon as our meeting as concluded. You will have the money for what you need. This project has the highest priority,' Vallaine assured him positively.

Surabar simply nodded again, his expression unchanging but his eyes distant. Vallaine took another sip of wine and rolled the liquid around his tongue gently, trying to use the rich flavour in his mouth to dissipate the stress of this meeting from the rest of his body. The General turned his gaze back to focus on the Emperor again and Vallaine automatically swallowed his mouthful of wine.

'I take it that you would like the leaders of these city disturbances brought before you, your Majesty,' Surabar suggested casually.

'That would probably be best, General. If I simply have them hanged without at least seeing them, word may spread and it might make the rest of your task more difficult. They will hang for their treason though. Much as I would like to throw them into the arena as fodder for the fighters or the animals, that would be too honourable a death for those who would defy the Seat of the Empire. They can hang from the city wall near the main south gate as a reminder for those who would seek to challenge my rule that I do not take kindly to treason. I already know who the main players are in this game, General, and I will not hesitate to hang every last one of them – even my lamentably deluded brother.'

The General took a deep breath and then got to his feet. He saluted with the same smart but casual ease as he had when he first entered.

'With your permission, your Imperial Majesty, I will go and get things moving. There is much to be done and it will not get done on its own,' he said brusquely.

'Of course, General, it was good to see you again,' Vallaine lied, smiling pleasantly at Surabar. 'Please do keep me advised of your progress.'

'Naturally, your Majesty.'

The General walked smartly out of the room and, even with his slight limp, his every movement was one of precision and efficiency. A dangerous man to cross, Vallaine thought as the door closed – a dangerous man indeed. However, this whole situation was now fraught with peril. Vallaine knew all too well that he was playing with fire and that one simple slip could prove very painful, maybe even fatal. The Sorcerer Lord of the Inner Eye broke into a chuckle at that thought, for when viewed in those terms his whole life could have been described in the same way. Intrigue, deception, malice and murder had stalked him since the day he had become a Sorcerer many years before. Being Emperor, it appeared, was a similar game. The problem was that whilst similar, this game had a lot more players with a breadth of strengths, abilities and resources that Vallaine had never faced before. Even though he held the position of the Emperor, much like the King in a game of chess, his moves were limited and his power on the board was relatively weak. All he could do was manipulate the others around him to ensure his survival, and if he had to sacrifice some pieces along the way to achieve that goal, then he had no qualms about doing so. Vallaine always played to win.

*   *   *   *   *

Femke reined her tired horse to a halt. The sun was just setting on her third day of travel out of Shandrim and she was already at the borderlands between Shandar and Thrandor. The spy had made excellent time despite having no natural ability as a horsewoman. Femke had felt sorry for her first horse and guilty for having had to work it so hard. Pushing ahead relentlessly, she had run the poor animal to the edge of exhaustion over the space of two days. Now her fresh mount was looking tired as well, after nearly a full day of travelling the roads at a steady run.

Once Femke had got beyond the stage of having to concentrate just to remain in the saddle, the long journey had offered plenty of time for thought. The puzzle of Shalidar and in particular his parting comments about her having failed to work out what was afoot in the Palace had played heavily on her mind. How had Shalidar known that the Emperor had sent her off on this mission, or had he just made a lucky guess? What was the assassin up to? Was he acting with the knowledge of the Emperor, or playing his own game? The web of intrigue in Shandrim had never been so tangled, yet the Emperor had sent her away from the city at a time when Femke felt that her skills and knowledge of the city had never been more valuable to him.

That made no sense at all and yet the Emperor was not foolish. He never did anything without good reason, so what was his reasoning here? Why had the Emperor assigned her this mission?

Giving a shuddering snort, Femke's horse walked to the side of the lane and started grazing at the long grass. A leg stretch was long overdue, Femke decided tiredly, and she slid down from the horse's back and staggered slightly as her legs protested at the change of muscle use.

'Oh, Shand!' Femke exclaimed, wincing with the discomfort. 'I'm going to walk bow-legged for months after this!'

Her horse was content to stand and chew grass, so Femke walked up and down going over everything that she could think of. Stopping for a moment, she closed her eyes and pictured again the parchment-strewn desk of the Emperor. Something about the desk had really bothered her and Femke felt that if she could just put her finger on one of the tantalising mysteries, then the rest would all fall into place.

Suddenly Femke's eyes opened wide and she took a sharp intake of breath. 'Of course!' she breathed. 'The Emperor isn't the Emperor at all. He's an impostor!'

Why she had not seen it before, Femke did not know. It just seemed so farfetched, but the more that she thought about it, the more little things fell into place. The strange feeling that she had felt in his presence that something was not right should have been enough right away, but the likeness was so good that it had to be a magical illusion of some kind. The voice was almost perfect as well. Just the odd inflection here and there had not sounded quite right and the diction was just subtly different, but otherwise it had been so excellent that she had fallen for it in the same way that everyone else obviously had.

'So no one in the Palace knows,' she reasoned. 'No one except Shalidar. The assassin certainly knew and that was why he had been so smug,' she said to herself softly. 'Yes, that's it. He knew and the Emperor – the impostor Emperor – must have guessed that I suspected something was going on. That's why he was so keen to keep me out of the way. First, he sent me on the strange trip to find Barrathos and now this mission. It all makes sense.'

Femke stopped pacing and smacked herself hard on the forehead. 'Idiot!' she scolded fiercely. 'Shand alive! There were more clues on that desk alone than loaves in a bakery!'

The reports written in a strange handwriting were from no spy, they were the impostor's own notes, which was why one had only been half finished. The inkpot had been to the left of centre, yet the Emperor had been right-handed and, of course, there was the most obvious clue of all, the wine. Certainly the Emperor had liked a drop of red wine, but he never used to drink in the daytime. Femke had just assumed that it was the stress of the political situation that had caused the Emperor to begin drinking earlier in the day. In fact, now that she thought about it, the Emperor had been drinking left-handed as well. It was probably a subconscious habit and she had somehow been blind to it for weeks.

So who was the impostor and how had he managed to get his features to match the Emperor's own so closely? There was really only one name that stood out from the possible list of suspects and that was the Sorcerer Lord, Vallaine. There were plenty of others who were capable of such a daring switch, but nobody with such obvious motives. Femke would bet a pound of pure gold against a copper sennut that her guess was correct. It all fitted. The Emperor had put out the hit on Vallaine, and the Sorcerer Lord in response had decided to strike right back. It was logical, she decided, pleased with that deduction. But where did Shalidar fit into all this, she wondered?

The light was failing fast now and the chill in the air threatened temperatures below freezing. Femke needed to decide what she should do in light of this major revelation. 'Do I go on with the mission, or do I go back to Shandrim?' she muttered to herself, shivering as the icy breeze began to run its fingers through her clothes and across her body.

The choice was not an easy one. If she went on with the

mission and tracked down this Thrandorian fighter, there was a good chance that she might learn more of Vallaine's plans for him. However, the pseudo-Emperor had conveniently given Femke a fairly comprehensive run down of his short-term goals before she had left. The plans that he had confided in her fitted well with the profile of Lord Vallaine and how she would expect him to think and act. He would have had little to gain by lying to her about those, as he would expect them to be all but reality by the time that she returned from this mission. Would the Thrandorian know any more? Femke doubted it, but there would probably be things he knew that would fill in many of the gaps in Femke's knowledge.

'This shouldn't be a snap decision,' she reasoned. 'I'm cold, I'm tired and I'm hungry. I'll stop at an Inn and get lodging for the night. Sleep should clear my head and a hot meal would be most welcome right now.'

With her mind made up, Femke decided to turn back to a village that she had passed through not long before, rather than go onward without any real knowledge of where the next suitable Inn would be. Climbing back onto her horse proved painful. Femke's thighs and bottom were seriously saddle-sore after three days of hard riding, so she prompted the horse forward at a sedate walk rather than resume the punishing pace that she had pushed along at all day. Even the gentle rolling motion of the walking pace was enough to set her back and thighs into spasm, and Femke decided that a soak in a hot bath would be high on her agenda at the Inn.

The walk back to the village took longer than Femke had thought it would, but despite having plenty of motivation to reach the comfort of the Inn, she could not bring herself to pick up the pace one iota. Femke was cold, stiff and sore, and now that she had made the decision to stop, her mental and physical drive had deserted her.

Eventually, the lights of the village drew closer and it was with a shared weariness that the horse and rider plodded along the main street to the front of the Inn. As they stopped outside, Femke could hear the sound of music wafting from within and a fair number of voices in raised conversation. It was obviously a busy night in the taproom. Normally Femke would have been delighted to hear the sounds, for a busy taproom where drinks were flowing was a mine of information just waiting to be exploited. Tonight, however, the spy would have been happier if it had been quiet as a deathwatch.

Femke eased herself out of the saddle and looped the reins over the picket post outside the Inn. Patting the horse on the neck, she reflected that the poor animal would probably not have strayed far if she let it loose. The horse looked as tired as Femke felt. Gingerly stepping across to the door, Femke opened it up and the noise from the taproom hit her with its full volume. If she could have, Femke would have turned around and gone somewhere else, but there was no choice so she pressed forward into the noisy room and weaved her way through to the bar.

Catching the barman's attention took a few moments, as he was busy serving other customers, but eventually he came across to serve her.

'What can I get you?' he asked briskly.

'I'd like a room for the night and stabling for my horse, please,' Femke answered tiredly.

'Well enough,' the man nodded. 'I'll tell the Innkeeper. He'll be along in a minute. Would you be wanting a drink while you wait?'

Femke was about to refuse, but then she realised that a glass of wine would actually be rather a pleasant relaxant, so she ordered one. Money was certainly no object, not that drinking out here in the country was expensive anyway, but Femke had visited the Palace treasury and drawn a significant amount of gold at the Emperor's direction before she left, so she had plenty of coin to live comfortably for quite some time. Having an open account with the treasury was a perquisite that Femke had never abused. Some jobs required that she act like a pauper and others like a queen and Femke enjoyed them almost equally for the different challenges that they presented. The money had never been a motivation for her choice of career, though the Emperor had always seen to it that she was well rewarded for her services. It was the excitement, together with the challenge and added spice of the danger of being caught that kept her fresh and interested. That had not happened in years, of course, for Femke was exceedingly good at avoiding being caught in the act of spying.

There were no vacant chairs at the tables, but Femke had no intention of stopping longer than it took for the Innkeeper to come and take her to a room, so she perched on one of the few free barstools and listened in to the conversations around her. Filtering through multiple conversations and focusing on the ones of interest was a skill that Femke had mastered long ago. The barman placed the goblet of wine that she had ordered on the bar next to her and she paid him for it absently, her mind unable to break the habit of several years of practice.

Several conversations seemed to be about the deaths of local livestock under strange circumstances. Sheep and cattle alike, it appeared, had recently been killed by some unknown creature or creatures that had struck and then disappeared without trace.

'A pack of wolves, I tell you. That's what's doing it,' one fellow insisted forcefully. 'Time was when we used to get raided by wolves on a regular basis.'

'Don't be a fool, Ethan. Wolves hamstring their prey and they don't kill for no reason. Wolves kill to eat. Some of the cattle were just killed and left. The few tracks I found didn't look like no wolf tracks neither. Too big by far they were. Never seen the like in my life.'

'Good thing is that whatever they are, they're heading for Thrandor by all accounts. The string of dead animals they've left across the countryside shows 'em heading as straight south as makes no difference, so I don't think we'll be troubled no more,' Ethan said with obvious satisfaction.

'True enough, and good riddance I say. Rumour has it the beasts killed a farmer and his whole family up near

Shakta. If it's true, then the sooner them beasts get into Thrandor, the better. Nobody as I've heard tell of has actually seen these beasts and I hope to Shand that I'm not the first. If I didn't know better, I'd have said it was demons' work.'

Several of the men in the group made superstitious warding motions with their hands at the mention of demons, and the hairs on the back of Femke's neck prickled with intuition as the men all glared at the speaker for his suggestion. It was almost as if they believed that by merely mentioning the evil, it would appear to devour them. The speaker laughed at their reaction, obviously not superstitious himself, and he took a long draw at his ale.

'Don't go bringing down evil on us by loose words, Malkiere,' Ethan said, his voice nervous.

Malkiere laughed aloud. 'Don't be foolish, all of you. Look at yourselves. The only person who could summon a demon is a Wizard and you don't hear tell of many these days. Besides, if it was a demon, then from what I've heard, you'd have to either be the Wizard's enemy, or be unlucky enough to get between the demon and the Wizard's enemy to need worry. The dark beasts are only ever called for a purpose – normally to kill those whom a Wizard wants rid of. Unless you fellows have been annoying Wizards recently, then I don't think you have much to worry about now that they've passed us by. Anyway, these ain't demons. They can't be. Ain't never heard tell of a Wizard fool enough to summon more than one at a time – far too dangerous. Nope, what we've had through here couldn't be demons.'

Femke jumped at a gentle touch on her shoulder and her heart felt as if it was trying to leap out through her throat. It was the Innkeeper. Femke had been so absorbed listening to the nearby conversation that with all the background noise around her, she had not noticed him approach. The spy mentally berated herself for the lapse, but she realised that extreme tiredness was largely to blame.

'Sorry, Miss, I didn't mean to startle you. I hear that you're looking for a room. Would you like to follow me this way and I'll show you what we have available?'

The Innkeeper did not fit the archetypal mould of those in his profession. From the look of him, Femke would have said that he had never touched a drop of ale in his life. He was quarterstaff thin and not overly tall. He looked fit and his face had something of a sad cast to it that was certainly not typical of someone who made his living offering entertainment and hospitality. His was probably a strange story, but it was not one that Femke needed to hear for she had more than enough to think about.

'Lead on, sir. I would very much like to retire to a comfortable bed and, if it is possible, a tub of hot water to bathe in would be hugely appreciated,' Femke replied, gesturing for the Innkeeper to precede her. 'Oh, and could you send someone out to tend to my horse and bring in my saddlebags? I'm just so tired that I couldn't find the energy to unload the poor girl. She's had a tough day, so if you could see that she's given a good rub down and a feed mix of oats and hay, then I'll be happy to pay any extra charge.'

'No problem, Miss. I'll send out one of the lads as soon as I've got you settled in your room. The tub of hot water might be a little longer, I'm afraid. As you can see, we're a bit busy this evening.'

'Of course, that's no problem. I need the tub so badly that if you have to wake me to deliver it, then I'll not complain,' Femke assured him with a weary smile.

'We have separate rooms for bathing, Miss. I'll get someone to let you know when one is prepared for you.'

'Thank you.'

They weaved their way through the common room to a door at the back, and no sooner had they passed through it than the reduction in noise level caused Femke to sigh with relief. It was amazing how a simple thing like a bit of noise could keep her stress levels so high, she thought, enjoying the relative quiet of the back of the Inn. The conversation that Femke had just overheard had really set her nerves jangling and it was hard to relax – even once out of the noise. Having just worked out that the Emperor was probably a Sorcerer in disguise, the last thing that Femke needed right now was more supernatural events to add into the equation.

The Innkeeper led her down a short corridor past the kitchens and up a square staircase onto the first floor. The lighting was dim, with just a single oil lamp at each end of the corridor and one at the top of the stairs, but it did not matter because the room that the Innkeeper led her to was only a few paces from the top of the staircase. He unhooked a big bunch of keys from his belt and, holding it up in the dim light, he fingered his way through them until he found the one that he was looking for.

'Here you are,' he said, inserting the key in the lock and opening the door. 'It's not that big, but it's comfortable enough for a tired traveller I'll warrant. Now, just you wait here a moment and I'll bring you a lamp.'

Femke waited by the doorway and the Innkeeper trotted off down to the far end of the corridor, retrieved the lit oil lamp and brought it back.

'I'll put another lamp down there in a few minutes. This has got more than enough oil left in it to see you bathed and into bed,' the Innkeeper assured her.

He preceded her into the room, placing the lamp on a small writing desk by the wall next to the head of the large bed, and then smoothed his apron as he looked around to check that everything was in order. 'I'll get your horse seen to next and have someone knock at your door when the hot tub is ready. The bathing rooms are just down the corridor to the right. There are towels in the top drawer of the press there and soap will be provided with the tub. Now, will you be requiring anything to eat tonight?' he asked inquisitively.

'No, thank you. This is all more than fine, thanks,' Femke replied, sitting down wearily on the edge of the bed.

'Very well then. I'd better get back down to the common room or the wife'll start hollerin' at me for slacking,' the Innkeeper said with a smile that did little to lift the sadness from his face.

The Innkeeper backed out of the room and Femke lay back on the bed and closed her eyes. Within seconds, Femke experienced a strange sensation of floating and weightlessness whilst her limbs simultaneously seemed to be weighted such that they were too heavy to move. It was extreme bodily weariness meeting a comfortable position and the opportunity to rest that produced the sensation, but Femke's mind was far too active to allow her to drift away into sleep just yet.

Femke could not help wondering whether Vallaine, if he really had taken the Emperor's place, was somehow responsible for other events going on as well. For some reason, Femke felt sure that demons, and not some other random large predators, had been responsible for killing the farmers' animals. The fact that the trail of these beasts was heading directly into Thrandor was just the sort of unusual coincidence that a spy was unable to ignore, but Femke had never heard of Sorcerers summoning demons before, making it unlikely that this was Vallaine's work. From what Femke knew of Vallaine, he was ruthless enough to employ any tactic that furthered his goals, but would a Sorcerer know how to summon a demon?

Then it struck Femke that the man, Barrathos, whom she had tracked down and taken to the Emperor, had possessed some very strange things in his bags. The Emperor had said that he needed Barrathos for 'a certain ability that he wanted to make use of'. If the Emperor was in fact a Sorcerer, why should Barrathos not be a Wizard? On the other hand, the whole thing might be a huge figment of her imagination and she might be about to embark on what the Emperor might deem to be a treasonous disregard for his instructions. The Emperor could be exactly who he appeared to be and Barrathos might have been a talented tradesman that the Emperor had wished to commission. Had her years in the espionage business affected her mind in such a way that she saw conspiracies where in fact there were none, she wondered? If she was wrong about all of this, she could easily find herself hanging on the wall next to the Governors who sought the Emperor's throne.

A gentle tapping at the door brought life back to Femke's limbs.

'Who is it?' she asked, sitting up on the bed again.

'Stable hand with your saddlebags, Miss,' replied a young man's voice.

'Come in,' Femke said and rubbed her face with her hands as the door opened and a teenage boy entered with her bags slung over his shoulder.

'Where would you like them, Miss?' he asked, eyeing her up and down appreciatively.

Femke covered her mouth with her hand to hide her smile and pretended to yawn. The stableboy was obviously awash with the raging hormones of puberty and eagerly looking forward to a chance to leap into what he saw as the qualification for manhood.

'On the chair at the end of the bed will be fine, thank you,' she replied. 'How is my horse?'

'She's pretty tired, Miss. You must have pushed her hard today,' the boy said, carefully arranging the bags over the chair and looking at Femke boldly again.

'Well, we had a long way to go. I'd really appreciate it if you'd give her a good rub down tonight and if you have a spare rug to throw over her, that would be very kind.'

The boy remained standing and looking at her, seemingly transfixed.

'Thank you,' Femke added with a tone that clearly dismissed him.

'No problem, Miss. If there's anything else I can do just ask for me. The name's Senhaile, Miss. Anything at all,' he offered and then winked at her before he closed the door behind him.

Femke collapsed on the bed in a fit of silent laughter. The poor boy, she thought, as she fought not to make any sounds of hilarity that might be heard outside. He would be vulnerable enough without her knocking him down flat by laughing openly at him.

The laughter subsided and Femke felt much more awake than she had before. It had been a long time since she had found anything to laugh at and the experience had made her feel altogether better. Femke was certainly awake enough to look forward to her hot tub and the decision about what to do tomorrow could wait until she felt clean and refreshed.

CHAPTER 7

Calvyn lodged another log of deadwood in the firepit, causing a cloud of glowing embers to leap into the air, spiralling upwards in a swirling mass of glowing motes that twirled and danced up into the clear night air like some fluted tower from an artist's imagination. Master Jabal coughed softly and Calvyn guiltily returned his attention to the Master so that he could continue with the lesson.

Jenna had just left to go and get washed at the stream and so Master Jabal had offered to give Calvyn another spell-casting lesson whilst she was gone. It was not that Calvyn did not want to concentrate on the lesson, but he found he was struggling to focus because of his concerns over the distinct feeling that something bad was happening, or was about to happen, to his friends. Master Jabal was right about one thing though – whatever was happening to Bek, Derra and the others was beyond Calvyn's ability to influence now. That fact offered scarce solace to his troubled heart, but it gave him something to hang on to.

'Sorry, Master Jabal, I was a little distracted. Please forgive my inattention. I'm with you again now,' Calvyn apologised humbly.

'Very well, Calvyn, let's see exactly what you know about spell-binding objects – and I don't mean dancing girls,' Jabal said, his eyes twinkling with humour in the firelight. 'You obviously know something, for you have woven spells into the blade of your sword. First of all, I'd like to establish what you know, then we'll progress your knowledge by studying the Staff of Dantillus and discussing what you think the Grand Magician did to spell-bind the Staff with such a powerful charm.'

Jabal paused for a moment and looked into the flickering flames of the fire.

'Shall we start with what Perdimonn taught you?' he suggested, still staring at the burning logs.

Calvyn smiled fondly at the thought of his old mentor and cast his mind back to the times that they had spent together by the sides of fires at similar campsites. The old Magician had not really taught him many spells at all. The incident with Selkor at the marketplace had precluded Perdimonn from teaching Calvyn any more than his first one or two spells. Perdimonn had simply taught Calvyn the sort of things that were achievable with magic, and how the combination of imagination and empowering runes could be used to achieve no end of amazing results.

Perdimonn had maintained that two things limited magic: the available power source and the Magician's imagination. That was why he had concentrated so much on the second element with Calvyn's studies.

'Well, Master Jabal, if by that you mean what specific spells did he teach me for the purpose of enchanting objects, then I'd have to say none,' Calvyn said slowly. 'We had really only just begun with spell-casting when Perdimonn insisted that we split up because Selkor was somehow tracking us. What he did do, though, was to give me his grimoire. Many of the spells in there were for making healing ointments and tonics that will cure all manner of ailments and injuries.'

'I see,' Jabal replied thoughtfully. 'So the spells that you put on your blade were in the grimoire?'

'Well, no, not exactly,' Calvyn said, scratching at the back of his neck as he tried to think how he was going to explain this diplomatically. He already knew that the other Acolytes at the Academy thought that he was reckless for inventing spells. What would Master Jabal think when he realised what Calvyn had done?

'Well then? What *exactly* were they then? Where did you learn spells that would bind magic into objects?'

'I... um... made them up, Master Jabal,' Calvyn mumbled.

'You made them up!' Jabal exclaimed in genuine shock. 'Are you serious? You just made them up – just like that?'

'Well, no, Master, it wasn't just a spur of the moment sort of set of spells, if that's what you mean. I worked at them for several days, arranging the runes into sequences that I felt would best provide the effects that I wanted. All of the spells that I cast on the blade were adapted from spells that were in the grimoire. I just sort of played with them a bit until they fitted what I wanted to achieve.'

'*Played* with them!' Master Jabal squeaked, his voice breaking with incredulity at what he was hearing.

Calvyn decided that he had better not mention the final spell and the disappearing rune that had come unbidden to him in the final moments of the sword's forging. Master Jabal already looked as if he was in deep shock from what Calvyn had told him, so to add more now might just be too much.

'I was confident that the spells would work, Master, and they did – every one of them,' Calvyn insisted. 'You have seen the spell that makes the blade my own at work for yourself. I worked other properties into it as well.'

Jabal drew a deep breath and looked Calvyn straight in the eye.

'Did Perdimonn teach you to just make up spells?' he asked seriously.

Calvyn was completely thrown. That was not a question that he had even really considered. The old Magician had always insisted that magic was infinitely flexible and that there were no limits to the combinations of the runes and the resulting effects. The limits, he had said, were only those of the wielder's imagination. Had he encouraged Calvyn to specifically design his own spells though? Calvyn could not remember precisely what Perdimonn had said that led him to think that it was acceptable to do so. He had just used instinct and his slowly increasing knowledge to guide his progress.

'No, not precisely, Master. Well, to be honest, Perdimonn didn't really get to teach me much practical magic as such. He just seemed to imply that there wasn't anything to stop me from doing it and the combinations of runes all made perfect sense, so...'

'So you just invented your own spells,' Jabal finished. He sighed heavily. 'Well, I suppose that I can't blame you for ignorance, but you are playing with worse than fire every time that you perform one of those spells of yours. It's a miracle that you haven't done yourself a serious injury in the process. Come then lad, let's have a proper look at what you've created. I only got a glimpse of it back at the Academy.'

Calvyn passed the sheathed sword across to Master Jabal and watched as he drew the blade. To Calvyn's astonishment the blade glowed with an unmistakeable blue light and for a moment Calvyn was at a loss for words.

'What's this?' Jabal asked with interest. 'The blade didn't glow like this when Akhdar drew it back at the Academy. I saw him do it in your quarters before we came back to my classroom to confront you with it. What does it mean?'

'It only glows like that in the presence of evil, Master Jabal,' Calvyn gulped and then leapt to his feet, looking around into the dark.

'Are you saying that I'm evil,' Jabal laughed, turning the blade in his hand and gently running a fingertip over the silvery runes seemingly embedded in the steel.

'No, Master Jabal,' Calvyn said nervously, 'but something, or someone nearby is. I think that I'd like my sword back for a while if you don't mind, and it might be a good idea to gather everyone else around the fire.'

'Ha! Very funny, young man. There's your sword, now let's get on with the lesson, shall we?'

'I'm serious, Master Jabal,' Calvyn whispered loudly, taking the blade and adopting a balanced fighting crouch and slowly turning around to scan in all directions. 'Deadly serious. Now, gather the others. Quickly! Before it's too late. The last time the blade turned this colour was when I was close to Darkweaver's amulet.'

Finally it seemed to sink in that Calvyn was not playing around and Master Jabal got to his feet. Lomand appeared from inside the tent and looked at Calvyn braced for battle as if he were mad.

'What are you...' he began, but Calvyn signalled him to silence.

Master Jabal walked over and whispered a quick explanation, repeating Calvyn's request to gather everyone around the fire, but he was too slow at getting the message across. Just then, several things happened at once. Calvyn realised that Jenna was out in the woods on her own at about the same instant that Lomand spotted one of the Naksa demons charging silently at Calvyn from behind. An instant later, Calvyn spotted the second Naksa angling in at him out of the dark.

Lomand moved incredibly quickly for such a big man. Racing forwards, he pushed past Jabal to make a diving intercept, his clenched fists punching into the demon's side and throwing its attack off course.

'*Ardeva!*' Calvyn yelled and, as his blade burst into flame, he braced himself to meet the demon that he could see bounding towards him. Calvyn had managed to learn a little about demons since the Gorvath had taken his soul. In particular, he had scoured every book in his room at the Academy for references on the subject, and though there had not been much in the Acolyte's reading list, what little he had found would prove very useful today.

Demons hated fire. That fact had appeared more than once, as had the advice never to look into a demon's eyes. The eyes of a demon were perhaps the most powerful of its formidable array of weapons. With its stare a demon could inflict a demon-daze on its victim, allowing the beast to use razor sharp claws and teeth to deliver a death blow. Its eyes, together with the soft tissues inside its mouth, were its only vulnerable spots, as the rest of a demon's skin was virtually impervious to any normal metal weapon. The only material that could easily penetrate a demon's skin was a special type of crystalline rock known commonly as demon's bane. Demon's bane was a rare material indeed, and the only samples that Calvyn had ever seen were the bits that Jenna had shown him. Unfortunately, he had no idea where she kept those and there was no time to look for them now.

Demons were also known to live in a primitive sort of caste system, classed mainly by power and intelligence. As Calvyn met the attack of the approaching beast, he judged this demon to be of low caste. It was almost dog-like in appearance, but it was bigger than the biggest dog that Calvyn had ever seen, and with its hugely muscled hind legs, it bounded more like a powerful cat than a dog. As it sprang, Calvyn dropped to one knee and used the momentum of the demon, as its weight crashed fully onto the point of his sword, to roll him backwards and so catapult the beast over his head.

For a moment, it felt like they were part of some aerial circus act, for the other demon, having had its attack deflected by Lomand's two-fisted body punch, flashed past Calvyn on a crossing trajectory and crashed headlong into the fire. Burning branches and embers scattered at its impact and the demon screamed out in pain and anger.

Calvyn rolled to his feet and managed to slash at the beast that had crashed into the fire, but his blade glanced from the demon's skin like any ordinary blade.

'That answers one question,' Calvyn thought in a flash and turned to meet the other demon, which had somehow turned and leapt at him again with terrifying speed. This time Calvyn swayed aside and slashed blindly towards the creature's face as it passed. Even in mid-flight the demon twisted and managed to rake its claws across Calvyn's chest. Momentum carried it by, and the burning sensation of torn skin and welling blood added urgency to his thought processes.

With a desperation born of intense fear, Calvyn muttered an abbreviated version of a spell that he normally used for lighting fires, but mentally directed the runes through his sword, imagining the blade spitting a ball of fire like an arrow from a bow. The demon that had just slashed him across the chest had already turned again, and Calvyn was aware that Lomand had somehow intercepted the other beast and was holding it at bay. Without a second thought, he pointed the tip of his sword and unleashed the spell. A ball of intense blue flame the size of his clenched fist shot from the tip of his sword straight into the face of the demon. It screamed in fear and pain as the flames scorched its eyes and it backed away in confusion.

Turning to help Lomand, Calvyn was horrified to see the big man with his hands determinedly holding around the demon's throat as the beast slashed and clawed at him with the claws on its hind feet. Lomand's body and upper legs appeared to be one huge mess of blood where the demon had already shredded his clothing, together with the flesh beneath, with its claws. Somehow, Lomand was still standing and holding the creature around the throat with his great hands and was squeezing with all his might.

Yelling something both incoherent and incomprehensible, Calvyn ran the few steps to Lomand's aid and thrust his burning sword up into the demon's mouth, piercing tissue and bone to strike into the creature's skull. The force of Calvyn's strike drove the demon out of Lomand's vice-like grip, but it did not matter for the beast was dead before it hit the ground. Lomand toppled down as well, but Calvyn could not afford to see how he was, for the other demon was gathering itself for another charge.

Calvyn wrenched his blade free and repeated his earlier fireball spell. With gritted teeth, he pointed his sword again and a second ball of fire erupted from the tip of the blade and struck the demon full in the face again. Its howl of anguish rent the night air with a cry guaranteed to raise the hairs on the back of the bravest of warrior's neck. Calvyn, although scared, did not hesitate, but ran forward and struck at the beast's face again and again, trying desperately to strike the eyes or into the mouth. The demon flinched from the blade at every strike, more likely from the flames that licked along the tang than from the threat of the metal itself.

A cry from the direction of the tent did not distract Calvyn, though he did spin past the demon so he had a chance to ensure that nothing else was about to attack him from behind. Out of the corner of his eye, he caught sight of the Grand Magicians scattering from in front of the tent and a huge shadow seemingly holding one of them in its clutches. Calvyn ignored it. He had enough to deal with here.

The Naksa was dancing around, slashing with its claws and snapping with its fearsome mouth of teeth, but the combination of the fireballs and the flaming blade had made it wary. It had tasted pain and seen its partner demon fall to the blade it was facing. Notably though, the beast did not retreat, but kept leaping left and right, constantly seeking an opening past the burning sword in order to slash and kill.

Calvyn ran his fireball spell a third time, but this time he adapted it, repeating the critical runes again and again and holding back on releasing it until he was in a position to make it really count. The demon snapped and snarled, and Calvyn flowed with the beast's movements, weaving and spinning around in a swirling merry-go-round of fire, fangs and death. Gradually losing its wariness, the Naksa made another strike forward with a vicious lunging snap of teeth and Calvyn released his spell, blasting fireball after fireball in a rapid-fire sequence at the demon's face. The Naksa flinched back with every strike and opened its mouth to howl in pain. Instinctively, Calvyn rammed the blade into the open mouth with the tip still spitting fireballs, and the creature's head exploded in an eruption of fire.

Panting with effort, Calvyn turned towards the tent and froze, trapped by a pair of mesmerising eyes. The great shadow that he had seen earlier moved forward slowly and, with an air of indifference, it negligently cast aside the lifeless body that it had been holding in its claws. Calvyn had no idea who the beast had killed. It was irrelevant. The eyes held him and his mind reeled with the knowledge that he was helpless. He could cast no spell whilst held and none could really harm the demon he faced, even if he was free to use his magic. This was a higher caste of demon altogether from the two that he had just been battling and the power in its eyes was far, far more compelling.

Silently cursing himself for his automatic reaction of looking up to the demon's face, Calvyn could only watch with an echoingly familiar sense of horror as the beast stepped slowly forward. It looked much as he remembered the Gorvath, Calvyn realised, his mind crashing into deep panic. He desperately wanted to lift his sword and at least attempt to fight, but the battle was all in the eye contact and it was a battle that he knew to the depths of his belly that he could never win. The eyes held him rooted to the spot – great, unblinking eyes, burning orange and filled with an unspeakable malice and evil. All control lost, Calvyn's arms fell limply to his sides and the burning sword dropped to the ground as his fingers lost their grip on the hilt.

There was nothing he could do. Demon-dazed and completely helpless, Calvyn watched as death advanced step by step towards him.

*　　　*　　　*　　　*　　　*

The second that the little arrow on Jenna's silver charm began to vibrate, everything fell into place: the feelings of dread and imminent danger, the charm continually pricking her chest and even Master Jabal not wanting her to leave the group. It all made sense.

'Oh, Tarmin!' she breathed and, straightening slowly, she scanned the woods around her for any signs of the demon, being careful to keep her gaze low in order to avoid accidentally making eye contact with it.

Every shadow suddenly seemed menacing, the bright moonlight giving everything a ghoulish cast. The noise of the stream dominated the still night air and Jenna could hear nothing but the gentle gurgling, splashing noises of the water. Nothing moved in the trees. There were no sounds or signs of life at all, but Jenna was not surprised, for she had experienced this before.

Suddenly remembering the demon's bane knife that Gedd had given her as a parting gift, Jenna's hand went to her hip in a flash. For just the briefest of instants, her heart had leapt in her chest as she thought that she might have lost it, or left it at the campsite, but as her hand settled on the hilt a warming feeling of relief flushed through her. That momentary panic left the taste of bile at the back of her throat and Jenna swallowed hard in an effort to clear the foul taste. It was no use. Her mouth had dried of saliva and, even with the clear running water of the stream at hand, Jenna knew that she could not waste the time to take a drink. Time was flowing faster than the stream behind her and Jenna could almost sense the last few grains of sand dribbling through the hourglass that measured her time to act.

With all the care and silence she could muster, Jenna slipped away from the stream and crept silently through the trees. Holding the silver charm in front of her with her left hand and gripping the knife for all she was worth with her right hand, Jenna slid soundlessly from tree to tree. The quivering arrow of the charm averaged out, pointing pretty much straight at the campsite and Jenna desperately found herself wanting to yell a warning at the top of her voice. A warning, though, might prove counter-productive, for it might cause the demon to strike before she was in a position to strike back.

A blood-curdling scream suddenly rent the night air, inhuman in pitch and full of pain and anger. Jenna knew instantly that stealth was no longer an issue and she sprinted forward, racing through the trees as fast as she could. A branch, hidden by the mulch of fallen dead leaves, caught her foot as she ran. The resulting trip sent her tumbling forward, and she crashed down hard onto the ground and dropped her knife in the process.

Jenna cursed aloud in frustration and then cursed again

in pain as she got to her feet only to find that her left ankle had twisted badly. It was agony to put any weight on it, and for a horrifying moment she thought that it might be broken, but there was no time to worry about that. Dropping back to her hands and knees, Jenna fought tears of pain and panic as she frantically scrabbled around amongst the leafy mulch on the ground around her, desperately searching for the demon's bane knife.

Another inhuman scream of pain, this one laced with fear, split the silence beneath the trees and Jenna felt like adding a frustrated scream of her own to it. Then she spotted the knife several paces away, stuck point down into a large tree root. Jenna scrambled forward on her hands and knees and wrenched the blade free at the same time as a shadowy shape came running at speed towards her from the direction of the campsite.

Instinct drew Jenna's arm back in preparation to strike and only the motion of the flowing cloak following the Master stopped her from throwing the knife at him. As he passed her, Jenna recognised Master Chevery's pasty features looking whiter than ever in the moonlight and full of terror at whatever he was running from. For a moment Jenna hoped that Calvyn was running every bit as hard, but she knew him too well to expect that. 'He's just too brave for his own good sometimes,' she cursed silently.

Gasping at the pain in her ankle, Jenna scrabbled to her feet and hobbled forwards towards the campsite as fast as she could manage. As she reached the tree line, Jenna could see that the demon had trapped Calvyn with its eyes and was closing in for the kill. There was no way that Jenna could cover enough ground to attack the demon with her knife before it killed Calvyn and her bow was in the tent. Her only hope was a knife throw, which was something she had never been good at.

Fesha had demonstrated knife-throwing skills to his fellow recruits one day whilst Jenna had been practising on the short range with her bow. Although she had been working on her archery skills, she had not been able to ignore the funny little man's bantering during his demonstration. Despite not even watching him for most of the time, Jenna had learned a few things from that demonstration and now she tried to remember every little piece of advice she had heard.

Unfortunately, as Jenna hurled the knife with every ounce of force she could muster, the inevitable weight transfer from right foot to left resulted in her weakened left ankle collapsing during the critical moment of release. Her brain, it seemed, attempted to correct for the loss of balance and the result was that Jenna knew even as she was falling to the ground that the knife would miss because the throw was too high, having been released an instant too early.

Time seemed to slow for Jenna, and even as she fell she somehow managed to follow the glittering arc of the thrown knife. Instinctively taking in a sharp breath and holding it, Jenna watched with breathless horror while her forearms took the impact of her body hitting the ground.

Even as the knife flew through the air, the Krill was exulting in the helplessness of its victim and, standing directly in front of Calvyn, it began to draw itself up to its full height in order to deliver the killing blow. As the demon reared up to its full height, so the knife met its target, driving with deadly force into the back left side of its skull.

All power left the demon's eyes and Calvyn staggered backwards away from the great beast even as it began to topple. The Krill hit the ground with a loud thud and Jenna's eyes filled with tears of relief. Silently she thanked the Creator that the demon had chosen that precise moment to stand tall, for the movement had surely saved Calvyn's life. A brief minute of quiet followed, then Calvyn's voice, sounding strained to breaking point, drifted on the night air from the campsite.

'Jenna, are there any more of them?'

More? Jenna had not even considered there being more than one, but the sounds that she had heard before reaching the campsite were consistent with there being more than a single demon. With a twist of her shoulders,

Jenna rolled onto her back and held the silver arrow charm up. It showed no inclination to settle in any one direction and Jenna heaved a sigh of relief.

'No, there aren't any more out there,' she called back. 'Are you all right?'

'Better than might be expected under the circumstances. You?'

'Twisted ankle,' Jenna said loudly. 'Maybe sprained, but I don't think anything's broken.'

'OK, Jenna. Just stay where you are for a minute and I'll come and give you a hand. I just need to help Lomand first. He looks in a bad way.'

Calvyn's mind still felt fogged from the demon's hypnotic influence, but he could see that Lomand was still alive. The big man's chest was still rising and falling with regular breaths, though he looked to be deeply unconscious. Probably just as well, Calvyn thought grimly to himself, for the pain of the huge number of claw wounds that he had sustained would be too horrible to think about.

Mentally blessing Perdimonn for his many healing spells, Calvyn ripped open Lomand's shirt and surveyed the wounds with as detached a mind as he could. There was a huge amount of blood loss, but Lomand was a big man and providing that Calvyn acted quickly, he would probably survive. There was nothing that would be life-threatening on its own, so Calvyn set to work weaving an intricate set of spells that drew the torn flesh back together and repaired the damaged tissues. By the time he had finished, Calvyn was gasping with the effort expended on such an intricate piece of magic.

The job was not finished yet though and Calvyn picked up his sword, which immediately burst into flame at his touch.

'*Darmok*,' he ordered, extinguishing the blue tongues of fire. Then, after noting that the blue glow that indicated the presence of evil was no longer shining, he set to work using the blade to cut Lomand's trousers from his legs.

Blood still flowed freely from the multiple lacerations that criss-crossed the man's thighs and Calvyn once again launched into a complex pattern of spells to repair the damage. By the time he had healed the last vestiges of trauma from Lomand's legs, Calvyn was fit to collapse himself. He had needed a lot of energy to complete the spells and had drawn heavily on his own resources to achieve the healing.

There was no way that Calvyn could hope to move Lomand into the tent and, even if all of the other Magicians had been there, he doubted that they would have managed to move him. However, Lomand, whilst healed of his injuries, was not safe yet. His body was in a state of shock and the air and ground were both extremely cold. If Calvyn could not do something to insulate Lomand from the cold fairly quickly, then hypothermia or shock might kill him just as effectively as the wounds would have.

Staggering with exhaustion, Calvyn stumbled across to the tent where he found the crumpled body of Master Ivalo. There was no need to check for a pulse – the Grand Magician was clearly dead – so Calvyn left him, entered the tent and gathered an armload of blankets. As he came out again Jenna was standing outside leaning on an improvised staff.

'You're injured!' she accused him, her voice seemingly ready to berate him for his carelessness.

Calvyn looked down at his torn doublet and noted the blood-stained tears across the front.

'Yes, but it's not bad,' he assured her. 'Here, help me get these over Lomand before he freezes to death.'

Together they worked to wrap the big man with several layers of blanket, managing to get material under him by rolling him onto his side and back again. A final blanket was folded to make a pillow for his head and then they sat down and rested next to the scattered remains of the fire. The main bed of ash and embers was still giving off a good amount of heat, and just with the bits and pieces of wood within reach Calvyn quickly managed to resurrect a small blaze.

'Come on, Calvyn. Let me have a look at your wound. I've

got some fresh water here, so I can at least clean it up for you,' Jenna offered once the fire was alight.

'That won't really be necessary, Jenna. I'll sort it out after I've rested a bit, but I wouldn't mind a swig of that water. My throat is parched.'

'Don't be foolish, Calvyn. You don't want the wounds to get infected. Come on. Off with that top.'

Calvyn smiled at her insistence, and when she started tugging at the front of his doublet he sighed tolerantly and eased it up and over his head.

'Now, can I have a sip of that water?' Calvyn asked, as Jenna winced at the sight of all the blood across his chest and stomach.

'Here you are,' she said, giving him her flask. 'Don't drink it all. I'm going to need some of it to clean that mess up. It looks like we're going to end up with matching scars, though I reckon that mine will still be more impressive than yours,' she added sadly.

'Matching scars?' Calvyn asked in surprise. 'I didn't realise that you were injured when you fought the Gorvath.'

'Well, actually, I gained the scars a little earlier than the final fight. I faced the Gorvath twice before we managed to kill it. The second time I was lucky to survive. I hope your wounds heal better than these.'

Jenna lifted the front of her shirt to show the great scars across her stomach from where the Gorvath had all but gutted her in Shandar, months before. Even now, the area of skin around the thick lines of white scar tissue was still a dark red colour, though not the angry red of a fresh wound.

'Jenna, I had no idea,' Calvyn said gently, as she lowered her shirt again.

'Ugly, aren't they?' Jenna said with tears in her eyes. 'I don't think I'll be able to lie in the sun and get a tan ever again. I'd be too embarrassed. I always knew that as a soldier I'd be likely to pick up scars but I suppose that I just never thought the consequences through.'

Calvyn leaned across and gently wiped away her tears with his fingers, then he shivered with the cold. Sitting in a temperature that was approaching freezing point with no shirt on was uncomfortable, but with the heat being given off from the fire it was bearable.

'Don't worry, Jenna. I'll fix it for you. Watch and see what being a Magician is *really* all about.'

Calvyn pictured again in his mind the spell for treating cut flesh, and tracing each cut with a fingertip he controlled the spell such that it healed like an eraser, wiping away each blemish with a single pass. Jenna's jaw dropped in amazement as she saw his skin whole again, and when he had finished she wiped away the blood from his body with a cloth only to find no sign that there had ever been wounds there at all.

'You can take away the scars?' Jenna asked breathlessly.

Calvyn smiled wearily. 'Yes,' he confirmed. 'I can heal your scars. Give me a moment or two to get warm and recover my strength and I'll rid you of them.'

'No, there's no need to do it now,' Jenna objected, wrapping her arms around him and hugging him tightly. 'They can wait until you've recovered fully. You're tired and it's a miracle that you're alive at all. I still don't know how you killed those other two demons without a demon's bane weapon.'

Easing out of the embrace, Jenna grabbed Calvyn's doublet from the floor and handed it to him along with his cloak, which was also lying nearby.

'Here – put these on. Much as I like looking at your bare chest, there's a time and a place for that and this isn't it. I'm going to dig out some food. I think that we could both do with something to eat.'

Leaning heavily on her makeshift crutch, Jenna got up and hobbled around the campsite, gathering food from several different packs. Bread, cheese, dried meat and travel cakes with a couple of apples made a meal that was more than sufficient to revive them. They washed it all down with the remainder of the water from Jenna's flask. Lomand began to snore as they ate, causing both of them to smile, for his shuddering snores were very loud. After a while the huge Magician rolled over slightly and fell silent, leaving the crackling of the fire as the only sound that broke the silence.

'I wonder how far the rest of the Magicians ran,' Calvyn said suddenly, his voice sounding loud after the long silence. 'They had a fair turn of speed on them for their age.'

'Master Chevery certainly wasn't hanging around when he passed me,' Jenna agreed. 'I'm beginning to wonder if they are going to be of any use to Perdimonn after all.'

'You mean that you think us all cowards who will run at the first sign of danger?' asked Master Jabal's voice from startlingly nearby.

The Grand Magician walked into the campsite from the darkness and fixed Jenna with a hard stare. Jenna met his gaze and returned it with one of her own.

'The thought had certainly crossed my mind,' she answered with more than a hint of a challenge. 'You were quick enough to run and leave Calvyn and Lomand to face three demons on their own.'

'That is very different from facing another Magician, Jenna. Demons are all but impervious to magic and neither I nor any of my brothers, are exactly fit for hand-to-hand combat with such creatures. Selkor is a different matter. We may not be able to defeat him, but we will not run from our duty to face him either... at least I won't.'

'Nor will I,' added Akhdar's voice, and he too seemed to materialise out of the darkness as he approached the campfire. 'Is Lomand...'

'Lomand is fine, Master Akhdar,' Calvyn anticipated. 'At least he will be after a good night's sleep. He was too heavy for me to move, so we just wrapped him in blankets where he lay. He's lost a lot of blood, so he may be a bit weak for a few days, but I healed his wounds so he should make a full recovery very quickly. Master Ivalo was not so fortunate.'

'I guessed as much when I saw that monster impale him with its claws,' Akhdar admitted. 'Where are the others?'

'I've no idea,' Calvyn said with a shrug.

'Not to worry, I'm sure that they'll return by morning.

CHAPTER 8

The next morning proved Master Akhdar half right. Master Kalmar had returned at some time after midnight, but of Master Chevery there was no sign. The three Grand Magicians conferred privately for a short while and then attempted unsuccessfully to contact Master Chevery by mind to mind contact. By the time that the campsite had been cleared and the horses loaded, they had obviously made their decision to continue without him.

'Leave his horse and suitable supplies for him. He'll find them eventually,' Master Akhdar ordered. 'In the meantime we need to keep pressing onwards. Those demons sought us out, which means that someone doesn't want us to get to our destination. Whoever sent them might try again, so let's get a move on and get to Mantor.'

Calvyn had a fairly good idea who had sent the demons and he was reasonably sure that it was not Selkor, but on reflection he decided not to pass on his suspicions to the Masters. If they thought that Selkor was trying to stop them from reaching Perdimonn it might give them the idea that Selkor feared the outcome, and give the Masters both some confidence and an even greater sense of urgency than he had managed to instil in them so far.

Lomand had risen early and gone about clearing the camp as if nothing had happened the previous day. He did thank Calvyn for healing his wounds when he discovered that it had been he rather than one of the Masters who had done it, and had complimented him on the job. Calvyn then went with Jenna down to the stream to help her fill all the water bottles before they moved on. Whilst they were there, he healed her scars and removed the last of the pain from her ankle.

Tears of joy rolled down Jenna's face in rivers as she ran her fingertips across the now unblemished skin of her stomach and Calvyn could not help but be touched by her reaction.

'One of these days I am going to thank you properly for this,' Jenna promised, the look in her eyes leaving no doubt in Calvyn's mind about what she meant. 'For now though, this will have to do.'

Jenna threw her arms around him and drew him into a prolonged kiss that left Calvyn both breathless and speechless. He had never really been intimate in his relationships with girls before and the combination of the promise and the kiss left him flushing red with a mixture of embarrassment and anticipation. Holding Jenna close made his heart pound until he was sure that she must be able to feel it thumping against his rib cage, seemingly trying to escape. It was a wonderful feeling and one that he was reluctant to end, but time and the pressure to reach Perdimonn weighed heavily on his mind. Eventually, he simply had to pull away with a wistful smile. He gathered his armloads of water containers and led a similarly encumbered Jenna back to the campsite.

If any of the Magicians felt that Calvyn and Jenna had been a long time fetching the water, none of them said anything. Lomand had tacked up the horses and once they had distributed the water between them, the six riders mounted up and moved out onto the road. Master Ivalo's horse was loaded with some of the equipment normally carried by the two packhorses and Lomand led the animal with a makeshift lead rope.

What the three Magicians had done with the bodies of Master Ivalo and the demons, Calvyn did not know. Though he was curious, Calvyn was not sure that he wanted to find out. It was enough that the campsite was clear and, although they were depleted by two, they were on their way again.

At about midday the Masters signalled a halt. Calvyn and Jenna, assuming they were stopping to eat, dismounted with the intention of getting lunch underway quickly. Master Jabal looked back over his shoulder and signalled to Calvyn to come forward. Calvyn handed Hakkaari's reins to Jenna and walked forward to see what the problem was. Jabal was quick to explain.

'There's a large body of armed men marching up the road in the opposite direction. What do you suggest? Should we clear off the road and wait until they pass, or should we press forwards and see if they make way for us?' Jabal asked earnestly. 'This is your country, Calvyn. What is the correct protocol here?'

Calvyn thought for a moment before replying.

'It very much depends on who is coming, Master Jabal. Can I see who it is and I'll give you my advice?'

Master Jabal moved his horse aside to allow Calvyn to walk through to the front of the party. At first Calvyn could not see what Master Jabal was referring to, because he was not as elevated as those on horseback behind him. Then he saw the banners moving above the hedgerows some distance ahead and he laughed.

'This is an unusual chance, Masters,' he called back to them. 'The black emblem with the blue cross is Baron Keevan's banner and the white one with the red running horse is that of Lord Valdeer. It appears that they're only just returning from the recent campaigns in the southern parts of Thrandor. If I may ride at the front of the party, then I should be able to gain us passage through the troops. The Baron will probably want me to give at least an outline report before we proceed, but that shouldn't take long. There's little point in going off road now, Masters, for both the Baron and Lord Valdeer will have sweep riders and scouts out as a standard marching order. I'm sure that they'll have seen us by now and will probably want to know our business on the road anyway. If you let me do the talking, then I should be able to minimise the delay.'

'Very well, Calvyn. We will eat while you give your report. Mount up and move to the front. Let's get this over with,' Master Akhdar ordered.

Calvyn ran back and vaulted up onto Hakkaari. As he did so, he noticed that Jenna looked a little apprehensive at the news that they would be meeting with the Baron. Calvyn smiled at her encouragingly before heeling Hakkaari forward to the front of the group. There would be no problems for Jenna from the Baron, Calvyn was sure of it. He could understand Jenna's nervousness though, for he was sure that he would feel the same way if their situations were reversed.

Leading the group forward at a steady walk, Calvyn sat straight in his saddle as they closed the distance to the approaching military forces. Whilst he might not be dressed to fit his title, he was not about to look sloppy in front of the Baron.

'Halt and declare your business,' ordered the banner guard, as Calvyn approached the front of the column of troops.

'I am Sir Calvyn, son of Joran, Knight of the Realm of Thrandor, Private. My business is my own. However, I wish to speak briefly with Baron Keevan and Lord Valdeer, so stand aside or provide a suitable escort, as you will. That way we can all be about our business,' Calvyn replied boldly, halting Hakkaari directly in front of the banner parties and speaking with as much authority as he could put into his voice.

'You wear strange garb for a Knight of the Realm, Sir Calvyn, but only a fool would make such a claim in front of so many armed men, unless he were an assassin trying to get close to the Baron. You shall have your escort, Sir. Please don't do anything foolish that might provoke those around you.'

'Understood, Private. Now, let's get moving, shall we?'

A group of soldiers were designated as escorts and some moved ahead whilst others fell in behind Calvyn and his followers. All eyes followed them as they moved through towards the centre of the army column where the Baron and Lord Valdeer rode. Several soldiers called out semi-respectful greetings to Calvyn as they passed, and one or two recognised Jenna as well. Calvyn gave each of them a smile and a nod of acknowledgement but although he recognised some of them, there were none that he knew well.

The fact that soldiers were acknowledging Calvyn and Jenna obviously relaxed the escort guard, for they realised that this strange group of people that they were taking to the Baron were at least friendly. Calvyn could not help but grin at the whole situation, for it was a real turn around of responsibilities for him to be leading the Masters in a situation where they were both regarded as strangers and potentially law-breakers. Only his status as a Knight of the Realm and the King's Adviser on matters magical gave them immunity from the law that made magic illegal. They would have to live under his protection and, whilst he knew that he could not milk the fact too much, it temporarily gave him a certain amount of power over them.

It did not take very long to reach the entourage of Captains that accompanied Baron Keevan and Lord Valdeer. Calvyn was both slightly surprised and amused when Captains Strexis and Tegrani both saluted him on sight. He returned the salutes smartly and gave one of his own to the Baron, who was just behind them.

'Hello, my Lords. Well met,' Calvyn said with a broad smile.

'Well met indeed, Sir Calvyn. I trust that your mission was successful?' Baron Keevan replied, his face maintaining its normal flat expression, but his voice conveying a degree of enquiring warmth.

'Well, my Lord, I got a little side-tracked from my original mission, though I would like to offer a report if we could gain a little privacy somehow.'

'You got side-tracked, did you?' Baron Keevan asked thoughtfully, looking at each of Calvyn's travelling companions in turn. 'I think that a short delay for your report might well be worth the time. Captain Tegrani, order the column to halt. Move them off the road into the fields either side, would you?'

'Yes, my Lord. Right away,' Tegrani answered, saluting smartly.

The Captain rode forward, bellowing orders as he went, and the Corporals and Sergeants sprang into action to ensure that those orders were carried out. The whole process was very orderly and practised, and before long the only people left actually on the road were a handful of Captains, the Baron, Lord Valdeer and Calvyn's party. Everyone dismounted and the Captains arranged for the horses to be picketed nearby. Calvyn then introduced his travelling companions to the nobles.

'Lord Valdeer, Baron Keevan, may I introduce Grand Magicians Akhdar, Jabal and Kalmar? This fellow is Magician Lomand and this is Private Jenna, whom I have borrowed from your service for the time being, sir. I hope you don't mind,' Calvyn added casually, almost as an afterthought.

'Not at all, Calvyn. It is good to see that you are still alive, Private Jenna,' Baron Keevan said graciously and Jenna bowed slightly to indicate her thanks for his concern.

'My Lord, much as it grieves me to admit it, I was forced to abandon my original quest to free Bek and Jez from Shandrim and leave that mission to Derra and the two Privates. I was contacted by my mentor, Perdimonn, of whom I've spoken before, and urged to go to Terilla to speak to these good gentlemen about Selkor. To cut a very long story short, my Lords, I'm now accompanying them to Mantor to meet with Perdimonn to attempt to stop the Shandese Magician, Selkor, from gaining any more power. It appears, my Lords, that the amulet of Derrigan Darkweaver is not the only item of power in his possession. He now possesses enough magical power to destroy Thrandor at a whim. We need to intercept him before he does anything of the sort.'

'This sounds like precisely the sort of event that the King gave you your current role for,' Lord Valdeer observed with a wry smile. 'You really need to report this to him if you are going to Mantor, you know?'

'Yes, Lord Valdeer, I will go and see his Majesty at the earliest opportunity. My heart tells me that we must press on to Mantor with all speed, because the last I heard Selkor was hard on Perdimonn's heels and Perdimonn was heading for Mantor. We can only pause our journey for as long as it takes to have a quick bite to eat and then we must press on. Please, my Lords, remain vigilant as you travel. We have already lost two of our party to demons. I suspect that you will not be troubled, as the attack appeared very focused on our party, but I do advise caution.'

'Demons like the one that took your soul before?' asked Baron Keevan, his eyes narrowing.

'Not exactly the same, my Lord, but deadly enough to kill one of our party. Another man is missing, so if you see an old man dressed similarly to the Grand Magicians here, please help him on his way. His name is Chevery,' Calvyn explained, trying very hard to keep his dislike for the man out of his voice.

The Baron and Lord Valdeer insisted that Calvyn and his party eat quickly with them, using the army's food supplies rather than their own. Also, the Baron ordered their supplies to be replenished and ensured that their horses were fed and watered. Although they ended up stopping for slightly longer than he would have liked, Calvyn judged afterwards that with the uplift of supplies, the slight delay had more than paid for itself. With the food that they had in the packs now, they should make it comfortably to Mantor with no need to stop again to purchase anything more. Calvyn's last request of the Baron was that if, on his return to the castle, he should find news of the rescue party, then tidings would be sent on to Mantor. The Baron was emphatic in his agreement with this and wished them all a safe journey.

When they moved on again, the Masters certainly

appeared happy enough considering the events of the previous twenty-four hours. Calvyn was actually so surprised at their levity that he asked Lomand about it. Less than a day had passed since one of their fellow Masters had been horribly killed and another had disappeared, and Calvyn could see little for them to be happy about.

'They are old men, Calvyn. Old men die,' Lomand answered him. 'When they left Terilla it was with the knowledge that the likelihood of any of them returning was remote at best. They came because they must, but just because they are continuing the journey without outwardly demonstrating their feelings for Ivalo's death and Chevery's... disappearance, doesn't mean they don't have any. Believe me, if Master Chevery doesn't come to Mantor, then he had better be dead or at least not show his face anywhere that the other three Masters get to hear of it. If he does, then Master Chevery will certainly feel the strength of their feelings.'

*   *   *   *   *

Perdimonn and the other Warders had been pleasantly surprised at the King's open-mindedness at what they had told him. The King and Baron Anton had heard them out and conferred briefly before asking them if there was anything that they could do to help. Having expected to be faced with straight disbelief, Perdimonn had been somewhat surprised by their apparent immediate acceptance of their story.

'I have seen too many strange things recently to dismiss you as crazy fools,' the King had said, with a knowing smile. 'I am sure that you understand my desire to have your story confirmed before I take everything that you've said at face value though, so please stay as my guests here in the Palace until Calvyn arrives to verify matters.'

Perdimonn had been more than happy to accept the King's offer, but had suggested that at least one of the four of them join the watch guard at the city gates on a rotating basis. Each of the Warders, except Perdimonn, had been fooled by Selkor's use of the Cloak of Merridom in recent days, so they were wise to the sort of tricks that Selkor might try. If they were going to confront Selkor, Perdimonn and the other Warders were determined that they would not harm anyone else in the process.

The King had seen the sense of Perdimonn's proposal and had called Veldan in to see that everything was set in place for their stay.

'Yes, your Majesty?' Veldan asked, bowing deeply as he entered the room.

'Ah, Veldan, thank you for coming so quickly. Please show these folks through to the West Wing Suites would you? They're going to be here as my guests for a while and I'd like them to be afforded every courtesy and comfort that we have to offer here at the Palace.'

'Yes, your Majesty. I'll see to it at once, your Majesty,' Veldan said deferentially, though he eyed the four Warders with a degree of distaste at odds with his tone. It was plain to see that he did not feel the odd looking group in their travel-soiled clothes looked fit to be in the presence of the King, much less be given suites in the prestigious West Wing.

Perdimonn winked at Rikath and his eyes sparkled with amusement at Veldan's obvious prejudice. 'Watch this,' he whispered to her as an aside when they were led out of the King's study. The Earth Warder moved forward until he was alongside the Head Butler and then looked across at him as if struggling to remember something.

'Tell me, Veldan, would I be right in assuming that you are the son of Nesrun, who also held the position of Head Butler some years back?'

'Yes, that's right. I am the last in a line of four who have passed the position from father to son,' Veldan announced proudly. 'Alas, I have no sons, so the family tradition will stop with me.'

'Ah, yes,' Perdimonn said, as if suddenly remembering a random fact that carried no importance. 'Of course, I had forgotten that Pallane and Favel were also related to you. That makes sense I suppose.'

'You appear to know a lot about Palace history, sir,' Veldan said, quite obviously impressed that Perdimonn could name his direct ancestors as far as his Great Grandfather. 'Is it a hobby of yours to study such things?'

'Oh no, Veldan! I was merely thinking that you were as full of your own importance as Nesrun was. When you reminded me that you were also related to Pallane and Favel, I suddenly realised that your manner is hardly your fault. It is obviously a family trait, for I remember Favel when he was promoted to the position. He was insufferable for months as I recall,' Perdimonn reflected, his eyes still sparkling with that inner mirth.

'You remember!' Veldan scoffed. 'I have been serving in the Palace for thirty-nine years, Sir, twenty-six of which have been as Head Butler. My father served twenty-nine years in the position before me and his father served twenty-four years. You are telling me that you can remember my Great Grandfather attaining the Head Butlership some twelve years or so before even that?'

'Actually, yes,' Perdimonn said with a bright smile. 'It was the fourth year after King Roath II came to the throne as I recall. It would not have been a memorable event at all though, had it not been for the hurricane that blew in across the Eastern Sea that spring. Do you remember, Rikath? It was the only *really* bad blow that I can remember that was a true easterly.'

'Oh, yes!' Rikath agreed, her eyes going distant as she cast her mind back. 'The surf that day in the Straights of Ahn was truly awesome to behold.'

'Even I remember that storm,' Arred laughed. 'The wind played over the entrance to my cave as if it was a giant bottle. I came out to see what was causing the racket and nearly got blown off the mountainside.'

'*You* remember!' Veldan spluttered. 'But that's preposterous! Why, you aren't old enough to remember King Malo attaining the throne,' he accused, pointing at

Arred. 'And you, young lady, you cannot be a day over...'

'Weren't you ever taught that it's rude to speak of a lady's age?' Rikath interrupted, raising her eyebrows at Veldan in mock surprise. 'Besides, if we are counting years here, then it is you that is the young man. Let's not argue over trivialities though. Would, perchance, the West Wing Suites boast a decent bathing facility? Frankly, I feel like something the tide washed in, but not so clean.'

Veldan looked outraged both at being interrupted and even more so at the fact that anyone could think that *any* Palace suite would not have a bath tub, let alone one in the West Wing. He quite obviously recognised that he was the butt of some joke that the three were having at his expense, and it made his manner even more sullen.

The Head Butler pointedly informed Rikath that, yes, there was in fact a small personal bathing pool in each of the suites, along with virtually any other facility that could feasibly be expected in a visitor's quarters. 'The Royal Tailors will be placed at your disposal to provide you with more suitable attire for wear around the Palace during your stay,' Veldan added pompously with another disdainful look at their clothes. After that, the Head Butler clammed up and pointedly ignored them until he brought them each to their own suite.

When Veldan left, the four Warders gathered in Perdimonn's suite and had a quick discussion about who would take the first watch at the city gates. Arred quickly volunteered to stand watch first. As it was an hour's walk down to the gate, they decided to hold a twelve-hour watch rota, running from midday to midnight. Arred was to do a slightly shortened first watch, and then the others would each stand a twelve-hour shift in turn.

It was agreed that whoever was on shift when Selkor arrived would call Perdimonn using the spell that allowed mind to mind contact. Perdimonn would then gather the others and manipulate time such that they could all go out and face Selkor together. They were all agreed that a one on one confrontation with him was out of the question.

None of them could face him on their own, but together they might be able to rattle him enough to make him back off.

Selkor knew three of the four Keys, but he did not know or understand the elements to the same depth that the Warders did. All of the Warders knew and loved the element that they had guarded for so long and, as Perdimonn pointed out to them during their brief meeting, all of them knew enough to block anything that Selkor tried with the three Keys that he now had access to. If Calvyn and the Council of Magicians arrived in time, they, together with Perdimonn, would counter anything Selkor tried with Darkweaver's amulet, the Ring of Nadus, or the Cloak of Merridom.

Arred left the meeting and made his way out of the Palace, to take up his post down at the city gates. The Palace itself was a bit confusing to navigate but, once Arred was outside, the way back down to the main city gates was straightforward. When he got there, Arred climbed the steps to the top of the city wall and walked along to the small guardhouse in the tower alongside the gates.

The Sergeant in charge of the afternoon shift gave Arred a look not unlike the one that Veldan had given him about an hour and a half before. It was a look that quite clearly conveyed the unspoken question 'What do you think you are doing here?' and added the 'You don't belong here, go away' sentiment all in one. Arred just smiled at the Sergeant and decided to explain the situation in a way that the Sergeant would have no choice but to listen to.

'Good afternoon, sir, my name is Arred,' he began, holding out his hand to the Sergeant for him to shake.

'I'm no 'sir', Arred. My rank is Sergeant and I have no wish to be lumbered with the nausea of being an officer,' the Sergeant replied, his face dour and his eyes looking at Arred's offered hand as if it were covered in something vile.

Arred's smile broadened as he took in the Sergeant's expression. Perdimonn would probably have words to say to him later, but Arred was not about to let this simple soldier, no matter what his rank, treat him as if he were something from the gutter. After all, Perdimonn had had his bit of fun with Veldan a little earlier. It was time that the Thrandorians started to wake up to Magicians and what they could do, Arred decided with increasing amusement.

'Well, my apologies, Sergeant. Forgive me, for I'm not really very familiar with the military. I've been living out in... er, a fairly remote area for quite some years now, so I've sort of lost touch with the civilised world and the way you do things,' Arred said, bowing his head slightly in apology but still grinning from ear to ear.

'What do you want, man? I can't stand here and chatter idly all day,' the Sergeant demanded irritably, obviously keen to be rid of Arred as fast as he could.

'Well, actually I'm here to help you guard the city gates. There is a powerful enemy of Thrandor on his way here right now and I, together with my three friends, are going to help you to prevent him from entering the city,' Arred explained.

'Oh really?' the Sergeant said sarcastically. 'Listen, Arred, or whatever you said your name was. I don't really appreciate jokes. I don't have time for them, do you understand? The city is perfectly well protected, thank you, so you and your friends can relax and let us do the guarding. If this 'enemy' comes, then I'm sure that we'll be able to handle him.'

Arred shook his head sadly and pursed his lips at the Sergeant's response. Quickly he checked to see that nobody else was up walking along the wall nearby, as he did not want to be responsible for any accidents.

'Unfortunately, Sergeant, you don't understand who it is that you will be dealing with. What will you do if the man in question melts your gates with a single blast of fire like this?'

Arred turned and shoved his left hand, palm forward out in front of him and silently completed the simple spell that he had prepared as he was speaking to the Sergeant. A huge jet of fire sprang from Arred's hand and roared nearly thirty yards along the top of the wall. The Sergeant leapt back inside the guardhouse and slammed the door shut. Arred extinguished the flames and gave a little bow to the people in the main street below. Virtually the entire street had come to a momentary standstill at his demonstration and several people now applauded, as they thought that they had just witnessed a new sort of street entertainer carry out his act.

A knock at the door brought no response, so Arred shouted with an exasperated tone as he hammered at the door a second time.

'Sergeant! For Tarmin's sake, man, open the door! I'm here to help you. If you were alarmed by that little display then you certainly don't want to meet Selkor. That's why the King wants us to help guard the city.'

At the mention of the King, there was a click and the door cracked open again. The Sergeant peered around the side of the door, whilst using it like a shield to protect his body.

'The King knows about this?' he asked uncertainly.

'Absolutely,' Arred replied firmly. 'I've just come directly from the Palace where my friends and I are currently staying – in the West Wing, if that means anything to you.'

'You're staying in the Palace?'

'That's what I just said, isn't it?' Arred replied, using a tone of forced patience. 'Now, Sergeant, let's start again, shall we? My name is Arred and I'm here to help you guard your city.'

Arred held out his hand again and this time the Sergeant gingerly reached out and shook it, apparently expecting the touch to be furnace hot. For a moment Arred considered making a hot spot, but decided that he had probably pushed the Sergeant around quite enough for one evening.

'So how did you do that fire thing? Doesn't it hurt your hands?' the Sergeant asked warily, watching Arred as if he expected the gangly, red-headed fellow to grow two heads, or explode into a million pieces at any second.

Arred gave him his best mischievous smile and raised his eyebrows suggestively.

'Do you really want to know?' he asked, interlocking his

fingers and pretending to limber them up for another spell. 'Only kidding! It's not something that I could teach you anyway. It takes years of study to master even the simplest magic spell, so it would be impossible to simply show you how it was done. That's the problem facing Mantor right now. A Magician is coming who is very powerful and you have no Magicians here in Thrandor to defend you, so... enter the cavalry! My friends and I, together with some others who are on their way here, are going to do our best to stop this man, Selkor, from causing you good people too much trouble.'

'Please, Arred, forgive my scepticism over this. I know that I saw your fire demonstration just now and, to be honest, it scared me witless. I still have a problem with the concept of a civilian, Magician or no, up here on the wall working alongside my men. I'm going to have to send someone up to the Palace to verify your story. I hope you understand,' the Sergeant apologised, spreading his hands in a signal that suggested he had little choice in the matter.

'Perfectly, Sergeant. Verify away! Now, to business: where's the best place to watch from, and have you got anything to drink up here?' Arred asked, his face serious.

The Sergeant nodded and directed Arred to the stairs in the back right corner of the room.

'If you go up there, the top of the tower is where our lookout post sits his watch. You can keep him company if you wish. He has a supply of fresh water up there and there's an urn of dahl keeping warm on the intermediate floor if you prefer.'

'Water and dahl, huh? No real drink then?'

'Not on duty, Arred,' the Sergeant said, sounding shocked at the very idea of drinking alcohol on duty.

'I had a feeling you were going to say that,' Arred said ruefully and shook his head in disappointment. 'Oh well, I'd best get to it, I suppose.'

At midnight, Arred handed over to Rikath. The Sergeant had confirmed Arred's story with the Palace during the afternoon, so Rikath had no problems getting up into the

Guard Tower. The guards took to her straight away and before long were falling over each other to bring her dahl and food. The Warder of Water was quite amused by all the attention. It was as if they had never seen a woman before, and yet women served in the military here in Mantor as they did in many of the private armies around Thrandor. When she handed over to Morrel at midday the following day, Rikath thanked the soldiers for their company and told them that she would be back in thirty-six hours time. Morrel then watched with mild amusement as the guards fought to get on a corresponding shift.

The more serious business of watching for Selkor and the Council of Magicians was uneventful. Morrel handed over to Perdimonn and he, in turn, back to Arred again with no sign of either party approaching the city. It was late afternoon during Arred's second shift when he spotted the first arrival. Unfortunately, it was not the Council of Magicians.

CHAPTER 9

As soon as Arred saw the figure in the black cloak, he knew it was Selkor. The Shandese Magician was making no attempt to disguise himself and he was riding a horse that stepped with the same proud, arrogant manner as its rider. Arred wasted no time. Selkor was still some distance from the city gates, but it would take him little more than five minutes to get to them.

'Perdimonn,' Arred called out, having initiated the mind-linking spell. 'We have company and it's not time to break out the welcome banners.'

'Understood,' Perdimonn sent back. 'Roughly how long until he reaches the gates?'

'Maybe five minutes at the outside.'

'Very well, we'll meet you by the city gates. Be very careful as you move. I'll slow him down until we can get there.'

'Will do,' Arred affirmed and, with one last glance down at Selkor from his vantage point up on the wall, he turned and made his way over to the stairs.

The strange lurch as Perdimonn manipulated time for the four Warders seemed more pronounced than Arred had remembered from his last experience of the phenomenon. It probably had something to do with what Perdimonn had done when he had anchored time to the Earth Key, Arred reasoned silently. This was no time to think about trivialities however, and it was with a fearsome level of concentration that Arred painstakingly made his way step by step down through the tower, out onto the wall and down to street level.

As before when Perdimonn had all but frozen time like this, everything was motionless and so weaving through the people in the street was fairly simple. Arred was extremely aware that he must not bump into anyone, as his real relative speed was incredible and the damage that he might do, both to the person he bumped and to himself, could easily be disastrous. Fortunately it was fairly late in the afternoon and so the main street was not overly crowded, making his short walk to the city gate a straightforward one.

The same eerie silence that Arred remembered from his trip in the rowing boat from Kaldea to the Straights of Ahn, made the hairs on the back of his neck stand on end. It was one thing to experience that silence far from land without another human being within sight, but to walk through a fairly busy city street and feel the same oppressive quiet was something quite different.

People: motionless, unresponsive and yet undeniably still full of the essence of life, posed in positions that varied from the mundane to the completely improbable. Everywhere that Arred seemed to look, someone in the process of stepping, jumping, or running had halted in positions that defied gravity, sometimes in mid-air. But then, in many ways, gravity was no longer working in the way that it normally did either. Arred's mind recoiled from that thought, because the more that he thought about what Perdimonn was doing in order to create this effect the less sense it made in every way. Logic told Arred that all sorts of dire things should be happening to his body if he applied the laws of nature to what was happening, yet this spell that Perdimonn had worked appeared to defy all logic. There were certain laws that even magic adhered to and yet Perdimonn seemed to have defied some of those as well. It really was most strange.

Arred reached the gates and sat down carefully just outside the city to wait. Sitting where he was, the Warder of Fire could see Selkor on his horse still a good distance from the gates and as motionless as everyone else. For an instant, Arred regretted his vow of pacifism, for it would be the easiest thing in the world to kill Selkor now and all of their problems would be solved. His vow, however, was sacrosanct. Nothing would make him break it – not even Selkor.

Perdimonn would have a plan. He always did, mused Arred, shivering slightly as he began to feel as if Selkor was watching him. It was a ridiculous feeling and Arred knew it, but within a couple of minutes it began to get the better of him. Rather than sit there and suffer a bout of nerves, however, Arred elected to move out of Selkor's line of sight. Rising carefully to his feet again, Arred stepped slowly back in through the city gates and opted to endure the eerie stillness of the city street over the imagined stare of Selkor.

To Arred, the wait for Perdimonn, Rikath and Morrel was interminable, so he set about trying to keep his mind distracted from his surroundings by practising his juggling. Time might be frozen for those around him, but it seemed to drag even more for the fiery-haired Warder. Finally, when movement caught his eye and he saw the other three Warders emerge from one of the streets that led up the hill to the Palace, Arred was ready to jump up and run to meet them. He did nothing of the sort, of course. Instead, he rose slowly to his feet from where he had been sitting, determinedly juggling five balls of fire in a complex set of mesmerising patterns. The balls of fire winked out in the instant that he spotted the other Warders and Arred carefully stretched his legs and eased the feeling of cramp from his muscles, having sat on the ground for so long.

'Come,' Perdimonn ordered simply. 'This will probably get ugly, but I've been explaining to the others how we might be able to work this confrontation to our advantage.'

Arred smiled broadly. Perdimonn always seemed to have a plan up his sleeve for every occasion and, as he had suspected earlier, today was going to prove no exception. The old Magician seemed to have a head for finding his way out of difficult situations, which was just as well because the rest of the Warders had spent many years wrapped up in their own little worlds and were not used to problem solving.

The four walked out of the main gates together and Arred pointed to the figure of Selkor seated on his horse. Perdimonn nodded and stopped them from going out any further from the city.

'All right,' he said, taking a deep breath. 'Arred, you stay here with the others and they can fill you in on the plan. I'll go out and see if I can liberate Selkor of a few of his burdens.'

Arred, although confused, did as he was told. He had thought the whole idea was to face Selkor together to prevent him from getting the fourth Key, but now Perdimonn was going out to Selkor on his own. Quite what logic Perdimonn was using escaped Arred, but as soon as the old man started walking forward on his own towards Selkor, Morrel and Rikath started bubbling out Perdimonn's plan. A moment later and Arred was laughing loudly as he grasped what Perdimonn was doing.

The old Magician walked carefully out to the stationary figure of the man whom he had tried so hard to thwart over the previous weeks and months. Although Perdimonn was fairly sure that his plan would work, getting this close to Selkor on his own was more than a little unnerving. He had managed to sound confidence itself to Morrel and Rikath, but moving right up to where Selkor sat upon his horse had Perdimonn's heart beating so hard in his chest that he thought it might explode.

Selkor was dressed in his usual black garb with high leather boots inlaid with fancy designs that had been worked with some form of silver thread. His whole bearing screamed arrogant superiority and yet the Shandese Magician's eyes glittered with a burning anger overlaid by ambition.

Perdimonn was glad that Selkor had not shown more prudence in his approach to Mantor. Perdimonn had been sure that the Shandese Magician would have tried to manipulate time by now, no doubt with painful consequences. It appeared that Perdimonn's assessment of Selkor was correct. The Shandese Magician apparently had thought that as he could no longer alter the flows of time to suit his purpose, then no one else could either. Perdimonn was sure that if Selkor had considered the possibility of others being able to manipulate time for even a second, then he would have used the Cloak of Merridom to approach Mantor in disguise. That would have made Selkor far more difficult to detect, but again, Perdimonn had considered that possibility.

Moving right up to Selkor's horse, Perdimonn walked around to the saddlebags. With infinite care the old Magician eased the buckles open and lifted the flaps to look inside. Gently he drew the contents out and laid them piece by piece onto the ground. There, at the bottom of the saddlebag, he found the Cloak of Merridom and his heart leapt.

'Perfect,' Perdimonn whispered to himself.

There was no way of taking back the Keys of Power that Selkor had stolen, and Rikath and Morrel had agreed with Perdimonn that trying to touch Darkweaver's amulet would not be wise. For all they knew, the amulet might operate independently of time, which made approaching its bearer a far more risky business than it would have been otherwise. However, the properties of the Cloak of Merridom and the Ring of Nadus were well known, making them safe to steal and fair game.

The Earth Warder was about to start repacking Selkor's supplies and gear back into the saddlebags when he realised that it would be easier just to steal those as well. That way, if they did manage to drive him away, the Shandese Magician would find his next night or two most uncomfortable.

Perdimonn chuckled. Whilst he could not do anything that might kill Selkor, he was certainly not above making the man's life uncomfortable. Instead of repacking the gear into the saddlebags therefore, he laid out the cloak on the ground and piled all of the other gear from the saddlebags into the middle of it. Wrapping the cloak around the pile, Perdimonn slowly folded it all into a neat bundle and left it on the ground whilst he looked for the ring of Nadus.

Perhaps not surprisingly, Selkor was wearing the ring on the middle finger of his right hand. Getting it off without seriously damaging Selkor's finger would not be easy, Perdimonn thought gravely, but if today's confrontation was not to turn into a disaster, then it had to be done. With infinite patience and care, Perdimonn gently prised Selkor's fingers from their grip on his horse's reins. Then, removing a small pot of ointment from his pocket, the old Magician smeared a dollop of the cream around Selkor's middle finger to help slip the ring off smoothly. There followed a delicate operation over what seemed like an age, of ever so gradually easing the Ring of Nadus fraction by fraction down Selkor's finger until it finally fell free into Perdimonn's hand.

Unable to suppress a grin, Perdimonn slipped the ring onto his own finger and then carefully cleaned the ointment from Selkor's fingers before repositioning them around the reins.

'So far, so good,' Perdimonn breathed, immensely satisfied with his unusual piece of thievery. Then, unable to suppress a quiet chuckle of amusement, Perdimonn picked up Selkor's gear in the neat bundle that he had made with the Cloak of Merridom and walked carefully back to the city gates.

The other Warders were all waiting anxiously at the gates to see if Perdimonn had been successful. All three heaved sighs of relief when the old Magician flashed the Ring of Nadus at them and lifted the bundle of equipment wrapped in the Cloak of Merridom.

'What's inside the Cloak?' asked Rikath, her face clearly showing her curiosity.

'Just the majority of Selkor's camping gear and food supplies,' Perdimonn replied innocently. 'Nothing of any great interest really.'

The other Warders all chuckled, looking at each other like

naughty school children that had just rigged their teacher's chair to collapse. It was a nerve-wracking prank at best, but it lightened the mood prior to what they knew would be a testing confrontation.

Perdimonn took the bundle and emptied the contents of it out onto the ground just inside the city gates. Passers-by would probably pick up most of it within a couple of minutes of the restoration of normal time, Perdimonn realised with a grin. Even if Selkor discovered the theft quickly, then collecting his gear back would not be an easy task. Having freed the Cloak of Merridom of its burdens, Perdimonn flung it around his shoulders and secured the ornate clasp at the top of his chest.

'All right then, is everyone ready?' Perdimonn asked, looking around at the others.

'As ready as we're going to be,' Arred answered with a grimace. The others nodded as well.

'Very well, let's get on with it,' Perdimonn said determinedly, and with an air of concentration he began working his shape-shifting spell.

Perdimonn had always hated shape-shifting, as he had never really been very good at it. Wearing the Cloak of Merridom made the process easy though, and the image of the person that he was to shape-shift into became vivid in his mind instantly. It was almost as if Perdimonn had been looking at the man only seconds before and within the space of a few short breaths the transformation was complete.

'Very impressive,' Rikath complimented with a grin. 'Now you almost look your age!'

'Very funny,' replied the voice of Grand Magician Akhdar sarcastically. Perdimonn gently touched his beard and hair, feeling the changes in the contours of his face and looking down at the changed appearance of his clothing. 'It's a shame the real Akhdar didn't get here in time, or this might have been significantly easier to pull off.'

Perdimonn concentrated again and began a new spell – one that he was both more familiar with and more practised at. After a couple of minutes he looked around at the others again and nodded.

'The illusions are in place on the walls,' he confirmed. 'Arred, are you happy that you'll be able to make it appear that some of them are casting fire spells?'

'I'll manage,' Arred said with a grin and momentarily started juggling balls of fire again.

'OK then, one final illusion...' he said and the Staff of Dantillus appeared in his hand, '...and it's crunch time.'

With that, Perdimonn reversed his time manipulation spell and the world lurched back into life and sound. The three Warders, together with what appeared to be Grand Magician Akhdar wielding the Staff of Dantillus, walked boldly out through the city gates once more to meet their approaching adversary.

When he saw the four figures emerging from the city, Selkor reined his horse to a halt and waited for them to come to him. His face settled into a derisive sneer as he identified them and he brought his hands together to finger the Ring of Nadus. As his fingers discovered the loss, Selkor's face momentarily dropped and his right hand sprang involuntarily to his chest, where Darkweaver's amulet gleamed balefully like a malevolent silver eye. Finding the amulet still there, Selkor's hand relaxed back down with the other again and his face twisted into an expression that managed to portray anger and satisfaction all at once.

'Where is the coward Perdimonn?' Selkor demanded loudly. 'You might as well order him out here or I will destroy this city of snivelling barbarians as I go in after him.'

'He has no need to face you, Selkor,' Perdimonn replied with Akhdar's voice. 'We jointly have enough power to prevent you from reaching him.'

'You think those poor excuses for Warders will stop me, Akhdar? Then you're a bigger fool than I gave you credit for. They're fools, one and all. Their presence will avail you nothing, and I've got more than enough power at my fingertips to flatten you and those other cowards thinking to ambush me from the wall.'

Perdimonn inwardly smiled. He had to give Selkor credit for sharp eyes. The illusional Magicians that he had created up there had hardly shown a cloak hem and Selkor had already spotted them. Could it be that Selkor was actually more nervous about this encounter than he made out, Perdimonn wondered?

'Turn aside from your pursuit of Perdimonn, Selkor, or you will regret this day forever.'

'I'll not turn aside now, you old fool. Have you no sense? I've pursued my goal over years and more hundreds of leagues than you've seen in your entire life, Akhdar. Today will see me become "The Chosen One", and there's nothing that you can do to prevent it,' Selkor retorted angrily.

'Get ready everyone. Here we go,' muttered Perdimonn under his breath.

Sure enough, Selkor invoked all three of the Keys that he knew in quick succession. Perdimonn made a flourish with his illusionary Staff of Dantillus as a distraction, whereas in reality he was preparing a spell to aim through the Ring of Nadus. Perdimonn fervently hoped that Selkor would not detect any difference. The old Magician doubted his own ability to tell the difference, so there was little reason to worry about Selkor doing so with everything else that would be happening.

With a roar like a thousand lions, a wall of flame rushed out from Selkor only to meet an instant gale of wind generated by Morrel, which turned the inferno of flames back upon Selkor. Perdimonn had anticipated that Selkor would use fire first, as it was his favourite element and so Morrel had been primed for the instant reply. Selkor was only saved from roasting by a shield of magical energy thrown around him from Darkweaver's amulet. Whether Selkor had initiated the amulet's power, or whether it had triggered automatically, Perdimonn could not tell.

Bolts of fire of a much smaller magnitude were raining down on Selkor from various places along the city wall, but they were like fire flies next to a forest fire in comparison with the monstrous first wave that Selkor had produced. Arred was merely initiating them to maintain the pretence that others were up there.

Perdimonn fired a few blasts of his own at Selkor, amplifying them with the Ring of Nadus. Although they would have been fatal had they struck home, Perdimonn knew full well that they would not do so with the amulet's shield now firmly in place. His attacks, also, were simply diversionary.

Selkor tried again with fire, this time striking out with lightning bolts. However, for every bolt he loosed, Arred met it with one of his own and the thundering cracks of those bolts meeting had people cowering in fright across the entire city. Selkor persisted for quite some time at this game, raining bolts of lightning from all directions, but Arred intercepted every one of them, firing counter-spells out with a determined grimace on his face and his fists tightly clenched.

Perdimonn switched to firing a mixture of distraction-type spells from the wall and the occasional heavy punch of his own. With carefully calculated blasts, he made the ground around Selkor erupt in showers of rock and mud with bolts of energy that he made appear from his illusionary staff.

Changing tack, Selkor turned towards the River Fallow and raised his hand in a commanding gesture. A wave rose from the river as the water gathered into a small hillock that raced at speed from the riverbed towards the four defenders standing before the city gates. Rikath raised her hands and the moving mound of water slowed to a halt. The giant mound of water shifted and changed shape like a great amorphous jelly, eighty feet high and a hundred feet across, that looked as if it was being squeezed and moulded by huge unseen hands.

An unseen war of wills ensued with the water shifting first one way and then another as force and counterforce were applied. The result was a stalemate, though Rikath was calm and unmoved whilst Selkor was now sweating and obviously beginning to struggle against multiple opponents. Every now and then Selkor would hurl a bolt of energy against the walls or at Perdimonn, or Akhdar as he saw him to be. Each of these attacks was met squarely by one or other of the Warders.

'Give it up, Selkor. You cannot win here,' Perdimonn shouted. 'Whatever you hope to gain by becoming "The Chosen One" is lost. You will never gain the last Key.'

'Tell that to your god, whoever it might be,' Selkor shouted back and hurled another scorching lightning bolt in his direction. A deafening crack split the air as Arred's bolt intercepted Selkor's in another huge explosion.

The shot was Selkor's last and he relinquished his hold over the great globule of water to Rikath, who flowed it harmlessly back to the riverbed.

Selkor maintained his shield, but wheeled his horse around and galloped off towards the Fallow Bridge. Perdimonn watched him go without comment and then looked around at the scorched grass and the cratered earth. Black scorch marks were obvious up on the city wall as well, and now that the battle was obviously over, distant heads began to appear up on the wall, curious to see what manner of people had just engaged in the most spectacular magical battle seen since Darkweaver's time.

Seeing that Selkor had crossed the Fallow Bridge and was still riding away without looking back, Perdimonn shape-shifted back into his own form and turned to face the other Warders.

'Well,' he said with a heavy sigh, 'that went as well as could be expected.'

*   *   *   *   *

Shandrim was swarming with soldiers and militia. Femke had barely got into the outermost fringes of the city and she had already been stopped several times by different groups, who had questioned her reason for being out on the streets. The military had seemingly got the city in a vice-like grip of control, which led Femke to think hard and fast over her initial destination.

The story that Femke gave each group of soldiers was consistent. Her aunt here in Shandrim was unwell and had written to Femke, begging her to come and stay for a while to aid the old lady's recovery. Femke pleaded unfamiliarity with the city and asked directions from each group that stopped her. Initially she asked to be directed just to an area of the city whilst she decided what to do. Should she find a place to stay so that she would have a base to work from, or should she gather some much needed disguise materials first?

Femke had several stores of clothing and equipment in various quarters of the city, but only one of them contained any military style clothing. Judging by the numbers of militia and soldiers in the street, any other disguise would be pretty much useless at the moment, so she made her way to the appropriate house. The risky part was the gamble of going back to one of her known storehouses, when the Emperor might anticipate her abandoning the mission and have her sources and storehouses watched for signs of her return. Consequently, Femke was extremely nervous as she approached the house and her heart was racing. Securing her horse outside, she fought the almost uncontrollable urge to scan the surrounding street area for possible watchers and did her best to walk coolly over to knock at the door.

For a long moment nobody answered and Femke's hyperactive mind quickly leapt to the conclusion that the house had already been raided and her contact dragged away for questioning. Then a slight sound behind the door alerted her to someone coming.

The door opened a crack and a familiar face peered through the gap for a moment, before the door opened wider.

'Oh, it's you,' the woman said in a low voice. 'Come in then, come in.'

Femke slipped inside and the woman closed the door behind her and gave her a raking look up and down.

'You really should eat more, young lady. You're thin as a quarterstaff. Come on into the kitchen, I've got some hot dahl on the stove if you'd like. It's not been there long, so it shouldn't be too stewed.'

'That would be wonderful, Mistress Lieza. Thank you,' Femke replied, genuinely grateful, for it was bitterly cold outside. 'I can't stop long though. I just need to collect a few things from my cupboard upstairs and then I'll be on my way. I've got a lot still to do today and not much daylight left to do it in.'

Mistress Lieza looked at Femke fondly and smiled, her weathered brown face gathering wrinkles as she did so. It was a warm and friendly face that gave the impression of a motherly attitude to any that were younger than she, and some that were older as well. Lieza would mother just about anyone given half a chance, but she did so with such genuine warmth that there were few who would take offence at her manner.

'You young people – always rushing around everywhere and never enough time to fit everything in. I don't know what possesses you, bless me if I don't. Still, you know your own business I'm sure, young lady. Come now, spare a moment to warm your hands around this mug and I'll take you upstairs to your cupboard.'

Femke smiled, partly with thanks and partly in amusement. Every time that Femke visited, Lieza insisted on taking her upstairs to the spare bedroom in which her store cupboard of clothes resided. On one such occasion, Femke had tried to say that it was fine and she knew the way to the spare room. Mistress Lieza had given her such a reproachful look that anyone seeing it would have thought that what Femke had suggested was somehow blasphemous. Then the motherly old spinster had led Femke upstairs anyway.

The brew was piping hot and Femke had to blow at it for a little while before she could so much as sip at it. Lieza had put in a generous spoon of sweetening without asking if that was how Femke liked it. Apparently she was quite unable to comprehend that anyone could wish to remain as slim and fit as Femke was. As it happened, although Femke would not have made the drink so sweet by choice, it brought a warming sense of energy that was most welcome after the best part of a week of hard and seemingly pointless riding.

Lieza bustled around the kitchen in an apparent effort to tidy things up, but there were just so many cooking pots and implements that all she seemed to be doing was moving things around. Ladles, spoons and spatulas were arranged in neat bundles along the walls, and strings of onions hung from great metal hooks in the corners of the ceiling. Shelves were piled high with pots, pans and baking trays of all sizes, and the work surfaces boasted racks of spices, herbs and jars of sauces that would have served a Tavern full of people, yet Femke knew that Lieza had no family and had lived here on her own for many years. Lieza simply enjoyed cooking and baking, and from what Femke had heard, half of the neighbourhood benefited from her hours spent in the kitchen.

Femke watched the stout little lady fuss around for a few minutes whilst she sipped at her dahl. It seemed only polite to accept a piece of fruit cake that Lieza virtually forced upon her, so Femke nibbled patiently at that as well, but time was ticking by and Femke was keen to get her things and move on. Eventually she felt the need to prompt Lieza again.

'Mistress Lieza, this is very nice, and I very much appreciate the cake and the dahl, but I really must get my things and be on my way,' Femke said apologetically.

'What, dear? Oh, yes! Of course you must. Silly me, what was I thinking? Come along then, follow me and I'll take you up there right away,' Lieza replied and she abandoned the pile of cooking implements that she had been rearranging, hitched her skirts with a hand at each hip and swished her way past Femke in a swirl of material.

The spare room was much as Femke remembered it, though there appeared to have been one or two additions to the myriad of little ornaments that littered every surface of the room. 'Lieza must spend her whole life dusting when she isn't cooking,' Femke thought to herself, as she fished inside her tunic for the string of keys that she kept around her neck. The string had nearly a dozen small keys on it, but Femke knew exactly which one she was looking for. It was a little brass key, with a head shaped like a butterfly and overlaid with pretty multicoloured enamel.

Lieza spent a moment or two rearranging ornaments and then left Femke alone and returned to the kitchen. Opening up the cupboard, Femke rifled through the various sets of clothes inside. The cupboard smelt a bit musty, but the clothes appeared fine other than the faint smell. Piece by piece she assembled a set of city militia uniform. Femke had only ever worn it once before, but it should still fit as she had not changed size or shape since that time. There was a sword in a scabbard at the back of the cupboard as well, but Femke had never bothered to get a crossbow as it had been unnecessary. Unfortunately, with the recent violence in the city, all the militia were carrying crossbows now and she would draw unnecessary attention if she did not have one. That would be a problem for later.

Bundling the uniform into a carisak also taken from the cupboard, Femke tucked the sword under her arm and prepared to relock the cupboard. As she closed the door, the young spy remembered one last very important item that she would need in order to make her disguise convincing. Opening up the cupboard again, she rummaged around until she found what she was looking for – two large bandage rolls.

Although Femke did not have particularly large breasts, her shape was sufficiently feminine that unless she disguised the unmistakeable curves, she would never pass as a young man. By binding bandages around her chest, she found that she could flatten herself sufficiently to mask her more feminine attributes and make her appearance manlier.

With the bandages also packed safely into the carisak,

Femke locked the cupboard and shouldered the pack. Now it was just a case of getting out of the house without Lieza cornering her into stopping for food. As silently as she could, Femke crept down the stairs and slipped out into the hallway.

'Thanks very much, Mistress Lieza. See you again soon,' she called out from the doorway, and before the old lady could reply, Femke slipped out of the door and darted across to her horse.

In seconds she was in the saddle and moving away up the street. Lieza knew better than to call out to her in the street, so Femke was safely away from the house, but on her way to where? Her normal selection of hideouts and night stops were out of the question, so it would have to be somewhere different, a place nearby that nobody would think to look for her. A woman did not carry a sword in Shandrim. It just was not done, so Femke was exactly what she did not want to be – conspicuous.

The only place that she could think of was an Inn just two streets away. 'The Golden Firedrake' it was called, and the man who owned it possessed a manner as pretentious as the Inn's name. Femke did not know the owner personally. Although she had never actually stayed there before, she had seen him fawning over customers with his false airs and graces when she had followed leads into the Inn. The owner was an obsequious, weasel-faced little man who had a habit of rubbing the palms of his hands together at frequent intervals, which in Femke's view only added to his distasteful appearance.

'The Golden Firedrake' would never have been Femke's first choice as a place to stay, but that was ideal because it reduced the chances of anyone watching for her there. With a silent prayer for the roads to be clear of soldiers between her and the Inn, Femke rode along the most direct route she could to minimise the chances of being stopped by a patrol. Whether her prayer cleared the way, or fate favoured her short ride, Femke did not care, for a couple of minutes later she arrived at 'The Golden Firedrake' unchallenged.

Taking her sword and carisak, Femke left the horse hitched to a post outside the Inn and went inside. The Inn was quiet for it was still only late afternoon and the owner was nowhere in sight. A woman busied herself behind the tap bar and she looked at the sword that Femke was carrying with obvious disapproval. Femke followed the woman's look down to the sword and smiled at her reassuringly.

'Oh, don't worry, it's not mine,' Femke said, holding the sword out for the woman to see. 'It's for my boyfriend. He's in the militia and his old sword has seen better days, so I bought him this today as a gift.'

'Good,' said the woman shortly. 'We don't normally like to see weapons in "The Golden Firedrake" at all. Obviously the military have little choice but to carry them, but it isn't fitting for a young lady to be seen with such a thing. Now, what can I do for you?'

'I was hoping to rent a room for a few nights if you have any to spare.'

'The prices are not cheap, young lady and I'm afraid that I must ask for money in advance for your anticipated stay.'

'Of course,' Femke said pleasantly, though inside she was annoyed, for she knew full well that this would not have been a requirement if she had arrived dressed in better clothes. 'How much will it be for a week?'

'A week? Why that would be five sen,' the woman said, plainly thinking that the price would be enough to drive Femke away.

'And would that include stabling, bath facilities and food?'

'Well, yes,' the woman said, drawing her brows together in a frown, as the price did not have the expected effect.

'Only five?' Femke said casually. 'Oh good! I'd have thought it would be more because my boyfriend said it was expensive here.'

In fact, five sen was an outrageously expensive price for an Inn like 'The Golden Firedrake', but the woman's attitude irritated Femke, making her want to rub this obsequious

Innkeeper's wife's nose in the fact that Femke's outward appearance hid a young woman of substantial means. Enjoying the moment, whilst keeping a perfectly straight face, Femke pulled out a purse overflowing with gold sen and opened it in such a way that the woman could see all too well that the only coins in the purse were gold ones. It would be fair to say that the woman's eyes literally bulged, threatening to pop out of her head at the sight of so much gold.

'Well, there's your five sen,' Femke said happily. 'Now, could you show me to the room, please. I'd like to get settled in and bathe away some of my travel grime, if that would be alright?'

CHAPTER 10

The distant cracks of thundering bolts of energy exploding through the air drove the Magicians to spur their horses into a gallop. The crackling crashes of sound rolling across the countryside came far too frequently for it to be natural lightning and there were no signs of storms in the air. The explosions could only mean one thing – a magical conflict involving vast amounts of energy. It did not take a huge leap of logic to work out who would be involved in such a battle.

'Follow me,' Akhdar yelled. 'We must reach Mantor before it's too late.'

The horses did their best, though they were already tired from having been ridden fairly hard for several weeks. Not surprisingly, Lomand's horse was the first to start lagging, and before more than a couple of minutes had passed the party began to spread out into a long string. The three Grand Magicians gradually pulled away from Calvyn, Jenna and Lomand. Calvyn and Jenna were still struggling with leading the packhorses, which was all but impossible at speed, and Lomand, as well as trying to lead the final packhorse, was simply too heavy for his horse to bear at a gallop.

Eventually the crashing thunder died away and there was a long pause. The party continued to ride hard, but Akhdar and Kalmar slowed for Jabal to catch up with them and they conversed as they rode. Calvyn saw them regroup, but the three Grand Magicians were too far ahead for him to be able to hear what they were talking about. Another solitary crack split the air, causing Calvyn's heart to leap again, but afterwards all was silent and there was still a good mile to go until they would crest the ridge to the north of the city where Calvyn and Jenna had fought against Demarr's army of nomads. That battle seemed an age ago now and it seemed almost unthinkable that it was actually less than a year since, as fellow Privates, he and Jenna had fought side by side in what had appeared to be a hopeless battle, no more than a mile and a half from where they now rode.

The silence after the ear-splitting thunder cracks of a few moments before felt terribly ominous, making Calvyn wish he knew the spell for distance mind to mind contact so he could attempt to converse with Perdimonn. He resolved to make a point of getting Perdimonn to teach him the spell at the earliest opportunity, deliberately forcing himself to reject the possibility that Perdimonn might not have survived the titanic explosions they had just heard over the previous few minutes.

As Calvyn and Jenna rode towards the top of the ridge that would give them their first clear view of Mantor, they found that the three Grand Magicians had halted and were surveying the valley for clues as to the outcome of the battle. Even at this range, the large area of scorched grass in front of the city was clearly visible and the peppering of craters in the ground around the scorched area gave a clear indication of how intense the conflict had been.

'What is it?' Jenna asked breathlessly. 'Do we know who won?'

The Grand Magicians looked at each other questioningly, but none would commit to a positive answer. It was Jabal who eventually answered her and his voice was heavy with caution.

'We don't know, Jenna. It's impossible to tell at this range and I would not hazard a guess at how this encounter has concluded. All I can say with any certainty is that our approach to the city must be made with all caution. If the Warders have failed to hold Selkor off, then he could well be in the city. Let's face it, without their support, we wouldn't have a prayer against him without the element of surprise. We should weave an illusion to mask our approach until we can determine exactly what transpired here today. That way we will build ourselves at least a small measure of time to prepare for any conflict of our own. Master Kalmar, you are probably our most talented illusionist. What would you recommend?'

Kalmar did not hesitate.

'A glamour,' he said firmly. 'Invisibility is just too risky and there is no way of masking sounds effectively. It would be difficult to effectively disguise all of us under normal circumstances, but if I may make use of the Staff of Dantillus, then it should be simple enough. A party of six with no wagons or goods would not pass as merchants, so I shall disguise Akhdar as a minor noble and the rest of us as his entourage. That will sufficiently explain our numbers and the extra horses. We should be able to ride right into the city without anyone raising so much as an eyebrow.'

Calvyn forbore to say that he could easily accomplish the same thing by the use of sorcery without any need to use the Staff at all. It would only have caused outrage amongst the Magicians, so he held his tongue and watched as the Magicians agreed and Kalmar prepared his complex spell. It was a shame that they were so inflexible, Calvyn reflected, because had he created the illusion by using sorcery, the Magicians could have held the power of the Staff ready should it become necessary.

Lomand finally caught up, his poor horse lathered in sweat. Whilst Kalmar was preparing his spell, the big Magician dismounted to give the animal a break. He pulled out a brush to start working away the sweat. Calvyn dismounted as well and suggested that they switch the packs from one of the other horses to Lomand's, and that Lomand should ride the packhorse down into the city.

'Yes,' he agreed. 'There isn't far to go now and I would hate to make the poor fellow lame for the sake of a couple of minutes work swapping loads around.'

Between them, Calvyn and Lomand manhandled the packs from one of the other horses, transferring them over to Lomand's roan stallion. They swapped over the saddles as well at Lomand's insistence. He claimed that his posterior had become used to the shape of his saddle and he really did not want to change, even for the relatively short ride ahead.

'You never know what will happen,' Lomand insisted firmly. 'We might find ourselves riding hard in an hour's time. I want to be on my own saddle if we do.'

By the time the rearranging of the saddles and packs was complete, Kalmar was ready to cast his spell. They mounted up in anticipation. The mare that Lomand had transferred to rolled her eyes in a look of disgust and resignation as the big Magician swung up into the saddle. Jenna chuckled as she saw the horse's reaction. Calvyn gave her a questioning look.

'Later,' she said with a grin.

When Master Kalmar completed his spell, everyone looked around at one another. Gone were the Magician's robes and travelling clothes of Calvyn and Jenna. In their place was a mixture of outfits that ranged from Akhdar's finery to Calvyn's mercenary guard outfit. Jenna was surprised to find that her outfit was nearly as fine as Master Akhdar's. Everyone's features had changed subtly as well, not so much that they would not be able to recognise one another, but sufficiently that they would not appear as they normally did.

'All right everybody, this is a quick who's who. Master Akhdar is now Sir Akhdar, a retired Knight of the Realm. Jenna, you are his daughter. Jabal and I are your servants, and Lomand and Calvyn are your men-at-arms. We will keep the same names to avoid confusion, but don't name one another unless it becomes absolutely necessary. Are you content, Brothers?'

'Most content, thank you,' Akhdar replied, looking around carefully at each of the others. 'Let's not tarry any longer. We must find out what has happened as swiftly as we can.

I would hate to find that having ridden so far, we're too late by such a small margin, but we won't know until we go and look.'

With that, Akhdar heeled his horse forward into a steady walk down the long slope into the valley while the others arranged themselves in suitable riding order behind him. Master Jabal dropped back and took the reins of the packhorse that Jenna had been leading, so that she could ride at the front with Akhdar. Master Kalmar did a similar swap with Lomand as it was more likely that servants would lead horses than hired soldiers.

Even at a walk, it did not take long to reach the city gates, and as the group approached they saw a growing number of people coming out of the city and appearing up on the wall to view the aftermath of the recent battle. Naturally, spectacular as the battle had been, those from the city who had seen anything of it were already exaggerating hugely to those who had not. Calvyn could hear people talking about dozens of Magicians who had appeared out of nowhere casting fire down from the city walls and then vanishing into thin air. Others talked of a wave of water a hundred feet high rising out of the river, and blasts of fire that simply had to be exaggerated. Calvyn knew how much energy it took to create even a small fireball. Even with the Staff of Dantillus, the sort of blasts that the people were talking about would be impossible.

Akhdar stopped before entering the city to ask someone what had happened, and he did not take long to find out the gist of it.

'Apparently, the Warders prevailed,' he passed back down the line to the others. 'They were last seen heading up the hill towards the Palace. Which way to the Palace, Calvyn?'

Calvyn's heart soared, and catching Jenna's smile as she glanced back happily at him, his face beamed in return. Perdimonn had somehow turned Selkor back a second time. That was fantastic news. Moreover, the old Magician was going towards the Palace, so Calvyn would undoubtedly see him there, as the King would surely require a lengthy report from Calvyn today.

'Turn left inside the gates, then first right and head straight up the hill,' Calvyn replied. 'It's still a fair ride as the Palace is at the top of the hill.'

The six riders passed into Mantor and made their way with less urgency than they had felt for several weeks. Calvyn was surprised to see that Akhdar and the other Magicians still had concern etched on their faces. They knew that Selkor had retreated and yet they looked graver now than they had before entering the city. Unable to contain his curiosity, Calvyn decided to ask Lomand rather than bother any of the long-faced Masters.

'What's the matter, Lomand? Why are you all so grim? The Warders won. Everyone said so,' Calvyn asked quietly.

'Yes, but at what cost?' Lomand replied in a rumble. 'For all we know, Selkor might now have all four Keys. Just because he's left the city, it doesn't follow that he was unsuccessful in meeting his objective.'

'Oh!' Calvyn said, understanding at last.

Unable to think of anything to add, Calvyn fell silent and remained that way all the way to the Palace gates. When they got there, Calvyn rode forward to the front of the group.

'Master Kalmar, would you reverse the glamour, please?' he asked politely. 'Then I should be able to find out if Perdimonn and the others are in the Palace and, if necessary, I will get us all inside.'

Master Kalmar took several minutes to reverse the glamour and Calvyn found that he was even more irritated that he had not felt able to offer his powers of sorcery as an alternative. Creating a relatively simple illusion like this would have taken no time, and to get rid of it again would have been instantaneous. When the wait was finally over and Kalmar completed the spell, Calvyn wasted no time in riding forward to speak to the guards at the gate.

'Good afternoon, gentlemen. Could one of you please relay the message to the Palace that Sir Calvyn is waiting at the gates? I require an audience with the King and I have a party of five others accompanying me.'

'You are expected, Sir Calvyn. Please wait just one moment and I'll have someone escort you and your companions into the Palace.'

'Expected? I take it that Perdimonn and three other Magicians are already here then? When did they arrive?' Calvyn asked inquisitively.

'Two days ago, Sir,' the guard replied. 'They caused quite a stir when they arrived. It's said that they cast magic spells right here in front of the Palace, Sir, though it seems they've been putting on an even more spectacular display today.'

One of the guards strode off into the guardroom and a whole group emerged shortly afterwards to lead away their horses and provide a small escort into the Palace grounds. Even though he had been here before, the sheer size of the Palace and everything about it imposed its presence over Calvyn's senses. He doubted that he would ever be able to approach the Palace without feeling the sense of awe and wonder that it inspired in him, yet he knew only too well that familiarity with even the most wondrous of things quickly bred complacency.

Once again, Calvyn and Jenna were led through the Great Hall and Calvyn's eyes automatically sought out the tapestry depicting the fall of Darkweaver. In some ways, Calvyn was not surprised to see that the tapestry had changed again, but the nature of the change was very curious. He nudged Jenna, subtly directing her attention to the tapestry and she frowned as she realised that the picture was not as she remembered it.

'That's not the tapestry that we saw there before,' Jenna whispered to him. 'But the subject material is strangely similar, isn't it?'

'Actually it is the same tapestry,' Calvyn replied in a similarly low voice. 'It's just the picture that is changing. I'm sure that the tapestry is magical in some way and it seems to be reflecting something of current events, but I'm not sure how to interpret it. The last time I saw the tapestry there were five Magicians fighting one. When we saw it together there were nine. Now there are only three, and two of those appear strangely ghost-like, as if they are fading away. The background has changed as well. That stone structure behind the characters wasn't there before. It's very strange.'

'We'd better ask Perdimonn about it when we see him,' Jenna suggested.

'My thoughts exactly,' Calvyn concurred.

The group was taken through to the King's private study where Krider was hovering outside the door. The Head of the Royal Household Staff was as immaculate as ever in a dark blue tunic, with gold trim and buttons, and a pair of black boots that had been polished so finely, they looked wet. He did not appear surprised to see them. Indeed, he appeared to be waiting for them, such that as they approached he knocked on the study door and announced their arrival to the King.

Akhdar signalled Calvyn to lead them through the door and Jenna followed him in, with the Magicians bringing up the rear.

'Your Majesty,' Calvyn said, bowing deeply to the King.

'Welcome back, Sir Calvyn. It's good to see you again. I have need of your support and knowledge to advise me, as I'm out of my depth with all these magical dilemmas.'

'I will give what counsel I can, your Majesty, but I bring with me others with far more authority to speak on such matters than I, and you already sit in the company of my mentor,' Calvyn replied, sparing a broad smile for Perdimonn.

The old man rose from his chair and Calvyn stepped forward to give him a brief hug. Jenna gave him a longer one, together with a kiss on the cheek, and Perdimonn's eyes sparkled with their usual inner mirth.

'Your Majesty, may I introduce my travelling companions. This is Grand Magician Akhdar, Grand Magician Jabal and Grand Magician Kalmar. They are the remnant of the Council of Magicians from Terilla in Shandar,' Calvyn explained, indicating each Master in turn. The Masters all bowed to the King as they were introduced.

'A pleasure to meet you, gentlemen,' the King responded with a nod.

'And this is Magician Lomand, your Majesty. He saved my life in a recent encounter that cost us two of our party,' Calvyn added, indicating the huge man, who bowed in turn.

'Doubly welcome, Lomand. I would have been sorely aggrieved to lose Sir Calvyn, as he has proven to be a valuable ally to date. As for you though, young lady, you I recognise. I have it in mind that we've met before – Private Jenna, isn't it?'

'You have a very good memory, your Majesty,' Jenna said, bowing rather than curtseying, as she felt it more appropriate, dressed as she was in her travel clothes.

The King smiled at Jenna's compliment and then finished off the introductions by naming Rikath, Arred, Morrell and Baron Anton to those who had not met them before. The King's large oval table had twelve chairs crowded around it and he directed everyone to take a seat.

'Ladies and gentlemen, this is an unprecedented meeting in my time as King. As you are all aware, magic has been prohibited in Thrandor, on pain of imprisonment or death, since the time of Derrigan Darkweaver, yet it is magic and the threat of Darkweaver's Legacy that we are gathered to discuss. Now, would someone please explain exactly what threat this Magician, Selkor, presents to Thrandor, aside from scorching my city walls and frightening my people with his pyrotechnic display earlier?'

'With your permission, your Majesty, I shall begin, though I'm sure that my learned friends from the Council of Magicians will have things to add to my information,' Perdimonn offered.

The King nodded and Perdimonn gave a brief account of the role of the Warders and the nature of the secrets that they protected. He then went on to tell of his previous encounters with Selkor and the Shandese Magician's quest to obtain items of power. In particular, Perdimonn concentrated on Selkor's quest for knowledge of the four elemental Keys and his seemingly unstoppable determination to become 'The Chosen One'.

'I'm sorry?' interrupted Baron Anton. '"The Chosen One?" What is that?'

'"The Chosen One" has been referred to by many Seers, Oracles and Prophets over the centuries as the person who will wield all four Keys of Power, Baron. Probably the most famous of these was a man called Drehboor, who predicted many things that over the years and centuries have proved to be accurate. He wrote little about "The Chosen One", but what he did write told of a man on a knife-edge, a man faced with a choice that will decide the fate of the world,' Perdimonn explained gravely. 'Selkor is the only man since The War of the Gods to wield more than one Key and he is but one Key short of becoming "The Chosen One". Despite the setback that we dealt him today, I cannot see him giving up on that goal.'

'I'm not so sure about that, Perdimonn,' Rikath objected, her face troubled. 'Something in his manner today when he left gave me the impression that he had little intention of coming back. It was as if he had resolved to pursue a new goal, but what that could possibly be I have no idea.'

'Well, I hope that you're right, for if I had to pick someone to decide the fate of the world, then Selkor would not feature highly on my list of candidates. Assuming that he does still desire the last Key and has merely retreated for the moment, we need to decide how we can prevent him from getting it.'

He fell silent, and for a moment or two nobody spoke. Everyone seemed to just stare into space, lost in thought, with imaginations running riot. Akhdar finally broke the silence, and when he spoke, he did so with a proud dignity that captured everyone's attention.

'Brother Perdimonn, my fellow council members and I have travelled hard to come to your aid. We may not have the power of magic that we had in our prime, and we have but one remaining icon of power to enhance our strength, but what we do have, we will endeavour to protect you with,' Akhdar stated.

Perdimonn smiled his thanks and acknowledged the sincerity of that offer with a slight bow of his head.

'As to icons, Brother Akhdar, I can hereby return these things into your care. I relieved Selkor of them earlier today and I'm sure that he'll not be best pleased to have lost them. That's one of the reasons why I feel that he'll be coming back. Not only did he fail to learn the last Key today, but he also lost the Ring of Nadus and the Cloak of Merridom into the bargain,' Perdimonn said, pulling the Cloak out from under the table and removing the Ring from his finger. Solemnly, he passed them both over to Akhdar.

The Grand Magician was stunned. He took the Cloak and Ring woodenly, unable to say anything except to mouth the word 'How?'

'How doesn't really matter, Brother Akhdar. What I did carried risks, but then everything we will do from now on will carry risks. We're gambling with the fate of the world here and I would prefer to stack the odds as much in our favour as I can. Now, would anyone like to hazard a guess as to what Selkor might do next?'

To Calvyn's surprise it was Baron Anton who offered the first opinion.

'If I were Selkor, I would try to work out what went wrong today, figure out a way around the problem and then strike back as hard and as fast as I could,' the Baron said thoughtfully. 'But that's based on a purely military perspective of course.'

'Nevertheless, it is a valid argument,' Perdimonn replied. 'My thoughts tend to lead along similar lines.'

'Should we restart the watch rota then?' Arred asked with a touch of anticipation in his voice.

'Well, we really need to decide if we're going to stay here, retreat elsewhere, or go after Selkor first, Arred,' Perdimonn answered quickly. 'I am very aware, your Majesty, that we are the worst sort of unwelcome guests here. We are breaking your laws and bringing trouble to your kingdom that you really don't need on top of recent events. What are your feelings on this situation?'

The King sat thoughtfully looking around the table at the strange group and he sighed. It was obvious that he was not happy with the situation as it stood, but no one around the table knew what line he would take to resolve things.

'You are correct in one thing, Perdimonn,' the King began after a tense period of silence. 'This has been a period of disruption in Thrandor that rivals any in our history. I can't say that I have any desire to prolong the troubles that my people have faced, yet neither can I shirk my responsibility to the future of the kingdom. You say that Selkor could potentially hold the fate of our world in his hands. I dare not ignore a man with such power. I've been guilty of ignoring things in the past and I'll not do it again.'

The King thumped his fist down on the tabletop in frustration and several people jumped at the force of the impact.

'Damn it!' he swore. 'I don't welcome any trouble, but I'll not evict you from the city. This Selkor fellow needs to be dealt with. I would obviously prefer it if the people of this city were not endangered in the process, but if you tell me that this is unavoidable, then I'll consider your plans and take advice on their merits.'

'Thank you, your Majesty. That is more generous than we have any right to expect. Now, does anyone have any other thoughts on what Selkor might do, or what we should do next? Should we wait for him to make another move, or should we anticipate?'

Calvyn had listened to everything that had been said so far with interest, but had not felt that he could really offer anything constructive. For some reason, he could not shake the feeling that everyone was missing something and he could not place his finger on what it was. The irritating thing was that the tapestry in the Great Hall kept coming back to the forefront of his mind again and again. No matter how Calvyn tried to focus on Selkor and the events at hand, the Darkweaver Tapestry kept niggling at his thoughts until eventually he felt compelled to say something.

'I'm not really sure how relevant this is,' Calvyn said hesitantly. 'It's just that I've noticed a certain tapestry in the entrance hall to the palace that seems to show the last confrontation between Derrigan Darkweaver and a group of Magicians.'

Perdimonn and the other Warders all exchanged looks that told Calvyn they knew exactly what he was talking about. From the way that they looked at each other, Calvyn felt sure they knew a lot more than he did about the tapestry and he wondered for a moment whether he ought to be saying anything about it.

'Go on, Calvyn, what about the tapestry?' Perdimonn prompted, giving him just the push that he needed to complete his train of thought.

'Well first of all, it appears to be magical,' Calvyn explained.

'Magical!' the King exclaimed. 'A magical tapestry in my hallway?'

'Yes, your Majesty. I meant to say something about it to you last time I was here, but somehow it slipped my mind.'

'It's one of the tapestry's properties, your Majesty. It fogs the minds of those who look at it, making them think that they are seeing what they have always seen there before,' Perdimonn chuckled. 'It has been there for a very long time and has been different every time that I've looked at it.'

'Fascinating!' the King said, clearly amazed. 'I'm amazed that such a thing has gone unnoticed in the palace for so long, but how is this relevant to our dilemma with Selkor, Calvyn?'

Calvyn paused, struggling with his thoughts and trying to decide whether he was about to make a fool of himself. It was too late to back out now though. Everyone was looking at him expectantly and waiting for his answer.

'Well, I might be wrong, your Majesty, but I don't think that the tapestry is showing the Darkweaver confrontation any more. I think that it's showing some sort of confrontation with Selkor – maybe one that hasn't happened yet. The frightening thing is that the number of people involved in that meeting seems to be reducing. The first time I saw the tapestry there were nine Magicians ranged against one. Of course, that might have been still showing the conflict between Darkweaver and the Council of Magicians all those years ago. However, the next time I saw it, there were only five Magicians and today there are only three. What's more, two of the figures seem to be fading.'

'Fading? Are you sure?' asked Morrel in surprise.

'Yes, sir. They looked ghost-like when we came through the hall just now. Also, there was something in the background which was very unusual, a rock formation that didn't look natural. I thought that it might give us a clue as to where Selkor might be heading at some point in the future. If we can work out where he's going and maybe beat him there, then whoever it is that does face him might gain some advantage by being prepared.'

'The young man has a good point, Perdimonn,' Morrel said positively. 'Nobody has ever tried using the tapestry like that before, but it could give us something of an edge.'

'An edge for what, Morrel? We need to be *very* careful about this. Are *we* going to force another confrontation?' Rikath asked uncertainly.

'Why don't we at least go and look at this tapestry?' Baron Anton suggested. 'Maybe we'll gain some useful clues from the picture that will offer guidance to our decision.'

'Good idea, Anton. I have a mind to look more carefully at this magical tapestry,' the King said decisively. 'We can come back here afterwards if you wish, but I think that viewing it would bring something fresh to our dilemma.'

The King's word was taken as final, and they all got to their feet to allow King Malo and Baron Anton to walk around the table and lead the way out of the study. Perdimonn hung back, walking between Calvyn and Jenna as they made their way through the corridors towards the entrance hall. He was keen to find out how Calvyn had fared with his lessons at the Academy and showed a certain amusement at the Masters' differing reactions to his rapid progress.

'Even Master Jabal was shocked that I'd been creating my own spells, Perdimonn,' Calvyn confided quietly, as they hung back a short distance from the others. 'I don't really understand it. The impression that I had from your lessons was that there were no restrictions on what you could do with magic, or how you arranged the runes of a spell. I thought that providing you used the correct runes and pictured the results firmly enough as you completed the spell, then *you* controlled the magic. I get the distinct impression from the Masters that they believe the exact opposite.'

'Have any of your spells ever failed?' Perdimonn asked with an amused smile.

'Well, no, but...'

'Then I'll let you draw what conclusion you will from that,' Perdimonn said, not allowing Calvyn to finish, and winking at him solemnly. 'Just remember that to be Masters at the Academy, they must have had an Academy education themselves. The knowledge that they impart is the knowledge that they have learned from their Masters before them. The unfortunate fact is that individuals will tend to shape knowledge to fit their own abilities and to demonstrate the best of their own talents. Individuals who have such a powerful influence in shaping the knowledge of others, especially over a long period of time, will therefore tend to have a distorting effect on the truth. It isn't necessarily a deliberate distortion, but time and tradition will turn one distortion after another into what eventually will come to be regarded as facts. A true student should question everything and a true Master is one who has learned his lessons by experience rather than rote. Think about it for a while and we'll talk about it again if you like.'

Calvyn certainly intended to think about what Perdimonn had said. It flew in the face of everything that the Academy believed, and Calvyn wondered why on earth Perdimonn had effectively sponsored him to the Academy if he did not believe in what it taught.

'So, young Jenna, you proved worthy of your quest to save Calvyn's soul,' Perdimonn said, turning his attention from Calvyn. 'I'm both immensely pleased and incredibly impressed. I knew from our mind contacts that you were a determined young lady, but if I were to be completely honest, I didn't really have high hopes for your success. I owe you a great debt of gratitude for going and doing what I could not.'

'Nonsense, Perdimonn,' Jenna mumbled. 'I didn't do it for you. My reasons were perfectly selfish. I actually have a confession to make though – I'm afraid that I gave most of your gold away. I'll repay it of course, but it will take me a while to earn that amount of money.'

'You gave it away, did you?' Perdimonn asked with a strangely pleased expression on his face. 'Might I ask who to?'

'Actually, it was to a couple who claimed to have met you before – Gedd and Kerys Arissalt.'

Perdimonn frowned for a moment as he thought, and then his face came alive with pleasure again.

'Kerys the healer? Lives in a village inside the Shandese portion of the Great Western Forest?' he asked.

'The same,' Jenna nodded. 'Her healing skills saved my life, and without Gedd's help I would not have survived the final battle with the Gorvath.'

'Then the gift was well given indeed,' Perdimonn assured her. 'There is no debt, Jenna. I need no money from you. There would have been no debt regardless of what you did with the money, for the money was given, not lent. It was yours to aid you in your quest and if it did that, then I consider it well spent.'

The three entered the huge hall some way behind the rest of the group. Everyone else was standing and looking at the tapestry already by the time that they caught up. Morrel in particular had a deep frown furrowing his brow as he gazed up at the picture, which marked him out from the rest of the group who were all looking with wonder at the two ghostly figures of Magicians that were now little more than shadows on the weave. Perdimonn walked straight to Morrel and placed a hand on the stocky man's shoulder.

'What is it, Morrel? What do you see?' the old Magician asked quietly.

'That stone to the left of the picture,' he said, pointing at an area of the tapestry which showed a stone that had quite obviously been shaped by a craftsman. 'Does that remind you of anything?'

Perdimonn looked and his eyes widened.

'So that's what he meant!' Perdimonn said grimly. 'He was being completely literal.'

'What, Perdimonn? What who meant?' Calvyn asked urgently.

'Selkor, this morning,' the old Magician answered. 'He said, "Tell that to your god, whoever it might be." He was being literal. That, Ladies and Gentlemen, is the Throne of the Gods. It appears that Selkor is planning to bring the gods back into this world.'

The outburst of comments and questions that followed was too confused for the next minute or so for anyone to be able to dominate. Eventually, King Malo raised his hands for silence and kept them there until everyone fell quiet. When finally he had the control and attention that he wanted, he quietly and calmly framed his question.

'Warder Perdimonn, how can you be sure that Selkor wants to bring back the gods? What could he hope to gain from such a deed?'

'The Throne of the Gods is the weakest point between this world and the realm to which the gods were banished after their war, many years ago. If Selkor is going to the Throne of the Gods, then there is little else that he could be trying to achieve. The Throne was the gods' seat of power, and they used to have a portal there that linked their world to ours. The portal was sealed, but it looks as if Selkor is going to attempt to reopen it.'

Perdimonn took a breath to continue, but was interrupted

by the last voice that anyone would have expected. Jenna was still looking at the tapestry, but not at the area that everyone else had been studying. Jenna was looking at the two remaining protagonists.

'Never mind what Selkor is trying to do,' she interrupted in a voice that betrayed her fear and horror. 'Look at who's facing him.'

Jenna turned to Calvyn and looked at him with an expression that caused his heart to pound.

'There's no doubt who this figure is, Calvyn. It's you!'

CHAPTER 11

Loitering anywhere near the Emperor's Palace was risky, even dressed as she was in a militia uniform, but Femke had to take an initial gamble in order to acquire her target. Despite having several other lairs around the city, Shalidar tended to stay in his suite at the Palace most nights. In that way, he and Femke were very alike, but the spy was not ready to accept many other similarities between them.

The back of Femke's neck and head felt very strange since she had cut her hair short the previous night. Her skin felt the cold air acutely and it was virtually impossible to combat the urge to keep running her fingers across the stubbly short hair on the back of her head. The tingling sensation that brushing it with her fingers evoked was both stimulating and addictive. Unfortunately, it was also a conspicuous gesture that was sure to be noticed if she kept doing it, so Femke made a point of stamping on the urge whenever she felt her hand wanting to rise.

Femke was more than a little pleased with her appearance as a militiaman. Diagonal leather straps across her shoulders broadened them sufficiently for her to pass as a slim young man, and subtle padding around her waist reduced her female curves. Fortunately, Femke's breasts were not that large to begin with, but with the bandages around her chest they were more than adequately concealed. The bandages did restrict her breathing a little, and Femke hoped fervently that she would not be forced to do any serious running, but otherwise they were not overly uncomfortable.

Subtle make-up had done the rest. Just the very faintest of shadows around the chin and upper lip added enough colour to hint at shaved facial hair, and a carefully placed shadow on her throat hinted at an Adam's apple. Anything more would have been too much, and expectation combined with imagination provided the rest of the disguise. After all, there were no women in the militia, so nobody would see her as a woman. It was that simple.

Femke knew only too well that the longer she waited around outside the Palace, the more chance there was that someone would question her presence. Being out in the open, she ran the risk of someone questioning her orders, but trying to remain concealed somewhere might give the idea that she was shirking a duty elsewhere. General orders seemed to have militiamen moving around in groups for the most part, and individuals were very few and far between. Femke felt that despite her disguise, she was standing out like a cow amongst sheep, but her options were severely limited.

Another group of half a dozen militiamen rounded a corner nearby and turned in Femke's direction. Several had passed her by without comment already, but something in the way that the leader's eyes latched on to her as soon as they had come into view, gave her the feeling that he was not about to ignore her.

Sure enough, as they approached he hailed her with a shout at almost precisely the same moment that she saw Shalidar slipping out through the Palace gates.

'You, lad,' the senior militiaman called out to her. 'What are you doing?'

'Not now,' Femke groaned. Shalidar was getting away from her again and she was helpless to prevent it. 'Yes, Sir?' she answered formally, flicking her eyes to watch which way Shalidar went. 'I'm just waiting for my Lieutenant to return from delivering his report in the Palace, Sir. He told me to wait out here for him. He should be out any time now, Sir,' she said, keeping her sentences short and punchy in typical military style.

'Very well, soldier. Carry on,' the militiaman said and continued with his group on their way.

Femke knew that she could hardly move until the militiamen had gone out of sight again, so she waited. It was as she was waiting and quietly clenching her fists in frustration that she suddenly became aware of a second figure leaving the Palace and setting off in the same direction as Shalidar. With a flash of realisation, Femke understood how the assassin had led her such a merry and totally fruitless chase before. He had someone of his own follow him to check for others doing the same.

With a slight smile of satisfaction, Femke let her hands relax. Her task had suddenly become very simple. All she had to do was follow Shalidar's own tail discreetly until the man was satisfied that nobody was following the assassin. Shalidar would almost certainly have a pre-arranged meeting place after a period of meaningless wandering. Once he was satisfied that he was not being followed, the assassin would probably dismiss his own man and then she could tail him directly. Even if he maintained the tail all day long, now that Femke knew he was there, she could either follow him, or work around him as the situation dictated.

The group of militiamen disappeared around a corner and Femke moved immediately into action. By marching smartly, it hid the worst of her feminine stride. Although she had mastered many skills during her time as a spy, walking like a man was not one of them. No matter how hard she tried, Femke could not completely lose the swing of her hips that branded her a woman, which was another factor that made this disguise so dangerously fragile.

Her mark turned from the main street into a quieter side street and Femke was careful to take her time in following. Much as she doubted that the man would expect to be followed, Femke was not about to assume anything. Shalidar was obviously no fool and she would not put it past him to throw in some added levels of self-protection, like watchers at whatever meeting place he might set with his precautionary shadow. Well, Femke was onto him now, and cat and mouse was a game at which she had become a master during her time as a spy. Shalidar would not give her the run around today, she decided firmly.

Peering around the end of the alley, she could see that the person she was following was making no efforts to check behind him. The man was completely intent on scanning ahead, so Femke moved into the side street and walked as casually as she could along behind him. Concentrating hard on trying to adopt a man's sauntering style of walking, the spy maintained a good distance back from her quarry and made a point of turning the opposite way out of the end of the side street.

Moving across the street before glancing back over her shoulder to see where the man was heading, Femke saw that Shalidar was not far away. The shadow walked past Shalidar, nodding at him as he passed. The assassin made no response, but moved back up the street towards Femke and she was forced to move ahead of him slowly to avoid attracting attention.

Shalidar overtook her a minute or so later and Femke slid her gaze across him as he passed on the other side of the street, being careful not to allow her eyes to dwell on him for so much as an instant. If the assassin felt for one second that he was being watched, then the game would be well and truly over. Keeping her slow strolling pace, Femke allowed him open the gap between them while she made a big show of casually inspecting every turn and alleyway that she passed. In reality she was actually checking to see if Shalidar had kept his shadow, but unless the man following Shalidar was much better than she was, which was most unlikely, then Femke was now the assassin's only tail.

Having established that she was clear to track Shalidar at will, Femke stepped up the pace and closed back up to a comfortable tracking range.

'Now then, Shalidar,' she muttered to herself. 'Let's see what you're up to, shall we?'

Shalidar did not mess around. To Femke's delight, he headed straight towards the district where the Legions had established their Headquarters. He was going to meet with his military contact again, Femke exulted silently. There could be few other reasons for his visit, because the military traditionally despised assassins. Shalidar would hardly go visiting somewhere that he would be almost universally shunned, without a very good reason.

Not surprisingly, the assassin did not go to the Headquarters itself. Instead he went to a residential area nearby where many of the more senior officers had taken up lodgings. When Shalidar got close to his destination, Femke, having worked out roughly where he was going, hung back a bit further. It was just as well that she did, for the assassin turned and had a good look around as he went up to a large house and knocked on the door. Femke managed to stay out of his direct line of sight, but also noted which house it was that he went into.

Watching for a couple of minutes until she was sure that Shalidar was not going to come straight back out again, Femke waited until she felt sure that it was safe for her to go and take a closer look at the house that he had entered. By chance, a Junior Swordsman from one of the Legions was marching past the house in the opposite direction as she approached.

'Excuse me, soldier, could you tell me who lives in that nice house over there?' she asked, keeping her voice husky as if she were fighting off a cold.

'That one?' the soldier replied with a laugh. 'I thought everyone knew who lived there. That's where General Surabar lives.'

'Really? The great man himself, huh? Well thank you, I'm much obliged,' Femke said and continued on up the road and away from the house as directly as she could. There was no point in hanging around and raising anyone's suspicions. There was certainly no chance of her getting into the house covertly in broad daylight, so Femke decided to go back to 'The Golden Firedrake' and think out her next move.

Shalidar meeting with General Surabar was something of a surprise to Femke, as the Emperor had given her the distinct impression that there was no link between the two. Of course, just because the Emperor was unaware of Shalidar's association with the General did not reduce the possibility that there was a secret plot being forged. The assassin had always played his own games and was probably as ready to betray this bogus Emperor as he had the real one, Femke reflected. What she needed to establish now was that the Emperor was indeed Lord Vallaine in disguise. Until that was established as fact, rather than a very firmly held theory, then Femke could not really act any further.

*   *   *   *   *

Calvyn felt sick inside. There was little doubt about it – the tapestry now clearly depicted him facing Selkor at a place that Perdimonn had identified as the Throne of the Gods. If Perdimonn had feared Selkor before the Shandese Magician had gained all these Keys of Power, to say nothing of Darkweaver's amulet, how much more should Calvyn fear him now?'

It was crazy, Calvyn kept thinking to himself. Why did the tapestry not show Grand Magician Akhdar or Grand Magician Jabal facing Selkor? Why was it going to be him; an Acolyte with virtually no experience of magic and certainly no experience of magical duels? The duel with Demarr did not really count in his mind, as his sword had automatically neutralised the magical blasts from the amulet during that encounter. Indeed, the only spell that he had cast was a protective shield spell that had disintegrated at the first blast from Darkweaver's legacy.

From the moment that the Magicians had confirmed what Jenna had first recognised, everyone had been treating him differently. The Masters were distant to begin with as they each wrestled with the question of why they were not going to be there to face Selkor. Were they not in the picture because they would not live to see the conflict, or was there some less drastic explanation for their absence? However, once they got over their initial shock, the Grand Magicians were all most insistent about teaching him as much as they could and filling his time with lesson after lesson in magic.

Aside from Perdimonn, the Warders seemed to treat him warily, as if he were some sort of dangerous animal that might strike out at them with no warning. Perdimonn did not seem very surprised by the revelation, but would not be drawn about his reaction. The King and Baron Anton were like proud parents of a child that had just achieved something momentous. Calvyn fervently hoped that their faith in his ability to turn around dark situations was justified, because this was one conflict that he felt both unready for and fearful of the outcome.

The most difficult person to face, though, was Jenna. Jenna had always been ready to share her dry sense of humour with him and keep him positive when he felt low, but now she had become quiet and withdrawn. It was not that she became physically distant, Jenna seemed more inclined now towards intimacy than she had ever been, but she did so silently, apparently unable to verbalise what was going through her mind. It really was not like Jenna at all and it was probably her behaviour more than anything else that was making him feel so on edge.

Calvyn fought down the bile that rose as he looked again on the tapestry. It was late evening and the Masters had finally left him alone and gone to their rooms. Calvyn was not yet ready for sleep though, as he had a multitude of thoughts and emotions to deal with. The tapestry clearly showed Selkor casting a spell and Calvyn holding his sword as if he were about to enter a sword fight. Why was he not shown casting a counter-spell, he wondered? Selkor did not appear to be carrying a physical weapon, so why was Calvyn shown ready to fight? Also, Calvyn would have thought that knowing the conflict he had to face, the Masters would have let him have the Staff of Dantillus rather than have him just use his sword. Master Jabal had already promised him lessons with the Staff tomorrow, yet what was the point? The Staff was not in the picture.

There was not enough detail in the characters shown on the tapestry to tell if he was wearing the Ring of Nadus or not, but Calvyn decided that he would ask for lessons with that as a priority. It was always possible, of course, that the picture would change again to show him wielding the Staff rather than his sword, but Calvyn decided to treat the picture as if it gave a reasonably accurate representation of what he could expect.

'Scared?' Perdimonn asked, his question making Calvyn jump, as he had not heard his old mentor approach.

'A little,' Calvyn admitted. Then he grinned at Perdimonn and shrugged. 'Petrified actually.'

'I understand,' the old man said simply. 'There's really no need to be afraid though. This is what you've been prepared for.'

'Prepared for? How have *I* been prepared to face down Selkor? He could fry me in an instant,' Calvyn said with a slightly hysterical edge to his voice.

'Oh, I don't think that he'll do that somehow,' Perdimonn assured him warmly. 'In fact, I'm confident that he won't.'

'And what makes you so confident?' Calvyn asked, his voice strained with the stress of trying to stay calm.

'It's a bit early to say, really, but the events of recent months have obviously prepared you for this confrontation in some way, or it would not be your figure on the tapestry.'

'Just because I'm on the tapestry doesn't mean that I'm prepared for this, Perdimonn, and you know it,' Calvyn replied accusingly.

Perdimonn sighed and smiled. 'Yes, you're right. It doesn't necessarily follow, I know, but you have been prepared in ways that you fail to see yet. Try not to let it get to you too much, Calvyn. By the time that you get there, you'll be ready. Trust me on this. Have I ever lied to you?'

Calvyn thought about that for a moment and smiled. 'Well, there was the time at The Black Cat Tavern when you promised you were just going to have the one drink,' he said slyly.

Perdimonn laughed and Calvyn joined in, feeling more relaxed for the release of emotion that came with that outburst.

'So when do we leave for the Throne of the Gods?' Calvyn asked, looking up at the tapestry again. 'And why is it called that anyway?'

'We leave tomorrow, Calvyn. We can't afford to risk the possibility that Selkor already has enough power to open a gateway that would allow the gods back to this world. As to why it is called the Throne of the Gods, well when you see it your question will answer itself,' Perdimonn said with a sly grin. 'Simply speaking, the Throne is huge. It wasn't built for a human to sit in, that's for sure.'

'So why don't we want the gods to return?' Calvyn asked, genuinely puzzled. 'Surely that would be a good thing, wouldn't it? After all, people all over the world worship a whole host of different gods. Don't you think they would be pleased if the gods were brought back?'

Perdimonn's face dropped into a frown and for the first time in a long while Calvyn noted that all hint of humour went out of his eyes. He looked deadly serious as he spoke.

'The gods that we are talking about here are not what you might think,' Perdimonn stated flatly. 'Certainly there are gods that people might consider "good", for they have some laudable traits, but the majority are not like those few. I would hesitate to compare them with demons, for they are not really that similar. However, they're from a different world, with very different values from our own, and whilst they have supernatural powers that have the potential to do wondrous things, they can be capricious in their use of them. When they shared this world before, the gods abused their powers, causing harm rather than bringing healing. They were banished for good reason, Calvyn. Giving them a means of returning to this world would be a disaster.'

'So why do people continue to worship them?' Calvyn asked, intrigued by the apparent anomaly. 'Why has the practice not died out if their influence has truly been removed from our world?'

'Everyone needs to have something to believe in, Calvyn,' Perdimonn answered sagely. 'Ignorance and man's instinctive desire to believe that all things are basically good have done the rest. It isn't so hard to understand really, but it's very important that *you* understand why you must prevent Selkor from achieving his goal. You have heard of the War of the Gods?'

'Yes, of course I have, Perdimonn. Everyone has heard of the War of the Gods.'

'Well, if Selkor succeeds and opens a gateway for the gods to return, then they will almost inevitably pick up that war where they left off,' Perdimonn said gravely. 'It would wreak havoc and disaster on a scale that will make your recent battles look inconsequential by comparison.'

Calvyn shuddered. 'You paint a grim picture, old friend.'

'It would be a grim day indeed,' Perdimonn agreed. 'Think about that tomorrow, my boy. For now I suggest that you get some sleep. It's getting late.'

'You're right. Goodnight, Perdimonn.'

'Goodnight, Calvyn. Rest well.'

Calvyn went back to his room and tried very hard to rest, but his overactive mind would not allow him to sleep for a long time. It was several hours later before he finally managed to drift off, and even then his sleep was fitful and filled with strange dreams. When Calvyn arose shortly after dawn, his eyes felt hot and gritty as if he had never closed them at all and his body felt drained of all energy.

Groaning, as he looked at his reflection in the mirror on the wall, Calvyn ran his fingers through his hair in an attempt to straighten it. He looked almost as rough as he felt. A splash of cold water across his face helped a little, but he still felt awful.

Perdimonn had not given a time for their departure today, but with no hint given of an early start, Calvyn was fairly certain that he had some time before they left. Unable to resist, he dressed and went back down to the entrance hall for another look at the tapestry. He did not really know what he was looking for, but he was almost disappointed to see that it was exactly as it had been the previous evening. Somehow, after his troubled night, he had imagined that the picture might have changed again – at least a little.

By the time that everyone else had risen and finished breakfast, Calvyn felt a little better, but the Magicians latched on to him straight away and started drilling him at spells and spell-casting. He thought that he would be given something of a rest when everyone gathered to leave, but one or other of the Masters seemed to be constantly at his side trying to impart more knowledge to him. If only they had treated him this way at the Academy, Calvyn thought wryly, then he might have learned enough to be more confident about this quest. As it was, he felt that most of what the Masters were trying to teach him was just washing over him. Very little of it was being retained, and Calvyn was beginning to wish they would just back off a little to give him some space to get used to the idea that he was being thrust to the forefront once more.

The four Warders, together with Calvyn, Jenna and the four remaining Magicians from Terilla, rode out from the Palace to a royal send-off. The King and all of his family, as well as Baron Anton and several of the other resident and visiting nobles, gathered outside the Palace to watch them leave.

'Good luck, Sir Calvyn. I shall expect a full report on your return,' the King said loudly, smiling up at Calvyn.

'I'll do my best, your Majesty,' Calvyn replied and gave him a smart salute.

'I also expect the rest of you to look after him to the best of your abilities,' the King admonished the gathered party. 'Please try to bring him back in one piece!'

'We shall do everything in our power to do so, your Majesty,' Perdimonn assured him, then with a final wave to the small crowd, the old man led the party out through the Palace gates and down through the city of Mantor.

'Have you got any idea where exactly we're heading?' Jenna asked Calvyn once they were underway.

'The Throne of the Gods,' answered Calvyn with a grin.

Jenna did not need to say anything. The raising of an eyebrow was enough.

'Actually, I asked Perdimonn the same question shortly after breakfast this morning. Apparently the throne is a huge carved stone seat at the top of one of the lower peaks in the mountain range that marks the southern border of Thrandor. It's not that far from White Falls Pass, if that helps,' Calvyn explained.

'Not a lot,' Jenna admitted. 'I've never travelled much south of Mantor before.'

'No, neither have I – aside, of course, from my brief visit to Kortag, and I didn't really have time for sightseeing on that trip.'

That was all the conversation they got on the ride through the city, as Master Jabal eased his horse forward alongside Calvyn's at that point and the bombardment of information resumed. Jenna listened in to what Master Jabal was teaching as well, for though it meant little to her at the moment, Jenna was now determined to learn quickly so that she could spend as much of her time as possible with Calvyn whilst she was an Acolyte. Besides that, there was little chance of any Master being so open again at imparting their knowledge as they were now.

It was as they were leaving the city that Jenna noticed the party of four riders coming down the road from the north. Even at a distance where individual features were not recognisable, the four had an air of familiarity about them. Jenna found her eyes tracking the group even as they turned west towards the Fallow Bridge.

'Sorry to interrupt you, Master Jabal, but do those riders look familiar to you, Calvyn?' Jenna asked, pointing across to their right.

Calvyn looked and squinted his eyes as he strained to make out details. The group was a long way away, but something about one of the lead riders reminded him of Derra. It was probably the upright stance in the saddle, he thought, as he considered the reason for that comparison.

'I'm not sure, Jenna,' Calvyn admitted. 'But it would be

good to make sure. Master Jabal, would you excuse us for a minute or two? This could be important. If we're held up for more than a few minutes, could you get the party to wait for us at the far side of the Fallow Bridge, please? Thanks.'

Calvyn did not wait for an answer, but wheeled his horse around to ride on an intercept course with the group of four. Jenna turned with him. They both heeled their horses into a brisk canter and the distance closed rapidly as they rode head to head towards the approaching riders. It did not take long before Calvyn could visibly see that it was Derra, with Fesha riding alongside her. The two rear riders were more difficult to see, but suddenly one of them turned his horse and accelerated past Derra and Fesha at a gallop.

Calvyn's heart leapt with joy as he recognised the dark haired rider.

'Bek!' he yelled, as he heeled Hakkaari forward into a gallop as well.

They closed incredibly quickly and both riders were out of their saddles and onto the ground before the horses had stopped. Calvyn was laughing with delight at the sight of his friend alive and well as he ran towards him, and so was totally unprepared for the look of pure hatred on Bek's face that stopped him in his tracks. They both stopped still for a moment about five paces apart.

'Bek?' Calvyn asked in confusion.

'Draw your sword and prepare to die, Shanier,' came the cold reply as Bek drew his sword and began to advance slowly forward again.

'Bek, it's me, Calvyn,' Calvyn pleaded. 'Shanier is gone forever. In truth, he died the moment my soul was returned. Bek?'

'Draw your sword or I'll cut you down anyway.'

The other four riders all closed in at a canter, every one of them yelling at Bek to stop, but he ignored them, closing them out of his mind in the same way that he had shut out the crowds at the arena. As far as he was concerned, the only other person in the world right now was the man he had sworn to kill, and nothing was going to prevent him from doing just that.

Calvyn backed away, hand on sword hilt but determined not to draw on his friend unless there was no other choice. Why did Bek think that he was still Shanier? Surely Derra and the others had told him what happened? Calvyn could not understand what was going through Bek's mind at all, but he had no illusions about how dangerous Bek was at this moment in time. What Calvyn needed was breathing space to talk to Bek – a chance to explain what had happened. Although he hated to do it, particularly as Bek thought he was still the Sorcerer Lord Shanier, the only way Calvyn could think of immobilising Bek without hurting him was by holding him with sorcery.

'Listen, Bek, I really didn't want to do this but you've given me no choice,' Calvyn apologised as he reached out with his mind to bind Bek with his power.

To Calvyn's complete shock, he could no more grasp Bek's mind than one could catch and grip the most slippery bar of soap. Calvyn's wave of sorcery simply seemed to slide off Bek's mind no matter how much power he threw at it. Bek chose just that moment to attack.

Somehow Calvyn managed to draw his sword and meet Bek's vicious rain of blows, barely deflecting his blade a full dozen times before he managed to retreat sufficiently to get out of Bek's reach.

'This is madness, Bek! Why are you doing this?' Calvyn asked, simultaneously throwing his full mental power at Bek with no effect whatsoever.

'I vowed to kill you, Shanier. I vowed over Jez's dead body and it's a vow I mean to keep,' Bek said, his voice flat and emotionless. His cold grey-blue eyes, though, were far from emotionless. The icy glare that had struck fear into fighters in Shandrim's arena was filled with a deep-seated anger and desire for vengeance that glittered with a mind-numbing intensity.

'Jez is dead?' Calvyn responded sadly.

'Yes, and now you're going to join him,' Bek growled and leapt forward to attack again.

If Bek had been at full fitness, Calvyn would not have lasted more than a few seconds. Even suffering intense pain at every forced swing and extended lunge, Bek was more than a match for Calvyn. Bek's arena training had given him a degree of skill that was unmatched by anyone that Calvyn had ever faced before, and Calvyn was forced to retreat with every swing of Bek's blade.

Suddenly, Calvyn realised that he was no longer alone. There were drawn blades to both sides of him and Bek stopped for a moment and backed off a step. Fesha and Jenna were standing to Bek's left and Derra and Eloise were to his right.

'Put down your sword, Bek,' Derra growled dangerously. 'Don't be any more stupid than you've been already.'

Bek was not ready to quit though. He simply drew his second blade and gritted his teeth in a snarl as he prepared to launch another attack. Blood was already beginning to bloom through his tunic where the recently healed wound in his side had split open again. Calvyn could see the blood and he knew that wherever it was coming from was none of his doing. He had barely managed to fend off Bek's attacks and had not even thought about counter-attacking, let alone landed a blade on Bek.

Desperate to prevent Bek from attacking again, Calvyn forced himself to race through all the spells he knew to try to find something quick that he could use to stop Bek from attacking again. A sudden thought struck him like a bolt from a crossbow, and without pausing to consider any further, Calvyn launched into the simple spell.

Even as Bek propelled himself forward in what would probably have proved a painful attack for both Bek and those who faced him, Bek's feet lost their purchase on the ground and he found himself rising up into the air above his line of opponents. He could still move his arms and legs but he could not move himself relative to the ground. He floated, suspended some ten feet in the air and unable to do anything about it.

'Now,' Calvyn said firmly, 'are you going to listen to me,

Bek? Or am I going to have to leave you up there to stew? Open your eyes, man! It's me – Calvyn. Not Shanier – Calvyn. Lord Shanier died in the moment that Jenna and Demarr killed the demon that held my soul. You cannot kill him, Bek. He's already dead.'

'Aaargh!' Bek yelled in frustration and threw his blades at Calvyn.

'Tarmin's teeth, Bek! Look, will you? Look at *our* friends, Bek. Look at Derra, Jenna, Fesha and Eloise. I haven't bewitched them, Bek. They have seen and conquered Shanier between them. They won *me* back – Calvyn – the person who I thought was one of your closest friends.'

'You sent us to die in the arena. You can't possibly be my friend,' Bek spat.

'Lord Shanier sent you to fight in the arena, Bek, and yes, I know that Lord Shanier was me – sort of. He was me without a soul. I have my soul back now though and I can only grieve at what you've gone through, as I grieve for the loss of my friend Jez. You have no idea how much I've thought about what I, as Shanier, did to you. I wanted so desperately to come to your aid once I'd got my soul back. It was at the forefront of my mind every day.'

'Then why didn't you, Calvyn? Why didn't you come?' Bek shouted, his voice cracking as his anger vied with his wish to believe what Calvyn was telling him. 'Jez believed in you, Calvyn. He believed in you to the day he died, and look what good it did him.'

A lump settled in Calvyn's throat at Bek's words, and he was at a loss as to how to reply. How could he tell Bek that something else had come up which was more important? Jenna saved him from having to by speaking up on his behalf.

'Bek, if you won't listen to Calvyn, then listen to the rest of us. I've been travelling with Calvyn all the way from Terilla, and not a day has gone by that he hasn't mentioned you and Jez, wondering whether Derra and the others had managed to save you. He told me of the torment that he went through when he was faced with the decision to leave his rescue mission in order to carry his mentor's message to the Council of Magicians. I'm sure that Derra and the others have told you how he set out with them but was forced by circumstance and duty to turn aside. You know that I haven't been cooking up this story with them, Bek, because they didn't even know I was alive until just now. It's true – all of it. This is Calvyn, the Calvyn who went through training with us, the Calvyn who fought with us here on this very field last year, the Calvyn whom I love. I'll stand and die for him here rather than let you near him with a sword in your hand, Bek.

'Jenna's speaking the truth, Bek. We've been telling you this all along,' Derra added with her distinguishing gravelly tones.

'Let it go, Bek. It's the Bek we knew at Keevan's castle that is missing here, not Calvyn,' pleaded Eloise.

Bek's mind railed at the idea of breaking his vow. He had pushed himself to the limits of his ability and endurance in order to keep the promise of avenging Jez's death. How could he just give it up now? Yet, the fact that all his friends and colleagues were telling him the same story gave him the uncomfortable feeling that maybe his oath had been overtaken by other events.

'I can't do it. I can't!' he cried. 'I promised over Jez's body to avenge him. I can't let him down.'

'You have avenged him, Bek. You defeated Serrius in the arena and someone else destroyed Shanier. The fact that you didn't free Calvyn does not matter one iota. Your promise has been fulfilled. The vow that you're clinging to is based on a lie. Calvyn is no longer Shanier. You can't do anything further to avenge Jez, so it's time for you to open your eyes and see things as they actually are. Now, are you going to listen to us, or do I have to have you chained until you see sense?' Derra asked, her voice fierce and uncompromising.

Bek looked down at Calvyn and found that part of him wanted to believe what everyone was saying. His gut instinct still refused to give up the vow because it had driven him to survive over the last few months. The vow had made itself a part of him, deep within his heart. However, as he looked at Calvyn, he could see nothing of the cold-hearted man who had condemned him to the arena. Instead, he saw the young man who had been his friend in Baron Keevan's army and his eyes began to blur as tears threatened to fill them.

'I never meant to harm you, Bek. On my life, I promise you that I'm speaking the truth. I can only apologise for what you've been through, though it's clear that saying sorry is woefully inadequate. It pains me to see you like this and I desperately want to convince you of my genuine remorse. If there's anything that I can do to convince you, then name it.'

Bek scoured his mind and heart, trying to think of something to challenge Calvyn with that would help Bek to resolve his dilemma. The problem was that the conflict of emotions created by both wanting to believe Calvyn and the others, yet not wanting to let go of the driving force that had given him strength and purpose for so long, left his mind in a fog. In the end the truth and sincerity in Calvyn's eyes and words overcame the steel of Bek's vow and something snapped within him.

Bek had known all along that it would be difficult to fight his old friend. Although he had felt extreme anger and bitterness about Shanier sending he and Jez to the arena, there had always been a deep seed of hope within him that the whole situation had somehow not really been Calvyn's fault. He had always known that the inner battle between that seed of hope and the raging fires of anger and revenge would dictate the outcome of this encounter. He had been sure that the thought of Calvyn's friendship was locked deep enough that it would not influence him when they met, but now, as he let go of the anger and inner pain at what had happened, a wave of emotion overcame him and he wept with relief.

Tears rolled down Bek's cheeks and his shoulders sagged in a mixture of defeat and a release from the stress of the vow. His were not the only eyes to weep. Calvyn's cheeks were also streaked with tears, as were Jenna's. The thunder of approaching hooves caused the five friends on the ground to look around at the approaching group of Magicians.

'Is everything alright, Calvyn?' Perdimonn called out, as he reined his horse to a halt.

Calvyn looked up at his silently weeping friend and nodded.

'Everything is fine, Perdimonn,' he replied slowly. 'Everything is just fine.'

<u>CHAPTER 12</u>

Femke walked jauntily up to a service gate into the Emperor's Palace. Gone was the uniform and sword, for it would not get her where she needed to go today. Instead, Femke was dressed in the livery of the Imperial Palace Staff. The only way that she was going to be able to find out if her hunch about the Emperor was correct was to catch him off guard, Femke had decided. That would entail spying of the most delicate kind – catching him both off guard and in such a way that he would not realise that he was being watched.

'Who're you, son?' the gruff guard at the service gate rumbled in a deep voice. 'I've not seen you around here before.'

Femke had decided that having cut her hair so short she could hardly pose as a female member of the palace staff, so she had maintained her persona of a young man and simply changed uniforms. Actually, she really quite liked the white tabard with the bright red insignia of the Imperial lion's head over crossed swords. It did look very smart.

'Dragonclaw one, one, two,' Femke answered in a low voice, so that there was no danger of anyone other than the guard hearing it.

'What? Er, I mean, really? Well you'd better be on your way then, lad,' the guard spluttered with surprise, waving her inside with a hasty gesture.

Femke grinned as she passed the guard. The password that she had just given identified her as one of the

Emperor's inner circle of spies. Of course, the guards had no idea how many were in that circle, and if she was truthful Femke was not entirely sure either. During her time working for the Emperor, Femke had identified eleven others that she either knew for definite were amongst those elite, or most probably were. However, the only person who could have confirmed her suspicions was the Emperor himself and he was highly unlikely to do that.

Spying was a very competitive and dangerous business. Spies quite frequently crossed paths in the pursuit of information, and if that meeting was significant enough then someone often ended up dead. The biggest problem with espionage at pretty much every level was that it was very difficult to tell for certain exactly who was working for whom, therefore, when faced with another spy working towards the same end, it was natural to assume that the other spy was working for someone else. That made the other spy as good as the enemy.

Of course, bloodshed in the Palace was strictly taboo. If spies crossed one another there, they waited until they were outside the Palace to settle any outstanding scores. It was also true that more spying went on in the Palace than anywhere else in the Empire. After all, spies followed power like moths were attracted to a light, and where was there more power than in the Palace?

Femke slipped in through one of several doors into the service wing of the Palace and, brandishing the scroll of parchment she was carrying like a sword, she bustled her way along the corridors as if she were carrying the most important document in the world on an errand that could not stop for anything.

Looking busy was an art form that Femke had long since learned from observing servants of many wealthy people. Some lived their lives making work of doing nothing in a way that made everyone think they were run off their feet – and in some ways they were – for to be good at avoiding real work took an energy and drive all of its own.

'Hey, boy!' called someone to her, as she weaved through

a group of servants carrying boxes of supplies to a storeroom.

'Sorry, can't stop,' Femke replied briskly and waved the scroll over her head.

Without so much as looking in the direction of the caller, Femke strode down the corridor and around a corner. Avoiding eye contact was a large part of the key to not getting stopped. So long as she focused her eyes on a point ahead of her and kept moving quickly, she should get to where she wanted to go. After that the tactics would have to change, for she could hardly walk at pace around one small area of the palace for any length of time without attracting attention.

Femke had that worked out as well, of course. As a top class spy she did not go into any situation without being as thoroughly prepared as she could be. The plan she had was not without risks, but those risks had been carefully calculated. Everything depended on her analysis of the situation and the carefully thought out message that she had written to the Emperor on the scroll that she was carrying. If he took the bait, then Femke would get her chance. If he did not, then she would have to go back to square one and come up with another plan.

There was always a servant loitering near to the Emperor's study door, ready to answer the ring of his bell and to introduce visitors. It was that person who was the key to her plan. Femke moved with a genuine sense of purpose through the hallways and corridors of the Palace, and that authentic urgency added extra credence to her assumed persona. A few minutes later, she approached the servant who was idly looking at pictures on the wall of the corridor, pictures that he had no doubt studied countless times before.

'Excuse me, would you mind passing this message to the Emperor. I'm told that it's very important, but it's taken me a while to find this place. I'm new here and I've been gone too long as it is, so I'd better get back to the library before I earn myself a beating,' she said in a rush, pressing the scroll into the servant's hands and then turning back up the corridor and walking quickly away.

The direction that she set off down the corridor was in the correct general direction of the library, though she had no intention of going that far. As soon as she could get out of the line of sight of the servant, Femke did so and stopped to listen for the servant to enter the Emperor's study. The timing of the next few seconds was critical.

Femke heard the servant knock on the door and open it, at which point she knew that he would be focused on moving into the room. Femke had seen the servants enter that study on dozens of occasions and they all did it in the same way, stepping in through the inward opening door and closing it behind them whilst making their bow to the Emperor.

Praying that the corridor would remain empty for a few seconds, Femke sprinted silently back along the corridor, hearing the door latch snick into place even as she was approaching it. With a grin of satisfaction, she sped straight past the door and along the corridor until she reached a quiet side corridor which she darted into and pressed herself against the wall out of sight. Working hard to control her breathing, Femke waited for the inevitable outburst from the Emperor's chamber. She did not have to wait long.

'Who gave you this?'

Despite the closed study door, Femke heard the Emperor's angry voice, and though she could not hear the servant's response the sound of the study door opening and the subsequent short conversation was very clear.

'New boy? Well go and fetch him here immediately,' the Emperor's heated voice ordered.

'Yes, your Imperial Majesty,' the flustered servant stammered in reply.

'No! On second thoughts you can take me to him. Come. Lead the way to the library and you can point him out to me,' the Emperor decided, obviously thinking better of giving the servant the chance to question the boy before bringing him to the study.

Femke smiled with satisfaction. Her heart had sunk for a moment when the Emperor had ordered her assumed persona brought before him, for that would have ruined her plan entirely. The whole idea of the scroll had been to get the Emperor out of his study, and she had written the words that she felt sure would get the best response:

'Barrathos is a fat old fool of a Wizard whose demons were about as much use as those poor souls you feed to the arena fighters each week. I know who you are. Your days are numbered.'

The reaction of the Emperor to those carefully chosen words was almost condemnation enough on its own for Femke, but she wanted to be one hundred percent sure and that meant seeing Vallaine in his true form. The only places that she was likely to see him so were his study and his bedchamber. Nobody that Femke had ever heard of had ever managed to spy on his Imperial Majesty within the sanctity of his bedchamber, which left only left her the option of the study.

Femke knew that there was a purpose built compartment for spying in the study. The Emperor had had it installed secretly himself so that he could pre-place a spy inside and then host visitors in the room. By always making sure that the visitors were shown into the room before he arrived, staff could serve them with drinks and leave them alone to talk. The Emperor was then briefed after the meeting as to what his visitors had discussed and looked at before he arrived. A perfect traitor trap which Femke now intended to use in reverse, for she was guessing that Vallaine had no idea of its existence.

That was the risk – she was simply guessing. If Vallaine did know about the chamber, then Femke would be boxing herself into a corner with no escape. It was not a comfortable thought, for Femke did not normally do anything without a carefully thought out escape route. In this case, however, the spy was willing to make an exception.

Femke heard the unmistakable sound of the Emperor locking the door of his study, and she ventured a quick glance around the corner. The Emperor and the servant were moving off down the corridor in the direction of the Library. Waiting until there was no chance of one of them inadvertently glancing back and seeing her, Femke dashed out into the corridor, only to stop dead in her tracks. The sounds of approaching conversation made her do a quick about turn and dart back out of sight. Two of the Imperial House Staff came strolling down the corridor chatting about cleaning rosters and who was not pulling their weight on which shift.

Femke was almost beside herself with frustration in wishing them on their way. It would not take long for the Emperor to reach the library and discover that nobody had seen the boy he was looking for. He would almost inevitably come straight back to his study afterwards, so her time was tight without this unforeseen delay.

The two staff members stopped not far from the side corridor in which Femke had concealed herself. Femke edged back a little way down the corridor and flattened herself into a recessed doorway.

'OK, well I'd better get up to the sleeping chambers and see how they're getting on,' said one voice.

'See you later then. Evening meal at the sixth hour?'

'I'll be there.'

They moved away, and much to her relief neither turned down Femke's corridor. The damage was done though and a lot of precious time had been lost. For a moment Femke hesitated further. Was there enough time left to get into position? If she was caught, she was as good as dead. Throwing caution to the wind, Femke decided to try. She raced out from her hiding place and sped down the corridor to the locked door with her lock pick already in her hand.

On reaching the door, Femke dropped to one knee and carefully inserted the lock pick. A bead of perspiration trickled its way down her forehead to nestle against her right eyebrow, but Femke stoically ignored it as she carefully manoeuvred the pick into position. Seconds ticked by as Femke expertly explored the innards of the lock with her pick, and more droplets of perspiration broke out on her forehead as she felt for the all important catch inside. With a click it released and Femke opened the door, slipped inside and started working to drop the lock back into place. For some reason it did not want to lock again. Femke could feel that the pick was in the correct spot, but the bar of the lock just did not want to budge.

The sound of voices brought Femke's heart to her throat. It was the Emperor returning. Her time had run out. There was no time left to finish locking the door.

'Well, I want him found,' the Emperor's voice was saying angrily. 'Search the Palace. Have everyone stop whatever they're doing and comb the Palace until you find him.'

Femke ran silently over to the drinks cabinet and began feeling for the catch that allowed it to swing away from the wall. Her only chance now was to hide and hope for the best. The one time that the Emperor had concealed Femke in the compartment, he had opened it up so she did not know exactly what she was feeling for even though she knew roughly where it was. Whatever the release mechanism was, Femke knew that she had scant seconds to find and activate it, for the Emperor was almost to the door. His voice was heated and getting very close.

'I don't care if you have to dismantle the blasted place brick by brick. I don't want excuses, do you hear me? Find him and bring him to me here – immediately!'

There it was – a button – low down at the back right hand side of the drinks cabinet. Femke pressed it and prayed that the cabinet would make no sound as she swung it out. It was blessedly silent and she wormed into the hole behind and pulled the cabinet back into place.

Fortunately, the tiny click of the cabinet locking back into place coincided with the sound of the key being placed into the lock of the study door and Femke, barely able to move in the tiny space, tried to relax and calm her breathing. Spots of light from tiny holes scratched through the mirror substance that backed the glass rear of the tall drinks cabinet, combined with a thin line of light from the edges of the recess, gave some light to Femke's well hidden retreat. Femke did not dare to peep out through those holes just yet. Instead, she held her breath for a moment and listened for the reaction to the unlocked door.

Femke could clearly hear the key rattling in the door lock as the Emperor tried in vain to open the already unlocked door. Then she heard the handle of the door being turned and the slight creak as the door to the study opened.

'Shand's teeth!' Vallaine cursed softly as he slowly opened the door and cautiously peered inside. There did not appear to be anyone in the room, but he was not about to take any chances. 'That sleen spawn Shanier lured me away from the study and then slipped in whilst I was running around looking for him,' he thought silently to himself. A careful mental scan of the room for illusions revealed nothing, but Vallaine was not about to be caught napping. Slowly drawing a dagger from his left boot, the Sorcerer Lord readied himself to enter the room. Then he stopped.

'Don't be crazy,' he said aloud to himself. 'You're too old for cat and mouse games like this.'

He looked up and down the corridor and waited until he saw a couple of servants trotting along the corridor, obviously already part of the search for the boy.

'You there,' he called.

'Yes, your Imperial Majesty?' answered the nearest servant.

'Search my study. Someone's been in there and may still be hiding inside somewhere. Be careful. He may be dangerous.'

'Yes, your Majesty,' the man gulped.

Cautiously, the two servants entered the study and warily searched the room together, whilst Vallaine watched from the doorway. They checked behind all the chairs, tapestries and the desk without finding anything, and finally, when he was satisfied that he was not going to be attacked, Vallaine entered the room.

'Thank you,' he said to the servants with a wave of dismissal. 'You can get back to searching the rest of the Palace now. Oh, and spread the word to apprehend anyone unfamiliar, not just the boy. I have a suspicion that our intruder might be a Sorcerer and therefore able to change his appearance at will.'

'Yes, your Majesty,' the servants replied, wide-eyed at the thought that they might be searching for such a person.

'Well? Don't just stand there! Get going.'

'Yes, your Majesty. Right away, your Majesty.'

The two servants dashed off at a run and did not look back. Vallaine closed the door and went straight to his desk to see if anything had been touched. Breathlessly Femke strained her ears to listen for anything unusual, and put her right eye to one of the little peepholes to try to see what the Emperor was doing. The cabinet was not really ideally situated for looking towards the Emperor's desk, but Femke did get glimpses of him moving around it, carefully examining everything for any evidence of tampering.

'Damn it, Shanier! What are you up to?' Femke heard him mutter angrily.

There was a rustling of papers and then the unmistakeable ring of a crystal glass being knocked. The ringing noise cut off abruptly as a hand grabbed the glass to stop it from falling.

'Wine, that's a good idea,' the Emperor's voice muttered.

Footsteps approached the drinks cabinet and Femke saw the Emperor move into view with his glass in his left hand. He stopped in front of the cabinet, initially looking down at the decanter of wine as he poured himself a glass, and then Femke's heart nearly stopped as he looked directly at her. A smile twisted up onto the Emperor's face as he seemed to look straight through the mirror at her and, as she watched with horror, his face blurred and settled into the unmistakeably evil features of Lord Vallaine.

*   *   *   *   *

When Calvyn lowered Bek to the ground, he was quick to embrace his weeping friend and to share his grief at the loss of their mutual friend, Jez. Jenna and the others crowded round them and added their support to what was an awkward and delicate reunion.

After a minute or so, Akhdar coughed pointedly.

'Much as this is a touching reunion, Calvyn, we really should be on our way. Selkor has already got a day's head start on us and we cannot afford to let him gain any more time on us,' the white-haired magician observed.

'Of course, Master Akhdar,' Calvyn replied quickly, 'but my friend here is bleeding. Surely we've got time to heal him before we ride on? I suspect that they won't want to be left behind either and Bek cannot travel any further in his current state.'

'Very well, but don't be all day about it,' Akhdar said impatiently, clearly not pleased with the delay.

'Come on Bek, let me have a look at that cut for you. I'm sure that I didn't get close to touching you with my blade, so... good grief!'

Bek lifted his tunic and Calvyn's eyes opened wide with horror as he saw the blood-filled bandaging and padding beneath. As carefully as he could, Calvyn unwrapped the wound and he gasped again as he removed the final sopping pad.

'Sit down, Bek. This is beyond my skill, but today is your lucky day,' he said, lending an arm of support to his friend as he helped him gently down to the ground. 'Perdimonn! I need your help. This looks beyond any healing spell that I know.'

Perdimonn immediately dismounted and handed the reins of his horse to Rikath while he quickly stepped across and knelt down next to Bek. Ever so gently, the old Magician probed around the entry and exit wounds and his face drew into a frown of concentration.

'This is no fresh wound. How long ago did you get this, young man?' he asked without looking up.

'Best part of a month ago now,' Bek replied somewhat

breathlessly as he fought against the pain from Perdimonn's investigative fingers. 'It's never really healed up totally.'

'Nor will it whilst you leap around waving those blades of yours about,' Perdimonn said, smiling to take the sting out of his words. 'Never mind, I can fix it for you. Now try to sit still for a moment.'

Perdimonn's face took on an expression of intense concentration, and Calvyn could see his lips moving fractionally as Perdimonn crafted a silent spell of healing. The spell was far from simple, as Perdimonn wove a web of runes and power that not only healed the surface wound, but also all the internal damage as well.

Initially, nothing visually appeared to happen, but Bek could actually feel his body knitting together inside and his eyes went as wide and round as Shandese sennuts at the sensation. The area of skin around the visible wounds was heavily puckered with scar tissue and still had a wide dark red area around that, but as Perdimonn's spell entered the final stages and magical energy repaired the damaged tissues, Bek and his friends watched in fascinated wonder as all signs of the wound faded away.

When Perdimonn had finished, he offered a hand to Bek and pulled him up to his feet. Bek poked experimentally at the area where the wound had been and was delighted to find that he felt no pain. There was no sign that he had ever been wounded at all.

'Thank you, sir. I owe you a great debt. I thought that I'd be weakened by that wound for a very long time, if not forever,' Bek said, bowing to Perdimonn.

'And so you would have been,' Perdimonn replied, acknowledging the bow with a slight nod. 'I'd still try to take it easy for a couple of days or so if I were you. You've lost a lot of blood and I can't replace that. Eat well and allow your body to replenish the lost blood and you'll soon feel as if you'd never been injured at all. Now, as I get the distinct impression that Calvyn is going to want you and your compatriots to join us, you'd better mount up and we can get underway again. Akhdar is quite right – we've no more time to waste here.'

Calvyn embraced Bek with another quick clasp of a hug. Those who had dismounted then retrieved their horses and vaulted up into the saddles. Within a minute the enhanced party of riders set out at a steady walk back down towards the Fallow Bridge, and Calvyn drew Hakkaari alongside Bek's horse.

'Nice horse, Calvyn,' Bek observed, looking at the beautiful stallion approvingly. Then his eyes noted the insignia on the saddle and they widened a little in recognition. 'Is that what I think it is?' he asked, pointing at the symbols that announced a Knight of the Realm.

Calvyn's hand went instinctively to the embossed symbol on the pommel of his saddle and he smiled with pleasure at that touch. The Master of the Royal Stables had insisted that as Calvyn was no longer travelling incognito he should have his new saddle and tack for this journey, and Calvyn had been more than happy to take it. He had not had time to go to the Royal Tailors to pick up his entitlement of clothing bearing a Knight's insignia, but just riding with the specially marked saddle was treat enough for now. If he lived to return to Mantor, Calvyn promised himself that he would go straight to the Royal Tailors.

'Yes, I'm surprised that Derra and the others didn't tell you,' he replied, glancing over his shoulder at the Sergeant who was riding directly behind them.

'We didn't want to spoil the surprise, Sir Calvyn,' Derra said with a wolfish grin.

'*Sir* Calvyn – it has a good ring to it,' Bek admitted slowly. 'Listen, Sir Calvyn, I'm really sorry about what happened back there...'

'Save your apologies, Bek. You had good reason to be angry, and please call me Calvyn. The honorific really isn't necessary,' Calvyn interrupted firmly.

'Oh yes it is, Sir Calvyn,' Derra's voice grated from behind him. 'You are a Knight and you'll act like one, or I'll be forced to take you to one side and remind you of a few of the lessons that I thought I'd taught you during your basic training.'

Calvyn flushed an embarrassed shade of red and laughed ruefully.

'Yikes! I might be a Knight of the Realm but I still can't get anything past Sergeant Derra,' he said with an apologetic shrug.

'I'm glad that you see it my way, Sir Calvyn,' Derra purred with a satisfied grin.

Bek laughed and Calvyn could not help but join him. Somehow, being ordered around by Derra made things seem to click back into place. It was just like old times.

'What are you all doing here anyway, Sergeant? Why aren't you at Baron Keevan's castle?' Calvyn asked with a frown. 'Don't take this the wrong way, but I'm surprised that you allowed Bek to bypass the castle with that wound,' Calvyn added, leaving no doubt in his tone that he felt that Derra had done Bek a disservice by letting him travel so far.

'The Baron reached his castle the day after we did and he told me of your meeting on the road. When the Baron told me that you wanted him to send word to you about us, I immediately volunteered our services again. Bek was adamant about finding you and when you weren't at the castle, I saw little point in having Bek restrained there against his will. I know him well enough now to realise that he would have followed us, or got himself into a lot of trouble trying. The Baron was a bit reluctant to allow all four of us to come, but I managed to persuade him of the sense of sending a small party, rather than a single message rider, and I didn't mention Bek's wound to him,' Derra replied.

'You persuaded the Baron? That must have taken some fast-talking. Baron Keevan is not slow-witted, and I'd have thought he'd see through any scam to get away for a bit more excitement.'

'Well, maybe I'm just naturally talented, Sir Calvyn,' Derra growled with an amused grin.

'Of that I have no doubt, Derra,' Calvyn laughed.

When they had stopped laughing, Calvyn decided to try to

put his mind at rest about the one aspect of their encounter that still bothered him. Why had Bek been able to resist Calvyn's attempt to stop him with the use of sorcery? Calvyn had tried with all of the power that he could muster, but his efforts had simply seemed to slide over Bek as if meeting an impenetrable barrier.

'Tell me Bek, have you had lessons in sorcery since we last met?' Calvyn asked curiously.

Bek started laughing again, thinking that Calvyn was asking in jest.

'Me?' he chuckled. 'You can't be serious?'

'Actually, yes, I'm very serious,' Calvyn replied. 'Before you made your first attack I tried to stop you with sorcery, but I couldn't seem to gain any purchase on your mind. It was as if you had managed to erect some form of impenetrable mental barrier. I've never encountered anything like it before.'

'No, Calvyn, I know nothing about sorcery. Just before I attacked, you say? Curious,' Bek said thoughtfully, fingering the ring on the middle finger of his right hand.

'What's curious, Bek?'

'It's just that immediately before I attacked, my right hand felt very strange. It was as if my ring had turned to ice and my entire hand felt cold from it.'

'Ring? You never used to wear jewellery,' Calvyn observed with a touch of surprise. He looked at the thick band of gold on Bek's finger and something triggered a strange sense of familiarity, as if he'd seen the ring somewhere before. Why he should think such a thing, he had no idea, for it was just a plain band of gold. 'Where did you get it?' Calvyn asked, intrigued to see if the ring was somehow responsible for the strange mental block.

'It was given to me by the Emperor of Shandar after my last fight in the arena. Come to think of it, he said something about it helping me when I faced you. Don't ask me to remember exactly what he said, because I honestly don't recall it. I'd just been run through with a sword and I wasn't able to think all that clearly, but I do vaguely remember him saying something about the ring helping me when I faced you.'

'But how could the Emperor know of me, or that you would come and find me?' Calvyn exclaimed in surprise.

'Well, he probably doesn't know about *you* as such,' Fesha interjected from behind them. 'He does know about Lord Shanier though, and as you and Lord Shanier are – well, one and the same – it stands to reason that he knows of you. According to the buzz on the streets of Shandrim, you're a rogue Sorcerer who betrayed the Shandese legions and he's desperate to have you slain. He was certainly very keen for me to come and do the killing.'

'A rogue Sorcerer?' Calvyn laughed. 'Well, that pretty much sums me up I suppose, though it's interesting that the Emperor should possess such a ring, much less give it away. There's something about that gift which sends cold shivers down my spine, and not just because he meant you to kill me. After all, I did arrange for five of his legions to be pretty much wiped out and that can't have made his rule popular. Let's hope that he'll leave Thrandor alone now and concentrate on his affairs at home.'

'I think that we could all say a hearty "Amen" to that,' Jenna agreed.

'Here, Calvyn, take the ring. I want nothing of powers of sorcery and magic. You're much better equipped to handle such things,' Bek said decisively, removing the ring from his finger and passing it over to Calvyn.

'Are you sure, Bek? It was a present to you from an Emperor.'

'Yes, but it was a gift with a barb. It might well have enabled me to inadvertently kill a friend and what gift is there in that? Take it. I'm sure that you'll have more use for such a thing than I.'

Calvyn was touched by Bek's gesture and he settled the ring on the middle finger of his left hand. He half-expected to feel something unusual as he put it on, but to all intents and purposes it appeared like any other piece of inert jewellery. In the back of his mind, he noted that the ring appeared similar to one that Lord Vallaine had used to wear. Maybe that was why it looked familiar. Perhaps there were more than one of these extraordinary shields, Calvyn mused.

Later that day, when the party had stopped to make camp, Calvyn was confused and more than a little irritated by the Masters' insistence on teaching him things that appeared to be irrelevant.

'Why am I practicing with the Staff, Master Jabal? The tapestry clearly showed me holding my sword and was not clear on whether or not I was even wearing the Ring of Nadus.'

Calvyn paused for a moment in what he was doing and looked at the Master with a quizzical expression. Master Jabal looked him squarely in the eye and smiled.

'I'm hoping that by the time you get to face Selkor, the tapestry will show you holding the Staff and not your sword, Calvyn. Of course, we won't know if I succeed or not until we return to Mantor. Whilst it's cleverly made, your sword wasn't spellbound to convey magic the way that the Staff and the Ring were. You're practising with the Staff first because it's the less powerful of the two. Quite simply, to have you practise with the Ring would be like giving a child your sword and asking him to chop vegetables. The child would be clumsy and dangerous and so would you. The Staff is more easily controlled. Once you've got the hang of that, then we'll progress to the Ring.'

Calvyn nodded thoughtfully at Master Jabal's answer and then grimaced. It would only take them a few days to reach the mountains and they were riding pretty much straight towards the peak that held the Throne of the Gods. Time was short and Calvyn knew it all too well. If the Masters had been more inclined to teach the sort of magical lessons that he was receiving now whilst he was still back at the Academy, he might feel more prepared to face such a powerful Magician in a duel of magic. The truth of the matter was that Selkor had Calvyn beaten for experience, knowledge and power. There was only one area in which

Calvyn might have an edge, and that was not in magic but in sorcery.

Selkor had to be a fairly powerful Sorcerer as well as a Magician, Calvyn reasoned as he contemplated his adversary. There was no other explanation for what Selkor had done at Mantor during the battle with the Terachite Clans. To affect the minds of a huge number of people such that they were immobilised was not the work of a Magician, Calvyn mused. Well, no, that was not totally true, because it would be possible with magic, but it would require a very complex spell and a vast amount of energy. At the time of the battle, Selkor had neither shown any evidence of casting a complex spell, nor had he been in possession of a large enough power source to make such a spell work. Sorcery was the only rational explanation, yet he knew that if he mentioned it to any of the Masters, the theory would be dismissed out of hand. After all, what true Magician would ever lower himself to the practice of what were viewed as the 'lesser arts'? Also, even if he had done so there was no room in their thinking for the use of such a talent to defeat a Magician of such power and subtlety as Selkor.

'Very well, Master, what spell would you like me to cast?' Calvyn asked.

Jabal considered for a moment, subconsciously rubbing at his chin as he tried to decide.

'I think that we need to give you something to work with that requires control, but that you're already adept at. The spell that you used to lift your friend there off the ground would be a good one. You showed excellent control with that earlier, so let's see how you do when you use the Staff. I don't think that lifting a person would be a good idea though, so let's choose an inanimate object, shall we?'

'Very well, Master,' said Calvyn, looking around him for something suitable. 'Should it be big or small?'

'It doesn't really matter either way,' Master Jabal answered with an amused smile. 'Either will present its own difficulties.'

'How about this then?' Calvyn asked, picking up a fist-sized rock.

'That will do just fine. Now, set it down on the ground and use your spell to lift the rock up to just above head height,'

'With the Staff?' Calvyn asked.

'No, not yet. Just use your own magic for now.'

Calvyn did as he was told, picturing the rock rising from the ground and mentally feeding the runes into the rock, as if doing so would make it somehow lighter than air. In perfect control, the piece of rock lifted off the ground and climbed to hang in the air at the prescribed height. Master Jabal nodded with a pleased expression.

'Now I want you to hurl the stone at that tree over there with all the force that you can muster,' Jabal ordered, pointing to a huge old oak tree. 'Really let loose with as much magical energy as you can draw.'

Calvyn's brows drew together as he concentrated not so much on power as on the result that he wanted. Remembering what Perdimonn had said about picturing the result, Calvyn imagined the rock smashing into the tree as if it had been fired from a great catapult. Then he released his spell. The results were impressive and Master Jabal's eyebrows raised in surprise at the crack as the rock powered into the trunk of the tree so hard that it left a deep gouge in the bark.

'Good! Very good indeed, Calvyn. I actually felt the energy drawn from the very air around us for that.'

The Master walked over to where the rock had come to rest on the ground and he brought it back and set it down where it had first been lifted from.

'Now,' he said with a slight smile. 'Let's see you try that again, but directing your spell through the Staff.'

Calvyn took the Staff of Dantillus and held it out in front of him. Closing his eyes he mentally directed the runes through the Staff, imagining them emerging from the clasped gem at the top of the Staff and flowing into the rock. As he released the spell, Calvyn opened his eyes and was amazed to see the rock shoot up into the air far faster than he had pictured it. It took every ounce of control that Calvyn possessed to prevent the rock from racing skywards, and even with his firm mental picture and his most disciplined stream of runes, the rock peaked at twice the height he had intended before slowly descending back to where he wanted it.

'Excellent!' exclaimed Master Jabal enthusiastically. 'Really well done, Calvyn. I expected to have to catch that from a great height. Now, let's see you throw it at the tree again.'

Calvyn took a deep breath and mustered his spell. Having experienced the unexpected amplifying power of the Staff on the simple lifting spell, he fully expected the results to be spectacular. Perdimonn caught Jenna's arm and pointed across to where Jabal was teaching Calvyn.

'Watch this,' he whispered to her with an amused grin. 'It should be entertaining.'

There two loud cracks as Calvyn released his spell, for the rock ripped through the air so fast that the vacuum it left in its wake caused a sonic crack, which was instantly followed by another as the rock drove into the bole of the tree. The impact was so fearsome that the rock shattered and its fragments drove deeply into the wood.

'Wow!' exclaimed Jenna in awe.

'Wow, indeed!' Perdimonn agreed with a smile. 'The boy really packs a punch with that Staff, doesn't he?'

CHAPTER 13

Later that evening, Perdimonn gathered the Warders and together they walked some distance away from the campsite. The night air was crisp and still and the moisture in their warm breath condensed into plumes of miniature cloud with each expiration. Once they were out of earshot from the rest of the party, Rikath turned to Perdimonn and asked him why he had called this meeting.

'What do you think of young Calvyn?' Perdimonn asked her in return.

'Nice young man – very genuine – plenty of raw talent,' Rikath responded quickly. 'Why do you ask?'

'Well, do any of you give him a hope of successfully facing down Selkor?' Perdimonn prompted.

'Not a chance,' Arred said sadly.

'Me neither,' Morrel concurred.

'Unfortunately, I'd have to say the same,' Rikath agreed.

'Then you believe all is lost before we even reach the Throne. Selkor has already won.'

'Not necessarily,' Morrel disagreed. 'Even though Selkor will probably defeat the boy, there is no certainty that he could open the gateway without the fourth Key. It might be that the encounter is not really that critical at all.'

'That is true enough,' Perdimonn admitted. 'But let's just assume for a moment that Selkor does have enough power to open a gateway. Where does that leave us?'

A long silence followed the question as the Warders considered the situation. The idea that Selkor could open a gateway and allow the gods back into the world was not a comfortable one, and all of the Warders' minds were filled with dire images of the consequences.

'Do I detect another of your plans here, Perdimonn?' asked Arred suspiciously. 'You didn't bring us out here tonight to depress us with thoughts of failure, did you?'

'No, I didn't,' Perdimonn said slowly. 'I've had a plan in mind for some time now, but it will require us to be as unanimous as we were with the time issue. Also, there might prove to be a bit more debate over this plan, because it's going to be significantly more contentious.'

'Well? Come on then – spit it out,' Arred prompted impatiently.

Reluctantly, Perdimonn started to outline his idea and watched as the jaws of the other Warders all dropped in amazement.

'You've got to be joking!' Rikath exclaimed when he had finished. 'That's the craziest thing I've ever heard.'

'No, Perdimonn. Absolutely no way will we do such a thing,' said Morrel flatly.

Arred just stood there, his eyes distant and his mouth open with shock, as he tried to come to terms with Perdimonn's radical idea.

Perdimonn sighed heavily. 'Well, I suppose it would have been a bit much to expect you to just accept this as a necessary step, but here, let me explain why I think we have little choice...'

*   *   *   *   *

Femke's heart had all but stopped when Vallaine had revealed himself. For a terrifying few seconds, by the expression on the Sorcerer's face Femke had been convinced that he had sensed her presence. He had seemed to look right through the mirror with his malice-filled eyes and that stare had drilled into her with an icy coldness that had her shivering even now with the memory.

It had to be at least late evening, if not early morning by now, Femke thought. The spy tried again to reach the button that would unlock the cabinet and allow it to swing away from the wall. Vallaine had been gone at least an hour and Femke doubted that he would return tonight. The Sorcerer Lord had stayed in the study for the rest of the afternoon and all evening, changing his appearance to that of the Emperor at every knock at the door.

Femke smiled to herself as she recalled the Sorcerer's irritation at the reports from servants as they continued to bring updates on the search, all with negative results. Lord Vallaine had inadvertently given her the perfect alibi for being back at Shandrim during this time. The Sorcerer Lord had muttered away to himself about Shanier so frequently that it quickly became clear that Vallaine was convinced his nemesis was here in the city. As the Emperor had sent her to look for Shanier and kill him, where else should she be but here? This gave her a much wider scope for manipulating events and people and Femke fully intended to make the most of it.

Before she could do anything, however, Femke first needed to escape the tight little prison that she had locked herself into. This was not proving to be easy. The space behind the cabinet was so small that Femke could not turn around and could hardly bend her legs at all. This made reaching the button that unlocked the cabinet all but impossible to reach. The hidey-hole had never been intended for self-use and anyone using it was normally secured inside by someone else, then released when the job was done. Femke was now beginning to realise that getting out by her own efforts was not going to be an easy task.

Grunting slightly with the effort of forcing her hand down towards the button, the spy contorted herself as best she could and stretched as far as possible. Head twisted up and shoulder down, forcibly squeezing her body down as low as she could, Femke reached out to where she knew the release button awaited the touch of her fingers. With a walking motion of her fingers against the back of the cabinet, she tried with all her might to gain an extra few millimetres, but it was no use. The button was beyond her reach.

With a sigh of defeat, Femke then had the struggle of straightening back up into a more comfortable position again. There had to be some way for her to extend her reach far enough to press the button, but she was not carrying much that she could use that way. The only thing she had was her lock pick and she was worried about the possibility of breaking that. It would not help her cause much to escape this miniature prison only to be trapped in a larger one. Still, Femke had few options, so she felt around until she managed to locate the lock pick in a pocket and then carefully extracted it and positioned the little wooden handle between the thumb, index and middle fingers of her left hand.

In a repeat of her earlier contortions, Femke squeezed her body down as low as she could and reached out with the lock pick to feel for the button. Gently sweeping the tip of the pick back and forth as she felt lower and lower down the back left hand side of the cabinet, Femke finally felt what must be the button sitting proud of the rest of the rear surface. With a pained grimace, she put the end of the lock pick on the button and tried to press it, but with her fingers extended as they were, Femke could not quite get the leverage to press the button.

Twisted as it was, Femke's body hurt in several places and she knew that she could not maintain the position for long. Pressing the handle of the lock pick against the cabinet, Femke used the cabinet itself to provide the leverage she needed and, just managing to reach the metal shaft beyond the wooden handle with her middle finger, she pressed the tip of the pick as hard as she could against the button.

Tears rolled from her eyes at the effort, and when the button finally clicked and the cabinet swung away from the wall, Femke fell out of the hole virtually distraught at the panic that she was beginning to feel. Although the cabinet swung away from the wall quite quickly, the spy was able to prevent it from banging against its end stop. Fortunately nothing in it was broken and noise was minimal. Once Femke had taken a moment or two recovering her composure, she carefully swung the cabinet back into place and moved silently across to the Emperor's desk to have a quick nose around before she left.

Taking careful note of where everything was before she touched anything, the spy then quickly leafed through the pile of reports on the desktop. The light was not very good, for the only illumination was from high internal windows that opened into the corridor outside the door. There were obviously torches burning in the passageway outside, but the light diffusion from the corridor into the study was not that good and Femke found Vallaine's spidery handwriting difficult to read. About the only thing that was certain was that Vallaine was set on invading Thrandor. Why that should be was not clear, but Femke decided better of delaying her escape any longer. The risky venture had proved more profitable than Femke could have hoped for, but in order to capitalise on it she still had to escape the palace without getting stopped.

Femke carefully replaced everything on the Emperor's desk as exactly as she could, then she climbed up on a chair so that she could pull herself further up to be able to look out of one of the high windows and check the corridor. There was nobody in sight. That was yet another bonus, because Femke had half-expected there would be a guard on this room after today's events.

With no time pressure, Femke naturally picked the lock in seconds and the click of the latch withdrawing sounded unnaturally loud in the otherwise silent room. Cautiously, she cracked the door open and peeped out into the corridor. Once happy that there was nobody around, Femke slipped out into the corridor, closed the door behind her and quickly used her expertise to drop the lock back into place.

It suddenly struck Femke that trying to leave the Palace dressed as she was would be very foolish, even at this late hour. Her chances of getting away unnoticed were very slim. The obvious answer was not to leave at all, but to go to her room here instead. It was a fair distance from this part of the Palace, but if she could get there unnoticed then she had all the changes of clothing that she could possibly need in her dressers. Not only that, but she also had wigs that would disguise her short hair and make-up that would change her appearance sufficiently that no one would connect her with the young servant boy whom everyone had been busy searching for today. Given the alternatives, making for her room in the palace suddenly seemed a sensible option.

Racing down the quiet corridors and pausing at each turn to listen for any signs of movement, Femke made it to her room without being spotted once. With the door closed and locked behind her, she heaved a sigh of relief and slowly undressed, neatly stowing her servant uniform away at the bottom of a drawer and getting out a suitable outfit to wear the next day. Then, with the stress and excitement of the day finally behind her, Femke flopped into bed and instantly slipped away into a deep sleep.

*   *   *   *   *

'Perdimonn?'

'Yes, Calvyn?'

'Something really strange happened last night and I wondered if you might be able to explain it,' Calvyn said, keeping his voice low so that nobody else would hear.

'Really?' Perdimonn asked with obvious curiosity. 'Strange in what way?'

'Well, it was a dream, or at least I think it was a dream. I dreamt that I was outside of the tent in my nightshirt, but with my sword belt around my waist. I remember feeling a compulsion to draw my sword and hold it up in front of me. Then I started casting more spells on the blade, but I also remember thinking at the time that the spells didn't mean anything. They weren't gibberish exactly, but I couldn't even hazard a guess at what the spells were supposed to achieve.'

'Yes, that is a little strange, but as you said, it was

probably just a dream so I shouldn't worry too much about it,' reassured Perdimonn with a sympathetic smile. 'I know that you're under a lot of stress at the moment. I'd try to forget it if I were you and concentrate on your lessons.'

'If that was all, then I'd gladly listen to your advice Perdimonn, but there's more. At the end of each of the spells one of the runes on my sword glowed briefly, then changed and finally disappeared altogether.'

'So?' the old Magician asked. 'Strange things happen in dreams.'

'I've just had a look at my sword, Perdimonn. The runes have gone. It's as if they never existed at all and yet the last time I drew the blade they were clearly visible, which makes me wonder whether I was really dreaming at all. If I really did cast spells on the sword then it wasn't of my own volition. Also, if I was being controlled it begs the questions, by whom, and for what purpose?'

Calvyn drew his sword and held it out for Perdimonn to look at. The old Magician studied the blade carefully for a moment and then raised his eyebrows quizzically at Calvyn.

'Well, I can't argue with you. There are no runes on the blade,' Perdimonn agreed quietly, doing his best not to attract attention to their conversation. 'Does the blade still have the same properties as it had before?'

'I don't know,' admitted Calvyn nervously. 'I haven't tested it yet.'

'Give it a try as soon as you can and let me know what happens,' Perdimonn suggested. 'I can't explain to you what happened last night, but if the properties of the sword are unaffected, then does it really matter that much?'

Calvyn thought about that for a moment, his features drawn in a frown of concentration.

'I suppose not,' he shrugged. 'But I just don't like the idea that somebody out there might be manipulating me against my will. What if it were Selkor? If he has somehow forced me to taint the blade with some spell of his, then I might as well cast it aside now.'

'Did the compulsion feel like Selkor?' Perdimonn asked

quickly.

'Well... no, not really. The compulsion didn't feel evil, or unwholesome, but beyond that I couldn't tell you anything.'

'Alright then, I shall think on what it all means,' Perdimonn promised with his most reassuring tone. 'Leave the matter with me, Calvyn, and I'll consult with my fellow Warders. Maybe they'll know something I don't.

'Thanks, Perdimonn. I really appreciate that.'

Calvyn rejoined his colleagues with a much lighter heart as they made quick work of dismantling the campsite and loading the packhorses. It was good to hear all the old banter picking up again between his friends and particularly good to see Bek in a jovial mood.

For Bek's part, he had good reason to be happy. Ever since his rescue from the Arena in Shandrim he had not allowed himself to open up to Derra, Fesha and Eloise, in case they somehow managed to soften his heart on the issue of his revenge against Calvyn. With the release from his vow to avenge Jez's death in the arena, Bek had apologised to his three rescuers at the fireside the previous evening. Derra and the others held no grudge, as they were more than pleased to see him acting like his old self again.

Eloise had been particularly pleased. Although she had been deliberately playing her relationship with Bek cool, the Private was finding herself increasingly attracted to him. Even during her recruit training back at Keevan's Castle, Eloise had harboured a soft spot for the talented Corporal, and she was really pleased to see him acting more like the man she remembered. His lessons in sword drill had often left her flushing with more than the heat of the exercise, and she had felt from the beginning that he would make an attractive partner. The problem, as Eloise saw it, was that she wanted to keep her focus on learning to be a good soldier and really did not want the complications that a romantic relationship would bring – particularly a relationship with someone of senior rank. Now that she had established herself as a Private, though, she was beginning to become more open-minded to the idea.

There had been a lot of hugging and shoulder slapping between the friends the previous evening, and by the time they had retired to bed, all of the awkwardness that had been present through the day had been dispelled. The next morning, Eloise felt ready to banter the Corporal into some physical contact, though not exactly of a romantic nature.

'Hey, Bek, are you going to pull on that rope, or just stand there all day enjoying the view?' Eloise asked in a loud voice.

'That's Corporal Bek to you, Private Eloise. Why? Do you want to make something of it?' Bek replied with a wolfish grin.

'If I did, you don't think I'd be stupid enough to challenge you with a blade, do you?' Eloise replied, hands on hips and tossing her head to clear her hair from her eyes. 'Look at you! You've not done any real exercise in weeks, Corporal. I could kick your sorry-looking, saggy backside in hand-to-hand combat anytime.'

'Is that right?' Bek answered, his grin widening even more. 'Come on then, Eloise. Let's dance.'

Bek cast aside the rope he was holding and moved to face off against Eloise, whilst she in turn interlaced her fingers and clicked her knuckles. Then, with deliberate provocation, Eloise put her hands out in front of her, palms up, and made a couple of small beckoning twitches with her fingers. Derra and Calvyn exchanged a glance and Derra made a little circling motion with her right hand that let him know she was perfectly happy with what was going on. With hindsight, Calvyn suspected that Derra had actually put Eloise up to the whole thing.

The time spent in training in the Shandrim arena had caused Bek's upper body mass to increase significantly, but he had lost much of the muscle tone during his long convalescence. Eloise on the other hand, although significantly lighter, was in perfect trim and awaited Bek's first move with a confident air.

Bek lunged forward, trying to gather Eloise into his powerful arms, but she danced to one side, catching his left wrist and twisting it hard. In doing so, Eloise forced Bek to lean forward whilst she drove her right knee up into his stomach, causing him to expel the air from his lungs with an audible 'oof' of pain. Even as Bek gasped for his first breath, Eloise let go of his wrist, sprang back slightly to generate space and spun on her heel to land a kick to the side of Bek's face that sent him sprawling to the ground.

'So much for the macho "First Sword" image,' Eloise laughed. 'With reflexes like that I'm surprised you survived half a minute in the arena.'

It was a deliberate goad and Bek saw straight through what was happening, but he also saw the sense in it. He had not had the opportunity to do any sort of physical training during the previous month or more, and now that Perdimonn had healed his wound he needed to get back into shape.

Rubbing his jaw ruefully, Bek pulled himself slowly to his feet. He was not in the slightest bit annoyed by Eloise's comment, but he launched another attack anyway in the full knowledge that she was probably more than able to counter anything that he could manage in his present state.

A flurry of arms and legs whipping vicious looking blows, blocks and counter blows followed, as Bek and Eloise ran through several rapid sequences of attack, defence and attack again. The sounds of the thudding blows drew the attention of both the Magicians and the Warders.

'What's going on?' Perdimonn asked sharply. 'Stop them, Calvyn, or I will.'

'Don't, Perdimonn – please. This is an essential part of Bek's recovery. He needs this,' Calvyn pleaded. 'Just leave them be for a minute or two. Derra and I will make sure that it doesn't get out of hand.'

Perdimonn snorted slightly in disgust at that.

'I don't see how beating each other's brains out can help any sort of physical recovery,' the old man said acidly, wincing in sympathy as Eloise managed to land a second spinning kick to Bek's face. 'That's got to hurt.'

Calvyn was not about to argue that point. He had almost

felt the sting in Eloise's blows and he reflected silently that he was glad it was not his face on the receiving end of them.

'Nevertheless, I would very much appreciate it if you stayed out of this.'

Bek had staggered at the latest kick but not fallen, and when Eloise tried to follow her successful kick with a second one, she suddenly found that it was her turn to go spinning to the ground. Bek had caught her foot by the heel with both hands, absorbing the kick and using the momentum to throw Eloise totally off balance. The result was a very smug looking Bek moving forward to make use of the advantage he had gained, but his confidence was premature. Eloise swept his legs out from under him and even as he fell, she cracked another wicked-looking kick with her other foot into his stomach. That was enough for Bek and he curled up into a foetal position, holding his middle with both hands.

'Enough,' he gasped, trying to laugh and get his breath back at the same time and failing on both counts. 'You win this time, Eloise. I'll get my own back later on. Perhaps you could give me a little bladework practice at some time today as well?'

'If the Private won't, then I will,' Derra growled. 'You've become far too soft with all that laying around. You'll have no credibility with the troops at all if you let Privates kick you around like that.'

Bek managed a sort of wheezy chuckle. 'Fair enough,' he nodded. 'I'll take whatever practice you're all willing to give me, but don't expect to knock me about like this for long.'

Eloise had got back up and now offered a hand to Bek. He took it and she hauled him upright. Eloise smiled, her green eyes sparkling with pleasure and her cheeks dimpling slightly.

'I wouldn't bet heavily on that if I were you, Corporal. I'm going to be heaving that saggy backside of yours out of the dirt for some time yet, if I'm not mistaken.'

Bek was at a loss for words as the effect of her smile struck him with its full devastating power. Eloise was simply shining and her beauty, which had become increasingly attractive to him since his rescue, brought feelings that he was not ready to deal with. He gulped hard and tried not to look stupid as he realised that his eyes were virtually on stalks and his mouth had dropped open slightly. He failed.

Placing a single finger under his chin, Eloise closed his mouth and walked past him to return to the dismantling of the tents. 'Come now, Bek,' she said brightly. 'Drooling will get you nowhere.'

Bek looked around quickly in embarrassment at Calvyn and Derra, who were doing their best not to laugh at him. Both were wearing smirks and Bek inwardly groaned as, with his cheeks flaming red, he hastily strode across to help Eloise. It was quite obvious that he was not going to hear the last of this for some time.

*   *   *   *   *

'How's the boy doing, Jabal?' Master Akhdar asked, deliberately keeping his voice low as they rode in their usual place at the front of the party. His tone was bland, displaying no concern or emotion. His eyes, however, told a different story. Akhdar was not simply asking out of curiosity, for the fate of the world might hang on Jabal's answer. The old Magician knew that time was running out and there was little that he, or anyone else, could do to affect the path that history was following.

'Calvyn is exceeding all my expectations, Akhdar. He truly is an extraordinary young man. His control, power and mental discipline is well beyond his years,' Jabal replied, also keeping his voice low.

'I sense a "but" coming,' Akhdar sighed, his piercing gaze seeing straight through Master Jabal's brave words.

Jabal grimaced.

'Unfortunately you're correct. The boy is a prodigy, but he's no match for Selkor. He would certainly stand a chance if Selkor hadn't gained knowledge of any of the Keys. The fact of the matter is, though, that Selkor can use the full force of three of the four elements. Even with the Staff and the Ring, Calvyn wouldn't survive a confrontation with the sort of force generated by one element, let alone three. He'll fail, Akhdar – I just cannot see any way that he can possibly succeed.'

'What if the Warders were to block Selkor's use of the elements like they did at Mantor, Jabal? Would that swing the balance in Calvyn's favour?'

Master Jabal stroked his chin thoughtfully as he considered that.

'It would certainly even things up, but the Prophecy said nothing of the Warders being present at this confrontation. I don't think that we should count on such a circumstance.'

'But if they were present?' Akhdar insisted. 'Would he be able to defeat Selkor?'

'It's possible,' Jabal conceded, 'but very unlikely. Selkor still has Darkweaver's amulet and a host of years more experience to draw on. Even if the Warders could block Selkor's use of the Keys, I would still have to favour Selkor in a duel. Calvyn is a resourceful young man, but that is unlikely to be enough.'

Akhdar nodded. He knew that Jabal's assessment was likely to be very accurate and it was in line with his own thoughts. This strengthened his belief that if it were to come down to a one on one encounter between Selkor and Calvyn, this whole quest was something of a futile gesture. Strangely, though, this hardened his resolve even more to help Calvyn as much as he could.

The old Magician looked over his shoulder at Calvyn. The young man was laughing and chatting with his friends as if he had not a care in the world, yet the world and everyone in it might very much be depending on him within the next few days. He was only calm through ignorance, Akhdar thought morosely. If he truly understood what was going on here, the boy would be rigid with fear. There was no way that Calvyn would be able to maintain any semblance of calm if he truly comprehended the gravity of the situation. The question foremost in Akhdar's mind was whether to explain to the boy exactly what was at stake here, or whether to leave him in blissful ignorance. What would be most beneficial to his last minute preparations? Perhaps speaking to Perdimonn about it might prove useful, Akhdar wondered, shifting his gaze beyond the group of soldiers to the strange group of four who followed them. It was certainly worth thinking about, if only to gain the old Warder's thoughts on the matter. Perdimonn probably knew the boy better than anyone.

'Give him two more sessions with the Staff, Jabal, then I'll introduce him to working with the Ring of Nadus. I'll not deny that the outcome looks bleak, but I've not dragged myself this far from Terilla to just roll over and die for Selkor now.'

'Very well, Akhdar, I can see that it will be necessary to push him on to using the Ring as soon as possible, though I'll be honest and say that I don't like it one bit. The boy packs quite a punch with his spells through the Staff, but whether he will appreciate the subtle differences between using that and the Ring in time for it to give any appreciable increase in his overall effectiveness is debatable. It might be better just to concentrate on the Staff and work on giving him a few useful surprises to deal Selkor when the time comes.'

'You could be right, Jabal, but given how fast Calvyn has learned everything else that we've thrown at him, I think that this young man will continue to surprise us and adapt to using the Ring just as quickly. I'm not going to pass up the chance to add to his arsenal before he meets Selkor. I get the distinct impression that this is our task in this whole affair, you know? How we prepare him might just be the critical factor. We just don't know, so let's do everything we can, shall we?'

'Oh, absolutely, Akhdar,' Jabal agreed fervently. 'I'm not trying to deny him in any way. I was merely suggesting that the most effective preparation might not necessarily be what we perceive it to be. We need to remain sensitive to Calvyn's progress and advance him in whatever ways will bring the biggest short term gains, was what I was trying to suggest.'

Akhdar smiled wearily at his fellow Grand Magician.

'I know,' he said softly. 'We all want to do our best for him now. I just hope that whatever we manage to do, somehow it might prove enough.'

The two old men looked back at Calvyn again, but if he was aware of their scrutiny then he showed no outward sign of it. All outward appearances indicated that Calvyn was intent on his conversation with his military friends. Perdimonn on the other hand did notice the looks of the two Magicians, and catching their eyes he smiled at them encouragingly. They nodded back politely and then looked forward again quickly.

'Perdimonn knows something that we don't, I'm sure he does,' Akhdar grumbled sourly. 'Why else would the old fox be so confident in the lad's abilities?'

'I don't know,' Jabal replied, scratching at his chin for a moment. 'Maybe you should ask him. We are all on the same side after all.'

'Hmm, well, perhaps I'll do just that. In the meantime, what are you going to work on in the next session? It would be good to know what you are teaching so that I don't duplicate unnecessarily.'

*   *   *   *   *

Bek was feeling inspired after his tussle with Eloise earlier and despite taking a lot of banter, particularly from Fesha, he decided to run alongside the riders in a bid to begin his return to peak fitness. Jenna took some of the heat off him by handing the reins of her horse to Calvyn and jumping down to run with him.

'I really need to work some of the kinks out of my legs after all this riding,' she laughed as she fell into step with a very determined looking Bek. 'Besides, I really quite enjoy running and I haven't done any for quite a while.'

'Enjoy running!' Fesha exclaimed. 'Are you sure you're feeling alright, Jenna? You're looking a bit feverish to me.'

'Laugh all you like, Fesha. I'm going to run for an hour or so and I'm sure that I'll feel a lot better for it afterwards.'

'Oh I don't think he should laugh too loud,' interrupted the harsh voice of Sergeant Derra. 'It will be his turn to run for an hour after you, Jenna. And to make sure that he doesn't slacken our pace at all, Eloise and I will be running right behind him to chivvy him along,' she added, looking pointedly at the grinning face of Eloise. The raven-haired Private's grin turned rueful, and she shrugged slightly as she acknowledged the implicit order in Derra's statement.

Calvyn laughed aloud.

'Ah, the joys of a Sergeant Derra run, I remember them well,' he chuckled.

Derra turned to him with one of her dark, sharply angled eyebrows raised questioningly, but even Derra's most intimidating look could no longer quell Calvyn's mood and he waggled a finger at her in amusement.

'Though you may find this funny, *Sir* Calvyn, it is most serious to me and I would request that you treat it as such. Indeed, I should point out that all that sedentary study at the Magician's Academy is starting to show around your middle, Sir. Might I suggest that you join us before you allow all that valuable training time that I invested in you to degenerate into flab and blubber.'

'Flab and blubber!' Calvyn exclaimed in mock outrage. He knew full well that despite the Sergeant's tone and carefully chosen words, she knew he had not gained so much as an ounce of weight since he had left for Terilla. 'I'll have you know that I'm in fine physical condition, thank you Sergeant.'

'Well in that case a little run won't hurt you then, will it?' countered Jenna.

'Is this a conspiracy or something?' Calvyn asked suspiciously.

'We're only concerned for your health, Calvyn,' Jenna replied with a grin and looked across at Derra with an exaggerated innocent expression. 'Isn't that right, Sergeant?'

'Absolutely,' Derra replied with a straight face.

'Don't listen to them, Sir. You know they're just manipulating you. Surely you're not going to fall for this?' Fesha advised almost pleadingly.

Derra fired a vicious stare at Fesha, who did his best to ignore it.

'Well...' Calvyn started indecisively. 'I haven't actually done much real exercise in a while, so a run probably wouldn't do me any harm.'

Derra and Jenna exchanged a brief satisfied look and Fesha put his hands out and raised his eyes heavenward in a look of sheer disbelief. 'I don't believe it!' he exclaimed with a heavy sigh. 'I've just lost all faith in the phrase "Rank has its privileges". Surely if it held true, then a Knight of the Realm would not find himself running next to a perfectly healthy horse at the whim of a Sergeant.'

'Nonsense, Fesha,' Derra disagreed. 'Sir Calvyn isn't doing this at my whim. He's going to run because he wants to. That's right, isn't it, Sir Calvyn?'

Calvyn laughed and shrugged. 'Of course it is, Sergeant.'

'You're a traitor to the male cause, Sir Calvyn,' Fesha said sulkily, though his eyes were lit with mirth even as he said it.

For much of the rest of the morning the party moved on towards the southern boundaries of Thrandor at a good pace. Calvyn was lectured in spells whilst he rode and the old Magicians made no complaint or comment when he declared that he was going to run with some of the other soldiers for a while.

During the rest stops for food, Derra organised sword drill for Bek and the others in turn whilst the Warders prepared the food for the party. Calvyn was fascinated to watch Bek running through his double sword callisthenic drills on his own after drilling with single blade against Eloise. Bek's grace and precision of movement were a wonder to behold, and the two blades really did seem to be a part of him as he moved. Despite the slow, deliberate movements of Bek's initial programme, he was sweating freely at the concentration of effort even before he moved into the more energetic speed drills that he followed it with.

'How can you follow an opponent who uses two blades at speed?' Calvyn asked his friend when he had finished his workout.

'Well, the drills help a lot. My tutor, Hammar, was an excellent teacher,' Bek replied. 'Once you're used to the interlocking motions, the anticipation and observation of the opponent's balance and motion is much the same as following a single weapon. The co-ordination and balance for swinging the blades is different of course, but the end results can prove devastatingly effective once you've mastered the intricacies of the dance.'

'I can imagine,' Calvyn said appreciatively.

'Of course, it's a useless skill outside of solo fighting,' Bek admitted with a grin. 'You could never fight in a battle line with two blades. It would be impossible to get any sort of timing with those either side of you and I doubt very much if Baron Keevan will allow me to have a second blade in any sword skills tourney, so I guess that it's a bit of a useless ability really. Still, having gained some ability at it, I feel obliged not to just allow that ability to fade through neglect. It would feel like a betrayal of Hammar's efforts somehow, do you know what I mean?'

'A bit like my running for Derra,' Calvyn chuckled.

Bek laughed.

'Something like that,' he nodded, grinning broadly. 'Only for some reason I have a sense that I might need it some day. It's as if I've been trained for a reason other than the fight with Serrius. Strange...'

'What's that?'

'Well, it's just a strange sensation. The sense that fate is somehow leading me by the hand down a predetermined path, but I have no idea what it is, or how it's going to turn out.'

'Tell me about it!' said Calvyn sarcastically.

CHAPTER 14

A tingle of excited anticipation coursed through Selkor's veins. He was at the base of the mountain on top of which sat the Throne of the Gods. The voices in his head were whispering ever more frequently now, urging him on with an exultant chorus of encouragement and it was all that he could do to restrain himself from trying to push his horse into a gallop.

The time was at hand for Selkor to show the world his power and do what no other Magician had come close to achieving. He felt destiny reaching out to him and he knew in his heart that when he opened the gateway that would allow the gods to return to this world, there would be a place alongside them that would be his forever. Who amongst even the greatest of the Magicians whose names littered the history books could claim to have become a deity? Yet that was what he had been promised, and he felt the power and truth in the whispers that filled his mind with ideas and pictures of what such power and authority would be like to wield.

Millions would worship him. Kings would kneel before his feet and beg for a benevolent touch or a blessing. By opening the gate he would unlock the door to eternal life itself and the passage of time would cease to be the curse that he had always fought to overcome. If all went well with the opening spell, age and past conflicts could be but shadows of memory by the time the sun set. All conflicts, that is, except one – Perdimonn would pay for his obstruction and his meddling.

Selkor smiled grimly to himself at that thought.

'Ah, Perdimonn,' he breathed with satisfaction. 'You will regret that you ever dared deny me that which it has always been my destiny to wield.'

As a god he would merely have to command Perdimonn to reveal the secret that he guarded and the old man would squirm beneath his gaze. Selkor would be denied nothing, and would be capable of anything a mortal mind could imagine and much more besides. Perdimonn would no longer be so much as an inconvenience, Selkor mused, chuckling quietly to himself. There would be nowhere the old man could hide and nothing that he could do to keep Selkor from plucking the Key from his mind whenever he chose. In some ways, it might be quite fun to let the old fellow run for a while, just to prolong the pleasure of finally having the Earth Warder precisely where Selkor wanted him. On the other hand, Selkor had waited too long to play a cat and mouse game now. No. He would see to Perdimonn quickly and have done with it.

The beginnings of a pathway leading up the mountainside began to emerge ahead, though Selkor needed no visual clues as to where to go. The voices directed him constantly now, with tones that raised in concern if he deviated by so much as a hair from the way they suggested, and virtually purred at him as he progressed directly towards his goal.

'Not far. Not far now,' the voices whispered gleefully. 'Just one last climb and you will be exalted forever.'

The pathway led under an archway of natural stone and then up what appeared to be a strangely formed ledge that climbed steeply up the side of the mountain towards the summit. Just a glance around at the sheer faces told Selkor that this was certainly the only easy way up to the peak. It also told him that the path was unsuitable for his horse, but then what use would a god have for a horse anyway?

Just before the archway Selkor dismounted and gathered the few things that he wanted from his packs before turning the horse loose. Even this small delay caused the voices in his head to raise in protest and it took a lot of determination and discipline to follow through with what he knew to be a sensible set of actions.

Once released, the horse trotted off down the more gentle slopes of the mountain base and Selkor stepped forward and under the arch. Distracted as he was by the constant urgings of the voices in his mind to press onward towards the top of the mountain, Selkor received a double shock as he walked under the archway.

Firstly, the voices cut off as if instantly frozen and Selkor clapped his hands over his ears in surprise as for a moment the silence threatened to overwhelm him. Then, even as he was reeling from the abrupt quiet, two figures stepped out onto the path ahead, one emerging from each side of the narrow way.

Selkor stopped and took a moment to gather his composure. The two men ahead were each armed with swords and were now marching shoulder to shoulder towards him with deadly purpose glittering in their eyes.

'Who are you and why do you threaten me?' Selkor asked aloud, annoyed that he could not keep a note of sudden fear from his tone.

'We are the Guardians of the forgotten mountain,' they replied in unison. 'Who are you that seeks to tread the path to the Throne of the Gods?'

'I am "The Chosen One". It is my destiny to climb this mountain and meet with the gods,' Selkor stated boldly, his voice regaining its surety and composure.

The two men looked at one another for a moment and then looked back at Selkor with eyes cold as ice.

'You're lying,' they accused together, their voices so perfectly in time that they sounded as one. 'You do not wield all four Keys. You're an impostor. Set foot under the arch again and we will kill you.'

'With your swords, I suppose?' Selkor asked contemptuously, his self-confidence now back at full strength.

He did not even wait for an answer. Without a merciful thought in his mind, the Shandese Magician formulated a fire spell and directed it through Darkweaver's amulet at the two swordsmen. A torrent of white-hot fire leapt from the amulet in a great stream that should have killed the men in an instant, but to Selkor's astonishment the fire did not touch either of them. For a moment, the Shandese Magician thought they had managed to raise some sort of magical shield that protected them from his assault. On closer scrutiny, however, the truth of the matter was even more disconcerting. Incredible as it seemed, the raging blast of flames was simply melting to nothingness about two paces in front of them.

The icy stares bored into Selkor with a cold disdain as the two swordsmen marched forward in unison. Selkor backed away at the same pace that the two men advanced, maintaining what he judged to be a safe distance between them. As he retreated, Selkor kept up the fire for a few more seconds and then ended the spell with an irritated flick of his fingers as he pictured the final rune disappearing like a burst bubble. Neither of the men batted so much as an eyelid in response. It was obvious that magic, even powerful magic, held no fear for these Guardians.

The two men stopped and Selkor followed suit, studying the two warriors intently as he wracked his brain to try to decide what to do next. It was a real conundrum. The Guardians knew he did not hold all four Keys. How they knew was a mystery, but that hardly mattered. Somehow they knew. Also, they seemed impervious to magic, so Selkor decided to try a slightly different approach. Over the years Selkor had studied nearly all of the arcane arts to a greater or lesser degree. He had always had a flair for sorcery and so, as he could not blast them with fire, he decided to try to overpower their minds.

Drawing a deep breath, the Shandese Magician reached out with the full power of his mind with the intention of simply freezing them where they stood. To his further amazement though, his mind encountered nothing to overpower. It was as if the two warriors were illusions set to scare off the faint-hearted.

'Strange,' Selkor thought. 'Very strange. What manner of being is impervious to magic and appears to have no mind upon which to make an assault? Could they be demons in the guise of humans? Or some form of zombie maybe?'

One thing was certain to Selkor: whoever, or whatever, these two characters were they were not about to let him take a casual stroll up the mountainside, and that would not do. For a moment, Selkor was tempted to Key all three elements that he possessed knowledge of and to blast the two men into mush. 'No,' he chided himself silently. 'That should only be held as a final resort. I will need all my strength to open the gateway. There are plenty of other things that I can attempt before it comes to that.' And there were, though most required time and concentration, so Selkor sat down cross-legged on the ground a short distance in front of the arch and got to work.

The two warriors held their ground, silent and unmoving underneath the archway and seemingly uncaring as to what Selkor was up to. They appeared relaxed and confident, which in itself was unusual, Selkor reflected silently as he carefully prepared his next ploy. Soldiers were normally brought up with superstitions and indoctrinated with strange phobias about the supernatural. These two were different. Very different indeed, for not only did they not fear magic or Magicians, but they had some strange form of protection against them.

'Well, let's see if you've met an Enchanter before,' Selkor muttered to himself as he finished scratching strange symbols in the earth in front of him with a small stick. With that, he began to chant in a strange, low, melodic voice and the two soldiers both turned their heads slightly to listen more closely.

The chant was both tuneful and rhythmic as Selkor's baritone voice rose and fell, creating an almost hypnotic series of sounds. Like the gentle rolling of surf on a beach or the melody of a waterfall, Selkor's subtle song hid the suggestion of sleep within its elusive strains. It was a chant designed to change subtly at every stanza, drawing the listeners' ears to subconsciously search for the variations and thus suck them into the power of the enchantment. With a slight smile of satisfaction, Selkor noted that he was gaining a response. Both soldiers were listening intently within a few seconds of him starting. 'It will not be long,' he congratulated himself silently. 'Now I've got them. The hypnotic suggestion won't take long to work.'

He was wrong. In fact Selkor was not just wrong, he was *very* wrong. The men appeared to listen closely enough, but the suggestion that Selkor endeavoured to plant in their consciousness designed to make them put down their weapons and go to sleep, appeared to have no effect. After several minutes of trying the Shandese Magician gave up in disgust.

'Oh, don't stop,' said one of the warriors mockingly. 'I haven't had anyone serenade me for a *very* long time.'

Selkor looked at him with a mixture of dislike, disdain and distrust, and something began niggling at the back of his mind.

'Have we met before somewhere?' Selkor asked the soldier. 'You seem strangely familiar somehow.'

The two warriors looked at one another for a moment and the one that Selkor vaguely recognised gave a rueful grin.

'Ah, the price of fame,' the other soldier sighed, and then laughed gently.

'No, I don't believe that we have met before. I'm sure that I'd remember meeting a Magician who deigned to learn sorcery and the skills of an Enchanter. You must be fairly unique in that. Most Magicians that I've ever met before always seemed to feel that the other arts were beneath them somehow.'

Selkor grunted, unconvinced, and looked carefully for the first time at the two fighters. The strangely familiar-looking man was slightly shorter than the other one, and his hair was lighter in colour. Both were lean with not an ounce of fat evident on them anywhere, but the one really distinguishing feature of the man that Selkor found haunting a niggling corner of his mind, was his fancy-looking sword.

To Selkor, who had never had an interest in weapons, a sword was a sword. However, even he could see that the blade that this strange young fellow carried was special. The blade was almost like an elongated leaf shape rather than the straight blade of his compatriot, and it gleamed with a bright silver colour that set it apart from any sword that Selkor had ever seen before. The other man's sword looked positively dull in comparison. Was it the sword that he had seen before, he wondered? Surely he would have remembered seeing such an unusual weapon, he chided himself. Normally Selkor only had to begin thinking about something familiar and the answer would spring to the front of his mind as if catapulted. Having spent years training his mind and his memory until it became his greatest asset, Selkor found it intensely disturbing that the hint of familiarity did not want to resolve into a firm memory. Who were these two men?

'Whoever these men are, they are no ordinary Guardians,' Selkor thought grimly. 'It would not do to have come this far only to fail through being hasty here. Some study is required before I do anything else.'

So, despite his frustration at having come so close to his goal, Selkor settled himself to observe the two fighters, to comb his memory and to consider other possible ways past them.

*　　　*　　　*　　　*　　　*

'Enter!' Vallaine ordered imperiously at the sharp double knock on his study door.

The door swung open and the ever-dangerous assassin, Shalidar, herded three very harassed-looking individuals into the room.

'The traitors, your Imperial Majesty,' Shalidar announced smoothly.

'Ah, yes! Well done, Shalidar. Well done indeed,' Vallaine

congratulated, his eyes glittering with sadistic pleasure and his voice purring with satisfaction as he surveyed the dishevelled trio. 'Well, well – what are we going to do with such ungrateful and untrustworthy individuals?'

Almost without thinking, Vallaine rose and walked around his desk to the drinks cabinet. Silently he withdrew a glass and poured himself a glass of red wine. True, it was barely the tenth hour of the morning, but a moment like this was one to be savoured and Vallaine found that a glass of wine always helped to enhance the pleasure of an enjoyable event.

'Under normal circumstances I would ask you gentlemen to join me with a glass of something to ease across the palate. Unfortunately, these are anything but normal circumstances, are they, Governor Sammanis?'

The Governor said nothing, his head hanging forward limply on his shoulders and his eyes seemingly fixed on his feet. Vallaine paused a moment, giving Sammanis ample time to reply before moving on to target his next question at the next in line.

'Treason, Governor Daraffa, is a serious crime in Shandar, is it not?'

'That it is, your Majesty, but it is not I who has committed the crime against Shandar. You are the one who deserves to hang for the debacle in Thrandor. What sort of Emperor commits an army to a campaign without a military leader and at the advice of a Sorcerer? I'll tell you – a senile fool of an Emperor, that's who.'

'Ah, and a single error of judgement gives you the right to rabble-rouse in my capital city, does it? If you think that my unfortunate mistake is going to cost me my position as Emperor, Daraffa, then think again.'

Vallaine took a sip of his wine, pleased to see that at least one of his enemies had the gall to speak against him to his face. As his eyes slid along to Governor Maritsa, he realised that there was no such fire in him. Before he even addressed his supposed brother, the man was blubbering and begging for mercy.

'Mercy, Maritsa? You beg for mercy? That is strange coming from one who only yesterday was calling for my head on a pole. Don't even think to use blood as a lever, for you ceased to be my brother the moment you took to the streets in an effort to depose me. No, you deserve no mercy and you shall be shown none. You have all been leaders of treasonous rebellion against the legitimate Emperor of Shandar – me. As a result, you shall each face the consequences of your actions.'

Vallaine turned, walked back around his desk and sat down. Drawing another sip of the rich red wine into his mouth, he rolled it over his tongue, savouring the flavour even as he savoured the moment. His position as Emperor was secure. Even the real Emperor's own brother had not recognised Vallaine for the impostor that he was. Victory was sweet on the tongue, Vallaine mused, as he prepared to pronounce the inevitable sentence.

Even as Vallaine drew in the breath with which he intended to condemn the three Governors, there was another knock at the door and Vallaine sighed out the breath in frustration.

'Enter,' he ordered sharply, muttering 'This had better be good' under his breath as he waited to see who was disturbing him at such a moment. Whomever he had expected, it was certainly not the slim figure who stepped through the door.

'Your Imperial Majesty, I hope this isn't an inconvenient time, but I really need to speak to you about a matter of the *utmost* urgency,' Femke said, giving her most formal curtsy and lowering her head and eyes in respect.

All pleasure in the sentencing of the traitors drained out of Vallaine in an instant. Since he had been posing as the Emperor, Vallaine had not heard the tone that Femke now employed and he judged that whatever she had to say was going to be vital to his future.

'Of course, if it cannot wait,' Vallaine said, being careful not to name his spy. 'Shalidar, see that Sammanis and Daraffa are hung where their bodies will serve as a reminder of the price of treason to their followers. Have Maritsa publicly flogged and then parade him through the main streets.'

'Thank you, brother. Oh, thank you for your merciful sentence,' Maritsa blubbed, obviously overwhelmed that he was not to be hung with the others.

Vallaine paused for a moment, looking at his supposed brother with intense disdain and dislike.

'And when you've finished parading him, I want him beheaded. Let it not be said that I offer lenience on account of blood ties,' Vallaine added, his tone icy.

'Yes, your Imperial Majesty. It will be done,' Shalidar confirmed in a steady voice and he led the three Governors out of the study and closed the door behind them, Maritsa blubbing uncontrollably all the way.

Femke noticed that Shalidar gave her a very searching look from just outside the door, but she chose to ignore him and concentrate on Vallaine. What she was about to do was every bit as dangerous, and possibly as foolhardy, as the treasonous acts that had just seen the three Governors sentenced to death. If ever there had been a time when she had needed her wits about her, it was now.

The thud of the door closing, followed by the click of the latch, was a release to Vallaine's tongue.

'What are you doing back so soon?' he hissed, beckoning her to come closer to his desk and keeping his voice low. 'Surely you're not here to tell me that you've completed your mission already? You can hardly have reached the Thrandorian border and returned in the time you've been gone?'

'In that much, you're correct, your Majesty,' Femke answered with a nod, also keeping her voice low and conspiratorial. 'The border was as far as I got before events forced me to make a sudden about turn. Strange things are happening outside of Shandrim, your Majesty. Demons are abroad for one thing and it was perhaps a strange coincidence that my path followed theirs for some considerable distance towards Thrandor. That was not what caused me to turn back though. I returned to Shandrim because by pure luck I stumbled across Lord Shanier's trail heading in the opposite direction. The reason that I am here, your Majesty, is because I have good reason to believe that Lord Shanier has come to Shandrim.'

'Ah!' exclaimed Vallaine. 'Just as I thought! Go on, Femke. How did you pick up his trail?'

'Well, your Majesty, as I said, it was largely by chance. I had managed to find the occasional hint of the Thrandorian fighter and his companions heading out of the city to the South, so I followed what few leads I found and very quickly started to hear rumours of strange creatures also heading in the same direction.'

Femke was pleased to note the quietly satisfied expression on the Emperor's face when she mentioned the demons, and she decided that her suppositions that he had been involved in their summoning had been correct.

'The trails led straight towards the Thrandorian border and I travelled with all possible speed southward. I'm sure that I was gaining on the Thrandorians, but the demons seemed to be well ahead of me all the way and all I heard of them were whispered dread rumours everywhere I travelled. They obviously move very quickly and were arrowing towards Thrandor as if released from a bow.'

Femke paused for a moment and raised her eyes slightly as if casting her mind back to the journey. The young spy had experience of lies and deceit, both at spotting the traits in others and performing convincingly herself. With the knowledge that she had of Lord Vallaine, Femke had more than enough of an edge on the Sorcerer to be able to make herself convincing. Lord Vallaine knew that she suspected something was not right with the Emperor, but she in turn knew that he knew. It was the sort of confused and dangerous situation that made Femke feel alive inside. The thrill of the danger and the possibility that her duplicity could be discovered with one slip of the tongue made her heart pound with excitement and kept her mind alert and focused.

'Apparently, the demons often killed cattle and sheep, seemingly for the enjoyment of the kill rather than from any hunger driven need. I heard several tales of slaughter amongst livestock and one or two of horrific murders on remote farms, which were most likely demon work as well. Anyway, I was nearing the Thrandorian border and it was late in the evening. I was exhausted from several days of hard riding so I decided to stop at an Inn for a short night's rest. I fully intended to rise before dawn and set out into Thrandor at first light, but something I overheard in the taproom whilst I was negotiating for a room with the Innkeeper caused me to change my mind.'

'What? What did you hear?' Vallaine asked eagerly.

Femke had him on the hook now and she knew it. He had taken the bait and she had set the hook perfectly. All that remained now was for her to reel him in.

'Three men speaking in fairly low voices, talking about a very unusual stranger who had come through the village only a day or so before. In a big hurry they said. Anger in his eyes and carrying a wound on one arm that he was trying to conceal.'

'A stranger, you say? What makes you think that it was Shanier?'

'I was coming to that, your Majesty. It seems that two of the men had actually seen the stranger and they were describing him to the third man. One described him as young of face with fair hair and angry blue eyes. The other described his long black cloak and shining black boots, but there were some things they both mentioned – that the man was some sort of Magician for one, and that he was heading towards Shandrim for another.'

Femke's voice dropped into a deeper tone as she clearly imitated one of the men.

'I wouldn't like to be wearing the shoes of that young fellow's enemy,' she growled dramatically. 'Well, as you can imagine, your Majesty, I couldn't ignore what I'd heard. From the description, it was fairly clear that the stranger was Shanier. How they knew he wielded magical powers they didn't say, but they did seem very sure. I was suddenly faced with a difficult dilemma. Should I go on and follow the original trail to its end, following the Thrandorian fighter and his companions? Or should I follow this new trail and track the stranger, who appeared most likely to be Lord Shanier himself? As you can see, I chose the latter option and I did so for two reasons. The first was that it appeared likely, given that the stranger sported an injury, that he had recently confronted the Thrandorian fighter, or the demons, or both. Therefore it was likely that those trails were not going to take me much further. And secondly, if, as I suspect, this Sorcerer Lord is coming to confront you, your Majesty, I judged that it would be best if I did my utmost to return to Shandrim with all speed and warn you. I hope that you feel my decisions were soundly made, your Majesty.'

Vallaine's eyes glittered from the Emperor's face as he absorbed the story.

'Indeed, Femke. Your judgement was perfect, though I have reason to believe that Shanier got here before you.'

'I know, your Majesty. I rode with all speed, night and day, but somehow he managed to stay ahead of me. From what I could gather from the men at the Inn, Shanier had about a day and a half's lead on me to begin with. The knowledge of that was frustrating in the extreme, for it meant that we had probably passed close by each other sometime on the previous day without me being aware of him. I gained ground all the way here, but I couldn't catch him before he entered the city and I judge that he probably came into the city yesterday evening. I'm sorry, your Majesty, I came as fast as I could, but it was not quite fast enough to catch up with him.'

Vallaine nodded thoughtfully, his mind racing through the possibilities of what Shanier would do next. What had the young man wanted in his study last night? Had he found what he was looking for? These questions played on his mind, but underlying them was the worry that without the protection of his ring, he might not have the power to stave off an unexpected assault by the young Sorcerer. Shanier's mind did not possess the power of some of Vallaine's previous challengers, but now that Vallaine no longer had the ring to protect him, he knew that it was possible Shanier could succeed where many other more powerful Sorcerers had failed before.

'You did well, Femke. You did very well. What you have told me confirms my suspicions that Lord Shanier penetrated the Palace last night. What I do not know is the purpose behind his trespassing. I know that you must be very tired after your hard travelling, but I find that I must ask you for more help. I need to catch or kill Shanier quickly before he can do any more damage to the Empire. It's a tall order, I know, but I want you to start searching for him immediately.'

Femke nodded wearily.

'Of course, your Majesty, but might I make a suggestion?' she asked, with an air of reluctance and thoughtfulness.

'You may.'

'Well, I am but one spy, your Majesty. I am good, but I can't be everywhere at once. Why not bring General Surabar in on this? He has a huge number of men at his command who, with the right orders, could make moving around a positive liability to Shanier. Also, your top assassin, Shalidar, is extremely talented at dealing with this sort of... er... problem. Why don't we all get together in an hour or two and discuss a course of action? I feel sure that between the three of us we should be able to flush out and deal with this Sorcerer.'

'An excellent plan, Femke,' Vallaine agreed enthusiastically. 'Get to work at arranging a meeting at the earliest possible hour. I shall be here in my study for the next few hours, so you can send them straight here at – what do you think? The midday call? Then we'll organise things as quickly as we may.'

'Very well, your Majesty. I will go at once.'

Femke curtsied again, keeping her head down and being careful not to allow any of the jubilant feelings bubbling inside her from showing in her eyes or her body language. One small slip now and she knew that she would dangle on a gibbet before she could blink. Vallaine was not a man to cross lightly, but as she left the room, Femke was confident that everything was falling together nicely. Providing that she moved swiftly, the bogus Emperor should not have a chance to realise what was going on and his grasp of power and control would slip through his fingers like water.

Vallaine watched Femke leave the room, but his mind was locked on Shanier and oblivious to her machinations. As the door closed, so did Vallaine's eyes and he opened his mind so that his consciousness could sweep through the surrounding areas of the Palace in a powerful and penetrating pattern of force. If Shanier were there then he might take the opportunity to strike, Vallaine considered, a momentary pang of fear touching his cold heart. However, Shanier was unlikely to expect Vallaine to reach out at him with such power, Vallaine decided. The advantage of surprise would be with him now that he knew the young Sorcerer was out there.

'He will be confident that he is still unlooked for at the moment,' Vallaine said to himself silently. 'His confidence will be his downfall.'

Vallaine was disappointed when he discovered no immediate sign of his erstwhile protégé. A quick end to this would have been preferable under the circumstances, although Vallaine had always found cat and mouse games highly stimulating. As he allowed his consciousness to return to his body, the old Sorcerer found himself strangely elated that Shanier had not proved himself to be careless and cocksure. It would make the eventual victory far sweeter to know that Vallaine had outsmarted him in a deadly game of wits.

Relaxing back into his chair, Vallaine took another sip of his wine. If there were one thing that the Sorcerer Lord heartily approved of, it was the former Emperor's taste in wine. The vintages at his disposal really were exquisite and they did much to keep him from flying apart with the extreme stress of his current situation. Becoming Emperor had seemed such a good idea at the time. True, it had removed the immediate threat of assassination, or at least reduced it for a short while. However, the political situation had not calmed as he had anticipated and now he found himself with even more restricted options than he had enjoyed before.

'I could always just walk away,' he muttered to himself thoughtfully.

It was not the first time this thought had surfaced and it was certainly tempting. He could disguise himself in any form he chose and simply walk out of the Palace, never to be recognised again. The catch to this was that Vallaine's ego could not stand the idea of admitting defeat in such a major way. The Sorcerer Lord had never been one to run away when the going got tough. He normally managed to find some resourceful escape that kept his reputation and pride intact. The only exception to that had been when news had first filtered back from Thrandor about the duplicity of Shanier. The rest of the Sorcerer Lords had turned on him en masse and he had been fortunate indeed to escape from the High Council with his life. Indeed, without the protection of his ring, he would not have managed it. Now the ring was on the hand of a Thrandorian fighter who had no idea of the power enshrouded in the gold. What was more, the man that the Thrandorian had set off to kill was here and the fighter, apparently, was not.

Vallaine ground his teeth slightly in annoyance at the thought of having given his ring away unnecessarily. It had been a bad choice – one of several, apparently, for good news had been in short supply recently. The capture of the rebel leaders had been the first really positive thing to happen in some days, and even that had now been tarnished by the confirmation of Shanier's proximity. Still, Femke was good at what she did and she was right in what she had said – between Surabar, Shalidar and Femke, they would be able to deal with Shanier. At the very least they should flush him out into the open and then Vallaine would get his revenge.

At that thought, he sat back in his chair, placed his glass on the table and interlocked his fingers in an arch. A slow smile of satisfaction spread across his face and his eyes glinted with an almost demonic evil.

CHAPTER 15

Selkor was both frustrated and more than a little irritated. He had sat for the remainder of the day, all through the night and well into the morning of the next day, observing the two Guardians who blocked his path to the Throne of the Gods. In response, they had watched him and they had displayed neither impatience nor fatigue at the task. In that alone, the two soldiers showed themselves to be very atypical of their trade. In Selkor's experience, most guards were easily bored and distracted, but not these two. True, they did not just stand still and watch him for all that time, but there was no denying their constant vigilance.

The Shandese Magician stretched out his legs and climbed stiffly to his feet. He was tired from lack of sleep and the long period of concentration, but he had long ago found that with discipline he could stave off the effects of fatigue for several days if necessary. The instant that he moved, the two Guardians moved swiftly to stand side by side about ten paces in front of him, precisely placing themselves between Selkor and the path that he so wished to tread.

'Gentlemen,' Selkor announced, brushing dust from his leggings and stamping his feet slightly to restore normal circulation and loosen his leg muscles after his prolonged spell of sitting still. 'I would ask you to allow me passage to the Throne of the Gods, or I will be forced to start getting nasty,' he warned ominously.

'Where is your champion?' asked the taller of the two men

quietly. 'You may pass if you bring a champion who can best one of us. Choose your weapon.'

'Ah! I see,' Selkor breathed, understanding flooding in like light into a room where the shutters had just been thrown open. 'I have no champion with me, I'm afraid,' he added with more volume.

'Then you may not pass,' the man replied in a matter of fact tone.

'Ah, but just because I do not have a champion with me does not mean that I cannot summon one,' Selkor said casually. 'I don't really want to do this, but you leave me with little choice.'

Feeling around in several fastened pockets about his person, Selkor finally found what he was looking for. It was a small black bag of what looked to be a soft, velvet-like material fastened at the top with a golden coloured pull-cord. With an almost reverential care, the Shandese Magician opened the bag and reached inside to scoop a little of the contents into his hand. Then, with a precision that spoke of practice, Selkor walked in a perfect circle, allowing a tiny trickle of the dust-like substance that he had drawn from the bag to fall in a constant fine stream from his hand as he went. The dust glittered in the air as it fell and, strangely, the slight breeze that tugged and billowed under Selkor's cloak did not seem to touch the substance as it dropped slowly to the ground.

As Selkor completed his circle of steps, so the last of the dust fell from his hand to complete the glittering circle on the ground. The two soldiers looked at one another for a moment and Selkor could almost feel the link of understanding that seemed to flow between them. He was fairly certain that the two understood what he was about to do, but neither of them seemed in the slightest bit afraid. The idea that they were unconcerned about the prospect of facing a demon chilled Selkor to the core. Was he wasting his time? Were these two warriors impervious to any sort of assault? Grabbing a firm grip of his senses, the Shandese Magician clamped down hard on the feelings of doubt that surged within him. Doubt had no place in one's heart when summoning a demon. Holding any sort of uncertainty in one's heart whilst summoning a creature from the other world invariably ended in disaster for the one doing the summoning.

Selkor took a deep breath and with an ironclad will he began the summoning chant. In some ways it might have been safer for him to use the Keys and blast the two into nothingness. Selkor was reluctant to do this for fear of draining his own resources so far that he was unable to complete the task that he felt driven to achieve, but wizardry was always a risky business and Selkor had never been more than an indifferent study at this particular branch of the arcane arts. It was too late to worry about any of that now. The chant had been initiated and there was no backing out once the circle was complete and the first stanza had been uttered.

Not one to be totally reckless, Selkor had opted to summon a demon that he felt more than up to handling. He had settled on a medium sized Krill, as he felt that the shadow demon would be more than a match for two men, even trained fighters with swords. After all, demons of the Krill caste had skin that was virtually impervious to weapons of steel, and their razor sharp claws would rip through all but the toughest armour and these two fellows were not wearing any armour.

The strange rhyming chant of the Wizard's incantation was in some ways similar to that of an Enchanter, yet at the same time it was inherently different. Where an Enchanter used the pace, intonation and power of the verse to beguile the minds of his listeners, a Wizard rarely had listeners to worry about. Anyone with any sense would run a mile at the first hint of a Wizard beginning a summoning, even if they knew that the demon being called was not being directed specifically at them. Demons were not exactly known for their discernment when it came to killing, and as summoning them had an uncanny way of being highly unpredictable, a prudent person would not be found anywhere near a Wizard whilst he was practising his art.

The strange amorphous grey blob that heralded the imminent arrival of a demon started to form in the centre of the circle of sparkling dust that Selkor had drawn, and the two fighters glanced across at one another again. A bead of sweat trickled slowly down Selkor's forehead as he intensified his concentration even further. These were the crucial few moments on which everything hung and even the slightest falter now could prove fatal. When the demon appeared, Selkor knew that he had to remain the master of the beast, or die.

It was a mark of the man that when the heaving grey blob suddenly condensed into an angry, snarling demon with a gaze that would stun even the strongest will if its eyes were met, Selkor was instantly in control and the demon bowed its head at his mastery.

'Kill those two men for me,' Selkor commanded forcefully. 'Then return to your kindred. Your master has spoken.'

There was a slight flash as the circle around the demon vanished and the beast leapt at the two men with a mighty roar. However, neither of the men moved so much as a hair and Selkor's jaw dropped in astonishment at what happened next.

Both fighters stood their ground and simply watched as the vicious killing machine rocketed towards them. Then, just as the demon was about to rip into them, the beast vanished mid-roar. No chanting, no spell-casting, no magic of any kind was used that Selkor could determine, but one second the Krill was charging the two fighters and the next it had gone.

'Now you've gone *too* far,' Selkor yelled, incensed at this latest failure and not really thinking what he was saying. Without further thought, or even care for the consequences, the Shandese Magician pictured each Key in turn: first fire, then water and finally air, drawing at the vast expanses of power with a ravenous desire to be filled with a surfeit of magic and rid himself of these two troublesome soldiers in one fell blast of energy.

'Ah! You are "The Key"!' the taller of the two fighters exclaimed in surprise. 'Why didn't you tell us who you are?'

The two fighters bowed as one at Selkor and stepped aside in an obvious movement to allow him to pass. The Shandese Magician did not know whether to be jubilant at being allowed to pass, or furious at having the reason for his boiling anger removed before he had the chance to vent his fury on the two soldiers. For a moment, he considered blasting them anyway as his senses overflowed with the awesome power at his fingertips. With an iron surge of self-discipline, he quelled the desire to strike out, as he knew that he would simply be expending energy unnecessarily and he was now very suspicious of the nature of the Guardians. 'Besides, if those meddling Warders decided to follow, then they will also be faced with the conundrum of the two fighters,' he reasoned, as he gritted his teeth and let go of the raging power that threatened to overwhelm his senses. 'The puzzle posed by the fighters might just buy vital time.'

As the power of the elements left him, Selkor staggered at the sensation of great loss. Holding that amount of energy at his fingertips brought an emotional high that was simply beyond description and the act of letting it go left him feeling as if he were falling over the edge of an emotional cliff. Even activating the Keys had taken a huge amount out of him and Selkor knew straight away that he would need to rest a little if he were to be successful in his bid to open the gateway.

'The time for rest will be later,' he muttered to himself. 'For now, I need to get up to the summit.'

Completely ignoring the two fighters, Selkor moved forward and past them, his stumbling, irregular steps betraying his fatigue, but the determined set of his jaw and the fire in his eyes telling an equally vivid story. Moving under the archway of rock that the fighters had been guarding, Selkor knew that the final die of the game had been cast. There was no turning back now. Something in his mind niggled a tiny doubt into his heart as he contemplated the title of 'the Key' that the fighters had bestowed on him. He knew that he had read a text referring to 'the Key' at some point, but its significance eluded him. Then, as he emerged from the other side of the gateway, all constructive thought dissolved as the voices returned inside his head and drowned out any thought processes that he had begun to work through. Instead, Selkor concentrated on putting one foot in front of the other as he plodded his way up the steeply climbing path.

*   *   *   *   *

Femke had never actually met General Surabar and, though she was fairly sure that it had been him she had been tracking on the day of the strange incident up on the rooftops, the spy could not swear to having ever actually seen the man. All she knew of him was his reputation: a strong leader who led by example, intelligent, even-handed, cool under pressure... the list of his strengths was long and very impressive. Perhaps even more impressive was the fact that no one that Femke had spoken to had a bad word to say about the man. Most men who achieved the status and position that Surabar enjoyed made a few enemies along the way, but everyone seemed to have nothing but praise for the General. For once it appeared that Shalidar was actually backing a worthy cause. Making this man Emperor of Shandar would probably be both a popular choice and a good one, Femke mused silently.

Approaching the house where Surabar resided with his Commanders, Femke considered again what she was doing. A chain of events was now in motion that was extremely unstable. Each link in the chain was precariously weak and if a single one snapped, the outcome for Femke would not be pretty. There were still a couple of points at which the spy could potentially back out of her dangerous scheme, but at the moment her mind was firmly made up to follow it through to the end. Her initial goal was to expose Vallaine for his true self and have him removed from power. A secondary goal of installing a worthy successor as the next

Emperor had posed her with a difficult choice, but the case for backing General Surabar had been gradually gaining weight with every new and positive thing that she heard about him. Backing a man whom she had never met would be foolhardy though, so Femke certainly wanted to meet him before she finalised that goal. Whatever part she had to play in General Surabar's future, Femke was determined that she would demonstrate, both to him and to Shalidar, that she had been aware of their conspiracy for some time.

Femke knocked firmly on the front door of the General's house and waited on the doorstep feeling like an impudent schoolgirl knocking at the Headmaster's house to beg a candy treat. It seemed that Femke had hardly finished the motion of knocking when the door opened and a tall guard in full uniform, complete with sword and dagger, answered her knock.

'Yes? What can I do for you?' the guard asked, standing very straight as he eyed the young woman on the doorstep.

'The Emperor has sent me with a message for General Surabar,' Femke answered, both relieved and pleased that her voice sounded confident and convincing. Inside she felt as if she had a cloud of butterflies all trying to escape her stomach. It was not a pleasant sensation.

'And what is your message?' the guard prompted pointedly.

'My message is for the General,' Femke insisted firmly. 'May I come in and speak to him, please?'

The guard did not so much as hesitate.

'No, you may not,' he replied, his voice holding no promise of compromise. Femke decided that pushing the issue was not going to achieve anything, so she acquiesced.

'Very well. Could you see the General gets the message that the Emperor wants to see him at the midday call. The Emperor will await the General in his private study, which is in the heart of the Imperial Palace. I believe that the General knows his way there already, so I won't wait around to escort him unless he particularly wants me to.'

'Indeed? Did the Emperor disclose the nature of the

meeting at all?' the guard asked, his voice betraying his curiosity.

'Not to me, sir,' Femke replied in a shocked tone. 'I'm just a messenger, sir. Why would the Emperor confide such things in a lowly messenger girl?'

If the guard saw through her dissembling, he showed no sign of it. Instead, he thanked her politely for her message and promised that he would pass it directly on to the General. Femke bowed slightly and withdrew at an unhurried pace. 'So far, so good,' she thought to herself with a certain amount of glee. 'Now to trap Shalidar into the bargain.'

Finding the assassin, however, did not prove so easy. To her frustration, Femke found that she spent most of the rest of the morning leaving a trail of messages for Shalidar all around the Palace and at his more common haunts in the streets thereabouts. With about half an hour to the midday call, Femke gave up and made her own way back into the Palace to make her final preparations for the imminent meeting. There was actually no necessity for Shalidar to be there to enable Femke to follow through with her plan. The assassin's presence would have been a pleasant nicety, but so long as Femke liked what she saw of Surabar, then she intended to execute her plan anyway and Shalidar could find out in slow time. In some ways it would be even more satisfying for Shalidar to be behind on current events. He had been irritating in the extreme in his gloating over knowing more than she about what was going on in Shandrim. Now Femke was ready to turn the tables.

*   *   *   *   *

Calvyn looked around at his friends' faces and smiled. Whatever the next few hours had in store, he felt privileged to have gained the friendship of such a great bunch of people. Fesha and Eloise were still trying to get a rise out of Derra as they bantered her about the lesson in swordplay that Bek had given her the previous evening. Meanwhile, Bek managed to look embarrassed for the Sergeant, who in

271

turn was taking the merciless ribbing with reasonable grace. The occasional growl from Derra was hardly out of character, but for once she seemed to be keeping the bite out of her voice as she fell victim to one after another of Fesha's witty quips.

'He'll push it too far if he's not careful,' Calvyn remarked quietly to Jenna, who was riding tight alongside him.

Jenna laughed and her big brown eyes sparkled with amusement.

'He *always* pushes it too far,' she laughed. 'Fesha wouldn't be Fesha if he didn't.'

Calvyn smiled back and once again he marvelled at the love that was evident in Jenna's face. Love that filled his own heart welled in sympathy and he found his breath catching in his throat again as he considered how Jenna would fare if he did not survive his imminent confrontation with Selkor. If only he could just ride away with Jenna now, they could live out their lives together in happy obscurity somewhere. Unfortunately, Calvyn knew that he could not bring himself to do that. The burden of facing Selkor had fallen to him and he could not back away from the responsibility, much as he might like to. Too much hinged on the outcome of this meeting – possibly the fate of the entire world. Calvyn knew his duty and he was not about to shy away from it.

Perdimonn and the other Warders had all been acting very oddly for the last few days and to Calvyn's surprise, they had all watched Derra and Bek's practice session the previous evening with a great deal of interest. After Bek's conclusive victory, the four Warders had huddled together and entered into one of their secret little confabs. Whatever they were discussing quite obviously did not meet with the approval of all of the four as when they broke up from their tight little group, for not one of their faces was smiling.

Whilst Calvyn did not really consider Lomand and the remaining members of the Council of Magicians to be his close friends, they were his travelling companions and his teachers. As such, Calvyn felt strong ties to them, particularly after their concerted efforts to teach him as much useful magic as they could in a very short space of time. Considering that they were old men who were, at best, out of practice when it came to travelling, they had ridden remarkably swiftly over huge distances to get here. Regardless of what they thought of a young Acolyte going to face a Magician of Selkor's stature, power and experience, they had helped in every way they could to give him the very best chance of success.

Ahead of them loomed the mountain, atop which apparently sat the Throne of the Gods and, more ominously if Perdimonn was correct, the Shandese Magician, Selkor. Calvyn strained his eyes looking up at the peak, trying to see if he could make out anything that looked like a throne. There was certainly nothing visible that fitted that description.

The Warders had taken the lead today, with Perdimonn and Arred heading up the small file of riders. It appeared that Perdimonn knew exactly where he was going, but that did not surprise Calvyn at all, for Perdimonn seemed to have been just about everywhere at one time or another. That was one of the facets of the old Magician's character that Calvyn had always found appealing. Whilst they had travelled together after the death of Calvyn's parents, Perdimonn had always had stories to tell about virtually anywhere that Calvyn cared to name and many more besides. It was hardly a shock, therefore, to find that the old man had been here before.

The going was all uphill from that point on and, aside from Fesha who always had a quip or a ready remark on the tip of his tongue, the party fell largely silent as they began the long, laborious climb. Calvyn turned over again and again in his mind the little that he knew about Selkor, trying to fathom a potential weakness that he might exploit. The truth was that he actually knew very little about the man other than what he had seen of his manner and the power that he had displayed on the battlefield at Mantor. The more Calvyn contemplated that encounter though, the more he felt Selkor had in fact used sorcery rather than magic that day. The fact that Selkor had studied sorcery gave rise to the question of whether the Magician had studied any of the other arcane arts. Calvyn knew very little about the other arts aside from the fact that they existed. How he would counter anything outside his knowledge of sorcery and magic, Calvyn had no idea. His train of thought brought little comfort and only served to set his nerves on edge again.

Calvyn's recent progress in spell-casting had brought him a new level of confidence, particularly as he had demonstrated good control with both the Staff and Ring. If Selkor had only possessed Darkweaver's amulet, then Calvyn felt that he would have had a good chance of defeating him in a duel. Armed with three elemental Keys, however, Selkor still appeared unassailable. Calvyn was mulling over this depressing assessment and wondering whether Selkor might not expect Calvyn to have any real knowledge of sorcery. This could possibly be something he could use to his advantage when they approached the archway of the Guardians.

Perdimonn reined his horse to a stop a little way short of the curious rock feature and held up his hand to signal the rest of the party to follow suit.

'What is it, Perdimonn? Why are we stopping?' asked Akhdar irritably. 'Are we lost, or are we halting for yet *another* break?'

'We are halting for several reasons, Brother Akhdar,' Perdimonn explained, his tone both reasonable and patient. 'The first is that this is as far as you can go unless you have someone to champion you.'

'Champion me? What are you talking about?'

'You will see shortly,' Perdimonn said calmly. 'Everyone please dismount here. The path is not fit for horses from here onward and most of us will not be going any further anyway. Calvyn, you'd better come to the front with me. It would be safer to invite the Guardians out than to go into their archway.'

Nonplussed, Calvyn did as he was told, leaving Jenna holding Hakkaari's reins. He had no idea what Perdimonn was talking about, as he knew nothing of any Guardians. To Calvyn's knowledge, this was the first time that Perdimonn had mentioned it.

'Don't forget these,' Akhdar said, catching Calvyn's arm as he passed. The Grand Magician held out the Staff of Dantillus and the Ring of Nadus for him to take and Calvyn nodded at him with a thankful smile. 'And good luck.'

'Thanks,' Calvyn said gratefully and then moved forward to where the four Warders were waiting for him. As he joined them, Perdimonn turned and looked with an air of determination into the archway.

'Guardians of the holy mountain, come forth,' Perdimonn ordered in a loud, commanding voice. 'There is one here who would challenge to pass.'

Several of the party gasped as two men dressed in fighting garb and carrying swords appeared at the mouth of the archway and moved out towards where the Warders and Calvyn waited. The two strangers both looked fit and moved with an air of confidence that made it clear they were no amateurs when it came to fighting.

The sword in the hand of the shorter of the two fighters was very striking in both shape and colour. Calvyn had never seen its like before and was fascinated by it, but Bek recognised it immediately.

'Look!' he exclaimed in a loud whisper to Eloise. 'That's Silverblade!'

'Who?' she asked in a return whisper.

'Not "Who?" but "What?"' answered Bek, his voice sounding truly awestruck. 'That leaf-shaped silvery-looking blade that the fighter on the right is carrying must be Derkas Silverblade's sword. I can't imagine that there have been two such swords made. My understanding is that the blade is unique. It looks like it should be soft as gold with a finish like that, but legend has it that the blade is harder than diamonds. I wonder where he got if from.'

'Where did this Derkas die?' asked Eloise, her tone

curious. 'I'm sure that I've heard the name somewhere before, but I can't quite put my finger on it.'

'Can't put your finger on it!' Bek exclaimed, genuinely shocked. 'Did you never hear the stories of Derkas Silverblade? He was *the* warrior of his age and as for where he died, well no one seems to know for sure. Legend has it that he was blessed by the gods and given a task so great that it was beyond that of normal mortals. The only really certain thing from the stories is that he was never defeated and he disappeared at the height of his prowess. Many claimed to have killed him, but none could prove it and surely if someone had killed such a legendary swordsman, they would have kept his blade as a trophy, particularly as it was so unique. I wonder where this fellow got it from.'

'Who seeks to pass to the Throne of the Gods?' the taller of the two fighters asked, speaking directly to Perdimonn.

'I and my four companions here need to climb to the throne, Pallim,' Perdimonn replied. 'Has Selkor passed already?'

'You, we know, Perdimonn, and yes, the Key has passed. The secret you bear entitles you to passage, but these others we do not know. They must prove their right to passage by knowledge or test of arms.'

The man whom Perdimonn had named Pallim moved along the group and looked at each person in turn.

'Arred,' the Warder of Fire announced, and looking Pallim directly in the eye, he did something with his fingers that none but the two of them could see. Pallim's eyes widened slightly and he bowed in response.

'You may pass,' he announced, and then moved on to Rikath. A similar sequence of events followed with Rikath and Morrel, before Pallim came to Calvyn.

Calvyn looked the man straight in the eye and announced his name. He had no idea what it was that the Warders had done with their fingers, so he simply remained still, staring the man out.

'Strange,' Pallim said slowly. 'I feel something telling me that I should allow you to pass yet you do not have a sign.

No! I'm sorry, but I cannot allow you to pass. If you insist on proceeding then you must name your champion. You must prove your worthiness by trial of arms.'

'I don't need a...'

'I am his champion,' Bek interrupted. 'What is this trial of arms that you speak of?'

'No, Bek. I can look after myself. You don't need to get involved in this.'

'Oh, but I do,' Bek replied with a grin. 'If nothing else I'm curious to know where that fellow got Derkas Silverblade's sword from. Besides, I'm a superior fighter to you and you know it. I want to do this.'

'Name the trial of arms, sir. What is the challenge?' Bek asked Pallim again.

'The challenge is a fight to the death with either my companion, Derkas, or me,' Pallim answered seriously.

'Derkas? You mean he's assumed the name to go with the sword?' Bek asked incredulously. 'Well, that's tantamount to blasphemy in my book. Very well, I accept the challenge. I'll fight him,' Bek stated firmly.

'No, Bek! Don't do it. There's something very strange about these two fighters. I can feel it,' pleaded Calvyn, desperately concerned for his friend.

'It is too late,' Pallim announced. 'The challenge has been accepted. Your champion must now fight Derkas, or die.'

Calvyn had a really bad feeling about this fight, and whilst he knew Bek to be brilliant with a sword, he could not help but wonder what it was about these two fighters that gave him the creeps. Unable to stand the thought that Bek might die through lack of knowledge in this encounter, Calvyn leant towards Perdimonn and whispered his concerns to his old mentor.

'Who are these men, Perdimonn? There is something about them that doesn't seem quite... well, human somehow.'

'That is probably because they are *dem taqat*,' Perdimonn replied, also keeping his voice very low.

'*Dem taqat*? What does that mean?'

'It means almost literally "Warrior of the Age". They were both the most respected fighters of their time and, of course, undefeated in single combat,'

'Then that really is...'

'Derkas Silverblade? Yes, but...' Perdimonn put his finger to Calvyn's lips to prevent him from blurting it out loud. 'It'll do no good to your friend's concentration for him to be faced with that fact. Bek is extremely talented. Let's see just how good he really is, shall we?'

Calvyn could hardly believe his ears. For the first time since he had met Perdimonn, Calvyn was genuinely angry with the man that he considered to be his mentor. How could someone who claimed to be a pacifist let someone else unwittingly blunder into a fight with a legendary swordsman with the mentality of 'Let's just see how good he is'? It made no sense to Calvyn and he felt as if his blood were ready to boil with the heat that his anger was generating in his gut. In truth, Calvyn already felt guilty about Bek's time in the arena in Shandrim, so he was not about to stand by and see his friend killed due to a lack of awareness.

'Look out, Bek!' Calvyn called out, heedless of the stare that Perdimonn levelled at him for ignoring his suggestion. 'I don't know how it's possible, but that really *is* Derkas Silverblade.'

Bek was approaching the man with the strangely designed sword even as Calvyn's warning came, but there was not so much as a flinch in his progress as he drew his sword and gave an arena style salute to his opponent. If anything, Bek's eyes might have narrowed by just the tiniest of margins, but otherwise he gave no sign that he had even heard Calvyn's warning.

Derkas also said nothing, but he did return Bek's salute with a subtly different one of his own. Strangely, the florid gesture managed to convey an impression of the archaic, but then, with an unexpected suddenness, the two fighters crossed blades in a rapid exchange of strokes that sent an echoing ring of metal on metal resounding about the mountainside. There was certainly nothing archaic to find in the way that the two swordsmen tested each other's style and speed. The silvery blade that Derkas wielded glittered and flashed mesmerisingly, luring the watchers' eyes into following its every move. The only people seemingly unaffected by the blade's hypnotic appeal were the two combatants, who both seemed as if they were almost looking through each other, as they each studied the other for weaknesses of style or balance.

Suddenly they parted and began to circle slowly, each a study of concentration as they stalked step by careful step around one another.

'What will you do if Bek is killed?' Calvyn whispered to Perdimonn without taking his eyes off the two fighters. 'Do you intend to sacrifice my other friends as well?'

'*I'm* not about to sacrifice anyone,' Perdimonn replied softly. 'It was your friend's choice to meet this challenge.'

'But you knew about these Guardians and who they were before we got here, didn't you? What's more, you knew that my friends would champion me. You set this up. What will you do if Bek fails? If he can't win, then not even Derra at her best would stand much of a chance.'

Perdimonn sighed softly and glanced around quickly at the rest of the group. Everyone was captivated by the two circling fighters, but nevertheless, Perdimonn drew Calvyn slightly further aside before speaking again.'

'There is another way for you to pass, but I'm hoping to avoid using it, for in doing so we would compromise the greatest secret of this age. In a short while you'll probably understand what I mean, for you're the one person who's likely to learn of it one way or another. In the meantime, I suggest that we both pray for your friend to find inspiration with his blade.'

Perdimonn kept his voice very low so that there was no chance of anyone other than Calvyn hearing him speak, and even as he said the last word, Bek and Derkas sprang into action again. Calvyn's reply died on his lips as his jaw dropped in amazement at the speed and ferocity of the fight that followed.

Calvyn had not seen Bek fight in the arena, but Derra had been there for his encounter with Serrius. If anything, Derkas seemed marginally faster than Serrius had been, but somehow Bek was finding speed to match him. Of course, Derra had not been anywhere near as close to Bek's fight with Serrius as she was to this one, so it might be the proximity of the combatants now that made the deadly duel seem more furiously intense and blindingly fast, she reasoned silently. Nevertheless, Bek was holding his own in an exchange of blows that was faster than anything that Derra could ever recall seeing before. Even as the Sergeant watched, heart in throat like everyone else, she felt her respect for the young Corporal's sword skills grow even more profound.

Bek and Derkas disengaged again and Derra noted that the strange Guardian held respect in his eyes that matched her own for Bek's skills. Unexpectedly, he spoke for the first time and his voice was almost warm and friendly.

'You make a worthy opponent, Bek,' he said, his intonation making him sound almost grateful. 'I must ask, though, why do you carry a second blade if you do not use it?'

Bek's eyebrows shot up in surprise as if the answer were obvious.

'Well, it would hardly be a fair contest for me to use two blades against your one,' he replied with a slight smile.'

'Who said the contest had to be fair?' Derkas laughed. 'Still, I thank you for the sentiment. If it makes you feel better, Pallim, lend me your sword, would you?'

'Be my guest,' Pallim said, drawing his blade and tossing it over to Derkas, who caught it neatly.

'Better?' Derkas asked.

'Much, thanks,' Bek replied and drew his second blade.

Calvyn had been impressed by Bek's exercise programme with two swords, but the first few seconds of the fight that followed made Calvyn realise just how good Bek really was. Bek's words flashed back to mind about the premonition that he had felt about needing his skills again and a tingle ran down Calvyn's spine. It appeared the fate that Bek had spoken of had just stepped through the stone archway to meet him. Was there some higher being or force controlling events, driving all of them along predetermined paths to meet their destinies, he wondered? For some reason the thought brought little comfort.

The clashing of steel and the incredibly agile dance of the two fighters spinning and whirling, slashing and blocking, filled Calvyn's senses to overflowing. He was watching and mentally urging his friend to victory, but at the same time a terrible feeling of wrongness and inclement evil started to wash over him. The evil was nothing to do with the fight or the fighters, but with something dreadful that was happening nearby. Suddenly, although the fight was still important, Calvyn sensed that it was very peripheral to another far more personal struggle.

'Selkor,' he breathed.

'You feel it too?' asked Perdimonn, his voice worried. 'Time has run out. Selkor is beginning to open a gateway and I'm not even sure that it's possible to stop him now. Whatever we do when we get past the Guardians, it must be done quickly. Be prepared to climb the path to the summit swiftly, for it is you who will have to tackle Selkor initially until we four Warders can catch up and help in whatever way we can.'

Calvyn's eyes locked back on the two combatants still battling with unbelievable skill and grace.

'Come on, Bek. Finish him,' he urged through gritted teeth.

But it was Bek that took the first cut, a line of red opening across his shoulder and Derkas pressed forward with a devastating combination of strokes that fell so thick and fast that it seemed impossible that anyone could defend against it. Amazingly, Bek survived the assault with only the addition of one minor cut. Then in an apparently impossible reversal, Bek counter-attacked. Wondrous flashing patterns played in the air and the song of steel was a constant ringing across the base of the mountainside, as Bek forced Derkas back. Calvyn and the others could restrain themselves no more and they all began shouting encouragement, urging him to victory.

With a sudden cry from Derkas, the two fighters sprang apart and the warrior looked down at a shallow horizontal cut that ran almost the full width of his chest. It was not a mortal wound by any stretch of the imagination, but with a flourish the legendary warrior saluted Bek with both blades and plunged them both point down into the ground.

'It appears that it is my time,' he stated, sounding slightly surprised and somehow almost grateful. 'Well fought, young Bek, you are an excellent fighter. Nice to see you again, Perdimonn.'

For those watching what happened next was extremely strange, for Derkas appeared to fade away slowly before their eyes. Even as he faded, the swordsman turned one last time to Pallim.

'Goodbye, old friend. It's been fun...'

He was gone – dematerialised into thin air before their eyes. Before anyone else could say anything, Pallim turned to Calvyn and bowed.

'Your champion has won you passage. You may proceed,' he stated simply.

CHAPTER 16

Two guards were standing in the corridor outside the Emperor's study as Femke approached it this time, and whatever they had been briefed to be on the lookout for had certainly made them alert. No sooner had Femke rounded the corner than one of the guards called out to her in a firm voice.

'Halt! State your business in this part of the Palace.'

Femke was surprised, but not overly so.

'I am here to meet with the Emperor, General Surabar and Shalidar,' she replied confidently. 'The meeting time was set for the midday call and that is almost upon us. Now, may I proceed?'

The two guards glanced at each other for a brief moment and there was an exchange of nods.

'Very well, you may approach,' one of the guards said almost reluctantly.

Femke walked boldly forward and raised her hand to knock on the study door, when the same guard cleared his throat in a way that was clearly meant to attract her attention again.

'Er, excuse me, Miss, but I need to check you for weapons before you enter,' he said apologetically.

'Check me for weapons?' Femke asked, genuinely surprised this time. 'And pray what sort of weapons would you be looking for? I've been accused of having a smile to break a man's heart, and a body to die for, but aside from that I'm unarmed.'

The guards both smiled, but the one who had told her of the need for the check was clearly not ready to just take her word for it. Femke sighed and, turning towards him, she raised her arms to allow him to frisk her for weapons. The spy had bluffed her way through weapons checks before and she was fairly certain that this guard would be no more thorough in his search than any of the others that she had faced in the past. Sure enough, the guard went through the motions of feeling down the sides of her body and checking the tops of her boots for hidden knives, then he thanked her for her co-operation and allowed her to knock on the door. Consequently, he had no inkling that Femke had in fact got two concealed throwing knives about her person. One was strapped to the inside of her right forearm beneath the loose sleeve of her shirt and the other was hanging on a concealed necklace style holster between her breasts. Femke had no intention of using them, but she always felt that carrying them gave her more options should things start going wrong.

The Emperor's voice called her to enter and Femke opened the door to obey. As she did so, the guards accosted someone else and Femke glanced around in time to catch her first glimpse of General Surabar before she walked into the study. Somehow she had expected the General to be a bit taller than he was. The perspective from the rooftops on the day she had tried to follow him had left her with the distinct impression of a taller man, but the General was of medium height at best. Everything else that she took in from that glance though was as she had imagined: the strong facial features, straight back, proud tilt to the head – everything was as it should be. An archetypal high-ranking soldier, she decided.

'Ah, Femke, punctual as ever,' the Emperor's voice praised as she entered his study. 'I trust that you were successful?'

'Well, your Imperial Majesty, I did my best,' Femke replied, dipping in a properly respectful curtsy as she entered. 'General Surabar is just outside with the guards, but I failed to locate Shalidar. He can be quite elusive at times. I have left numerous messages for him and I can only hope that he receives one of them sooner, rather than later.'

'Ah, well,' Vallaine said, nodding his head understandingly. 'It cannot be helped. If I have to brief Shalidar separately later, then so be it. At least we can mobilise the General's forces into action now. That will certainly hamper Shanier's ability to move around too freely.'

'My thoughts exactly, your Majesty,' Femke agreed enthusiastically. Then she coughed and put a hand to her throat. 'My apologies, your Majesty, my throat is very dry. Might I be so bold as to beg a drink?'

'Of course, Femke. Help yourself. There are glasses aplenty in the cabinet over there. You do drink wine, I trust?'

'A glass of wine would be wonderful, your Majesty. Thank you,' she replied and began to move towards the wine cabinet. Then she stopped and turned back to face the man she knew to be Vallaine. 'My apologies for my manners, your Imperial Majesty. Would you like a top up whilst I'm pouring?'

Vallaine looked down at his half empty glass and smiled with genuine pleasure.

'Why not? That's an excellent idea, Femke. Talking is certainly dry work.'

Femke approached the Emperor's desk and took the half empty glass from his outstretched hand. Her timing was perfect, for at that precise moment the General knocked on the door and in the second that Vallaine's attention was diverted from her to the doorway, and before the General had a chance to enter, Femke made her most dangerous move.

As she turned away from Vallaine with the glass in her right hand, Femke passed her left hand over the top of it, whilst using her left thumbnail to trigger a tiny mechanism in a ring on the middle finger of the same hand. The gemstone on the ring hinged aside and a tiny drop of clear liquid dripped cleanly into the Emperor's glass.

As the General entered the room, Femke looked across at him and gave him a genuine welcoming smile. The General gave a curt nod of acknowledgement, but there was no real warmth in his manner. That might change in a few minutes, Femke reflected as she reached the cabinet and began to pour the wine.

Whilst pouring wine into both the Emperor's glass and her own, Femke was careful not to put her hands anywhere near the top of Lord Vallaine's glass. Femke could feel the Sorcerer's eyes following her every move at the cabinet. When she picked up the glasses by their delicate stems to walk back to the Emperor's desk, Femke noticed a slight tension drop out of the Sorcerer Lord's shoulders. There was no way for him to know that the very thing that he had watched her so paranoidly for had already occurred long before Femke had even reached the cabinet.

Femke passed the full glass across to Vallaine and lifted her own in a thankful salute before taking a sip. Vallaine placed his own glass under his nose for a moment and took a second to savour the aroma, but Femke had no qualms about him smelling her little additive, for it was odourless and tasteless.

'Would you care to join us, General?' Vallaine asked him, knowing full well what his response would be.'

'No, thank you, your Imperial Majesty. I try to abstain during the daylight hours.'

'Very good, Surabar, very good. Now then, I'm sure that you're probably wondering why I've summoned you today, but before I move on to that, I should really introduce you to Femke. Have you met the General before, Femke?'

'No, your Majesty. I've never had the pleasure.'

'Well, in that case... Femke, meet General Surabar. General, this is Femke, a truly remarkable young woman who is most talented in the field of espionage.'

'A spy?' the General observed quizzically, as he shook her hand in greeting.

'The best, General, as you will come to see before this meeting is over,' Femke replied with a cheeky smile.

'Really?' he asked, the right side of his mouth twitching up in just the faintest of hints at a smile. 'I do like to see youngsters with self-confidence. Sadly, it is all too often misplaced.'

'Well, in this case, General, the young lady has good reason to be self-assured,' Vallaine interjected. 'Femke has demonstrated her abilities at getting tough jobs done time and again for me and it is because of her latest discovery that I've called you here today. Lord Shanier, the Sorcerer who betrayed the Legions in Thrandor, has come to Shandrim.'

Vallaine paused to let the fact sink in and he took a deep sip of his wine. Mentally, Femke began counting. The substance she had used was potent and its effects would not take long to manifest themselves.

'I've called you here, General, to see if you have any ideas on how we could track him down. I would dearly love to see him swing from a gibbet next to those other three traitors that I sent out to die this morning. Have you got any ideas?'

The General scratched thoughtfully at his chin, and whilst he did so Vallaine took another sip of his wine.

'A Sorcerer, you say?' the General stated more than asked. 'So I take it that he is a master of illusion and disguise. He could be anywhere in the city and could appear pretty much as he wished. Hmmm...'

The General tapped his finger against his lips for a moment or two, carefully considering the situation before committing himself to anything.

'Tell me, young Femke – you, as a spy, will be familiar with the concept of blending into the background. If you were Shanier, how would you disguise yourself?'

'That's easy, General. With all the troops in the city at the moment, I would surely pose as a soldier,' Femke replied quickly.

'Hmm, as I thought,' Surabar said softly. 'I can certainly make it more difficult for an impostor, your Majesty. I'll instigate a whole series of challenge and response codes that will change at every call. The Commanders will issue the codes and I'll have checkpoints set up throughout the city. The codes do not need to be difficult, but they do need to change at frequent enough intervals to trap anyone not actually living in the barrack tents into making mistakes. Anyone who fails to correctly respond to the challenge code will be detained and...'

General Surabar broke off as his eyes raised to meet the Emperor's. The man in front of him no longer looked anything like the Emperor and Surabar was momentarily thrown.

'Go on, General. Your ideas make a lot of sense. This is just the sort of containment plan that I had hoped you might come up with,' Vallaine prompted, his eyes glittering in his wizened face. The Sorcerer was still completely unaware that his own deception had been unmasked.

Femke turned to the General and managed to catch his eye with her movement.

'Sorcerers are tricky fellows, General,' she said with a slight smile. 'Catching them off guard is quite a trick to pull off, but I think that we are making progress today, don't you?'

The General was fairly well speechless, but Femke was now confident that the poison in Vallaine's system had enough of a grip on him that his mind would be powerless to strike, so she pushed ahead.

'You see, the Palace here in Shandrim has always been a hotbed of deceit and trickery, but never more so than the last couple of months. I have always prided myself in knowing exactly what was what, but even I have struggled to pull together all the threads in the recent tangle of events. Now I think that I can pretty much tie them all together.'

'What are you talking about, Femke? Is there something that you have held back from your reports?' Vallaine demanded hotly, still unaware that his illusion was no longer in place.

'Oh no, *Lord Vallaine*, not at all.'

'Lord Vallaine? What are you insinuating, young woman?'

'I am insinuating nothing, sir. I am merely stating what is now obvious for anyone who cares to look,' Femke replied, raising her hand and pointing at him. 'You have been unmasked and I would simply like to introduce you to your successor before you pass away.'

'What the...?' Vallaine spluttered, looking down at his clothing and hands and discovering that his illusion had indeed disappeared.

'You were right to mistrust me with the wine, Vallaine. Unfortunately, you were looking at the wrong time.'

'What have you done to me?' Vallaine asked, his hands beginning to shake as he tried to get to his feet.

'I've poisoned you, Lord Vallaine. Why? What did you think I had done? I am no Sorcerer, so I was forced to fall back on what I know best. Finding a substance that would render a Sorcerer powerless quickly and yet give me enough time to ask that Sorcerer a few questions before he died was both difficult and very expensive. Fortunately, you had given me a large amount of gold from the treasury to complete my latest mission, so money was really no object and it's amazing what you can buy when you have enough gold.'

'You foolish girl!' Vallaine spluttered, his wrists and arms beginning to shake as well. 'Give me the antidote right now. Don't you realise what you're doing to Shandar?'

'Oh yes, Lord Vallaine. I understand perfectly what I'm doing. I am doing exactly what you did – killing the Emperor in order to make way for someone far more suited to the task. At least, that's the way I see it. You see, I know about your conspiracy with Shalidar and how, when the last Emperor sent out his assassins to kill you, you somehow managed to turn the tables such that it was he who died and you who replaced him. I also know about Barrathos summoning those demons that you sent after Lord Shanier. What you probably don't know is that Shalidar did not just sell out the last Emperor – he sold you out as well. This time, however, I find myself pleasantly surprised at his employer. For once, it seems that Shalidar might actually be doing the Empire a favour.'

'Who?' Vallaine croaked, his whole body now twitching and his sunken eyes glittering with frustrated malice.

'Why, General Surabar, who else?' Femke said casually.

'What!' exclaimed Vallaine and Surabar in unison.

'Oh, come now, General. Surely you are not going to deny it? I saw Shalidar enter a house that you then exited some hours later and on another occasion I followed him to your quarters. What other explanation would you offer?' Femke asked casually.

The General still looked genuinely shocked and was opening his mouth to reply when he suddenly clutched his hands to his head and cried out in pain. For an instant, Femke wondered what had happened to make the General screw his face up into such an expression of agony – then she found out.

With a cry of her own, Femke dropped to her knees and clamped her hands over her scalp as hard as she could. A searing pain lanced through her skull as if someone had driven a long steel pin into her forehead and out through the back of her head. Even as she landed on her knees, the spy looked up at the Emperor's desk to see Vallaine leaning forward on his shaking forearms with the most intense expression of concentration, hatred and pure evil that she had ever seen. The sight struck fear into her heart. Somehow, Vallaine still had some control over his sorcerous powers and unless she did something quickly then it was likely that the next person to enter the study would find not one, but three dead bodies.

Through gritted teeth Lord Vallaine, now shaking like a leaf, defied everything that Femke knew about the effects of the poison that she had given him to drink.

'You… will… not… live… to… celebrate… my… ruin,' he gasped and the pain level inched up to an even more excruciating level.

'Yes… I… will,' moaned Femke with equal determination, and with a flick of her wrist a knife appeared in her right hand. Another flick and the knife sliced through the air and struck Vallaine with a sickening thud.

The throw was not a good one really, as it only struck Vallaine's shoulder and the wound it inflicted was far from fatal, but it had the desired effect. Lord Vallaine fell back with a crash from the desk, attempting in vain to clutch at the new source of pain with his violently shaking hands, his concentration totally broken. The juddering thuds of the Sorcerer's limbs thrashing in violent convulsions behind the desk were still in full flow when the door to the study burst open and the two guards, followed closely by Shalidar, crowded into the room.

'Seize that man!' Surabar ordered in tones that few would question. His finger pointed squarely at Shalidar. 'He's to be held on charges of treason.'

The guards paused, momentarily confused, for the order was about the last thing that they expected. Unfortunately the slight pause was enough for Shalidar. He had assessed the scene in an instant and realised that whatever happened now, it was unlikely to be good for his immediate future. There was a flash of hands as Shalidar landed blows that felled both of the guards before they had a chance to move and he flung a dagger at Surabar so fast that even Femke, who had seen good assassins at work before, did not see the blade leave his hand. To Femke's complete astonishment, Surabar somehow swayed out of the path of the blade. Although the spy's instinct to draw and throw her remaining knife was fast, the ever-slippery assassin was faster. The throw that Femke made this time was much more positive than the one she had aimed at Vallaine, but Shalidar was so quick that the blade somehow slid past him, missing by a hair's breadth, and thudding harmlessly into the doorframe.

He was gone.

Vallaine's thrashing ceased and one of the two guards moaned softly on the floor by the door. The other guard was out cold and showed no signs that he would stir anytime soon. Femke turned her head and raised her eyes to meet the stare of General Surabar, which she could feel was fixed on her.

'Here, young lady, let me give you a hand,' offered the General.

Femke flinched slightly from his offered hand, for whilst his words were kind enough, the General's tone was hard as granite and his eyes held anger, together with many questions. Still, it was far too late to back away now. Events had progressed at a far faster pace than she had reckoned on and it was abundantly clear that she had misjudged the General's relationship with Shalidar.

Taking the General's hand, Femke pulled herself up to her feet and braced herself for the onslaught of Surabar's anger. To her surprise, it did not come. The General maintained an iron control over his temper and when he asked his first question, it was with a calm voice at odds with his flashing eyes.

'Well, Femke, for one so young, you certainly have an uncanny knack for finding trouble on a grand scale. Tell me, how is it that you managed to uncover such a devious and subtle conspiracy?'

'Natural skill, mixed with a bit of luck, I guess... your Imperial Majesty,' Femke shrugged with a cheeky grin, deliberately throwing in the title to bait a response.

'You can drop the "Imperial Majesty" bit right now,' stated Surabar firmly. 'If my guess is correct, Shalidar was conspiring with one of my Commanders. I've already got a good idea which one it was. I have no desire to take on the Imperial Mantle. I'm a soldier, not a politician.'

'Sir, with all due respect, you're an icon. You are just what Shandar needs right now. I apologise for the slur on your character by associating you with Shalidar. I must admit that I was surprised at my own deductions, because they didn't fit with the profile of you that I'd built before finding the apparent link to the assassin. If you take on the Emperor's Mantle now, the people will gladly follow your lead.'

'That's all very well, but I'm not of noble birth and as I just said, I have no desire for the power,' Surabar stated, his voice flat and very matter of fact.

'To be honest, sir, I don't think that you're going to have a lot of choice. Vallaine disposed of his nearest political rivals in typical brutal style this morning. Who else is there that you would back to be the next Emperor? I think that you'll find good candidates very thin on the ground. Unless, of course, the Commander that Shalidar was conspiring with would make a strong Emperor,' Femke suggested, watching carefully to see how Surabar reacted.

To her surprise, he gave a short bark of laughter.

'Ha! If my suspicion is correct, we will find the conspirator is a Commander called Vammus. Believe me, he is a Commander in name only. His father bought him the position in the hope that it might make a man of him. In my book, the father would have been better to let him serve in the ranks. As it is, Vammus is a bumbling fool who gets others to do all his dirty work for him. It would certainly fit his nature to hire an assassin, and I wouldn't be surprised to find that his target was not the Emperor, but me.'

'Well, sir, we won't be able to keep rumour of what has happened here quiet for long. I, for one, would be pleased to see you installed as the new Emperor. If you were to decide to take on the Mantle, even on a temporary basis, until someone that you feel is more suitable arrives, then I can have word of your rise to power buzzing in the streets before nightfall. The city has been in a state of widespread unrest for some time now. I'm sure that the people would rejoice to hear that you were their new leader – even if it was only to be on a temporary basis.'

The General's brow furrowed as he considered Femke's appraisal of the situation and he tapped his finger gently against his lips. Saying nothing, he turned, walked over to the Emperor's desk and looked down at the body of Lord Vallaine whose staring eyes, even in death, seemed to carry a glint that spoke of evil. Surabar sighed heavily.

'Reluctant though I am to admit it, Femke, you are right. The Empire has suffered greatly under the influence of

Vallaine recently. I can at least put a stop to some of the corruption and prepare the way for a more suitable Emperor. Very well, I'll take the mantle of Emperor, but I want word spread that I am only acting as Regent until a more suitable candidate presents himself.'

'Your Imperial Majesty,' Femke said, curtsying deeply and bowing her head. 'Might I suggest that you would be much better not actually announcing that fact to the world, or you will be inundated with Noblemen, major and minor alike, all claiming to be suitable candidates for the Mantle. Why don't you simply take the title and then bestow it on the most suitable candidate in your own time. If no one knows that this is your intention, you will be much more likely to see them as they really are.'

'Very good, Femke! Your logic is sound. You know, there are more than a few Commanders that I've worked with who could do with a dose of your powers of reasoning. So be it. Go and spread the word that Emperor Surabar is now in control and things are going to change.'

'Yes, your Majesty. With pleasure.'

*   *   *   *   *

'Quickly, Calvyn! Through the archway,' Perdimonn urged, almost dragging him forward past Pallim. 'There's no time for a full explanation now, but there is one thing that you must know before you push on to the top of the mountain. Let's get to the other side of the arch first, because this is for your ears only.'

The Warders all strode under the archway at a fast walk and Calvyn gave a quick farewell wave to his friends and grasped Bek's hand in a warm handshake. Before he could follow the Warders, Jenna ran up to Calvyn and caught him in a tight hug.

'If you think that I'm going to let you go up that mountain without at least giving me a farewell kiss, then you're sadly mistaken,' Jenna breathed into his ear.

Calvyn flushed bright red as he kissed Jenna, and his friends smiled at his discomfort.

'Make sure you come back in one piece, Calvyn. I didn't trek halfway around the world for you to get yourself killed by Selkor,' she whispered before squeezing him one last time and then giving him a gentle shove in the direction of the Warders.

'I'll do my best, Jenna,' Calvyn replied in an intimate tone, still red-faced with embarrassment at her public display of affection. 'Don't worry – Perdimonn and the other Warders will keep me out of trouble.'

With a last smile at his friends, Calvyn turned and ran up under the archway after the Warders with words of good luck ringing in his ears, as those left behind shouted out their support.

Just at the other side of the rock archway, the Warders stopped and Calvyn joined them, breathing heavily.

'I'll take the Staff for you,' Perdimonn offered, holding out his hand. 'You won't be needing it.'

'What do you mean I won't be needing it, Perdimonn? Am I going to face Selkor, or not?'

'Yes, you'll be facing Selkor, but you won't be using the Staff against him. Think back to the tapestry, Calvyn. What were you holding in the picture?'

'Well, it looked like my sword,' Calvyn replied slowly, but surely you're not going to suggest that I face him with that alone. The Staff of Dantillus was made by a Grand Magician. My sword is a toy in comparison. Selkor said as much when he looked at it after the battle of Mantor.'

'That's irrelevant,' Perdimonn stated calmly. 'Even if I allow you to take the Staff, it would not be in your hand when you faced him. You would lose it, or Selkor would destroy it. Either way, the Staff would not be involved significantly in your conflict. You have the Ring and your sword. Between them, they will be enough.'

'But the tapestry has been changing so much. How can you say with any certainty that the picture doesn't show me holding the Staff now?'

'It's quite simple, Calvyn – I'm not going to allow you to take it and therefore the tapestry will show you holding your sword. My fellow Warders and I effectively blocked Selkor from ever being able to get the fourth Key a few weeks ago. The problem was that when we realised what Selkor was attempting to do, we also realised that there was little that we could do to stop him. You are the only one who can do that. Whether you realise it or not, you have the abilities and the resources to do it. Don't write off your sword too quickly. It is a much more potent weapon than you might think and Selkor really doesn't have anything in his arsenal to match it. Trust in yourself, Calvyn. We'll catch up and help you just as quickly as we can, but none of us are as fit as you are, so you'll have to keep Selkor from opening the gateway until we arrive.'

Calvyn did not know what to say.

'I'll do my best, Perdimonn, but what if he uses the Keys?'

'Then you'll rise to the challenge,' said Perdimonn with a smile. 'You have to. We wouldn't send you if we didn't think that you had a chance of success. Go. There's no time to waste. Whatever Selkor's doing is ripping the very fabric of this world in a way that will cause huge repercussions regardless of whether the gateway opens properly, or not. Be careful, Calvyn. Waste no time, but do be careful and trust your instincts. The gods must not be allowed to get through that gateway he's constructing.'

Calvyn did not need telling again and he had no words to express his fear of failure to the Warders, so without any further delay, he turned up the narrow pathway and started out at a run up the mountainside.

'Remember, it's your destiny to meet Selkor today. It was woven into the tapestry. Someone is guiding you along this path, Calvyn. Don't give up hope,' Perdimonn called up after him.

Despite his recent running practice and being quite fit naturally, Calvyn found that he could not run for very long up the steep incline. However, the feeling of extremely powerful magic thrumming in the air and an overwhelming sense of impending terror and doom spurred him to push the limits of his strength and endurance. Every time he

was forced to slow to a walk, the very air around him was so
alive with the atmosphere of magic that he broke back into
a run within seconds and he drove his body upwards with
strength that he never knew he possessed.

Doubts hounded him with every step. It was true that he
could now direct spells with a certain amount of skill and
accuracy through the Ring of Nadus, but even with the
added punch to his magic, Selkor had more than enough
power to counter anything Calvyn could hurl at him.
'Someone is guiding you,' Perdimonn had called, but
guiding him for what purpose? The words seemed to mock
him the more he thought about them. Guiding him to his
doom most likely, Calvyn thought morbidly, but even bound
as he was by fear and doubts he continued to doggedly
force his legs to propel his body up the viciously steep path
as fast as he could.

The pathway wound around the mountainside like a
snake coiled around a rock. Most of the time it was narrow
but perfectly safe. In one or two places, however, the path
became more like a ledge and the footing seemed less like a
path and more like a test designed to turn back any who
were not truly serious about reaching the summit. 'As if the
Guardians were not enough,' Calvyn thought grimly, as he
edged along the latest narrow and crumbling section with
his back firmly against the mountainside and his eyes
trying not to focus beyond where he was going to step to
next. Bits of stone crumbled and showered down the
mountainside as a badly placed footstep resulted in a small
section of the ledge breaking away. Then he was past the
tight section and he forced himself to run up the wider
section that followed.

Some time later the path ahead began to step upwards in
a broad, natural-looking stairway and Calvyn looked up to
try to see the mountain's summit. He had no idea how far
there was to go, and did not really want to guess, but magic
pulsed in the air with an urgent beat and he felt certain that
it could not be much further to the top. As a precautionary
measure Calvyn drew his sword and, holding it ahead of

him, he proceeded to try to spring up the steps. He had barely climbed a dozen or so of the broad steps before his tired legs lost their spring, and from then on it became a case of forcing first one leg and then the other to step up onto the next shelf of rock.

The stair-like climb seemed to go on forever, and after a short while Calvyn put his sword away again and he used his hands to push down on his knees to help his exhausted leg muscles push his body up to each new level of rock. By the time that he did reach the summit, he was so physically tired and unaware of anything other than the next step that he was almost at the throne before he realised Selkor was just ahead.

It was fortunate for Calvyn that Selkor was equally focused, or Calvyn would probably have been blasted out of existence before he had a chance to recover from the amazing sight of the carved mountaintop. The Shandese Magician was standing in front of the massive throne and completely lost in the thrall of his magic. It was no wonder that this place was called the Throne of the Gods, Calvyn marvelled, as he took in the size of the great stone seat. It would have taken a small army of stonecutters a considerable time to carve the giant of a chair. The entire throne was worked with clever carvings, and the arms, carved in the shape of a pair of leaping panthers, were worthy of masterpiece status on their own. It took a moment for his eyes to take in what he was seeing, but after a second or two of wonder at the sight of the virtually modelled mountaintop, Calvyn's attention was drawn to the Shandese Magician and the spell that he was casting.

There, in front of the throne, Selkor was standing with his hands outstretched in front of him and energy was pouring from his palms in a flood. The streams of magic appeared to be collecting in a sort of a ball of fire just a few feet in front of him. Shimmering with every colour that Calvyn could imagine, a combined flow of force was flowing from the fireball into what Calvyn could only think of as a sort of whirlpool in the air some yards away.

Calvyn had no idea what Selkor was doing, so how could he stop him? There was so much energy being committed into that vortex that if he were to break the flow of power there was no telling what might happen. For all Calvyn could tell, the result of interrupting a spell of this magnitude might be as devastating as the disaster that rendered the Terachim a desert.

For a moment, Calvyn simply stared at the vortex and the power flow, feeling lost and helpless. Why had it become his responsibility to stop Selkor? He was not even a fully trained Magician and yet here he was, alone and facing an adversary who had spent years in the pursuit of power and the study of magic. What should he do? Should he just aim a spell through the Ring of Nadus at the combined flow of power and blast power through it to try to interrupt it somehow? If he did, would he then be seen as the perpetrator of any disaster that might ensue? He could always just go and run Selkor through with his sword, but then, with the spell incomplete, who was to say what might happen to that vortex? For all Calvyn knew it might just continue to grow until it engulfed the entire world. Without any knowledge of the nature of the swirling, sucking hole of nothingness, could Calvyn ever hope to control it? Of course, the Warders were on their way up the mountain and they would probably have more of an idea of such a thing than Calvyn, but there were still no guarantees.

What should he do?

By hesitating, Calvyn lost his chance for action. With a final pulse of blinding energy, the fireball ejected a massive dose of magical force into the vortex and then the ball itself was sucked in as well.

Taking a deep shuddering breath, Selkor's shoulders slumped slightly with fatigue. Then, with a start, he became aware of Calvyn watching him and the Shandese Magician's lips curled slightly into a malicious smile.

CHAPTER 17

'So, Perdimonn has sent his cub to try to do his work for him,' Selkor said, his voice full of disdain. 'He seems to have been delegating a lot recently. And I see you brought your sword with you. That's good, because I was meaning to come and find you so that we could have another chat about your little lightning rod. It seems that I do have a use for it after all, so if you'll just hand it over, then you can be on your way and I'll not harm you. Ah, excellent! I see that you've brought the Ring of Nadus. I was most perturbed when that went missing, but as you've kindly brought it back to me, then I'll have that back as well.'

Calvyn started to raise a mind block as he felt Selkor's wave of sorcerous mind power sweep over him. To his surprise, it proved unnecessary. The ring that Bek had given him completely negated Selkor's attempts at mental control and the metal of the ring turned cold on his finger. Calvyn allowed himself to smile as he felt the Shandese Magician's mental fingers of power slip over the surface of his mind like a duck sliding around on a frozen lake. In a slow, deliberate motion, Calvyn drew his sword and prepared his shield spell, pleased to be able to focus all his attention on the problem of countering Selkor's inevitable barrage of magic.

'This *cub* has grown one or two more teeth since we last met, Selkor,' Calvyn replied, surprised by the calm that he managed to convey in his voice. In reality he felt anything but calm, and the threat that panic might overwhelm him seemed to linger like a dark cloud in the background. The aching in his legs and the throbbing of his feet after the rapid climb up the long mountain path were an added distraction, as they gave a constant nagging reminder of his fatigue. Calvyn had always excelled at mental control exercises though, so blocking out the pain was one thing at least that was achievable. 'Now, might I suggest that you undo whatever mischief you have just done here. Allowing the gods to return to this world is really not a good idea. Reverse your gateway spell now, or I'll be forced to do it for you,' he added with as much authority as he could muster in his voice.

To reinforce his attempt to turn Selkor from his path, Calvyn reached out to Selkor's mind to try to sway the Shandese Magician's will to his own. However, where Calvyn had excelled at certain disciplines of Sorcery, straight mind power had never been one of his strengths and Selkor's mental barrier held.

'Ha, ha, ha! Reverse the spell?' Selkor laughed through gritted teeth as he held off Calvyn's mental assault. 'Reverse my ticket to eternal life and power beyond your imagination? You're a very funny young man. The spell is not reversible, apprentice. In just a few minutes, the vortex that I've created will bore its way through the barrier between dimensions and the gods will be able to step from their present existence into ours. Then life will become very different. Think of it: the gods will bring a return to the proper hierarchy, where Magicians are revered for their abilities rather than shunned. Kings will defer to us, the wielders of real power, and those of us who are strongest will rule the world at the right hand of the gods themselves.'

If the Shandese Magician was surprised at not being able to control Calvyn as he had at Mantor, or surprised at the young man's laudable attempt at controlling him, then he hid it well, but his laughter had little humour in it and he was clearly perturbed that he could not penetrate Calvyn's mind to gain a hold over it. It was obvious that if he wanted to take the Ring and Calvyn's sword, then he would have more of a job to get them than he had anticipated.

'As you can see, Selkor, I've progressed a little from the raw apprentice that you last met. Now I am an Acolyte, but I suspect you'll find that my training has been a little more comprehensive than that of most Acolytes of my years and experience.'

'An Acolyte,' Selkor spat derisively. 'So those doddering old fools from the Academy have got their claws into you as well, have they? Well, don't expect anything that they've taught you to be of much use. At least Perdimonn has some originality about him. Those fusty old idiots at Terilla are so blind to what magic is all about that they're completely hog-tied by their dogmas and traditions. You'd be lucky to find an original thought amongst the lot of them. Did they, for example, teach you how to cope with something like this?'

Calvyn did not hesitate. He released his shield spell through the Ring of Nadus. A fraction of a second later a fireball impacted the surface of it right in front of his face. Calvyn flinched automatically and closed his eyes against the flare from the collision. There was a sizzling, crackling noise as the energies met, but Calvyn felt nothing of the heat generated. A second or two later, when Calvyn opened his eyes, he took a calming breath and prepared himself for the onslaught that he knew would follow.

'Apparently they did,' Calvyn replied, raising his eyebrows slightly and trying once more to keep his voice calm.

This time Selkor was more than a little surprised. The Shandese Magician had put a lot of energy into the spell and it was certainly far more than any normal Acolyte would be able to handle. To see the fireball burn out harmlessly on Calvyn's rapidly erected shield of magical energy just tipped Selkor's temper over the edge and so, in a rapid sequence, he fired a series of high powered bolts of energy. Every one of them fizzed and crackled harmlessly against Calvyn's shield, and this time Calvyn managed to refrain from flinching. By the time Selkor had finished unleashing his anger, Calvyn could feel the heat of the final impacts and he realised with some trepidation that a few more blasts and the shield would fail.

'I should have known that Akhdar wouldn't have allowed you to wield the Ring of Nadus without some training,' Selkor muttered grudgingly. 'It won't avail you though. I can literally unlock the power of the elements themselves to throw at you if necessary. I would like to think that you've enough sense not to let it come to that. If I unleash that sort of power, I'll not only destroy you, but I also doubt that the Ring or your sword will survive either.'

'Selkor, it is *you* that should think again. You can't seriously think that the gods will allow you to rule anything once they've come through that gateway of yours? I might not have the sort of power that you've managed to accumulate, but I'm not ready to give up my world in a foolish bid for immortality. I'll spend my last breath attempting to stop you if I must, but that gateway must close before it's too late.'

'You! Stop me? You've been listening to those old fools too much.'

'Perhaps you're right, Selkor, but I've come too far to turn away from my responsibility now. No one else is here to stop you. There *is* only me, so I guess that we'll both have to come to terms with the idea. Close the gateway, Selkor. This is your final warning. If you don't, then I'll be forced to go on the offensive and I'm very sure that you won't want to be on the receiving end of some of the other spells that I've learned.'

Calvyn was amazed that his voice sounded so calm and authoritative. For a brief moment, he thought that he might even be getting through to the Shandese Magician, but the moment was short-lived.

'NO!' Selkor shouted, his eyes hardening. 'Are you a complete fool? Don't you understand anything? I'm moments away from immortality. I've not come this far to be denied my prize by an upstart. If you want the gateway to close, then you're going to have to close it yourself, *Acolyte*, and I'm not about to just stand by and watch you try. Come, do your best if you will, but you haven't even begun to see what I'm capable of yet.'

With an arrogant gesture of defiance, Selkor raised his hands and keyed one after another of the elements. Clouds began to boil up above the mountaintop in great black towers that seemed to blossom in a matter of seconds to a vast height, and the wind that had been little more than a breeze suddenly picked up to a swirling gale that whistled and howled through the rocks. A flash of lightning rent the sky between two of the great storm clouds and a crash of thunder followed a split second later. Rain, the like of which Calvyn had never seen before, descended in a deluge and within a few seconds Calvyn was drenched to the skin and freezing cold.

'Where are Perdimonn and the other Warders?' Calvyn wondered, looking up at the heaving mass of brutal looking clouds with a growing sense of trepidation. 'How am I supposed to cope with something like this? A single strike from one of those monsters and I'll be roasted like a chestnut.'

Even as his thoughts teetered on the edge of despair, Calvyn's determination welled within him. Narrowing his eyes against the flood of rain that was teaming down on the mountaintop, Calvyn formed the weather shield spell that Akhdar had used during their journey to Mantor and released it through the Ring. Instantly, a tight bubble of magical energy enveloped Calvyn once more.

Selkor was standing in his own bubble not far away and a maelstrom of wild, unnatural weather blasted the mountaintop with its fury. The Shandese Magician pointed a finger at Calvyn and a bolt of lightning struck Calvyn's bubble shield with a blast that should have fried him to a crisp. The shaft of superheated energy clasped and crackled against the bubble. Calvyn could physically feel the bubble weaken and knew that at any second the shield would fail. Surprisingly, it held. Selkor was astounded, and Calvyn was also more than a little amazed. Selkor pointed again and Calvyn knew that the shield would never hold against another such blast, so he sprinted across the mountaintop towards potential cover. The lightning struck and Calvyn's bubble of energy burst instantly. The lightning struck the rock behind Calvyn's feet and he felt the exploding shrapnel of shattered rock strike him in several places up the back of his legs and across his back.

The next blast struck in front of him and Calvyn was thrown back off his feet, the burning white flash of energy momentarily blinding him. Selkor was laughing insanely and Calvyn realised that the Shandese Magician was now just toying with him. With a twisting gesture of his hands, Selkor lifted his arms skyward and a huge spinning tornado whirled from the bottom of the nearest great storm cloud and began to tear at the mountaintop with its ferociously powerful winds. Calvyn could not think, his eyes were still struggling to recover from the flash of the lightning bolt, and before he knew it the base of the tornado was on him and he was sucked into the swirling throat of the whirling tube of force.

Lifted from his feet and spinning upwards in a maelstrom of gigantic proportions, Calvyn could just make out the mountaintop falling away beneath him. The pain in his ears from the huge drop in pressure was agony, and for a moment Calvyn's heart told him that this was the end, but at the same time a deeper, more primal survival instinct caused him to formulate a simple wild spell of desperation. Stabbing his sword back at the earth, Calvyn released his spell through the blade and a line of force from the tip of the blade shot down and hit the mountaintop, clinging to it with a limpet's stubbornness.

Hanging on with a grip like death, Calvyn seemed to spin even faster, attached as he was by the magical grappling rope to the ground, but somehow he managed to grab the handle with his other hand as he spun like a stone being whirled in a sling. The whirlwind sucked him upwards with dreadful force and the howling wind that whipped Calvyn round and round as he hung, inverted in the tornado, ripped at his clothing and threatened to drive all thought from his mind. Even as it did so, an image of Jenna facing down the Gorvath in order to save him formed clearly in his mind and feelings of love and responsibility filled him with renewed determination. Forming a new set of runes in his mind, Calvyn began to cause the safety line of magical energy to slowly contract, drawing him inch-by-inch back down towards the mountaintop.

Calvyn emerged from the side of the snarling tornado about twenty feet above the ground and with the sudden loss of dragging force holding him in the air, he fell headfirst to the ground. There was no time for any magic to soften the landing and although Calvyn managed to roll as he hit the ground, the hard impact produced a fresh wave of pain through his body.

Rising slowly to his feet, Calvyn's eyes smouldered with a fierce determination and anger as he faced Selkor once more. Still holding his sword in a tight two-handed grip, Calvyn swung the blade as if making a defiant gesture at the tornado that was still roaring nearby. Calvyn cast the spell that he would normally use to lift objects into the air and drove it through his sword at the tornado. The results were stunningly spectacular as the swirling tunnel turned in on itself and the sudden opposing winds ripped the tornado to shreds within a couple of seconds.

Thoughts of using the Ring of Nadus were gone and Calvyn advanced on Selkor, wielding the sword like the weapon it was. Selkor pointed at Calvyn and another huge bolt of lightning struck down from the cloud. Calvyn did not even think. He simply batted the bolt aside with his sword as if he were swatting a ball with a bat. Another bolt followed and another, and Calvyn dealt with each in the same fashion.

It took a few seconds for Calvyn to register that he was actually still alive and had not been fried on the spot, let alone the fact that he was not even feeling any heat from the gigantic blasts. Somehow, his sword was more than coping with the ravening gouts of energy that Selkor was directing at him. Something very strange was going on here. When Calvyn had faced Demarr and his sword had come into direct conflict with Darkweaver's amulet, the sword had heated up to the point that the handle had physically burned Calvyn's hands. Afterwards, Selkor had described the blade as a magical lightning rod and Calvyn had believed him.

During the encounter with Demarr, Calvyn had never thought to direct any spells through the blade. The sword had somehow drawn the magical fire from the amulet to its tip and absorbed it. This time was very different. The magical fire that Selkor was flinging around was of a whole new magnitude. It was being flung with the full force that the elements of nature had to offer. Calvyn was now using the sword more in the fashion of the Staff of Dantillus or the Ring of Nadus, yet he had never worked any amplifying spells into the blade, so how was he dealing with Selkor's monstrous strikes so easily?

A darting thought flashed through Calvyn's mind as he suddenly realised why Perdimonn had been so keen to relieve him of the Staff of Dantillus and make him use his sword. First, there had been the strange spell that had come unbidden to him when he had woven the original spells into the blade. More recently though, there was the strange experience of the dreamtime spells that he had apparently cast on the blade that had made the three silver runes change and disappear. The more that Calvyn thought about it the more he suspected that Perdimonn's claims of ignorance were all a sham. The old man had known exactly what was going on. Although Calvyn could not remember how the runes had changed before they had disappeared, he was willing to bet that Perdimonn and the other Warders would know all too well what the runes looked like.

What was it that 'The Oracles of Drehboor' had said? Something like 'The Chosen One will wield all four Keys.' That had to be it. Calvyn *was* wielding all four Keys. They were in his blade. It was the only explanation. Selkor could throw anything he liked at him, but providing Calvyn directed his spells through the blade of his sword, then whichever elements were required for the spell would activate automatically and the full force of that element would be employed.

'I am "The Chosen One",' Calvyn laughed aloud. Then he repeated it as a loud shout for Selkor to hear. 'I am "The Chosen One", Selkor, do you hear me? I am "The Chosen One"! Back down now, or face the consequences.'

For a split second, Calvyn saw fear register in Selkor's eyes as the full implications of the shouted statement sank in, but the Shandese Magician was far too committed to his course of action to be turned aside now.

'Enough is enough, Selkor,' Calvyn yelled, knowing that his cry would more than likely be ignored.

Calvyn had no intentions of allowing Selkor the chance to hurl anything else at him. The strange vortex that Selkor had set in motion before Calvyn had reached the mountaintop seemed to be growing by the second. Unless Calvyn did something about it soon, then Selkor might yet win the day. The gateway that was swirling into existence would have to close, but Calvyn somehow had to deal with Selkor at the same time. Even though the Masters had taught him some offensive style spells, Calvyn did not really feel comfortable when casting any of them. The spells that were still foremost in his mind were the healing spells from the grimoire that Perdimonn had given him and it suddenly occurred to Calvyn that he might just be able to adapt one of them to this occasion.

In a flurry of movement, Calvyn sprinted across the mountaintop to a position that put Selkor between Calvyn and the vortex. The Shandese Magician was surprised by the sudden move and from his hands he fired a couple of lightning bolts, which Calvyn deflected again with his sword. Realising the power available in his blade, Calvyn re-cast his shield spell and watched with satisfaction as the following bolts of energy fizzed harmlessly against the adamantine wall of energy produced by the sword.

Selkor was not ready to give up though, and suddenly

changing tack completely, he directed a series of spells through Darkweaver's amulet. To Calvyn's horror, they cut through his shield like a hot knife through butter. Each of the spells diverted to impact on the tip of Calvyn's sword at the last second and the blade bucked and kicked in Calvyn's hands with each impact.   Apparently, Darkweaver's amulet used magical power that was of a different sort entirely to that of the Keys.

Within seconds, the pommel of Calvyn's sword began to heat up in his hands just as it had when he had faced Demarr, and he knew that his sudden inspiration of a plan to finish this would have to be executed quickly, or it would be too late. Setting his jaw with defiance, Calvyn mentally built the picture of what he wanted to achieve and then set to work with the runes. All the while, the sword seemed to writhe in his grip like a snake, constantly twisting and turning in his hands with the impacts of incoming bolts of flaming energy. Also, it continued to get hotter in his hands until the agony of holding the roasting hot handle was excruciatingly painful. It was with huge relief that Calvyn released the final spell through his sword.

A wall of energy leapt up in front of Selkor. Initially it seemed to bend around him until the ends of the wall were parallel to the entrance of the swirling vortex. Then, it was as if the wall contracted, drawing Selkor back as it flattened back into a straight wall. The Shandese Magician suddenly found himself being forced backwards step by step towards the opening gateway behind him. He had no time to create a counter-spell and before he knew it, he was at the threshold of the vortex.

'I didn't want to have to do this, Selkor, but you left me no choice. You want to sit at the right hand of the gods – be my guest. Give them my regards.' Calvyn called out, as the Shandese Magician suddenly realised what was happening.

'No! You fool! The gateway isn't fully open yet. Stop. Don't do it! Pleeeease...'

Selkor launched a final withering blast of energy through the amulet that literally blasted Calvyn's sword out of his hands and, for the briefest of instants, the figure in black seemed to hang in the maw of the vortex before being drawn into the spinning vacuum.

Calvyn fell to his knees and heaved a huge sigh of relief. Selkor was gone. It was difficult to believe, but against all the odds he had defeated the Shandese Magician. The only problem was that unless he finished the job and closed the gateway, Selkor might well step back through the gateway with an army of gods right behind him at any moment.

Battered, bruised and hurting in just about every part of his body, Calvyn retrieved his sword. The handle of his sword further singed the flesh of his hands as he picked it up, but he knew that he could not close the gateway without using the power locked in the blade. With an iron discipline, he blocked all pain from his thoughts and mentally pictured the gateway as a wound in the body of this world and then proceeded to launch healing spell after healing spell at it, driving each of them through the blade of his sword. To his dismay, nothing seemed to be working. The comparison between damage to a human body and the damage to the fabric of time and space appeared to be just too contrived for the spells to have any effect.

In sheer desperation, Calvyn got back on his feet and gripped the handle of his sword as hard as he could. Narrowing his eyes, he mentally imagined the clear air at the edge of the vortex as unblemished skin. Firing a stream of runes into the sword, he stabbed it into the clear air next to the vortex like a needle dipping into the edge of a wound. With all his strength, Calvyn then tried to draw the blade in towards the centre of the spinning hole in the air. Even hanging on the sword that was somehow embedded into, what appeared to be, thin air did not seem to have any effect and Calvyn was about to withdraw the blade and try to think of something else when a shaft of glowing orange energy struck the vortex to his left. Another shaft of sea-green energy struck it an instant later and Calvyn became aware of a third and fourth striking it to the other side of him.

'Don't stop now, Calvyn,' shouted the familiar voice of Perdimonn. 'Try again.'

It took every ounce of Calvyn's strength to pull the edge of the vortex down, but with a loud groan of effort he pulled with his entire weight against the blade and the round shape of the spinning gateway gradually began to change shape. Slowly but surely, Calvyn managed to drag the edge to what had been the focal point of the gateway. Then he repeated the process and heaved the bottom of the vortex up to meet it. With a final sequence of runes, Calvyn drew the tip of his sword along the resulting line in the air, joining the two edges together as he would a simple cut. Even as he did so, the streams of force from the Warders focused at his sword tip and the line in the air disappeared as if it had never existed.

As the last few inches of the vortex were sealed, the rain slowed, first to a more normal showery sprinkle, then stopped altogether as the storm clouds began to disperse. The wind dropped back to a cool breeze and all signs of lightning and thunder vanished. Calvyn staggered over to the huge stonework of the Throne of the Gods and sat down heavily on a great block of stone that could only be described as the footrest.

'Well done, Calvyn. You never cease to amaze me, you know,' Perdimonn said, with a tone that held both pride and admiration.

Calvyn had not expected to see the Warders for some time yet. The whole conflict with Selkor had lasted no more than a few minutes and Calvyn would have expected the Warders to struggle for some time on the long winding path up the mountain.

'Why didn't you tell me, Perdimonn?' Calvyn asked wearily.

'Tell you what, Calvyn?' the old man replied casually.

'That I was "The Chosen One".'

'He knows,' Morrell muttered softly, his voice concerned.

'Of course he knows,' Rikath chided him with a soft laugh. 'If he didn't, he wouldn't have survived.'

'You realise that you must never reveal that fact to anyone?' Perdimonn asked seriously.

'I sort of guessed that secrecy might come into this somehow,' Calvyn sighed with a nod. 'Of course, I understand that the Keys are very important and must be kept secret. It will be quite easy really, because I don't actually know any of the Keys anyway. It was a guess based on the results of a spell guided through my sword that led me to understand what you had all done, but weren't you taking something of a risk by not telling me?'

'Life is all about taking risks, Calvyn, but our oath of secrecy kept us from revealing the Keys to anyone and much as I would have liked to tell you, I was bound by my oath.'

'But you wouldn't have been revealing the Keys, because I still wouldn't have known what they were.'

'I know, but my fellow Warders and I discussed it and the consensus was that we would be breaking our oath by telling you. Here, don't worry about it any more. Let me have a look at you. You've done quite enough magic for one day.'

Calvyn was more than glad to let Perdimonn heal his wounds and, tired as he was, the walk back down the mountainside took a lot longer than the original climb. By the time that they emerged from the archway at the bottom of the path, it was late in the afternoon and Derra had got a very organised looking campsite set up no more than twenty yards or so outside the stone arch. The Grand Magicians were keeping watch from various strategic points in case Selkor came through the archway, while the rest of the party loitered with weapons to hand. When she saw him, Jenna virtually flew into Calvyn's arms and squeezed him tight against her as she buried her cheek in his shoulder.

'It's over,' he said simply, stroking her hair gently with his freshly healed hands.

Seconds later everyone crowded around, either shaking Calvyn's hand or patting him on the back. Questions bubbled at him from all directions. Initially, he found it impossible to respond to any of them, as he could not sift through them fast enough to formulate any reasonable answers. Calvyn was prepared with a fabricated story of how he defeated Selkor, but he knew that it would be difficult not to spill out the revelation that he was 'The Chosen One'. He did not really want to lie to his friends and he felt sure that the Grand Magicians would see straight through the untruths that he was going to tell them, but Perdimonn and the other Warders had made him swear an oath that he would maintain the secret at all costs. In some ways, Calvyn felt that this confrontation might actually be more difficult to cope with than the battle on the mountain.

In the event, the story that he spun about having surprised Selkor and tipped him through the gate that he was in the process of forming had enough elements of the truth in it to hold up to all the questions that followed. Calvyn made out that the storms on the mountaintop had been a by-product of the Warders collaborating to force the gate closed after he had pushed Selkor into it. The Grand Magicians seemed content with his explanation, as the fact that an Acolyte had defeated such a powerful enemy by luck, fitted perfectly with their perceived natural order of things. Master Jabal had looked very thoughtful after Calvyn told his story, but if he suspected anything, he did not voice his suspicion aloud. He did say though, that he was looking forward to finishing Calvyn's education at a more proper pace. Akhdar and Kalmar echoed his sentiment, which in Calvyn's mind meant that from now on he would undoubtedly have to put up with the tortuously slow progression to his robes that all of the other Acolytes endured.

'Still,' he reasoned silently with a wry smile. 'Why should I get any special treatment? It's not as if I just saved the world or anything!'

Perdimonn and the other Warders all corroborated Calvyn's story and throughout the afternoon and into the evening there was a general air of jubilation around the campsite. The only person who seemed slightly out of the general celebratory mood was Bek, but when Calvyn asked him about it, he refused to be drawn. The reason for his subdued demeanour only became apparent the following morning when the party prepared to break camp and start the journey back to Mantor.

'Come on, Corporal, saddle up! What's up with you this morning?' Derra barked, clearly irritated that it was one of her soldiers who was causing a delay.

'He's not coming with us,' Perdimonn said quickly, not giving Bek a chance to reply.

'Not coming? What are you talking about? Of course he's coming. Get on your horse, Bek, and don't take all day about it.'

'He's not coming with us,' Perdimonn repeated. 'Bek has no choice in the matter. By defeating Derkas in the duel yesterday, Bek has become one of the Guardians. He must remain, Sergeant. There's no force in this world that can drag him from this place, so you might as well leave him be.'

Bek's head hung low on his shoulders, and he pursed his lips and shrugged helplessly at the Sergeant. Derra's eyes softened slightly and Calvyn and the others from Baron Keevan's army all climbed down from their horses and went over to Bek, not quite yet believing that they were going to have to leave without him.

'How long have you known?' Eloise asked, her voice barely more than a subdued whisper.

'From the moment that Derkas faded away,' Bek replied. 'I felt something in me change at that moment and I spoke with Pallim about it last night and confirmed my suspicion. Somehow I knew from the moment that I defeated Derkas that it was my destiny to remain here. I'm really sorry that I'm not coming with you, but don't worry about me. I found out last night that Pallim has been here even longer than Derkas and he claims that he's never been bored. He says that he's a better swordsman than Derkas was and he's promised to teach me how to improve my swordplay even more.'

'This is a pretty drastic way of escaping your instructor duties, Corporal. I know that having to teach us fumbling idiots how to use a sword was painful for you, but doing guard duty for evermore is a rather extreme alternative,' Fesha joked. But his voice held no conviction in the humour that he was trying to bring.

Bek smiled weakly in response and patted Fesha on the shoulder in thanks for the effort to lighten the moment.

'I'm going to miss you all terribly, but as Perdimonn said, I have no choice. I must stay. Still, it's not as if you won't know where I am. I do expect you all to come and visit me every now and then. I appreciate that I'm not exactly just around the corner out here, but it would be great to know that I can look forward to you coming to see me.'

'Of course we will,' Eloise said straight away and was echoed by Jenna, Calvyn and Fesha.

Derra looked with hard eyes at Perdimonn and walked over to his horse.

'Are you sure that there's no way of releasing Bek from being a Guardian?' she asked, her face stern and her voice predictably hard and uncompromising.

'I know of no way to break his bond to this place,' Perdimonn replied, looking Derra straight in the eye. 'Bek has taken on the role of Guardian and the only way that he can relinquish it is to be defeated in combat. From what I understand of the Guardians, he will not be able to deliberately lose a fight and as long as he remains here, Bek will not age. He has now, to all intents and purposes, become immortal. There are many who would give everything they had to gain such a prize.'

'And did you know this before Bek fought with Derkas?' Derra demanded.

'Yes, I did,' Perdimonn admitted, his expression not changing in the slightest.

'You knew, but you didn't warn Bek of the consequences,' she accused, her eyes flashing dangerously.

'Yes, Sergeant Derra, I knew *exactly* what would happen if Bek challenged one of the Guardians, but could you have given me an alternative way of stopping Selkor from returning the gods to this world? Calvyn was destined to meet Selkor at the Throne of the Gods. The only way that Calvyn could meet that destiny involved getting him past the Guardians. I'm sure that you'll agree that Bek was the obvious choice to make the challenge. I didn't ask him to do it. No one did. He chose to fight of his own free will. I honestly believe that it was his destiny to fight Derkas. For all I know, the hand of a higher power has been guiding his every footstep to reach just that end. There's certainly a great deal of power in this place and only the very best fighters ever get to be Guardians. For all I know, the Creator Himself has had a hand in the last few days. The timing and results certainly don't lend themselves to being the work of a minor power, or I'm sure that the minor gods would be wreaking havoc throughout the world as we speak.'

'You could have at least warned him,' Derra growled.

'Yes, I could, but would it have made any difference?' Perdimonn sighed wearily. 'Bek, would you have challenged Derkas knowing what you know now, or would the fact that winning meant becoming a Guardian have made you think differently?'

'I'd have fought him anyway,' Bek replied without hesitation. 'Calvyn needed a champion. I was not about to let anyone else have the privilege.'

'Question answered,' Perdimonn said with a slight shrug.

Derra did not look happy, but she did turn from Perdimonn and returned to speak once more with Bek before they left. Standing in front of him for a moment, the Sergeant took everyone by surprise when she stepped forward and gave him a hug.

'Farewell, Bek. I still think you deserve better than a lifetime on a mountainside in the middle of nowhere, but if I ever get the chance, then you can rely on me coming to see you and we'll have a friendly re-match,' she said gruffly.

'Thanks, Sergeant. I'm looking forward to it already,' Bek replied, genuinely touched by the Sergeant's uncharacteristic show of affection.

The others all said their goodbyes in turn, until only Eloise remained. Bek looked into her eyes wistfully and the raven-haired beauty returned the look with tears welling in her eyes. Neither was able to articulate their feelings in the end and, rather than fumbling with words, they just held each other in a long embrace. When they parted, both had tears in their eyes, but neither said anything other than 'goodbye'.

Everyone mounted up again and with much waving and reluctant backward looks, the party moved off northwards towards Mantor.

'Safe journey,' Bek called after them in a loud voice and with a final wave he walked back to where Pallim was waiting for him under the stone archway.

'Now that's over with, are you ready for a spot of sparring?' Pallim asked with a friendly smile.

'Ready and waiting,' Bek replied with a grin and he drew his sword with an enthusiastic flourish.

*   *   *   *   *

Several weeks later, Calvyn, Jenna and the Magicians were in the Palace at Mantor, where they had been explaining to the King what had happened. Calvyn felt awful about lying to Malo about what had happened, but at the end of the day he was not prepared to compromise the secret that Perdimonn and the other Warders had made him swear to keep. It came down once more to a question of loyalty and priority, and in this case Calvyn felt justified in sticking to the prepared story.

If Jenna had been affectionate before the journey to the Throne of the Gods, she was doubly so now and Calvyn was enjoying her company in the privacy of his suite in the Palace where they spent a lot of time together talking about the future. They both knew that they would have to go to Terilla soon. Calvyn, out of earshot of the Masters, had given Jenna as much detail about life in the Academy as he could. Of course, as Calvyn had never visited the female half of the Academy, he had no idea if the girls would be treated any differently, or how often the two of them would be able to spend time together. Those were questions that could be posed to the Masters on the long journey ahead though, and for now they simply enjoyed the chance to spend time together with no burning responsibilities hanging over them.

Preparations to continue on their journey back towards Terilla were beginning to get underway. Perdimonn and the other Warders had dispersed the previous week and Derra, Fesha and Eloise were readying themselves to accompany Calvyn's party as far as northern Thrandor. Calvyn and Jenna were relaxing, curled up in a cuddle on the large sofa in Calvyn's living room, when a knock at the door to Calvyn's suite proved to be Veldan with a message from the King.

'Sir Calvyn, the King requires your presence in his Courtroom. A delegation has just arrived from Shandar. They are claiming to be the Ambassadors of a new Emperor. King Malo would like you present just to make sure that there are no Magicians or Sorcerers hidden amongst them.'

'Of course, Veldan. I'll come right now,' Calvyn assured him.

The King was waiting with Baron Anton at his side when Calvyn arrived. Both of them looked slightly uncomfortable, which Calvyn decided was unusual for men who were used to dealing with diplomacy on a day-to-day basis.

'Ah, Calvyn! Thank you for coming so quickly. Veldan, just give me a moment or two with Sir Calvyn and then send in the Shandese delegation, would you? I don't want to keep the Ambassador and her retinue waiting.'

Veldan bowed and withdrew, drawing the doors closed behind him.

'I've called you in because this is really most unusual, Calvyn. We've never seen a female Ambassador from Shandar before and I want to be sure that if this is some elaborate ploy, we're best placed to spot it.'

'I'll do my best, your Majesty.'

'I know you will, Calvyn, and I trust your judgement implicitly. We have been hearing no end of strange things from our small intelligence network in the north. Everyone agrees that there has been a change of leadership and a major power shift within Shandar, but no one knows what the new Emperor's intentions are when it comes to foreign policy. With any luck, we should get something of an insight into that today. Just keep your ears and eyes open and watch for any signs of magic being used.'

'Of course, your Majesty.'

At that moment, there was a loud warning knock and Veldan entered, leading a richly dressed young lady, flanked by three unarmed men, each carrying a small box.

'May I present Lady Femke, Ambassador of Shandar, your Majesty?'

'Welcome, Lady Femke. It is always a pleasure to receive a peaceful emissary from our nearest neighbours. What brings you to my humble kingdom?'

Femke smiled warmly and her eyes sparkled.

'His Imperial Majesty, Surabar, Emperor of Shandar, wishes to send you greetings and offers gifts of compensation for the recent unwarranted invasion of your Sovereign territory by our troops. He wishes to convey his apologies on behalf of the Empire and initiate a new era of trade and co-operation with Thrandor,' she pronounced, her voice both a model of confidence and reflecting the warmth in her smile.

Responding to her gesture, the three men who accompanied her opened the boxes they were carrying to reveal a mixture of gold, loose gemstones and items of exquisite jewellery.

The King raised his eyebrows in surprise and glanced across at Calvyn. In anticipation, Calvyn had already cast a spell sweeping the room for objects with magical powers and found none but his own. He gave a very subtle nod, but noted instantly that the King was not the only one to see it. This Ambassador had sharp eyes, he decided. Friendly or not, this young lady looked to have her wits about her and Calvyn felt sure that diplomacy with Ambassador Femke would prove most interesting. This was more than likely to be a tricky encounter for the King. Still, diplomacy was not Calvyn's area of expertise, and he was sure that the King would enjoy crossing diplomatic swords with the Ambassador as much as Bek enjoyed duelling with real blades. The recent spate of battles might be over, but somehow Calvyn felt sure that life would continue to throw up plenty of less violent challenges to keep everyone busy for a long time to come.

The End... for now.

For information about further stories by the same author, see www.swordpublishing.co.uk